D0912124

be my enemy

By the same author

QUITE UGLY ONE MORNING
COUNTRY OF THE BLIND
NOT THE END OF THE WORLD
ONE FINE DAY IN THE MIDDLE OF THE NIGHT
BOILING A FROG
A BIG BOY DID IT AND RAN AWAY
THE SACRED ART OF STEALING

be my enemy
or,
fuck this for a game
of soldiers

christopher
brookmyre

LITTLE, BROWN

A *Little, Brown* Book

First published in Great Britain in 2004 by Little, Brown

Copyright © 2004 Christopher Brookmyre

Blackjack written by Art Alexakis. From the Everclear album *Slow Motion Daydream*.
Copyright © 2002 Evergleam Music/Montalupis Music/Commongreen Music/
Songs of Universal (BMI). Lyrics reproduced by kind permission of Art Alexakis.

The Heater words by Don McGlashan, music by Don McGlashan, Ross Burge, Alan
Gregg, David Long. From the Mutton Birds album *Salty*. Copyright © 1994 Warner
Chappell/Mana Music. Lyrics reproduced by kind permission of Don McGlashan.

Envy of Angels written by Don McGlashan. From the Mutton Birds album *Envy of
Angels*. Copyright © 1997 Warner Chappell/Mana Music. Lyrics reproduced by
kind permission of Don McGlashan.

The Heater and *Envy of Angels* also appear on *Flock: The Best of The Mutton Birds*.

The moral right of the author has been asserted.

All rights reserved.
No part of this publication may be reproduced,
stored in a retrieval system, or transmitted, in any
form or by any means, without the prior
permission in writing of the publisher, nor be
otherwise circulated in any form of binding or
cover other than that in which it is published and
without a similar condition including this
condition being imposed on the subsequent purchaser.

*All characters in this publication are fictitious
and any resemblance to real persons, living or dead,
is purely coincidental.*

A CIP catalogue record for this book
is available from the British Library.

HARDBACK ISBN 0 316 72522 6
C FORMAT ISBN 0 316 72614 1

Typeset by Palimpsest Book Production Limited,
Polmont, Stirlingshire
Printed and bound in Great Britain by
Clays Ltd, St Ives plc

Little, Brown
An imprint of
Time Warner Books UK
Brettenham House
Lancaster Place
London WC2E 7EN

www.TimeWarnerBooks.co.uk

For Roger Dubar

Thanks: Marisa, Art Alexakis, Don McGlashan

When everything is simple in the white and the black
You will never have to see the grey anymore
You will never have to be afraid . . .
Please don't tell me that this isn't what you asked for . . .
Be careful what you ask for

Blackjack, A. P. Alexakis
from *Slow Motion Daydream* by Everclear

Prologue:
Burial and Exhumation

November 11, 2001

'Bin Laden? A fucking charlatan.'

'Be serious for a minute,' Williams told him.

'I am being serious. That's my point. Everybody's so reverent about this guy. Strip away all the mythologising and hocus-pocus and what have you got? Patty Hearst with a beard. Bored rich kid playing at soldiers. He's in the huff with his family, for Christ's sake – the psychology's pitifully mundane. If he'd been born into a semi in Surbiton he'd have painted his bedroom black, got himself a Nine Inch Nails T-shirt and hung around swingparks drinking cider from plastic bottles.'

Fotheringham's rant was attracting admonitory glances, more in disapproval of the growing volume and vehemence than the content, which wouldn't have been clearly discernible above the whipping wind. Raised voices were not decorous at a funeral; they suggested that your thoughts were not respectfully concentrated upon the memory of the departed, even if, in Williams's case, that was not strictly true. Nothing was more prominent in his mind than the man they had just buried or the consequences of his loss, not least the fact that Williams now had his job.

Fotheringham gestured apologetic acknowledgement and Williams led him in the opposite direction to the dispersing mourners.

'Bin Laden's about a lot more than thrill kills and power trips,' Williams chided, measuring his condescension precisely. 'And there's three thousand dead people in New York of the opinion that you should be taking him more seriously.'

'I'm taking him entirely seriously, sir. I just don't think it will help us if we buy into the hype and start thinking of him as some kind of formidable genius. Look at the Black Spirit, if you need a primer. Remember what a bogeyman he was? Turned out to be a fucking oil-biz wage slave from Aberdeen.'

'Quite. Something, I should remind you, that we only learned after the fact. Didn't make him any easier to catch, did it? And besides, I don't think there's much ground for comparison. For all his theatrics, the Black Spirit was essentially just a mercenary, prepared to do horrific things on other people's behalf if they paid him enough. Bin Laden represents the possibility of *ten thousand* Black Spirits, all of them prepared to do horrific things merely because it's Allah's bidding. We've never had to face this kind of fanaticism before: there's no fifth column to cultivate, no disaffected factions to encourage, no waverers, not even anyone we can bribe and corrupt. Just total, unquestioning, homicidal, *suicidal* commitment to the cause.'

'With respect, sir, that's what I mean by believing the hype. For one thing, there is no cause. Bin Laden's too smart to marry himself to anything as cumbersome as a coherent or even consistent political ideology, because such a thing could be debated, held up to scrutiny, and, worst of all, alienate potential followers. "The cause of Islam" is expediently nebulous. You scream loud enough about Allah and nobody's going to ask you to clarify any awkward specifics before signing up. Through religion, Bin Laden can posture as all things to all Muslims. But there's one specific he does deliver, and that's the thing he needs more than Allah, the thing that's really motivating your "unquestioning" footsoldiers.'

'What? The promise of all those virgins in paradise?'

'An enemy. Somebody to hate, somebody to blame. The US, the Jews, the West. The Muslim fundamentalists aren't

4

looking to Bin Laden because he's a genius. They're looking to him because he's the one who's currently got a team together to give the infidel a kicking. That's his main leadership credential: that right now, he's the one doing some leading.'

Williams grimaced a little, his features hardening less against the growing drizzle than in strain at tolerating his subordinate's less-than-focused reflections. David Fotheringham was tagged in Williams's mental files under 'Useful But Flaky', sub-section 'Intelligent But Scheming'. He'd been indispensable as an infiltrator ten or fifteen years back, boyish looks allowing him to pass for someone much younger, combined with a sly talent for winning people's trust. He wasn't out in the field these days, partly because his knowledge and experience were more valuably applied in managing the operatives who were, but also because there were question marks over his ability to remain emotionally detached. It was a charted symptom of chronic exposure to his particular field of analysis: spend all your time identifying potential threat and subversion and your instincts could get a little defensive, to say the least. Revulsion was a natural response, but hatred clouded your judgement. Now that Selby was gone and Williams was in charge, it would be up to him to harness Fotheringham's abilities: the trick was finding a way of loosening his leash but keeping him on-side.

'Forgive me, Fotheringham, maybe it's the circumstances this morning, maybe it's last night's whisky and maybe it's just the damp, but I'm having trouble understanding why one of my most respected intelligence officers is standing before me doing a very good impression of trivialising the biggest threat to security that this nation currently faces.'

'I'm not trivialising, sir. I'm saying these guys – Bin Laden, Al Qaeda – are only as dangerous as they've been allowed to be.'

5

Williams looked around the cemetery, thrusting his hands into the pockets of his coat.

'Where are you going with this, David? It's fucking freezing out here and I've a pressing appointment with a sausage roll and a pint of bitter.'

'Are sausage rolls still mandatory at official funerals?'

Williams gave a small, stiff grin.

'Sausage rolls are mandatory at all funerals, even vegetarian ones, and I couldn't half do with one right now. So enough procrastination: what are you saying?'

Fotheringham took his own turn at casting a slow eye across the headstones.

'Do you know the joke about the two hunters, out of ammo, who come across a lion in the grassland?'

'Can't say that I recognise it so far, no.'

'Well, the lion clocks them, so one of them drops his gun and just starts running. His mate tells him he's mad, there's no way he can outrun a lion. The first guy says: "I don't need to outrun the lion: I only need to outrun you."'

'Al Q hit the Twin Towers because the Yanks made it easy for them. I'm saying we should make it no fucking picnic to be an Al Q operative in the UK: present ourselves as the hardest option and let the rest watch their own backs.'

'Far be it from me to pour cold water on your enthusiasm, but I'm obliged to remind you that counter-terrorism isn't really your area of expertise.'

'No, sir. My area of expertise is idealistic half-wits looking for some cause to make their lives seem meaningful and their selves feel important. I've seen them of every stripe, every colour, every political hue, and the one thing they all have in common is, to use an appropriately jingoistic phrase, they don't like it up 'em. For every truly committed suicide bomber, there's two dozen easily-led romantics who'll go looking for a new hobby if things start to get hot.'

'Meanwhile my sausage roll is starting to get cold.'

Williams began walking as directly towards the carpark as the headstones allowed. 'I came here to bury a colleague, not to listen to your head unravelling, Fotheringham. Sounds like you should stay out of what you clearly don't know.'

'With every respect to his memory, I know our departed boss has exited the stage not a moment too soon.'

Williams checked his stride, casting an eye towards the dispersing mourners and the growing cavalcade of slow-departing cars.

'Gracefully,' Fotheringham continued, 'with his legacy and dignity intact, before the likes of Al Qaeda exposed him as an anachronism. They've changed the game beyond anything Selby could recognise, ripped up our definitions of the unthinkable and made it easier for the next nutter along to contemplate atrocity. This isn't a war, not even a cold one. You said it yourself, there's no generals to assess or outsmart, no rifts or factions to exploit, and you don't get to see troops massing before the strike comes.'

'Justin Selby was a man of honour and principle.'

'Unquestionably, sir. He believed in democracy and good old-fashioned fair play. These fuckers don't.'

Fotheringham stopped and stood still. Williams ignored his punt at dramatic effect and ambled onwards, charting a straighter course towards the exit.

'It's time we started playing dirty too, sir. I'd like to see how many of their "disaffected loner" recruits and so-called fanatics remain quite so committed once they start picking up their teeth.'

Williams shook his head. 'So a few public floggings, maybe a beheading in Trafalgar Square, that what you have in mind?' He walked backwards as he called out his disap-pointed scorn, then turned again and proceeded in the direc-tion of that much-vaunted sausage roll.

Fotheringham stood his ground, undaunted by Williams's departure.

'I'm talking about OFP 857.'

Williams stopped and turned around. OFP 857 was one of MI5's more badly kept secrets, and it was no surprise that Fotheringham should know about it. The question was, given his ratified flaky status, how much he really knew, or how much he'd merely bought into the myth.

'Did I hear you right?'

'Yes, sir. Since September 11th we've found ourselves facing a real monster: multi-headed, poison-tongued, murderous and entirely ruthless. I think the time is right for us to unleash a demon of our own.'

Williams had to stifle a laugh. Ever since Selby's colossal fuck-up in not burying it properly when he should have, this was a story that had rattled around the organisation down the years, in rumours, half-truths, speculation and out-and-out bollocks.

'What do you know about OFP 857? Seriously. Do you know what it stands for, for a start?'

'Omega File Prisoner 857. Imprisoned without trial, detained indefinitely, in order to cover up his activities. Also known as army sergeant Maurice Shiach, assigned to train Territorials and student OTCs around the country. Originally recruited as an informant by Special Branch in the Seventies, investigating suspected extreme right-wing factions in the TA. In the Eighties he was unofficially given free rein to recruit and assemble—'

'Bollocks he was.'

'Just the way I heard it, sir.'

'That's the problem. There's so much hair grown on that sorry tale, a lot of *Boys' Own* shit that people want to believe in. What else do you know, from "the way you heard it"?'

'That he ran a prototype covert assassination unit, to take out subversive elements without raising suspicion over the motives of their deaths. Accidents, suicides. That's why I brought it up. The people we're facing these days love to

8

have martyrs. It fuels their cause. This way, we could deny them that while taking crucial heads.'

'You believe we can enhance the security of our country by killing certain of the people who live here?'

'People who are planning to undermine that security, yes. If we'd popped Bin Laden coming out of Highbury one afternoon, several of our citizens might not have died on September 11.'

This was Fotheringham in full flake mode. He wasn't the first to be seduced by the Shiach myth: who wouldn't like to believe we had a secret unit who could almost invisibly wipe out the people who threatened us? The reality was less romantic, a repeat of it unthinkable. It was high time Fotheringham was disabused of his misconceptions, though if he seriously had the stomach for what he was deludedly contemplating, Williams might yet be able to use that. If nothing else, he had brought to the top of the agenda one of the unsolved problems Williams had just inherited from Selby.

'You start with Bin Laden, but where do you stop, David? Who's going to make that call? Me? You? Shiach?'

'Desperate times call for desperate measures.'

'We're not that desperate yet. Believe me, he wasn't some 007, licensed to kill. Shiach was a nightmare looking for someone to dream him: someone feeling like you do now, angry and frustrated and wishing you could just blow the bad guys away. He was a psychopath in need of a cause to justify his bloodlust, and Shiach was more interested in the blood than the cause. He was little more than hired muscle, impatient to provide the way if someone else had the will.'

'You mean the Architect?'

'Ah, you've heard that nonsense too. Shiach's *own* myth-making, that one. That was how he seduced his recruits: told them about his silent partner who was in MI5, giving the impression that what he was up to was sanctioned. Trust me, what he was up to was entirely off his own back. He was a self-deluding nutter, and the myths came about because Justin Selby inadvertently fed his delusion by covering the whole mess up.'

'What exactly did this mess consist of?'

'Shiach's "unit" murdered some lefty activist lawyer and made it look like suicide. To this day, the widow doesn't know any different. Nobody does. Selby found out, though. He'd been worried about Shiach for a while and engaged the time-honoured paranoid ploy of sending an informant to inform on his informant. He got nothing from the main man, but one of Shiach's TA recruits spilled his guilt-ridden guts, and not a moment too soon, because it wasn't all clever little suicides they were planning. That's the myth: that they dreamt up subtle, invisible ways to make inconvenient people disappear. Not Shiach. He wanted mayhem. Hide in plain sight. The more messy and insane, the harder it is to see the motive.'

'What happened to the recruit?'

'Topped himself, ironically.'

'You sure he topped himself?'

'Oh, yeah. Shiach was locked up by then. I say ironically because there were no repercussions for him, apart from his own guilt, it would seem. Selby had to make the whole thing go away, and he impressed upon the guy that there'd be no murder case to answer as long as no-one knew there'd *been* a murder. But Shiach didn't just need to be silenced, he needed to be stopped. That's where Selby screwed up. He should have thrown the whole thing open to the cops, but he was terrified of the political damage. You can say the phrase "rogue element" as many times as you want, but when you've got someone connected to both the security and intelligence services wiping out dissidents and making it look like suicide . . .'

'I can see the headlines, yes.'

'And you have to understand, the way Selby's mind worked, he wasn't protecting a government or a political party. He was protecting the very office *of* government, because what credibility would that office have, home or abroad, if we were perceived to be assassinating dissenters? He had to cover up the whole thing, and he had to get rid of Shiach. Me? I'd have given him a taste of his own medicine, suicided the bastard. Unfortunately, Selby's stubborn principles ruled that out. He considered what Shiach had done an affront to everything he believed this country stood for, which included not killing people just because you find them inconvenient.'

'So it's true he had him imprisoned without trial?'

'That part is true, yes. His identity has been effectively wiped, his files sealed and the only thing anyone on the inside knows is that he doesn't have a parole date. Selby made him disappear in his own bloodless way, no doubt feeding Shiach's delusion that he's some kind of martyr, wronged patriot or detained secret agent. "Omega File Prisoner 857". He must have loved that. Good job he doesn't know what happened to Omega File Prisoners one through 856.'

'What?'

'Nothing. There weren't any. It was Selby taking the piss because he knew Shiach drove a white VW Beetle.'

'I don't follow.'

'Herbie's registration was OFP 857.'

Fotheringham laughed. Williams knew he could now consider the myth officially debunked. The sausage rolls would all have been scoffed by now, but it had been worth it, as it looked like he now had the answers to two of his inherited problems: namely yoking Fotheringham's loyalty and erasing Selby's big mistake.

'The bastard's been rattling around various prisons since 1991, out of sight while his legend gets bigger and wilder.

11

And now that Selby's gone, he's my responsibility. Out of sight but not out of mind, it would be fair to say. There's safeguards in place to stop him talking to anyone on the outside, but nothing's perfect, and you can imagine the fallout if his story ever did reach the public domain. It was a risk Selby was prepared to live with for the sake of his principles, but let's just say he was a better man than I.'

'I think I hear you, sir.'

'You still think certain individuals' deaths would benefit our national security?'

'I do.'

'Well, I might just have a job for you.'

December 16, 2001

Shiach stared into the blackness ahead, above, below. Everywhere but behind.

Behind, there were search beams, bright and penetrating, sweeping the decks in automated arcs, while sirens, klaxons and shouts rang pointlessly into the void. The ship was a tiny island of noise and light, its rage and ferment an insignificance amid this vast, indifferent nothingness. From the edge of such nothingness, it was easy to see just how small his world was, what little he would be leaving behind if he chose to make the leap.

Somewhere within the cacophony, and despite the rush of wind in his ears, he heard the shriek of metal that announced his makeshift barrier had been breached. Two guards emerged on to the rain-lashed deck, looking urgently around and quickly spotting him as he gripped the rim on the starboard bow. They shouted something, lost to the night, then split up, preparing to move in cautiously from two sides.

Time to decide. Cold, unknowing blackness ahead; a vivid, endless certainty behind.

He'd been offered a starker version of this choice before, and in a way it had been available to him every day since. Until now, there had been more reason to remain upon this tiny world, even if that reason was little more than hope, or even merely defiance.

'You could, of course, save both our consciences a lot of trouble,' Selby had said, placing a jar of sleeping tablets and a bottle of whisky down on the desk. The whisky was a cute

13

touch, deliberately archaic, Selby's revenge for Shiach telling him he belonged in a bygone era. 'I know it should be a revolver, but I didn't think that would be a wise thing to be giving you.'

'You never had anything to fear from me, Selby. You're the one who thinks we're on different sides.'

Selby didn't reply to that, just left the room and closed the door, the last time Shiach ever saw him. He wasn't going to stay and argue when he knew he'd made all the points he needed to, especially as solitude would be more conducive to the resolution he sought.

There would indeed be 'a lot of trouble' for the sake of Selby's conscience; trouble Shiach had no intention of sparing him, because his conscience was clear. No amount of whisky was going to elicit any remorse for his past, but it was more likely his future Selby thought he'd recoil from. Imprisonment without trial, no sentence, no parole, no judges to appeal to and no-one he could tell his story. Leaving aside the fact that nobody would believe him (and the stinging irony that he had been fastidious in wiping out the evidence himself), there was the inescapable conundrum, as Selby had so sincerely pointed out, that it would be entirely self-defeating. If he somehow managed to make the truth known, he would achieve only the destruction of the things he had sought to protect, and deliver everything into the hands of the very people he detested. He would disappear, leaving no trace of what he had done, to enter a world where he could tell nobody who he was. There would be no communication, no trace to be left for anyone to follow, and in seven years he would receive a legal declaration of his own death, but in reality there would be no such definite end in sight.

The whisky and pills option was presumably supposed to look that bit more attractive by comparison, and Shiach would admit that for a bleak few moments it did. However, the problem for Selby was that it wasn't a limited-time offer. If he decided he couldn't take it any more, Shiach could check out any time he liked, and every morning he woke up alive was another day on which the world, the country or even just the right minds could change.

That possibility was the price Selby would be forced to pay for his principles, just as silence was the price Shiach would be forced to pay for his. The difference was, Shiach trusted Selby's moral resolve far more than was apparently reciprocated, given the series of obvious MI5 plants he sent in to monitor him down the years.

At first he considered it deeply insulting that Selby should think his agents wouldn't be spotted by a man of his experience, but in time it dawned on him that perhaps it was only the screws (and maybe even their own handlers) they were supposed to deceive. It was Selby's way of letting him know he still had his eyes and ears on him, no matter how many years passed, no matter what changed in the world outside.

The world on the inside changed little, even when it changed completely, as upon the two occasions he was moved to new prisons, each supposedly surpassing the security of its predecessor. Like he could ever have escaped. Escape was for lucky and audacious opportunists, exploiting lapses and complacency, or for schemers who masked their intentions behind a placid, anonymous face in the crowd of a teeming population. There would never be complacency around Omega File Prisoner 857, nor would any screw be allowed to think at any time that he posed no threat. He didn't have an iron mask welded round his bonce, but it was still pretty obvious to the hired help that his was a special and extremely sensitive case. Their lack of even casual inquisitiveness, despite natural curiosity, was as telling as it was conspicuous. He would occasionally ask *them* how much they knew about him, but the most expansive response he'd ever got was that they were told 'the information is on not so much a need-to-know basis as a what-you-don't-know-can't-hurt-you basis'. And that went right up the chain, within a system that was too busy, too strained just getting on with itself to allow its functionaries to dwell long upon one little mystery. Even an intrigued governor would have simply too much else on his plate to get hung up on questions he had no hope of receiving answers to. OFP 857, or less formally 'Prisoner John Smith', with all his added security consider-ations (no visitors; no mail, out or in; no phone cards nor ever to be unescorted in an area containing a telephone; no recording devices; no blank paper; periodicals only to be read – and replaced, intact, unmarked – under supervision; etcetera, etcetera, etcetera) would send any intelligent mind into bouts of speculation at first. Then soon enough he'd just become part of the furniture, an albeit colourful permanent fixture, but as such one that, like all other permanent fixtures, everybody got used to.

Everything becomes banal in prison, even mysteries. Whatever aura surrounds you when you walk in soon wears off once everybody's seen you getting on with the same routine as all the rest, day after day after day. There was this strange unspoken code that you never asked about each other's crimes. You could open up about your own, but you didn't ask, recognising an invaluable right of privacy. Thus he would not have been conspicuous for never discussing why he was inside, if it wasn't that, whether they spoke about it or not, everyone always knew what everyone else had done. Everyone else except John Smith, OFP 857. Christ knew what they guessed about him, but nothing they dreamed up could be as disturbing as the truth.

He had suffered a gross miscarriage of justice, but he couldn't complain that the state had got the wrong man, and anyway he wasn't comfortable considering himself some hapless victim. He would not disown his acts even if he could seek absolution, so there was no journey of self-rediscovery to embark upon. And given that successive governments would be deftly protected from knowledge of his existence, he could hardly be considered a political prisoner.

However, he had been incarcerated indefinitely and without trial, for following what he believed in: for having the guts to carry out the deeds necessary to protect the way of life and freedoms enjoyed by the very people who would most vehemently condemn him. That was the moral cowardice of the unaffected. Easy to say over your *Guardian* and croissants: 'We must find better solutions than violence.' Meaning YOU, some other bugger, must find better solutions, while we'll be busy getting on with our comfortable lives.

He was a prisoner of conscience.

He had acted – just as now he silently endured – out of patriotism. There, he'd said it. Patriotism: a word devalued by a million halfwits waving plastic Union Flags, who bought a Piccadilly tourist-shop notion of what their country represented. A word scorned by a million liberal malcontents cutting off their noses to spite their collective face, considering it untrendy to stand up for a country that enshrined the very values that saddled their every high horse.

Patriotism was about knowing what your country stood for, and not being prepared to let anyone desecrate that, be they enemies foreign or domestic.

Oscar Wilde called it 'the virtue of the vicious', but then he was an Irish poof, so what could you expect? And maybe he was right, but that didn't mean viciousness was without virtue. If there's a cleaver-wielding rapist at the door of your teenage daughter's student flat, would you rather she owned a sweet-natured and placid sandy Labrador or a snarling, one-hundred-and-eighty-pound black Rottweiler?

Humiliating as it was to recall, Shiach had never expected to see out even one year. Selby would be reined in by a superior, or perhaps Shiach's very existence within the system would throw up too many awkward anomalies for his secret incarceration to be sustained. He'd envisaged secret meetings, confidential memos, factional lobbying and wrangling over this vital and explosive issue. What he didn't appreciate was that he had ceased to be vital, explosive or even remotely important. The issue was closed when he was locked away, and the entire point of the exercise was that he would be out of sight, out of mind, gone and officially forgotten.

And then, just two weeks ago, it happened.

'Smith, OFP 857. You have a visitor.'

The impossibility of this functioned on two levels. The first was the official, being the conditions that stipulated he wasn't allowed so much as a piece of paper and an empty milk bottle with which to communicate to the outside world. This initially made him suspect that 'visitor' was a figure of speech, and that some form of HM Prison Service officialdom was about to make itself manifest, particularly given that it was around two o'clock in the morning. However, the second level of impossibility, militating even against this more mundane scenario, was that his current accommodations were aboard HMP *Attendant*, a converted Royal Navy medical frigate presently afloat upon the North Sea a couple of miles east of Grimsby. There had been a few latter-day hulks converted in recent years, mainly to alleviate overcrowding in onshore facilities, but *Attendant* was commissioned specifically to be the last word in escape-proof confinement. While the others remained anchored in bays, really just floating cell-blocks cheaper than fresh construction, Shiach's home for the past three years was fully seaworthy, only putting in twice a week for supplies and highly vetted, closely monitored, one-on, one-off visits to prisoners.

He was led to a secure, windowless room containing only two chairs and a table. It wasn't the visiting room, he knew, as according to fellow inmates, that had two-way mirrors concealing an observation gallery, microphones monitoring all conversation and triangulated video cameras picking up anything the restricted perspective behind the glass might miss.

A good place for someone to have an accident, he mused as he stepped inside, two screws remaining in the corridor behind him.

He took a seat and waited only a couple of minutes before the door opened and everything in his world suddenly changed. The MI5 emissary had arrived unheralded in the darkness, on a helicopter that no doubt officially never left the hangar, to conduct a meeting that never took place, with a prisoner who did not exist.

It was almost unsettlingly businesslike. He had a thousand questions, but knew he could ask none. Facts and statements, laid down flat. Conditions and parameters, time and date, special instructions and then an on-the-spot demand to accept or decline.

Not the toughest question he'd ever been asked. Accept or decline. Take this one and only chance or rot inside for the rest of your days, which were unlikely to be many given that Mike Williams was clearly prepared to be more, ahem, pragmatic than his predecessor when it came to eliminating risks.

For yes, Selby was dead. Nothing lasts forever, and no-one lives forever either.

Accept, he said. To which Fotheringham responded with one final stipulation, under the circumstances more difficult than anything else he'd be required to pull off.

'When you leave this room, you look like you've been kicked in the gut, that whatever you learned in here just trashed whatever was left of your hope.'

He didn't need to explain further. Speculation about himself and his status wore thin according to the law of diminishing returns, but something like this incident was bound to have the screws' jungle telegraph buzzing. It was in his best interests to infer that his dark and secret burden had just got heavier, maybe even unbearable.

What truly was unbearable was the ensuing fortnight. Short time was the hardest time, according to those inmates with a parole date to aim at. To Shiach's mind, few of his days or weeks had ever passed quicker or slower than others, but that had been when he had no reason to count them. However, if there was one benefit, it was that when the time came, he was entirely focused and ready, able to act without thought or hesitation, deliberate to the point of automatic.

Shiach always suspected Selby had screws working for him – placed agents or otherwise – as well as the more obvious plants among the various inmate populations, so it was no surprise that Williams could call upon similar unseen hands when the time came.

It didn't take mass orchestration; it just took *enough* orchestration: perhaps only three, even as few as two people acting as instructed, more than likely ignorant of each other's existence, let alone activities, and certainly ignorant of the intended consequences. Even Shiach himself would never know who they were, nor they that it was him they were helping. Things happened that shouldn't happen, and things happened that no-one could plausibly anticipate, far less improvise spontaneously to take advantage of.

A fight broke out in the canteen, quickly escalating (and thus revealing itself as a deliberate prelude) to a hostage situation as four screws became isolated at the port end of the dining area, next to the kitchen. Shiach had chosen a table right at the back, accompanied as ever one-on-one by a screw (on this occasion one Officer Doyle) because the canteen area offered access to a phone via the kitchen. When the intended nature of the trouble was revealed, Shiach's escort knew not to present himself as a fifth possible hostage and made for the starboard exit, which accessed the 'non-secure zone', the part of the ship housing staff facilities and accommodation.

Shiach followed him to the door, which through a glass panel he could see a screw unlocking from the other side.

'I've got no part of this,' he said, hands raised. 'Fuck's sake, don't leave me in there. It's not as if I'm gonna go anywhere, is it?'

Doyle stepped aside and ushered him through, before getting the right side of the door himself. Having spent the past fortnight giving off an air of almost desolate resignation, Shiach knew he wouldn't inspire much fear, especially with more pressing security issues to consider. And there was always the matter of being several miles out in the North Sea to allay those escape worries.

'We'll cuff this one and take him to the Rec room on B Deck,' Doyle told his colleague. 'We're gonna need all hands down here, so we need to lock him up someplace and it has to be somewhere that doesn't have a phone.'

'Christ, does that matter so much right now?' the other screw protested.

'Only if still having a job next week matters. Don't forget this is OFP 857,' Doyle insisted, to Shiach's great relief. These considerations had, he now understood, been accurately anticipated by Fotheringham, who had briefed him on the two locations he would most likely be taken. Individual staff quarters were the most secure, but nobody was going to leave a prisoner in there with access to their own property. The entire admin suite was just a communications play-ground, and the engine room was a massive no-no given fire and other sabotage possibilities. Thus, it was always going to be the staff showers or their recreation den, with

21

the toss-up being between them preferring the risk of him squashing all their ping-pong balls to pissing on their towels.

He was cuffed, hands in front, and taken to B Deck, keeping his head down and steadfastly maintaining his now familiar expression of defeat as nervy and agitated screws passed him hastily in the corridors. There was no time for explanations, it being enough to see him escorted by two colleagues for them to file the otherwise irregular sight under The Least of Our Problems.

Doyle and his mate deposited him unfussily at the Rec room, commitments elsewhere causing them to eschew the expected lecture about what would happen to him if he abused these circumstances. Instead, Doyle settled for: 'There's a kettle, some tea, milk and stuff in the fridge. Help yourself. Don't screw up.'

Shiach nodded rather pitifully, like he'd barely have the motivation to make a cuppa, never mind get up to mischief. Satisfied, they withdrew and locked him in. The lock was a sturdy, modern, five-lever fixture, indistinct from those in the secure zone apart from there being only one fitted to this door. However, the door was not his intended means of exit. The interiors of the staff decks had been remodelled with far less concern for containment considerations, meaning that many of the partitions consisted of no more than gypsum board and wallpaper mounted on aluminium frames. The shower room's walls were constructed of sterner stuff to support the necessary ceramic coverings, but the changing area would have offered a joint-equal point of least resistance.

He folded up the ping-pong table and flipped down its castors, then got his shoulder behind it and rammed it into the wall. It took only two attempts for the whole table to smash through into the corridor.

Water began pouring from the sprinklers as he emerged behind the table, accompanied by the sound of fire alarms

22

to add to the emergency klaxons already ringing around the tub. It was possible the inmates had set something ablaze in the kitchen, but also a tactical consideration that the screws had activated the system to make things cold and uncomfortable for the miscreants, dousing spirits rather than flames. Whoever did it, for whatever ostensible motive, was quite probably obeying secret orders, because either way, the upshot for Shiach was that the exterior deck access doors were automatically unlocked for evacuation purposes.

The cold of the sprinklers' output was a reminder that things weren't going to get any more cosy from here on in, but having been numb for more than a decade, it was exhilarating to feel anything at all. Nor could he afford any time to ponder what was ahead until he had made sure of getting there, which became complicated by the unexpected investigatory reappearance of Doyle and partner at the end of the corridor. The chancers had evidently been in no hurry to get back to the fray, and so hadn't got as far away from the Rec room as he'd anticipated when he began his demolition. Shiach pulled a lever to unfold the table sideways across the passageway, the ends of either half tipping the walls at about thirty degrees to the horizontal, then he turned and ran for the door to the stairwell.

He lunged up the stairs three and four at a time, pausing in front of the door to the exterior deck so that he could remove a fire extinguisher from its strapping. The door, unlocked by the fire system, opened outwards as he plunged the handle, but not without the stiff resistance of the wind whipping rain against the metal. Shiach barrelled through and narrowed his eyes against the downpour, letting the door slam heavily behind him. He took the steel cylinder he'd lifted and wedged it between the door and the lip of the first of four short steps leading on to the open deck. It hardly constituted an insurmountable barrier, but it would buy him the seconds he needed.

23

He picked his way carefully across the slippery surface towards the starboard bow, staring out at the night, a prison the only visible vessel offering safety amid dead black nothingness.

When you leave this room, you look like you've been kicked in the gut, that whatever you learned in here just trashed whatever was left of your hope.

Who would be asking questions if an apparently depressed and possibly desperate prisoner seized the moment to end it all, given that he didn't officially exist and had been legally dead for years anyway?

The next step was literally a leap of faith.

Yes, he'd been here before all right, but unlike Selby's pills and whisky, with the two screws cautiously closing in, this one was a limited-time offer. Its options were also more clear-cut. Rejecting the pills and whisky was easy, because it bought time and time offered possibilities, time offered hope. Fotheringham had been dangling a whole new future in front of him, the very possibility he'd been holding out his hope for. If it was actually just bait, then it meant the end of hope. Either way, there was nothing left to live for on this ship.

Fotheringham was down there with scuba gear and handcuff keys, a speedboat floating unseen half a mile away, or Shiach was about to erase himself for Mike Williams's convenience. He pulled at the rim with his fettered hands and hurled himself into the darkness, betting on the former. One of them would be right to have trusted Fotheringham, and the odds were it would be the one who had known him longer: the one who knew him as the Architect.

Friday, October 25, 2002

Margaret Thatcher's Rotting Corpse

'You know, I kind of miss the Eighties,' Parlabane said, gazing disinterestedly at the passing countryside.

'Mmm,' Vale replied. 'Mobile phones you could ram a castle drawbridge with. Ghetto blasters bigger than the actual ghetto. Big hair, big shoulderpads, big eye make-up, and that was just the men.'

'What would you know about it? You probably spent most of it in dingy Eastern European hotel rooms, peering through grimy windows at trilbies and Trabbis.'

'Indeed. You really nailed the experience there; unsurprising, I suppose, in one so informed.'

'Fuck you.'

'But I did catch the odd glimpse of life in the West on those sixteen-inch, black-and-white East German televisions. Believe me, you've never really seen *Dynasty* until you've seen it dubbed into Polish with Czech subtitles. Came as quite a shock to hear Linda Evans didn't actually sound like a shot-putter in drag.'

'Don't knock the big hair and shoulderpads. I can get quite fetishistic about those if I let my mind wander. Probably because that's what the women I fancied were wearing when I had no chance of anything more than a Christmas kiss from an elderly auntie.'

'So is that what the good lady doctor togs up in for a special treat on your birthday?'

'Don't go there.'

'Mister P, I do believe you're blushing. I can picture it now. The intermingling erotic musk of Boots hairspray and

27

Poison perfume, A Flock of Seagulls on the stereo—'

Parlabane slapped the dashboard.

'Ah, see you were doing well there, but you blew it with that Flock of Seagulls remark.'

'How so?'

'You picked it up from Nineties American movies, proving you really did spend the decade in that dingy hotel room. Every fucking American movie that harks back to the Eighties goes on about A Flock of fucking Seagulls.'

'To give them their Sunday name.'

'It's become a self-reinforcing myth. Anyone who remembers the Eighties – and by that I mean anyone who didn't spend it cooped up in a Berlin B&B stroking his telescopic sight – would know that A Flock of fucking Seagulls blipped onto the radar screens for about a fortnight, mainly because of that stupid cunt's ridiculous hairdo, then failed to trouble the chart compilers ever again. But any time a Yank scriptwriter needs a quick Eighties cultural reference, bang, there it is, remembered from the last movie *he* saw that mentioned the fucking Eighties, and thus the myth lingers on.'

'And do you genuinely feel this strongly about it, Mr P, or were you simply trying to get me away from speculating further about the more embarrassing aspects of your conjugal rites. Because I haven't forgotten.'

'Keep your eyes on the driving, Tim. You've already got us off-track in our conversation. What I meant was, sometimes I miss the ideological simplicity of back then. No grey areas, no middle ground, just them and us, the good guys versus the bad guys, on every issue. East versus West, left versus right, rich versus poor, the Tories versus the miners, the Tories versus CND, the Tories versus homosexuals, the Tories versus Bob Geldof. I mean, you really knew who to hate in those days. Now it's too muddled, so I just hate everybody in case I miss anyone out.'

'Maybe it's the ideological simplicity of yourself you miss.'

'You having a go?'

'Would I? No, seriously, I've been there too. The world, politics, conflicts . . . it didn't all become more complicated, it was always that way, but when you're younger you don't know enough to appreciate that. The more you learn, the more you understand, the greyer the tones get. You're not missing the Eighties, Jack, you're missing your youth, and the comforting certainties of ignorance.'

'Maybe, maybe. But I can't refrain from observing how that sounds pretty ironic coming from a Cold War veteran.'

'Not ironic at all, if you think it through. In fact, I believe you've just reinforced my point. The Cold War might have seemed a very black-and-white ideological conflict to you, and clearly in many ways it was, but remember that my field of operations was entirely in the grey area.'

'Turning agents and all that?'

'And all that, yes. An appreciation of just how flexible this apparently rigid divide really was was one of the most crucial means of surviving it.'

'So is that how agents ended up getting tapped by the other side? Too long sleeping with the enemy, looking at it their way, losing sight of those comforting certainties.'

'Well, only for those who forgot *the* most crucial rule of survival: don't bring politics to work. Your job is to play the Us versus Them game. If you start thinking too much about what makes them them and us us, you're either going to be ripe for turning or a mindless zealot, and neither make the most effective agents. The former lose their purpose and the latter their judgement. You couldn't afford to be an extremist in my line of work.'

'Must have made for an interesting perspective upon the people you ultimately worked for at that time.'

'I ultimately worked for you, being the ordinary Brit,

something else it paid never to lose sight of. It didn't matter what I thought of Thatcher or Reagan any more than it mattered what I thought of Carter or Callaghan. Just because you disagreed with the Poll Tax and detested Margaret Thatcher—'

'Detested is a little inappropriate,' Parlabane said. 'Maybe closer to say I spent the entire Eighties wishing I was pissing on her rotting corpse.'

'Which, to underline my point, still didn't make the KGB nice people.'

'Agreed, but my point was that there were extremists at the top of the command chain. Margaret Thatcher being the topical example. My understanding of politics may have been less sophisticated back then, but even looking through the retrospectoscope doesn't change my perception of someone who really did render the political world black and white. She cultivated division as a matter of policy, talking about whether you were "one of us" or "the enemy within".'

'And you miss that, that's where we came in, yes?'

'Yes. No. I mean . . . Fuck, I don't know. Maybe I'm starting to feel my age, but I wish I was still as sure of what I believed today as I was back then; or even just as sure of what I hated. Believe me, Tim, it's tough being a bleeding-heart liberal in a world full of bampots.'

'Or as Bertrand Russell had it, "The problem with the world is that the fanatics are so sure of themselves while the wiser people so full of doubts."'

'Elegantly put and impressively remembered. See, that's what I love about your generation. You know these things chapter and verse and can pluck them from your skull on cue. What can we quote? Song lyrics, sitcom gags and philo-sophical soliloquies that sound pseudo-Shakespearean until you remember they were spoken by Jean-Luc Picard.'

'My generation. Cheeky little twerp. But to my wisdom and knowledge I'll add good grace and accept your compliment. That said, I think you're selling your generation short. It shouldn't devalue the words you remember that they derive from popular culture rather than high art. The second usually starts out as the first, and time filters the dross.'

'You know, I can only take so much of you being so damn reasonable. It's winding me up.'

Vale laughed, a sonorous, chesty cackle that was part tormentor and part amused parent. It rattled around the inside of the Land Rover like a trapped bat.

'You're bored, aren't you, Jack?'

'Out of my fucking skull, Tim.'

He laughed again. Nailed. There wasn't much you could hide from Vale. The guy was born to be a spy.

'Is journalism getting too much like working for a living these days then, Mr P?'

'Why do you think I accepted this ridiculous assignment? At least it's getting me out of the office to do more than watch some New Labour blowhards having a circle-jerk.'

'You accepted the assignment because you were flattered by the invitation.'

'Why would I be flattered by some bunch of self-publicising charlatans thinking I was the right guy to beta-test their holiday camp?'

'They had your number, Mr P. Flattery doesn't necessarily need to take the form of praise. Being specifically requested for a junket involving precisely the kind of nonsense you are on the record as detesting was all but guaranteed to get your attention.'

Parlabane said nothing, and couldn't help a resentfully embarrassed bashful smile. Vale was on the nose, as usual. The self-publicising charlatans' efforts to hook him had been transparent, but they had also been irresistible. It had been Maria Scoular, the *Saturday* magazine editor, who'd received the invite, but only as a conduit towards deploying the name upon whose attendance the junket was conditional.

'Fancy this, Jack?' she'd asked, smirking a little as she waved it in front of his desk with clearly no intention of handing it over until she'd had her fun trickling out the details. '"Work hard, play hard, and by Monday morning you'll know who you and your colleagues really are."'

'What is that, the latest motivational missive from management?' he asked. 'I know exactly who my colleagues are. The scum of the earth. Oh, did I say that out loud?'

'It's not from management. It's from a company called Ultimate Motivational Leisure. They're having a junket to hawk an upmarket team-building course, or "experience" as they call it. Posh digs and yomping through the hills to make ageing execs feel all up-and-at-'em.' She put on a cringingly duff American accent, the kind it was politest and most humane merely to pretend wasn't happening. '"The ultimate test of what you're made of, the ultimate journey of self-discovery, the ultimate vision of what you could become." Plus canapés and a turning-down service. Tick box for vegetarian dining option.'

Parlabane reached for the letter, but it still wasn't forthcoming.

'Why is everything "ultimate" in the world of marketing?' he asked, feigning ambivalence about the true question at hand, viz, why she was brandishing this thing at him. 'I used to put it down to some pre-millennial culminatory thing, but the dawn of a new century didn't seem to extinguish this absurd need to claim everything as the last word. Nobody's selling good experiences or even great experiences: it's always ultimate experiences. Sounds pretty final to me. If only. "The ultimate shaving experience": I'd buy that if it was true. "The ultimate reality TV experience, then we promise to fuck off and make something that won't have Lord Reith's coffin burrowing rapidly towards the Earth's core."'

'I saw one on holiday advertising the ultimate bungee-jump experience,' Maria told him. 'Can't say it filled my head with thoughts of safety and assurance. But these guys are making some ballsy claims for what can't amount to more than an activities weekend in the Highlands.'

'Of course they are. They know their target market. They're not pitching to Herbert Grey-Suit who's looking for somewhere a bit different this year for the sales conference. They're after the high-end macho types, guys who want to think they're facing some challenge that not everybody would be up to meeting. But I'll bet we're talking seriously posh digs, because the same target market will also want to indulge their self-image as the refined and cultured elite who need and appreciate the finer things. Easier to hurl yourself face-down in the mud or wade across a ford if you know there's a claw-foot bath waiting for you at the end of the day.'

'McKinley Hall. Recently refurbished. STB Four stars. Taste of Scotland award. There's an uncanny prescience to your cynicism.'

'I'd hardly call it that. But as you're dwelling on the quality of the accommodation, I'll call on the same powers and predict this is the part where you ask me if I want to go. Your own supernatural gifts should be sufficient to divine my answer.'

Maria cocked her head to one side and assumed a deliberately transparent I-know-something-you-don't-know expression. He imagined she liked to think of herself as 'coquettish' in such moments, when in fact she was treading precariously close to frenzied strangulation. She'd been brought in to 'lend a lighter touch' to the weekend glossy; so light, in Parlabane's opinion, that it surely separated itself from the rest of the paper of its own accord and floated into readers' bins without their fingers soiling its delicate pages. The editor, however, saw it differently, mainly because Maria had lent a lighter touch in precisely the way he had hoped and anticipated: namely, filling half of it with fashion spreads of youthful female models (who would otherwise be described in solicitous email spam as 'barely legal teens') invariably in diaphanous garb. The ed's thinking was that it appealed to female readers 'because women like pictures of clothes', and as far as the male reader went, there'd be no complaints 'as long as you can see their nipples', something never in doubt when you were shooting outdoors and braless in Scotland. Most depressingly, the ed was probably right.

Parlabane didn't dislike Maria, but it amused him, indeed amused both of them, to play up to the images of themselves each perceived the other as harbouring. It was probably also known as flirting, or from Parlabane's side as close to it as his sexual self-consciousness would allow in the everlasting aftermath of a tabloid newspaper informing him (and everybody else) that he had been cuckolded by 'a smouldering young doctor'. The story had been part of a far more elaborate stitch-up that landed him in prison and certain others in the ground. People had died, careers had been ruined, a conspiracy was unmasked, a killer jailed and Parlabane had lost several feet of intestine in the process of getting to the truth, but the main thing anyone remembered was that his wife had shagged some surgeon bearing, according to the cheque-book testimony of a former conquest, 'a very big scalpel, if you know what I mean'. Yes, dear, there are partially developed foetuses who know what you mean. That's one holding the tape recorder.

'Aren't you curious as to why I'd even be thinking of offering something like this to you?' Maria asked.

'You mean to me in my capacity as an investigative journalist with better things to do than write advertorial guff for your Travel pages, or to me in my capacity as a cantankerous cynic who thinks any company bearing the word

Ultimate in their name should be summarily asset-stripped and its named directors forced into alternative careers as performers in coprophile fetish hard-core videos?'

'Vividly put, as ever. But I mean to you in your capacity as the person named specifically on the invitation.'

Parlabane grabbed in vain for it once more. 'Where?' he asked, less incredulous than intrigued.

'Mr Parlabane has struck us as precisely the kind of glib and opinionated hack who turns a profit denigrating things that he knows little about and which secretly pique his numerous insecurities. For that reason, we would like to challenge his prejudices and expectations by throwing down the gauntlet and telling him to smell the glove.'

'Aye, very good. You were doing well until the glove remark. I saw *Spinal Tap* on the telly at the weekend too. What does it really say?'

'"Glib and opinionated prick." Nah. It's a formal press release apart from a header paragraph which does request you specifically and exclusively. I couldn't think why, so I phoned the PR company up, and they *did* have the right guy. They know you're the resident hatchet-man and they know you've been through a few scrapes in your time, so they thought you'd have an interesting perspective.'

'Interesting sounds too gentle a word.'

'Oh, they're aware you're likely to slag them off. The girl was a bit coy here and there, as if they're quietly confident you could be in for a pleasant surprise, but they're ready for a kicking.'

'So why waste the freebie on me? Can't they get some chinless wank from the *Daily Mail*?'

This was Parlabane's revenge for the 'glib and opinion-ated prick' remark. Maria's ex bidey-in now worked at the *Daily Mail*. He'd have referred to the guy as her ex-lover, but it was impossible to imagine anyone on that paper being in possession of a functioning penis.

'If some chinless wank from the *Daily Mail* trashed the new Tarantino movie, would it put you off seeing it?'

'No, it would be the best recommendation I could think of.'

'Well, it cuts both ways. Presumably a thorough panelling from you would be just the thing to convince those high-end macho types you were talking about that this is the kind of experience that would blow their hair back. And in the unlikely event that you write something positive, they can say look, even a complete prick like Jack Parlabane thinks we've something to offer.'

'Was it the *Daily Mail* remark?'

'Yes.'

'Good. So either way, they get what they want. What do you get?'

'Good copy, I would hope. Come on, Jack, it'll be fun.'

'It will not be fucking fun.'

'Well, at least you'll be able to have fun saying how little fun it was.'

Parlabane thought about it, or at least pretended to. He was sold way back, on the flimsy and admittedly pathetic basis of the offer's implicit ego-stroking, for even back-handed compliments were compliments nonetheless. There was also the element of challenge being less intentionally presented by a company negligently deluded into believing there really was no such thing as bad publicity.

The downside was actually having to go on the fucking thing, to say nothing of the prospective company of the kind of twats who would sign up for this crap voluntarily. It was for this reason that he told Maria he'd do it on the condition that he could bring his own photographer. There was no way he was putting himself through something like this without an ally, and he had just the man in mind.

'Who?'

'A friend of mine.'

36

'Does he have much experience taking pictures? Maybe a CV or a portfolio I could take a look at?'

Parlabane thought about Tim Vale's CV, at least the little he believed he knew for sure about it, and his photographic 'portfolio'. It would have been a dream to see how coquettish Maria's face looked across the light-table as he laid some of Tim's work down upon it for her evaluation. 'This is an extreme-range telescopic-lens study of two middle-ranking Politburo members engaged with a Finnish call-girl in what is technically referred to as the spit-roast position. What do you think of the composition? Do you think there's too much glare off this subject's arse-cheeks? And here we have an earlier work, an infrared sequence of a dissident being tortured by Stasi agents in a lock-up in Leipzig. Yes, those are wire-cutters. Oh, and mustn't forget his more minimalist period, as typified by this microfilm of documents pertaining to the true extent of the Chernobyl disaster and its projected economic and infrastructural ramifications.'

He settled for: 'He knows what he's doing.'

And lo, it came to pass, that the pair of them were chugging up the A9 in Vale's well-weathered ancient Land Rover, the unrepentantly shoogly and rugged pre-Freelander type that was seldom seen without at least two sheep or four squaddies hanging out of the back.

'So how come you're bored? I thought you were doing rather well these days. Didn't you win an award or something like that?'

'Oh, Christ, everybody wins an award these days in Scottish journalism. I was right up there in the pantheon alongside Best Fixed Odds Prediction Compiler.'

'I think Story of the Year or whatever it was probably carries a little more weight than you're allowing.'

'More weight than I was comfortable with. Blowing the lid off Moundgate turned out to be something of a mixed blessing in terms of career moves.'

'I take it, getting you out of jail and off a murder rap appears in the credit column here.'

'Granted. When I got out of jail the first time, I was practically unemployable, despite what I had to offer in terms of the things I do best. Then the second time, after the big story broke, everybody wanted to hire me, and now I'm practically unfireable despite no longer *offering* the things I do best. That story made me famous; famous enough, anyway, in circles where I was most effective only if I was anonymous.'

'But didn't you do that big undercover thing last year about the Big Firm or whatever you call them?'

'The Old Firm,' Parlabane corrected. Vale was referring to his through-the-looking-glass discovery of how either side of the Glaswegian footballing fault-line perceived the other. They didn't consider themselves extreme – they each hated the extremists on the other side. Each had painted a picture of the other lot's intolerance and extremism in beliefs and attitudes, but Parlabane had failed to find much evidence of these beliefs or attitudes actually being held. In effect, he found a lot of angry folk who thought the world would be a better place without people like *them*, but *them*, the people as described, didn't exist, and the tragedy was that their world wouldn't be better if you could make them see that. They needed an enemy to project their anger and loathing on to.

'It was hardly undercover,' he went on. 'I just went to a few games, drank in a few pubs and earwigged a few conversations. It's easy to be anonymous among football supporters, especially the loud-mouthed numpties who want to believe the world is full of folk who agree with them. But these days there isn't a PR office or ministerial advisor who doesn't know exactly who I am.'

'You made yourself the story, that was your mistake. Same as the spy game, Jack: when you make it about you, you end up exposed.'

'To be fair, there were other parties scheming pretty hard to make it about me too. Beadie, for one.'

'And you played right into his hands.'

'Guilty. The consensus is that I subsequently redeemed myself, but in practical terms much of the damage was irreversible. I've got a bigger salary, lots of clout around the paper and more editorial freedom than I could once have dreamed of, but I can't help feeling like the pipe and slippers are upon me. Ratified respectable status. Ach, I don't know. Mid-life crisis shite, complaining about nothing, ain't I?'

'Sounds like it, old chap.'

'I mean, nobody's tried to kill me for more than three years. I should be pretty pleased about that. But part of me takes that as a sign of slipping standards.'

They both laughed, Vale bending forward over the steering wheel, his eyes narrowing as they did in moments of the greatest mirth and sincerity. Some people looked younger when they smiled, but when Vale did, his age simply seemed frustratingly indeterminate in a different, sunnier way.

'Seriously though, old chap, you've batted an impressive innings in that particular field. But there's glory also in having the judgement to know when it's time to declare.'

'I know you're trying to annoy me when you start using analogies pertaining to that bloody awful game.'

'To quote your fellow Scottish journalist, Bob Crampsey, I consider it a day wasted on which one passes up the opportunity to mention cricket. However, my point remains sincere. How many people have tried to kill you, Jack?'

'I don't know. I've never felt like counting them up.'

'Perhaps it's time you did, as an exercise in perspective. What you have to bear in mind is that the scoreline someone in your profession would – and should – normally be looking at is zero, apart from psycho ex-lovers and the like, which

39

don't strictly count as we're only looking at attempts caused directly by your work. Let me start you off with a big one: the then Secretary of State for Scotland, Alastair Dalgleish.'

'Nah, strictly speaking, Dalgleish didn't personally try to have me killed. It was Roland Voss he had killed, and I got in the way of the mopping-up operation. I'm not sure how much Dalgleish even knew about my involvement until it was too late. It was his ex-security-services hired thug, George Knight, who tried to have me killed; Sarah too, and Nicole who was holed up with us at the time, ironically for her own safety. Ah, yes, George Knight. Charming individual. Would have been a shoe-in for Home Secretary if Thatcher had been aware of his gifts.'

'So that's one: and oh dear, see? We've exceeded that "normal journalist" baseline already and we've only just begun. Who else?'

'Okay, let's see. Stephen Lime. He really did personally try to kill me. Sarah too, again. Sad how intemperately some people can react when you burgle their office, haxor their PC and derail their murderous plan to score a swift few mill.'

'Quite. That's two. And then there was the PR guru type, Mr Beadie, which makes—'

'No, we have to go back before we can go forward. Someone tried to kill me in LA, but that one'll have to remain anonymous: the prick with no name.'

'You didn't even know his name and he wanted you dead? That should tell you something: sounds like the homicidal equivalent of casual sex.'

'No, I meant it was a hitman but I never knew who sent him. Could have been one of . . . let's say I pissed off a lot of people over there, so it wasn't exactly a narrow field.'

'Thus you further my promiscuity analogy.'

'They didn't all want me dead, Tim. I hope. Just one of them. So him, or maybe even her, then Lime, then Knight.'

'And I'm assuming – nay hoping – Beadie was the last?'

'Yes and no.'

'Ye— How can he be yes and no: he either was or . . .'

'Lime tried to kill me again while I was in prison. I wasn't sure whether he counts twice.'

'For the purposes of what I'm trying to demonstrate, then yes. It's attempts we're counting.'

'In that case, you'll have to notch up another for Beadie, then. He only put up one contract, but there were two attempts to scoop the pot. I'm pretty sure he was also planning to kill Sarah, if you're keeping a tally of subsidiary murder attempts.'

'You bloody well should be. That's three times your wife's life has been in jeopardy because of your activities; few of which, I should add, would be recognised under even the most liberal definition of the word journalism.'

'Nah, only twice. The first time was as much her own fault as mine. And she was only my wife for the last one.'

'Oh, you're clutching at straws now. And no amount of pedantry changes the fact that there have been repeated attempts on your life and Sarah's, all because of things you've done for the sake of a byline.'

'That's a bit trite, Tim. There was a sight more at stake and you know it. I could as easily say you did as much – and a lot more – for the sake of a pay cheque and a pension. Neither of us was doing it merely because it was our job.'

'True, but only one of those jobs was *supposed* to involve covert surveillance, burglary, computer hacking and butting heads with professional assassins. Granted, you got away with it – even saved a few more lives than just your own, and hats off to you for that. But as I said, there's a wisdom in knowing when it's time to declare.'

'I have declared, Tim. Why do you think I'm reduced to looking for my kicks on this pitiful excursion?'

'But I'm sure I heard the good doctor Sarah say you

received a death threat only last month from some of those lovely Countryside Alliance types.'

'More like six months ago, maybe a year. All I did was suggest that the Kite mark should be temporarily withdrawn from Barbour clothing until it had been investigated whether there was a link between wearing it and certain, em, shall we say, neurological symptoms. Anyway, death threats don't count. You should see how many the sports editor gets. It doesn't take much to have the monobrows reaching for the green-ink biro and their double-spaced scribble-pad. You need to pose a lot more of a threat before someone genuinely attempts to rub you out.'

'I can understand your perverse pride in that, Jack, but I hope you appreciate that pride is all it's worth. I think you should be grateful to have snagged a spot in the comfort zone and survived to enjoy it, given the number of enemies you've made and the ways in which you made them. Don't worry that the grass is growing under your feet just because you're not collecting any new ones. And if it's bothering your ego that nobody's taken a punt at you recently, I'd recommend you find an alternative source of self-esteem pretty damn pronto.'

'It's cool, Tim. You can spare me the counselling. I've already had that particular dark night of the soul. The reasons for my past behaviour have been long since laid bare and dissected. Insecurities projected into isolationism, ego-driven desires to humble those who make me feel small, id-driven thirst for visceral thrill-seeking, to say nothing of a self-loathing manifested in a conditioned and channelled but nonetheless dangerous self-destructive streak. I'm down with the self-analytical shit, daddy-o. I am well aware of how insane some of my past deeds were, and of my less altruistic reasons for doing them, but that doesn't stop me missing it all now and again.'

'You're missing your youth, Jack, that's all. And who

doesn't? Do you think I want to be eating cold cabbage soup in a Bucharest basement tonight, blowing on my fingers so they're not too stiff to pull the trigger if my contact turns out to be setting me up? Do I buggery, but I still sometimes find myself wishing I was back there, wishing I was that person again, when what I'm really wishing is that I was twenty years younger. You don't want to be breaking into buildings, circumventing surveillance and playing dodge-the-Dobermann just to get a story for a newspaper that'll be wrapped round a deep-fried haggis by the end of the week, do you?'

Parlabane thought about it.

'I guess it should tell me something that it's the mention of deep-fried haggis that's got my juices flowing more than the B&E.'

'Exactly, old chap. And you certainly look like you could do with some junk food. I've never seen you look so disgustingly healthy.'

'I know. I got into a bit of a cycle after the stabbing. Started exercising more than I ever had before just to prove to myself that it hadn't done me any permanent damage. Plus I have to get my adrenaline fixes legitimately these days, so I've upped the ante on the rock-climbing. Physically speaking, I'm a disgrace to my profession.'

'Well, I just hope it doesn't extend to being on the wagon. I'm told this place has a rather choice wine list and I do believe our expenses are being met by our publicity-seeking hosts.'

'Trust me, Tim, if I was on the wagon, I'm damn sure what we're about to encounter would blooter me straight off it.'

'Oh come, come. Shake off that nasty cynicism, Mr Parlabane. It's the only thing holding you back from all the joy life has to offer. Let's have some full-blown Positive Mental Attitude.'

'Yes, sir, Mr Vale. I'm opening my mind wider with every mile closer you drive.'

'Well, that's the carpark dead ahead, so you better hurry it up.'

'I'm getting there, really I am. I can feel it starting to channel through me. There are no problems, only solutions. There are no strangers, only friends I haven't met yet. I am ready to learn, ready to be moulded. I'm feeling empowered. I'm feeling pro-active. Goddammit, I'm feeling ready to stick some David Gray on the stereo and scatter my shrivelled cynicism like ashes as the new me rises like a Phoenix from the . . . oh fuck, who are these bastards?'

'Looks to me like our fellow constituent ingredients in Ultimate Motivational Leisure's great team-building recipe.'

'Not a promising start. I haven't met any of them yet and I already want to kill that one there for wearing shades on his brow in October, and at the very least disembowel whichever one owns the BMW X5 with the "Fair Fuel for All" sticker. If those petrol bills are starting to bite, maybe you should consider driving something that gets more than two miles to the gallon and costs less than FORTY FUCKING GRAND.'

'Happy thoughts, Jack, remember, happy thoughts. Whistle with me, come on.'

Vale coasted the Land Rover into the picnic-area-cum-carpark, a wide oval of grey gravel and tree bark bisected by the road, which narrowed at the far side as it exited between two stone pillars. These each stood at the end of a low wall, continuing as a dry-stone dike and eventually, closer to the surrounding trees, wire fencing to denote the outer boundaries of the McKinley Hall estate. There was a large brass plaque on the left-hand pillar, elegantly inscribed with the name of the property, above a cluster of official tourist-board attributes.

There were already four other vehicles parked in the area, including the ostentatious urban wank-tank and a yellow minibus, which was sitting in front of the pillars and demonstrably preventing any vehicular progress into the estate. In front of it were a gaggle of fellow initiants into the rites and mysteries of UML, as well as a UML meeter-and-greeter, identifiable by his bright yellow company polo shirt, bright yellow company rainproof jacket and the obligatory clipboard. To the left of the vehicle, next to the side-sliding door, was a collection of light luggage.

Vale killed the engine. Parlabane sighed deeply, then caught his eye and they both laughed.

'Those who are about to die salute you,' Parlabane muttered.

'Speak for yourself. I'm here to get hammered on Merlot and single malt.'

They climbed from the Land Rover and walked slowly towards the gathering, Parlabane distantly wondering what kind of noises a Geiger counter would be making around those yellow togs.

'Good morning,' hailed Mr Obvious, before checking his watch and correcting himself. 'Sorry, afternoon. Donald Baxter, Ultimate Motivational Leisure.'

'I won't call you a liar for the sake of five minutes,' Parlabane assured him, trying his miserable best to seem bouncy and outgoing. 'Jack Parlabane, *The Saltire*. And this is Tim Vale. He's going to be taking the photies.'

Baxter extended a hand and shook each of theirs, briefly but firmly. He seemed warm but not over-ingratiating, which was a relief as Parlabane had set his cloying tolerance to its lowest setting. The guy, close-up, wasn't quite what Parlabane had been expecting. He looked passably lithe for his late thirties and seemed comfortable enough in what he was wearing to suggest he was no stranger to sportswear, but there was something of the indoors about his face, a pallid gauntness that spoke of cramped offices and communal fag-breaks round the basement entrance. A liberating career change, perhaps, God help us, from rat in

45

the office maze to life-embracing activities zealot. Or maybe he would be handling the indoor headgames, all the 'If you were a colour, which colour would you be?' and 'We're on a desert island and we need to build a hut' stuff.

'You're here to slag us off,' Baxter said, grinning. 'Or that's what everybody's expecting, right?'

'I'm here to give an objective and impartial account,' Parlabane insisted, with the level of sincerity that normally accompanied remarks such as 'We'll keep your CV on file' and 'I won't come in your mouth'.

'Don't worry,' Vale said. 'I'm here to make sure he looks like an arsehole in the pictures, so the piece will be fairly balanced overall.'

'This is going to be written up for the paper?' asked a voice. 'I hope you've the budget to clear the image rights if I appear in any of the photos.'

It was the guy with the brow-dwelling sunglasses, which turned out to be Oakley Magnesiums, and which were not the only upscale designer detail about his person. He looked like he was wearing Parlabane's mortgage. No question the wank-tank was his too, which was an uplifting thought, as it meant there was one fewer person present he already wanted to kill.

'Rory Glen, The Reflected Gleam Agency,' he announced himself. The accent was schooled in Edinburgh, that marbles-in-the-mouth, speak-without-moving-your-lower-jaw drawl that was either taught on the Lothian Posh Schools Official Syllabus or a post-op symptom of certain rugby injuries. Parlabane detected a hint of something else to it too, aspirationally trendy despite several generations of tweed-wearing in the bloodline. 'And this is Elizabeth Ford, also of Reflected Gleam. My, ehm, associate.'

Glen's ostensibly informal omission of Reflected Gleam's represented hierarchy was, Parlabane interpreted, intended merely to underline it. It was in the boss's gift to accord such apparent parity of status, his privilege to pretend to himself that he meant it. The woman acknowledged Vale and Parlabane with a smile so thin it was eligible for a Red Cross parcel drop, momentarily making Parlabane warm to the poor bugger who had to work with her. It was almost comforting to know there was someone present who wanted to be here less than he did.

'We're in advertising,' Glen offered, which did not come as a momentous surprise to Parlabane's ears. The guy announced it with a contented confidence that suggested he spent little time outside of circles where this was considered impressive. Parlabane resisted the urge to say: 'Wow, can I have your autograph?', remembering a period when he had once been bursting to tell people he was a reporter (though to draw a distinction, he had been half this guy's age at the time).

'Have you got the UML account?' Parlabane asked, switching to Best Behaviour Mode, a technique of affected credulous sincerity that was an essential skill of his trade.

'I'm not sure they could afford us,' Glen replied, laughing heartily at his own stab at what just about technically qualified as a joke. 'Nah, just kidding. We're going to do a deal soon, I'm sure, but we both agreed Reflected Gleam should sample the merchandise before we pitch.'

'So who's handled their PR so far?'

'Ian Beadie,' Baxter said, a glint in his eye as he looked at Parlabane. 'Big House Promotions.'

'Ian Beadie?' asked Glen. 'But I thought . . . oh, I see. Big House. Very good.'

'We're actually using a firm called Seventh Chime,' Baxter went on. Glen nodded sagely in a way that divulged he'd never heard of them and didn't want to admit it. Parlabane, for his part, was glad Baxter hadn't expanded on the unspoken significance of the Beadie remark, specifically his inconveniently publicised part in it. The former tabloid

47

editor and self-styled PR Rottweiler was serving four life sentences for various counts of murder, attempted murder, conspiracy to murder, blackmail and attempting to pervert the course of justice. As he had just admitted to Vale, certain of those counts related to Parlabane, and their ultimate failure had not come before he got to learn what a sharpened steel ruler feels like when someone's using it to stir your guts. It wasn't a period of his life that Parlabane was very happy to recall, far less discuss with relative strangers, and nor would it have made his fellow guests garrulous in his company over the coming days if they feared he was on some kind of sting.

'And have they sampled the merchandise?' Parlabane asked.

'We're waiting for them, as a matter of fact.'

This confirmed something that had hitherto confused Parlabane, mainly, admittedly, on account of his own expectations. While Glen had wasted no time in announcing his terribly impressive presence and introducing his visibly reluctant underling, there had been no indication that the rest of the gathering comprised the remainder of a Reflected Gleam delegation, imminently about to be subsumed into one dynamic corporate consciousness. Instead there was a lot of shuffling of feet and nervy, polite eye-contact between people who were clearly not yet comfortable together and who were probably even less comfortable at the prospect of just how intimate they might soon be forced to become.

'So this isn't all Reflected Gleam folks?' he asked. 'I'd assumed, with it being a team-building weekend, that the point of the exercise—'

'It's a little more than a team-building weekend, Mr Parlabane,' Baxter interrupted. 'As I'm sure you'll find out. In fact, this would be a good point to advise you to leave your expectations in the back of the Land Rover. But you're right. In future normal practice, the UML Experience will be aimed at groups of people who work together. The point of the exercise this weekend, this being a promotional undertaking, is to demonstrate to our potential partners and potential customers that if we can bind together people who don't even know each other, then just imagine the effect on a group of committed colleagues. We'll be waiting until everybody's here before formal introductions. Saves a lot of confusion and repetition.'

UML Experience. Parlabane could hear the capitals and see the trademark.

'Is it part of the UML Experience to park a mile outside the hotel?'

'Actually, it's more like two miles, the way the road winds round the river, but yes. And at risk of bringing down some of the scorn you've got primed and ready to tip, I'll explain that it's for psychological reasons.'

'I had just assumed it was so we couldn't escape.'

'That's pretty close to the truth. When they enter the estate, we want people to forget the outside world, leave it behind along with their expectations and prejudices. Your car is a big link to that, a visual cue every time you catch sight of it. It can break the spell, if you like, which can be damaging at certain more delicate points of the process. This is one of those experiences where you only get back as much as you're prepared to give of yourself, and the presence of a vehicle that you know can swiftly return you to your everyday life is likely to distract from that commitment. It's also been proven by experience that people are more likely to bail out when the going gets tough if they can do so privately and unilaterally. You can bail out of here any time you want, but to do so you will have to get one of us to take you back across the river. You'd be surprised what a barrier that can be. It's amazing how people can find an extra something in their locker when the alternative is admitting to everybody that they're giving up and running out.'

'How tough's the going going to get?' Parlabane asked.

'I can't say. You're all likely to find different aspects more challenging than others – but you'll *all* be challenged. Otherwise we'd just be wasting our time.'

'Wine list and *haute cuisine* notwithstanding,' Vale was compelled to add.

'I'd take nothing for granted if I were you,' Glen suggested. 'We might be on bread and water as a team punishment, or have to earn our meals like on BB.'

'BB?' Vale asked, apparently baffled.

'*Big Brother*. The TV show.'

Still Vale offered a blank countenance.

'Don't tell me you've never at least heard of it?'

'Mmm. Vaguely. Can't say it captured my imagination.'

'Oh, you're not one of these prudish types who gets all self-righteous about voyeurism and hidden cameras and spying on people?'

'Each to his own, I suppose,' Vale said with a poe-faced shrug. 'But I do find the idea a little distasteful.'

Parlabane, close to self-mutilation with his fingernails to avoid laughing, reminded himself never to play cards against the devious bastard.

Motivational Oratory (i)

'I appreciate more than anyone just how busy you all are, so I don't intend to take up too much of your time, but I do feel it appropriate to share a few words with you right now, on what I feel will be a very important occasion for our establishment.'

Sir Lachlan stood a few steps up on the grand staircase, looking as ever like a timid and embarrassed senior relative who'd been asked to make an impromptu speech at a surprise birthday party. His dress was unusually sober, perhaps because for once he would be taking something of a back seat with regard to the hotel's meeting and greeting duties; those, like a great deal else about the running of the place this weekend, being deferred to the UML lot. He had atypically eschewed the overbearing tartanry, sporting neither kilt nor trews, though Alison's keen eye detected the familial plaid on the inside lining of his waistcoat, which he fingered nervously at the left-hand seam as he spoke. Now that she came to think of it, this was as little tartan as she had ever witnessed or even imagined about his person, including pyjamas as observed during last month's nocturnal false fire alarm.

When she'd first arrived she thought he was doing it (or more accurately overdoing it) for the benefit of the tourists, or as part of an affected Scottisher-than-thou image projected by many members of the Caledonian upper orders, possibly in compensation for sounding like they'd seldom left rural Englandshire. In time she had become aware that it was not so much a uniform as an all-over comfort blanket, and the

51

more he wore, the more self-assured he behaved. It was unexpected, then, that on this day of all days, with so much at stake and his anxiety levels correspondingly high, he should be so uncomfortably in mufti, but Alison guessed it was evidence that the hand – or rather tongue – of Lady Jane had ruled the day. If so, it was a testament to the respect in which he held her judgement, or fear in which he held her wrath, that he was in obedience despite her absence, she having left for London via Inverness first thing that morning.

Lady Jane had been to the fore in brokering the deal with UML, she being the one with far more of an astute head for business. With so much riding on the success of the promotional junket, it had therefore been an inopportune time for her mother to break her hip and require the presence of her only daughter at her Kensington bedside. Lady Jane had been forced to depart with all haste, muttering darkly about the folly of octogenarian equestrianism, and leaving the success of this arguably make-or-break venture in the hands of her beloved but less than trusted husband. She had dispensed a lengthy staccato of instructions to Sir Lachlan as he carried her bags to the Range Rover, the last and most impassioned of which was: 'Stay out of the way as much as possible and for God's sake don't be strutting around in all that bloody tartan. It's not a bloody theme park.'

So here he was, left to rally the troops before the guests descended, almost bereft of his talismanic garb and more than a little hamstrung by his wife leaving the staff under no doubt that she shared their perception of him as a bumbling idiot. The staff were gathered in the entrance hall, the almost imposingly impressive sight that greeted guests once they arrived through the wide double doors. The reception desk was to the left as you came in, but the hall was dominated by the staircase dead ahead, sweeping widely up to a half-landing, from which it split in two and ascended to the first floor. The ceiling hung two high stories above,

wood panelling flanking the walls, this height accommodating a gallery on the first floor that overlooked the
entrance hall on all four sides. Pairs of crossed claymores
hung from the wooden panels, both a decoration and a testament to McKinley Hall's survival of less civilised times. The
half-landing also bore arms: family heirloom rapiers and
cutlasses inside a display cabinet, about which Sir Lachlan
would joke: 'In case of emergency, break glass.'

It was an unquestionably grand setting, but given the
scarcity of their numbers and Sir Lachlan's nigh-apologetic
lack of presence, there was an uncomfortable intimacy about
it, like the meeting may as well have been taking place in
the kitchen. Granted, Sir Lachlan wanted to impress a sense
of moment upon them, but the palpable reality of the gathering was a load of busy people obliged to listen to someone
who they all wished would just give it a bye, not least to
spare their mutual embarrassment.

'As you are all no doubt well aware, my family has
invested a great deal in the restoration of McKinley Hall,
and its transformation from a state of neglect into this proud
and beautiful building is to me a source of great . . . ehm
. . .' Alison winced in the tension of the silence as he groped
pointlessly for an alternative to 'pride', the poor soul doubtless imagining scorn and criticism in the minds of an audience who for the most part weren't actually listening. 'Pride,'
he eventually decided with an acknowledging smile. 'But
restoring a building is a straightforward matter in comparison with the, ehm, matter of restoring a reputation, and it
has been the challenge of, well, all of us here, to make people
think . . . the right thoughts about McKinley Hall. Rather
than the wrong ones, as they may have before.'

The right thoughts. Inspirational stuff. Adding to Alison's
empathetic discomfort was her knowledge of how
passionate and engagingly articulate Sir Lachlan could be
when he was talking about this very subject. His problem

was that he didn't do bullshit or business-speak very well, something of which Lady Jane was excruciatingly aware in laying the groundwork for playing host to UML. Alison didn't know much about this team-building outfit, but had garnered enough to guess that business-speak would be their stock-in-trade, with bullshit never running low in the supply cupboard.

'The right thoughts are that McKinley Hall is now a magnificent country hotel in a splendid setting, with a heady kind of atmosphere you can only find somewhere steeped in . . . history. A place with elegant accommodation, unrivalled tranquillity and, of course, the finest of staff.'

It was an indication that he was barely treading water that he had resorted to quoting the hotel's own brochure copy, but this actually counted as a decent recovery from the jolt of almost careering into the treacherous badlands of '. . . history'.

Peter Mathieson, the chef, cleared his throat ostentatiously. Sir Lachlan looked at him, a little startled, in fear that this was a form of heckling or confrontational disrespect, all the worse for its source being the person other than his wife whom he held in most cowering awe. Then his face visibly lightened in relief as he realised it was merely a humorous prompt, and for that as close as he could have hoped to get to audience rapport.

'And, sorry, yes, how could I forget, absolutely the finest of food. Thank you, Peter. We have indeed so much to offer, and with this weekend a very important opportunity to demonstrate that. I know you're probably thinking that what we all need now is for me to shut up so that you can get on with preparing for this weekend, but I wanted to acknowledge a few things, not least your efforts in what have sometimes been trying . . . times. We had to lay some staff off in the summer and I know the rest of you have felt you're spread rather thin as a result. We didn't have the best of luck and there's been times when I've felt the weight of . . . well, I suppose you could say, the past was against us here. But we've held it together, haven't we? And now we're looking at what we all hope will be a whole new beginning.'

The weight of the past. That was what he meant by 'the wrong thoughts', and what he had unintentionally stumbled towards when he mentioned history. These were all tentative references to something Sir Lachlan would never directly speak of or even formally acknowledge, and his staff would be skirting dismissal were he to hear them mention it.

Alison had been working there a little under four months, since leaving school at the end of June. Her sixth-year exam results, supplementing what she had already garnered in fifth, had earned her offers from a number of universities, but having spent all of her nineteen years in Inverness, she knew her restless feet would not be satisfied by mere relocation to Glasgow or Edinburgh, exciting as student life there would no doubt be. The limits of her world had been so narrow that the desire to expand her horizons grew in inverse proportion; so much so that she reckoned it was a good thing she wasn't from Dingwall, as it might have taken a trip to outer space to sate her wanderlust. As it was, she would settle for the Far East to begin with, and see how much farther east she could get before the money ran out.

That was why she was at McKinley Hall. With her name not being Jacasta and her parents inexplicably having failed to establish a six-figure trust fund for her further education and gaap yaah, she was going to have to finance her travels off her own back. It had therefore seemed a prudent – if a wee bit ascetic – course of action to get a job that would not only earn her some money but drastically curtail her opportunities to spend it. The McKinley Hall estates appeared on the Ordnance Survey map approximately four kilometres north of the Middle of Nowhere, so the only jobs offering fewer opportunities to go shopping and socialising were on platforms in the North Sea, where the time-on to time-off ratios were more forgiving. She slept there six nights a week, sometimes seven when she couldn't be bothered with the eight-hour round trip (minibus, bus, train) home to Sneck. The plan was to stick it out until Christmas, then take off into the great unknown in the new year with every penny she'd accrued.

She'd started in July as a waitress, but like almost everyone else in the place, found the definition of her duties more and more blurred as the summer wore on. Unfortunately, this was not because business was booming and the place stretching to accommodate its guests. Tourism in the Highlands was continuing to suffer in the aftermath of September 11 (and more locally, the attack on Dubh Ardrain), with the free-spending Americans just not travelling here in anything like the numbers they used to. But this summer, it had been a more powerful and even more merciless saboteur that had done the damage. The weather had been utterly bloody miserable, with the relentless rain and unseasonably low temperatures driving the suffering natives abroad in record numbers. So with the Yanks staying put and the Brits buggering off, the tourist economy was like a weakened heart pumping a depleted volume of blood: everyone was suffering, but the more remote you were, the worse it got. McKinley Hall, marketing itself on its isolation, was not best placed to ride out the storm.

Staff were laid off and their duties absorbed into the survivors' workloads, with eighteen-hour days not uncommon to accommodate every whim of what guests the place did attract. Neither the bar nor the kitchen would ever close as long as there was a credit-card-holder still conscious in the building. Alison didn't mind so much though, apart from when her treacherous alarm clock made its implausible claims that morning had come around again after what

felt like only twenty minutes' sleep. After months of relentless study, some good, honest, physical hard work still
seemed like an easier option than picking up another Chem-
istry textbook. Plus, a benefit of her expanded workload
was that over recent weeks she'd got to help out in the
kitchen, rather than just ferrying plates to and from the
diners.

The downside of this was that it was against the wishes
of the chef, who not only refused to teach her anything, but
harassed and abused her even more than previously when
she was only waiting tables. His problem wasn't that he was
being forced to accept the unskilled help of waiting staff in
order to keep the ship afloat (though that was hardly balm
to his inflamed ego), but that it was Alison who had been
given the nod to do so by Lady Jane. As opposed to Monica,
who'd got her jotters instead.

Monica had been there longer than Alison, so it was
natural that there would be some resentment about the
newer girl surviving the axe, but the more sober consensus
was that the decision was as unsurprising as it was inevitable
in this necessarily austere regime. Monica was, it was widely
accepted, in no imminent danger of death from hard work,
moaned constantly about what little she did get around to,
and her digits were rumoured to become spontaneously
adhesive in the vicinity of a cash register. Mathieson,
however, saw properties in her that he judged Alison lacked:
principally, big tits and being happy to let him shag her
without any complicating commitments such as acknowledging that they were engaged in any kind of relationship.

Mathieson didn't go a bundle on Lady Jane, either, though
he was less directly vocal in expressing this. To be fair to
him (something Alison was far from wont to do), he did
have to endure from his boss a degree of attempted inter-
ference that someone in his position might consider imper-
tinence bordering on provocation. Lady Jane fancied herself

as a cook, or more specifically 'the next Lady Claire Macdonald, except with a half-decent dentist' according to Mathieson. Consequently there were frequent battles, negotiations, compromises and tantrums over the menu, as the boss made her injudicious efforts at pulling rank over someone *she* had hired for his greater expertise. Lady Jane was truly steadfast and business-like in most of her dealings, but perhaps it made her more reassuringly human that she had this flawed compulsion, manifest in the catering equivalent of teaching her grandmother to suck eggs.

In Mathieson's eyes, then, Alison was not only a usurper, but an agent of the enemy: Lady Jane's spy. It was therefore left to the sous-chef, Ger, to make use of her and give her the pointers she required. This was how Mathieson got to have his huff and eat it too: there was a desperately needed extra pair of hands around the kitchen when it was most valuable, but he knew her contribution would fall within his assistant's remit. Thus he could keep up his aggrieved-objection performance without cutting off his nose to spite his face.

It was difficult to get an accurate handle on the dynamic between the chef and his right-hand man. Mathieson was in his early thirties, something of an aspiring culinary superstar who spurned no opportunity to give the impression that he thought this particular gig was beneath him, an inauspicious step on a career ladder that would inevitably lead to very high places. Alison hoped he got there too, all the way to celebrity chef, with his own publishing deal, TV show and homicidal psychotic stalker. Ger was a few years older, or at least looked a few years older in a hard-paper-round kind of way. The first thing anyone was likely to notice about him was the scar running up the right side of his face, from his jawline to just below his eye, but having worked closer beside him, she'd say that his real ruggedness ran deeper. Like Mathieson, the skin on his hands was rough, callused and riven with nicks, scratches and scars. Unlike Mathieson, however, in Ger's case they continued along his forearm as far as his rolled-up sleeves revealed. Alison had been fairly terrified of him the first time she set foot in the kitchen, seeing him picked out in profile as he perused the open fridge, a fearsome blade gripped in his right fist, long straggly hair secured for hygiene purposes in a thick ponytail.

In practice, she barely exchanged words with him for the first couple of months, other than the minimum required to receive and respond to orders, but had quickly learned that in the McKinley Hall kitchen, his was not the presence to dread. Mathieson doled out almost as much abuse to Ger as to everyone else under his command, which she found a little surprising, as it seemed the chef was placing a lot of trust in the invisible barriers of hierarchy to protect him. That most of Mathieson's barbs referred to criminality and prison struck her, if true, to further underline the precariousness of the chef's behaviour.

Ger, for his part, didn't say a lot to anybody, not even to rebuff Mathieson's insults, none of which seemed to penetrate anyway. He worked tirelessly, uncomplainingly and with very little outward sign of stress. It wasn't that he appeared to be tuning everything out, more that he was at one with the place, no matter how frenetic it got. Alison would sometimes catch a glimpse of him when things were getting fraught, and he'd have this small, private little smile about the corners of his mouth that suggested not mere content, but that he might actually be getting off on it. In that respect, he was a reassuring presence to be around, because he made it all – the heat, the din, the chaos, Mathieson's bluster – seem, well, not normal, but not something to shrink from.

She only really got to know him when Lady Jane ordered that the kitchen make more use of her. He talked more at times when Mathieson wasn't around, though perhaps this was partly down to Alison feeling more inclined to conversation herself when the chef's presence wasn't putting her on edge. Mathieson had always tended towards the crude, overfamiliar and downright leery towards the female staff, but now that she had been foisted upon him, he made a point of staring at her tits or making remarks he clearly hoped would make her uncomfortable. Ger tended to ignore this, but it couldn't be said he didn't notice or failed to respond: Alison was sure it was no coincidence that he spent more time teaching her techniques, as opposed to assigning her basic chores, when Mathieson was being obnoxious. Given that this was his default condition, it had meant that she'd very soon learned a lot, and the more useful she became, the clearer it became to all that Mathieson wouldn't be able to get rid of her.

As Mathieson's remarks suggested, Ger had been inside, though he was not expansive about either this part of his life or the preceding part that had put him there. 'I was a bit mental when I was younger. And pretty stupit,' was all he was initially prepared to reveal. Of his workplace demeanour, he explained that he was a guy who knew he was lucky to have a second chance. It hadn't been so long ago that he could never have imagined himself having a career, never mind imagined having a career doing this, so he knew to count his blessings and get on with ensuring he'd be doing it for a long time. When she asked him how he put up with so much abuse, he laughed, a very dirty-sounding cackle.

'I've put up with a lot worse than having to listen tae that wee bawbag,' he said, smiling. 'He's a good chef, and he sure knows it, which is why he's such a wanker. But just because he's a wanker doesnae change the fact that he's a good chef, and I can learn a lot from him. Course, when I've learned everythin' I can from him, I'm choppin' him up an' stickin' him in the freezer . . .'

However, despite this professed philosophy and customary calm, she noticed that he was becoming occasionally less sanguine in the face of Mathieson's excesses. He wasn't confrontational about it, but instead of ignoring the outburst, he would quietly warn Mathieson to calm down, or 'cool the jets', as he preferred to put it. It made Alison feel both a little guilty and a little excited that all of these interventions had been when the vitriol was directed at her. Mathieson, unfortunately, seemed to be taking note of this growing allegiance, and it wasn't making him any easier to be around.

The run-up to the UML weekend witnessed a rising tension throughout the entire place, and it was Alison's experience that whatever conditions prevailed elsewhere in the hotel would be multiplied in their intensity in the kitchen. This was exacerbated by an increase in the frequency of Lady Jane's visits, as her fussing and concern over the junket predictably prompted her to proffer some 'suggestions' for the weekend's special menus. No-one was immune from a sense of heightened anxiety, the words 'make or break' having been used by the lady of the house, with all the implicit ramifications for on-going employment.

The other phrase that had been used was 'new beginning'. McKinley Hall had had a few of those in its time, and even in its latest incarnation as a hotel there had already been a supposed new dawn when it opened its doors to the public. However, with the public not exactly flooding through those doors, the overtures of Ultimate Motivational Leisure had promised, if not a wholly fresh endeavour, at least a chance to kick-start what had stalled.

McKinley Hall had been operating as though at reduced capacity since the late-summer lay-offs, meaning that it couldn't offer all of its rooms even if there were guests enough to fill them. It was a short-term survival strategy, and one that wasn't looking entirely certain of paying off before UML came along and made a virtue out of it. They wanted to take over the entire place for the duration of their 'Experience', but were not offering anything like as many places as the Hall had rooms. They didn't want merely to prevent the intrusion of non-involved guests: they wanted the run of the place, access to every room and anything else that might facilitate the scope they required to play their little games and 'spring a few surprises'. As they would be paying around two-thirds of what the place might hope to make over a weekend at (thus far never achieved) full capacity, their every request, however unusual, was acceded to by Lady Jane. The plan was, all going well, for there to be one UML weekend per month, with that likely to increase as their reputation grew and business expanded. They wanted their relationship with McKinley Hall, Lady Jane reported, to be ultimately not an arrangement but a part-nership. UML couldn't think of a location more suitable for what they had in mind, and it would be a great way of spreading word of mouth about a hotel that was otherwise suffering from being so far off the beaten track. A new begin-ning indeed, but none of it would matter much if the promo-tional premiere weekend went in any way tits-up.

But if Lady Jane was uptight about the weekend being a success, her anxiety was, Alison suspected, quietly eclipsed by that of Sir Lachlan. Given what she had learned about the history of McKinley Hall and his family's relationship with it, she understood better than her less curious colleagues the extent of Sir Lachlan's desires that its new, restored incarnation should be a success; to say nothing of the depths of his fears should it fail. That was why, despite knowing how mutually uncomfortable it would be, he felt compelled to make his speech, and why he'd have made it even if his embarrassed wife had been standing a few feet away, glowering and tutting the whole time. So much had been taken out of his hands recently, he needed to feel he was doing everything that *was* in his power, even if he was merely an enfeebled football manager who knows he's helpless once his players cross the touchline.

'A whole new beginning,' he repeated, nodding to himself. 'A brighter future, and the success that God knows you all deserve. We've all had to work very hard of late just to stay afloat, and I think we all know we're going to have to work even harder to grasp this chance before us, but I also know we're the people to do it. So let's look to the future of McKinley Hall as it lies immediately in front of us, with this, our first Intimate Motivation weekend.'

Alison closed her eyes for a moment, not wanting to catch anyone else's look or be party to a smirk. Intimate Motivation. That was what he'd called it every time, with Lady Jane seething as she corrected him, and it always seemed the harder he was trying to remember the right name, the more the stress guaranteed he'd fluff it. When Alison looked at him again, however, he had a twinkle in his eye, and not just because the ordeal was almost at an end.

'And if you tell Lady Jane I called it that again, you're all fired,' he said, to polite and largely relieved laughter. 'Thank you, everyone. Now let's get to work.'

Purple Hail

Emily stood as near to the back of the semi-circle as she thought she could risk without it being apparent that she was trying to stand as near as possible to the back of the semi-circle. She was wearing a heavy yellow shapeless fleece with a thick-toothed zip, the kind of garment normally only worn by women whose idea of fashion shopping was a biennial trip to Mackay's. By rights the outfit should have been completed by a pair of sta-prest burgundy slacks with an elasticated waist, and beneath those a pair of pants that came up to just below the sternum. She couldn't decide if it was a consolation that everyone else was similarly garbed, as although it was preferable not to be the only one resembling an overweight shaved lemur, it was less than easy on the eye to see this hideousness everywhere she looked.

In her hands she held a paintgun, or as Francis Campbell, UML's über-motivator, described the same object, a 'Kestrel G4 semi-auto marker with compression-assisted power-feed, pro-performance nitrogen back bottle, precision diamond-cut muzzle break and a chronometrically calibrated restricted projectile velocity of 250 feet per second'. She had also been issued with a spare cartridge, a pair of protective goggles and a clip-on earpiece complete with a thin, levered boom-mike. Oh, and of course, the yellow fleece, which had been waiting for her on her bed when she entered the room, compliments of UML.

Surveying the tooled-up lemon assembly and listening to Campbell's interminable address, she had to concede reluctantly to herself that Jack Parlabane had a point when he'd questioned how all of this was going to make anyone a more valuable employee. He struck her as the type of guy who would be utterly insufferable when proven right, and worryingly struck her also as the type of guy who was, insufferably, proven right quite a lot.

Parlabane zeroed in on her almost as soon as she and Kathy had arrived, for reasons that it had failed to occur to him were entirely predictable and thus easily anticipated. She and Kathy ran the PR firm that had been – albeit tentatively – representing UML, so Parlabane, being here to rip the piss out of the whole venture, would be tapping them for anything he could construe as a negative comment. One remark from her, even in an understandable moment of high stress, suggesting she was having anything less than a richly fulfilling time, was worth any number of paragraphs of Parlabane's own vitriol. Forewarned was forearmed, but neither was likely to deter his persistence, so she had already resigned herself to seeing a lot of him over the next couple of days.

He'd piled into the seat in front of her on the minibus, cheerfully introducing himself and his photographer before pitching straight to the top of his agenda by asking: 'So, exactly how big a waste of time and money do you reckon this kind of carry-on is, on a scale from making your own crisps, to the Millennium Dome?'

'It's not costing me any money to come here, Mr Parlabane, so that's a moot point, and I think the moment to assess how well your time has been spent has to come after you've spent it.'

'I meant in general: all of this corporate team-building keech, like *It's A Knockout* without the funny costumes. All right, fair do's if you get a kick out of playing daft games, but is anybody here stupid enough to think it's somehow gaunny make them work better when they get back to the office?'

Emily had smiled and looked straight ahead, partly to convey that she wasn't going to be baited, but equally so that she could get a longer look at Donald Baxter, who was driving. Kathy had sat up front next to him, it having been agreed by the pair of them that they should split up and mingle from the off, no matter how tempting it became to circle the Seventh Chime wagons. With so many people milling around, luggage being loaded and questions being asked, she hadn't been able to make more than brief eye-contact with Baxter as he shook her hand. His face, though, had seemed unnervingly familiar, not so much a spark of recognition as a jolt of something much stranger. If it didn't sound so ridiculous she'd have said it was as though she'd known him in a previous life. She hadn't heard the name before UML approached Seventh Chime, and his voice hadn't rung any bells on the very rare occasion he'd called, it being mostly Campbell who did the moving and shaking. Her conversations with both had been as brief as they had been scarce, the pair preferring email correspondence in accordance with UML's stated belief in 'the electronic office'. (They had exchanged no snail mail, and come to think of it, Emily wasn't sure if she even knew their address.) However, the moment she clapped eyes on Baxter, she felt not only that she knew him, but that she had known him a long time. Unfortunately, she was at a loss as to where from, or just as frustratingly, why she couldn't remember.

It was a happy by-product of her confused scrutiny that she was coming off unflustered to the point of aloof towards her would-be interrogator.

'Given that you might be relying on their goodwill and cooperation over the next few days, Mr Parlabane—'

'Please, call me Jack if it would make you more comfortable.'

'You don't want me to call you what would make me more comfortable. But as I was saying, do you think it's a good idea to be insulting your fellow guests by implying that they couldn't recognise and avoid a waste of their time if they saw it looming ahead of them?'

'Isn't it more insulting to suggest that vacuous "pro-active" management-speak, or taking part in sub-drama-school role-playing games is gaunny make them perform better at their jobs? Or that it makes you closer to your colleagues to know that they caught you when you fell backwards during one of those trust exercises – which I fully expect to be engaged in before nightfall, by the way.'

'If it makes you feel any better,' she replied, 'if we *are* made to do one of those trust exercises you described, you can rest assured I won't attempt to catch you.'

Parlabane's name was familiar, to say the least, even before UML requested he be invited. It was part of her job to know, or at least know about, as many journalists as possible, and though he wasn't likely to be on her guestlist for a new gallery opening, she'd been aware of his byline and his reputation even before he became Ian Beadie's nemesis. Granted, little she had heard about him prior to that had been complimentary, but anyone Ian Beadie hated so much that he'd tried to kill him couldn't be all bad. Working at what might be termed the sunnier end of the PR industry – parties, junkets and launch events, mainly for fairly small, leisure- and media-based businesses – she had thus far no occasion to lock horns with Parlabane, nor had she imagined doing so unless his editor went insane and made him the food critic. This was something she was grateful for, and the reason she lobbied hard, if ultimately in vain, against UML's wish to invite him.

Emily had imagined him to be bigger, somehow. Older too, gnarled, nicotine-stained, beer-bellied and grey-skinned from a lifetime under flickering striplights: the grizzled old-school hack to out-grizzle all old-school hacks. What she'd seen standing by the minibus she had in fact taken to be part of the UML set-up, as he looked lithely fit and had something unmistakably of the outdoors about him. It wasn't just that his face looked healthily weathered by sun and wind beneath a dirty-blond mop that seemed likely to shed sand if he shook it; some people (and there were a few present) simply looked out of place away from their desks, their phones, their bar or their favourite table, and he conspicuously wasn't one of them. It probably enhanced the impression that he was standing next to the infamous Rory Glen, who had typically spent a lot of money on looking the outdoor type, but who had succeeded only in looking all the more like a yuppie on a weekend country break.

Parlabane's photographer was a surprise package too. With Parlabane having cultivated – some might say hammed up – his anti-establishment credentials through the self-image he conveyed in print, it seemed particularly incongruous that he be accompanied (as a condition of attendance, no less) by someone who could have walked out of a Noël Coward play. He was another who looked cut out for whatever the weekend might have in store, though she couldn't decide if he looked fit beyond his years or facially aged by his outdoor exertions. Neither could she decide of which thespian Fox brother he most reminded her, nor explain why she could as much picture him looking through a scope as a lens.

'I'd argue that any social activity – the more pleasurable the better – would bring work colleagues closer together,' offered Rory Glen. It was an intervention for which Emily was grateful enough to offer a conspiratorial smile, even at the potential cost of offering encouragement to a man whose reputation for promiscuity was often denoted by the phrase 'ferret up a drainpipe'. 'Actually,' he continued, 'it might be more accurate to talk about morale-building than team-building, if it's the latter you're so sceptical about.'

'So why not gather the staff and just go for a few drinks,

if it comes to the same thing?' Parlabane asked, turning in his seat to take on Emily's ally. 'Why come all the way up here with them?'

'Because you can get to have a few drinks up here too. It's what else this weekend might offer – and what your local pub presumably doesn't – that we're here to judge.'

'So if we're not the bestest of buddies by the end of it, I'll have proven my point?' Parlabane challenged.

Glen laughed, Parlabane too.

What else this weekend might offer. It didn't look promising through the minibus window. Their vehicle meandered slowly along a single-track road, its pace dictated less, she suspected, by the driver's desire to showcase their surroundings than by the tortuous bends and dips he was cautiously negotiating. They had disappeared under a canopy of greenery only yards past the gateway, the deciduous forest testament to the remoteness and historical isolation of the spot. Most tree life north of the central belt was planted conifers, vast acres of them in file and column like a Roman regiment. There was plenty of that too, only a mile or so south-west, but the borders of the McKinley estate were buffered by something darker and truly ancient. There was a stillness about it that was like a distant, estranged relative of tranquillity. This was the kind of woodland, she imagined, where the darkest tales, myths and metaphors had been born: treacherous pathways, primal temptation, ripe carnal fertility and bloody, carnivorous death. If any of Beatrix Potter's shower had ventured forth in here, their heads would have ended up on sticks.

Maybe it was just the weather. They emerged from the trees to cross a bridge thirty or forty feet above a wide stream tumbling energetically over rocks, unwearied by the efforts of carving this deep V into the landscape these past few million years. It would surely have been a beautiful sight on a bright, clear day, as would the woods with the sun

69

angling crystal beams through the foliage to the mossy floor. Under heavy clouds and swirling drizzle, there seemed a sense of harshness, even cruelty about the exposed isolation of the place, though this was probably exacerbated by the thought that she'd be spending a lot of time out in it. Such landscapes were really best admired through a double-glazed window with a cold glass of Sauvignon Blanc in front and a warm fire behind.

That would be happening at some point, of course, but she was not without trepidation about what might come first, *what else this weekend might offer*. Taking possession of her first paintgun did little to assuage her doubts, and that was before Campbell began his pep talk.

Within moments of the UML man opening his mouth, she could sense Parlabane's glee. Having all checked in and discovered their accommodation to be of a reassuringly luxurious standard (diminished only by the sartorial suicide note lying across the duvet), they were mustered under order in a grand, high-ceilinged drawing room. There was a glorious fire blazing in the cavernous hearth, causing Emily to survey the room with much the same longing she imagined Eve regarded the garden as the gates closed forever behind her. Instead of a comfy chair and a menu, she was issued with 'the tools of team-building': equipment the efficacy of which looked at that stage in some doubt.

Campbell stood before the fire, Baxter deferentially positioned a few feet behind and to the left. Campbell looked younger than his colleague, perhaps the youngest person in the room, but had been introduced by Baxter as 'the motivational genius UML head-hunted for this post from a short-list of one'.

'Good afternoon,' he began. 'And welcome to the UML Experience. I have to say, I envy you your position because you don't know what's in store, and I really wish I could

70

be in your shoes. I feel like a parent waiting to see his children opening their Christmas presents.'

'Well begun is half done,' one of Emily's primary teachers used to say, and from an 'enthusiastic pitch' point of view, she couldn't fault Campbell's opening gambit. Nonetheless, she'd wager that if old Mrs McQueen could have heard Campbell continue, she'd have changed her proverb to 'well begun is no guarantee that the rest won't be a complete fucking embarrassment'.

'What is about to be engaged with here is essentially a paradigmatic prospective assemblage intended to render a dynamic orchestration of employee energistics across multiple vertices. Through a system of non-apparent motive vehicles, we will seek to initiate from within the disintegrated participatory constituents an innovated focus-drive generating a core-gravity that will channel exertory critical impulses along complementary and bi-reflexive vortals . . .'

He looked up to a semi-circular gallery of jaw-gaping silence.

'Or is that what you were expecting me to say?' he asked. There was relieved laughter around the room, and a rather too self-satisfied look on Campbell's face, like a cheap stage magician overimpressed by his own trick.

'Okay, let that be lesson number one. If you have expectations, we're going to mess with them. If you have assumptions, we're going to debunk them. I'm not here to give you any lectures or to presume to tell any of you how better to do your jobs. Nor am I daft enough to preface what's about to take place here by projecting a standardised outcome from it. The only thing I can predict for sure is that you're all going to learn a few things you didn't know about yourselves and each other, and whether that helps you back in civilisation, who can say . . . though I'll be surprised if it doesn't. The main thing to bear in mind for what lies ahead, the absolute crux of the exercise, is that we're here to have some fun, okay?'

Not bad, Emily reckoned, and he'd pulled off a good gag; though she couldn't help suspect it had been coached rather than natural. Campbell still struck her as someone who'd have been more comfortable talking in management-speak than taking the piss out of it. 'Projecting a standardised outcome' had slipped in there fluently enough. And taking the piss out of something was often a cheap way of buying your indulgence in it: you make one joke about it and people are less aware of how seriously you're taking it the rest of the time. This suspicion was borne out by Campbell's subsequent reference to their overdue mutual introductions as 'an identity affirmation exercise'. It sounded second-nature to him, but plenty of people laughed, assuming he was still at one cool-ironic remove.

'Now, you were told as you entered the room that we were issuing you with the tools of team-building. Can you show me those tools?'

A number of paintguns were held aloft with varying degrees of enthusiasm, ranging from Rory Glen striking a macho pose, to cursory waves of the barrel, and of course Jack Parlabane pretending to shoot himself in the head.

'Wrong,' Campbell announced. 'And we'll call that lesson number two. You thought we meant the paintguns. We didn't. We meant your colleagues here in front of you. *They're* what you build a team from. And we're about to demonstrate that right now.'

They were each invited to come forward and introduce themselves to the rest of the room, whereupon they were required to thrust their hands into a black sack and pull from it a strip of cloth, either red or blue.

Again, participation ranged from the self-conscious to the over-assertive, with the conduct of the two Reflected Gleam delegates illustratively calibrating the spectrum.

The invitation had gone out to 'Rory Glen and guest', so it didn't reflect much of UML's gleam if Liz Ford had been the RG staffer who *most* wanted to attend. Reading between the lines, it was plausible to imagine a number of disappointed male employees whose enthusiasm for the jaunt had carried less lustre for Rory than the prospect of getting into Liz's pants amid the conducive informality of a boozy jolly.

Emily, despite having hung back until almost the last, announced herself with practised professional enthusiasm, beaming to the room with her invaluable PR technique of making eye-contact with everybody but focusing on no-one. She delved a hand into the sack and pulled one of two remaining strips from it. A swift tally of the assigned colours told her the last would be blue also, and she observed with a stifled groan that Parlabane was yet to draw.

'My name is Jack Parlabane,' he said, having ambled forward with a tediously demonstrable lack of haste. 'I'm from *The Saltire*. I'm here to have my expectations, assumptions and prejudices thoroughly confirmed, and if they're not I'll write that they were anyway, because I'm a journalist and that's what we do.'

So that made two people who were pretending to be self-deprecatory.

Emily and Kathy had set up Seventh Chime six years ago, both having worked most of their professional lives in the assorted tiers of public relations. Emily's introduction to the field had been as a press officer for an umbrella group of voluntary organisations, legacy of her guilt-ridden lefty past, while her fellow traveller Kathy, having studied drama, had discovered a greater talent for publicising theatre groups than for acting in them. They'd both seen the grotty and glam ends of the business, each having had uniformly brief corporate tenures and appointments at major media houses. When they decided to go out on their own, it was so that they could represent companies and organisations that they believed in, or were at least not ashamed of. They'd both witnessed the professional obfuscation their job could require, and neither wanted to be the 'spokesperson' on *Newsnight* squirmingly trotting out the corporate line in shamefaced defence of the indefensible, while at home a million viewers gave their telly the finger. It would be fair to put it that they didn't want to be representing the kind of people who would have them locking horns with the likes of Parlabane. What was it he'd written about Beadie? 'Personal contrition is realising you're in the wrong and consequently making amends; corporate contrition is realising you're in the wrong and consequently hiring Ian Beadie.' Something like that.

Seventh Chime was in the information business, and their philosophy was that it should always be about giving, not concealing. She had nothing to be ashamed of, and neither did UML. Even if this did turn out to be a pile of crap, nobody was being deceived and nobody was being hurt, so she wasn't going to let Parlabane make her feel like some corporate whore just for earning her living. She respected Jack Parlabane for what he was and what he'd done, but right now he was acting like a petulant teenager taken under protest on a family holiday. That he was drawn on her side was a double blow. Not only did it mean this first part of 'the UML experience' would have to be pretty special to unite the two of them in a team, but it meant she didn't even get the satisfaction of shooting at the fucker.

'So did anyone catch the rules at all?' Emily asked. They were standing around the hotel's outdoor tennis court, their blue favours strapped tabard-style over the mandatory yellow fleeces, headsets making them look like the world's worst-dressed teeny-pop group. 'I was paying attention, but I started feeling self-consciously girly around all these boy-toys. We basically have to shoot the other lot, is that it?'

As well as herself and Parlabane, the blue team comprised Liz Ford from Reflected Gleam; Toby Seaton, who ran some charity in Newcastle, the name or nature of which Emily hadn't caught, and Joanna Wiggins, an IT consultant from Liverpool. Though lacking any solid reason to overestimate the calibre of the opposition, Emily was predicting that the only team-building effect of this exercise would be to bond the blue lot through shared adversity and humiliation. During the brief gun demonstration-cum-practice session, the only person less accurate in their shooting than herself had been Parlabane, who had consistently failed to even hit the circular ringed target pinned on a lamp-post twenty feet away, never mind get anywhere near a bullseye. Toby had looked a little more gifted in terms of aim and basic hand-eye coordination, but he also struck Emily as so shy and unassuming that he'd be afraid to splat an opponent for fear of offending them. And then there was Joanna. She was the best shot of the group and seemed the most cheerfully enthusiastic about the prospect of the game at hand, but she was also, without wishing to put it indelicately, likely to present the largest and least mobile target.

'It's basic CTF stuff,' Joanna informed the group.

'CTF?'

'Capture the flag.' She pointed to the blue flag resting against the net in the centre of the court.

'Ah.'

'This is our base. There's a red flag in theirs. We have to get hold of their flag and bring it back here, while stopping them doing the same thing.'

'And if they get our flag to their base first, they're the winners? So it's like a race.'

'It's not a race. The winner is the first team to bring home the enemy flag while their own flag remains uncaptured. If they get ours, we have to get it back here.'

'Got it, I think. '

'Also, if they get hold of ours, we have to channel all efforts into a cross-steal before we even think about recovering our own flag.'

'To create a stand-off,' Parlabane suggested, to Joanna's approving nod. 'Buys us time.'

'And you all know the drill about getting hit?'

'I caught that part, yes. Like I said, I was paying attention, it was just . . . Sorry, doesn't augur well, does it?'

'Between the rules and learning to work the guns, it was a lot of information at once,' Toby assured her. It would have sounded patronising to the point of sarcasm from anyone else (well, from a specific one else), but there was a sincerity about Toby bordering on the apologetic. The phrase 'big drink of water' leapt to mind when she looked at him, but this was an uncharitable thought symptomatic of her growing discomfiture. It wasn't looking good for the UML experience that her first response to the situation was to develop irrational hostilities and begin identifying faults and weaknesses in her team-mates. So far she had subconsciously dissed Fatty, Weedy and Sarky before a shot had been fired. It was only a game, for God's sake. Get it together, girl.

'I'm lost too,' confessed Liz. 'But it's always worth bluffing a while in the hope that someone else elicits a recap.'

'Agreed,' said Parlabane. 'The trick that's let me snooze through a thousand press conferences. Sounds like you're the one distinguishing yourself as leadership material, Joanna.'

'Bollocks I am. I just know about it from work. Online CTF games are what office networks are really for. Why do you think the IT folk are always last to leave the building?'

'You serious?' Liz asked.

'Semi. We work late to get the job done, but it's a good way of winding down afterwards.'

'I thought that's what Shiraz was invented for,' Liz argued.

'Granted, but tell me any other circumstances where you can shoot your boss and still keep your job.'

'*Now* I see where you're coming from,' Liz said with a nasty smile, holding her gun at arm's length and peering along the barrel. 'Rory Glen, there's a paintball here with your name on it.'

'Just remember your boss can shoot back,' Joanna warned.

There were a few sage nods and 'mmm's as they contemplated the unknown quantity that was the opposition. The two teams had been given their weapons-and-rules briefings in separate locations, the reds by Baxter and the blues by Campbell. This was not only so that neither side would begin the game knowing the location of the other's base, but also to mask either team's individual strengths and weaknesses. Emily wondered whether it was also intended to make each side assume the other to be far less useless, but couldn't realistically envisage the perception being mutual.

'Rory'll be very, very up for it,' Liz mused, as if having pondered the same concern.

'Your mate Tim's going to be pretty handy too, isn't he?' Emily asked Parlabane. 'Let's face it, he's a press snapper. He's got to be adept at sneaking around and taking shots at people who haven't even noticed he's there.'

'Fair to say,' Parlabane replied. 'But he can't shoot film and paint at the same time. Or rather, I should say pixels and paint, but either way, he's got a job to do, so that should be a bit of a handicap. Plus, he's old. Even if he's hiding in a bush, you'll hear him wheezing from twenty yards.'

'Why do I suspect you wouldn't be saying that if he was in earshot?' Liz enquired.

Parlabane grinned.

'Didn't look that old to me,' she added. 'Distinguished, maybe, but not exactly decrepit.'

'Distinguished. He'd love that.'

'You tell him, you get a paintball in your mouth from point-blank.'

A horn sounded from somewhere above, one of those compressed-air portable klaxons. Emily looked to the hotel building. Campbell and Baxter were visible on the single tower that protruded from the central rear of the building, standing behind a safety rail on the turret. Campbell was holding the klaxon, and both were in possession of binoculars.

'So that's how they play referee,' Joanna observed.

'No, this is how we play referee,' said a voice in Emily's ear. They all looked at each other, indicating identical experience. 'Your comms systems are now active. Red team use channel one, blue team channel two, channel three is for UML and emergency use only. Due to the nature of the hardware, there is, unfortunately, nothing to prevent you monitoring each other's communications other than the spirit of fair play. And remember this above all: we can hear everything. Happy hunting.'

'Christ,' muttered Parlabane. He didn't say it – he *couldn't* say it, that was the point – but there was no question he was pissed off that he could no longer go ripping into UML without being overheard.

'Is it too late to talk about tactics?' Liz asked Joanna, the thought of taking on Glen evidently having sparked the group's only thus-far stated will to win.

'I'll stay back and guard the base,' Joanna replied confidently.

'Is that your role when you play online?'

'No, I usually attack, but when I play online my avatar's a six-foot blonde with pneumatic tits, legs up to her armpits

78

and the waistline of an end-stage anorexic smackhead. The real me's a trifle less nimble, but I'm also the best shot, so it makes sense I stay put and repel boarders.'

'Fair shout,' Parlabane said.

'Toby and Elizabeth—'

'Liz, please, everyone.'

'Toby and Liz, you both did actually hit something in practice, so you're the scouts.'

'Scouts?'

'You hang back in neutral territory,' Joanna instructed. 'You attack in the second wave, but your first priority is to get their flag and it's your job to intercept ours if they get away with it.'

'The second wave?' Emily asked, wondering how she'd missed the role of their predecessors.

'Yeah,' Parlabane explained with an unexpectedly bashful laugh. 'You and I are the first wave. Also known as cannon fodder.'

'And you doubted UML could make you feel a valued part of a team,' Emily told him, her levity borne of relief. It sure took the pressure off to be given a role she felt confident about fulfilling.

'Okay, one last thing,' Parlabane said, pulling down his protective goggles. 'Assume they're earwigging our transmissions.'

'Really?' Emily asked. She didn't mean to sound naïve, but wasn't sure how everyone else would respond to an unenforceable rule, whether the Corinthian spirit would be deemed more conducive to engendering trust across the whole group. 'I thought the rule was that we didn't. Just because there's no way of restricting the channels doesn't mean we should—'

'Assume it,' Liz agreed. 'Rory'll be listening. He'll want every edge he can get.'

'And what about your pal?' she asked Parlabane. 'He

79

struck me as the gentlemanly type, snapper or not. Wouldn't he have some views on fair play?'

'Indisputably a gentleman to the last. And his view as such would be to crush us proles using every advantage at his disposal.'

'Some friend.'

'Who? Him or me?'

'Both.'

'Fair shout. Let's go.'

Emily felt a strange sensation, a repeating shudder that came in waves, pulsing through her and causing the hairs on her neck to tingle. There was a tightening in her stomach too, and an inexplicable desire to stretch her toes and fingers, as though they would better conduct whatever it was as it passed through her system. It took an involuntary giggle as she ran headlong and gasped for breath to explain it to her: she was enjoying herself.

It had been a slow burn, starting as it did from the unpromising baseline of reluctance and mild embarrassment. However, what began as an overall nervousness about mere participation progressed to become a growing, tightening tension as she and Parlabane stalked on quiet feet under the cover of the trees. The silence nudged up her pulse as the on-going lack of sound became almost excruciating, taking her back more than quarter of a century to games of hide-and-seek-in-the-dark, when she had almost willed someone to catch her, if only to burst the rising balloon.

Toby had reasoned that the enemy base must be in the woods to the east: there was only open hillside and bare rock to the north; the hotel and its formal gardens formed a pre-described boundary to the west; and tellingly, Baxter and Campbell's turret vantage point offered only a limited view to the south. For reasons of fairness, Joanna ventured, it would be in some kind of open space but with limited points of entry, matching the pros and cons for attacking and defending their tennis court; perhaps a picnic site or play area. But whatever and wherever it was, the game would be won and lost in the thick of the woods.

The giggle came as she ran, upon Parlabane's signal, across a few yards of open ground to the cover of another tree, the pulse and tingle sparked by her fear and expectation of the sight of an enemy or the sudden impact of paint. He put his finger to his mouth, but it was as much to cover it against the sound of him giggling too. Visual confirmation that he didn't appear to be having an especially unpleasant time prompted her to realise that thus far *she* had actually been the one most apprehensive about UML's ability to deliver, made manifest in her spiky but professional hypersensitivity. UML, she now understood, didn't need or expect her to play guard dog against Parlabane, and maybe Campbell wasn't quite so crazy to have invited him.

'I'm shaking like a leaf,' she confided in a whisper.

'That's a point,' Parlabane replied, not only whispering but averting his boom mike with one hand.

'What?'

'I can see some leaves that aren't shaking, even when there's a bit of wind. Look.'

He was right. Ahead and to the right there was some foliage that seemed oddly still and uniform, but only if you were looking for it.

'I see it.'

'It's a camouflage screen. Dunno where the base is, but we're on the right track. This is where UML expected the action to—'

He cut himself off and put a finger to his lips again, then signalled Emily to follow him. She watched him pick his steps delicately across the ground, his footfalls absorbed by the moss-cushioned earth. He was heading for the far end of the screen, gesticulating to Emily to make for the near.

Barely daring to breathe, she ventured forward slowly, putting each foot down softly and on specific spots, like she was treading a path through the strewn toys of a sleeping child's bedroom. The concerns of such stealth were so automatically consuming that she had to remind herself to have a glance up now and again, her absorption momentarily reminding her of Elmer Fudd silently inching his way through the forest while failing to notice that Bugs Bunny was doing likewise about six inches behind him.

Parlabane held a fist aloft, which she eyed quizzically until it occurred to her that this signal meant 'stop'. She did, taking the moment to survey her surroundings, or 'check her six' as Joanna had advised. They were mere feet from the screen, standing about six yards apart. Parlabane held up three fingers. She nodded, feeling another ripple through her stomach and a ridiculously disproportionate sense of heart-thumping apprehension.

Parlabane put one finger down, then another. Emily held her breath.

One finger remained.

'Blue team, report status,' said a male voice loudly in their earpieces, startling the pair of them and causing them to turn away from the screen. Parlabane reflexively swept his weapon around as he scanned the area. There was nothing to be seen and no further sound to be heard. He held a hand to his chest and began laughing again, as silently as he could but helplessly nonetheless. Emily was a few moments longer in recovering from her heart's attempt to eject through the top of her skull, but found herself equally tickled by it. Remembering himself, Parlabane took a step forward and looked behind the screen, doing so casually and with none of the deliberateness of his approach, like he was checking there was milk in the fridge. Still laughing, he shook his head to confirm there was no-one behind it.

'Jack here,' he said quietly, for the benefit of the mike.

'With Emily. Status is two changes of trousers required. We were kind of in the middle of something. I guess I should have requested radio silence, Toby.'

'It's not Toby,' replied the voice.

Parlabane and Emily looked at each other, which was understandable, but at a cost of neither looking the right way as a second, unnoticed camouflage screen toppled forward opposite the first. Parlabane reacted and dived to the floor as Rory Glen and Kathy emerged from their cover, firing rapidly from a distance of twenty or thirty feet.

Emily not only froze to the spot, but even forgot she had the means to retaliate. She heard whizzing sounds and soft impacts, but felt nothing, and it took a long, incredulous moment to deduce that this meant none of the shots had hit her. Parlabane was rolling and scrambling across the ground towards the cover of a tree, arced paint splats following his progress like a comet tail across the camouflage screen. In the excitement of the moment, they had reacted to the moving target and fired at him, taking their eyes off the sitting duck (or frozen turkey) for a crucial half second. When they did return their attention to Emily, she had recovered from her paralysis and was charging for the cover of the screen, her progress assisted by Parlabane now returning fire, which required Glen and Kathy to take evasive action of their own.

She picked herself up from a bundle into a crouch, panting and laughing, the ridiculousness of it all being faded from significance by an unexpected competitive edge that felt natural enough to have its roots in survival instinct. A voice in her head was telling her there was nothing to be so worked up about, the worst that could happen was she'd get hit with a paintball and knocked out of the game, but right then, that actually sounded pretty disastrous. She wasn't bothered about winning – yet – but she was damn sure she wanted to be playing. It was a pure, uncompli-cated and innocently exhilarating experience, the kind of thrill you weren't supposed to get after the age of about thirteen. After that, you had sex, booze, drugs or power to trip on, if you could get them, but on this evidence there still remained an appetite somewhere in her psyche that those weren't designed, intended or remotely able to satisfy.

To her left she could see Parlabane, huddled against a paint-blotted tree, pinned down by enemy fire a few yards from cover. She leaned around the screen, a wood and wire-mesh construction supporting green camouflage-patterned canvas, thousands of leaves adhering to a tacky coating on the outside. Kathy was shooting from a kneeling position as Rory moved carefully sideways, intending to widen their triangulation of fire. Shouting to get their attention, she began pulling the trigger as fast as the bolt allowed it to recock, getting off five shots before retreating. She didn't hit anything, but when she peered around again, she saw Rory scurrying back towards the toppled screen to help Kathy pull it upright in front of them. Emily splatted a few shots against the screen in order to keep them there, as Parlabane hurtled on swift and light strides to join her.

'Having fun yet?' she asked him.

'I'm about to,' he whispered, masking his mike again.

'Glen, you're a devious fucker,' he said, his tone almost admiring. 'We figured you'd listen to our channel, but broadcasting on it was low. Nearly shat ourselves it was so sudden.'

'All is fair in love and war, mate,' came the reply via their earpieces.

'You mean you're this devious when you're trying to get a shag?'

'Stick your head up and I'll tell you.'

'I just might. You're almost as bad a shot as your pal Katie.'

'It's Kathy.'

Parlabane grinned at this with a silent satisfaction Emily didn't grasp.

'Join in. Keep them talking,' he whispered, before twisting the dial on his headset to change channel.

'You going to take that insult lying down, Kath?' Emily asked. 'I think he's sullying the honour of our company. Stand up and make him pay.'

'You're nearer,' Kathy replied. 'Why don't you shoot him for the both of us?'

While Kathy was talking, Parlabane was transmitting. 'Red team requesting urgent back-up at the screens, under attack from four enemy,' he said quietly but urgently, adopting a hoarse, low register that was intended to sound like Rory. He wasn't going to get a job on *Dead Ringers*, but it might be passable over crackly headsets to team-mates who'd only just met the guy.

Parlabane remained silent as she and their two opponents traded another few jibes over the airwaves. He then nodded and held up a thumb. That his subterfuge had worked was apparent from the impish, toddler-with-a-secret smile on his face; less so was what was so clever about inviting enemy reinforcements to outnumber them in what was currently a balanced stand-off.

Parlabane switched back to the blue channel.

'Blue team, for those wondering what all the witticisms are about, we are pinned down, two enemy engaged. We are about a hundred and fifty yards south-east of the gardens. Time is of the essence.'

'Don't bother yourselves,' Rory advised. 'We'll have splattered them and moved on by the time you get here.'

'What are you planning?' Emily whispered, levering the boom away. 'Bring more of their guys and more of our guys here for an even bigger stalemate?'

Parlabane was about to answer when instead he reacted to movement somewhere to his left, turning and firing four shots as a figure flashed between the trees. He then stood up and sent a volley towards the opposite screen to keep Rory and Kathy from responding to the development.

'Come over this side,' he urged, indicating Emily should take position next to him at the other end of the screen. He stood up again and unleashed another burst, allowing Emily to lean out and look for the third opponent. She saw nothing, then noticed Rory's head peeping out at ground level, his gun just in front. She withdrew as the paintballs whizzed past the side of the screen, their sound failing to cover that of hurried footsteps as this new interloper stole another few yards forward.

Emily thought she could hear his voice, low and muffled, but couldn't make out the words. Whatever he'd said, he repeated a couple of times before calling loudly: 'Rory! Kathy! Switch to the red channel for fuck's sake, I'm trying to talk here.'

Parlabane indicated to Emily to do likewise.

'. . . as soon as I could,' she heard.

'Why? You're supposed to be defending the base. You left Grieg on his own?'

'You said there were four of them up here. Grieg can handle—'

'I didn't say anything. I've been on the Bl—'

'Red team, this is Grieg. Base under attack. Repeat, base under attack.'

'Parlabane, you sneaky little bastard,' Rory shouted.

'I need help back here, I've got two oh fuck. Fuck. Sorry. I'm hit, I'm out. They've got the flag. Exiting north, side of the stream.'

'All is fair in love and war, Rory,' Parlabane called.

It got kind of hectic after that. Stealth, strategy and tension had had their moment. Now it was time for pace, noise and mayhem. Communications crackled in Emily's earpiece, too many simultaneous voices to even identify an individual, far less the specific content of anything that was being said. Parlabane started backing away, bent low and eyes flitting rapidly around the periphery. Audible and urgent shouts hailed that the enemy were doing the same thing.

'If they're smart they'll do what Joanna suggested and go all out for a cross-steal. But my guess is she's the only one here who really knows the game, so they'll try and intercept our flag carriers instead.'

'Operation Human Shield for us, then?'

Parlabane grinned. 'Only if we find our team-mates first. We'd best split up, improve the odds.'

'What about backing each other up?' Emily asked, a little nervous of going it alone, albeit more through the comfort of safety in numbers than any of the tactical proficiency Parlabane had exhibited.

'The hide-and-seek bit's over, I reckon. It's time for running and shooting. Two people together make a bigger target to aim your paint at.'

And with that, he was gone, disappearing swiftly through some shrubs and out of sight.

Emily felt the pulsing return, the hollow, tense sensation growing in her guts as she stalked her way towards the cover of another tree, bracing herself for an ambush with every inch.

'Ach, bollocks to it,' she said aloud, and began running instead. *Exiting by the side of the stream*, the felled opponent had said. Well, she didn't have the first idea where the stream was, so there was no point in attempting a specific destination; and arguably a virtue to not having one. Best to just charge blindly into battle and draw fire away from the flag-carrier. They'd survived longer than anticipated, but the role of the first wave hadn't changed.

The cries and half-formed sentences continued over the airwaves, mostly red-team voices on the blue-team channel, attempting to relay their own or their quarry's estimated positions but lacking the geographic frame of reference that would have made it worthwhile. She flicked to the red channel just for a bit of peace. This bore unexpected fruit shortly after her charge into the arboreal unknown, having slowed to a tired jog, had ended in a headlong tumble over an exposed tree-root. Without the distraction of voices sounding like they were inside her head, she was able to hear a lone male speaking aloud to himself only a few yards away as she lay, inconspicuous, on the forest floor.

'Oh fuck, here we go,' was all he said, but it was enough to give her the jump on him as he prepared to face down the approaching blue-flag carrier.

Emily couldn't see him yet, but she knew where he'd appear from. She spotted his target first, a ruddy-faced and excited-looking Liz, hurdling an ancient trunk and bearing a red flag in one hand, the burden unlikely to do much for her aim.

He made his move as Liz stumbled upon landing, the man emerging from cover and opening fire from a crouch on one knee, only four or five yards from his prey. Max was his name, if she remembered correctly. Liz completely lost her footing in fright at this sudden appearance and went sprawling to the ground, but not before two purple splotches had appeared on her blue tabard and a third criminally blemished the perfection of her yellow fleece at the right shoulder.

'Bastard,' she said, near breathless as her exertion and fright turned to laughter.

Emily had responded too slow, but not, as it turned out, too quickly. Having failed to spring up in John-Woo-style balletic slow motion and thwart Liz's assassin before he could pull the trigger, she at least had the sense not to play her hand too early. Even as he made his way towards the flag that Liz was obliged to discard, his oblivious back exposed and vulnerable, Emily could already hear further footsteps approach. Two sets, in fact, converging from different directions. Max heard them too, and made the mistake of freezing where he was as he looked for their sources. He (and Emily behind him) saw his team-mate Kathy first, which meant that by the time he saw Toby, Max had already been splattered by him and Emily had vanished from her work colleague's line of sight. Max dropped to his knees with mock gravitas, then collapsed, turning, to end up on his back, only feet from the now squatting and still laughing Liz. Kathy reacted astonishingly, clocking the angle of fire that felled her team-mate and practising an evasive forward roll, from which she emerged firing in Toby's direction. Toby took a single, decisive splat to the middle of the chest, all of his own shots having headed where Kathy *would* have been but for her spontaneous acrobatics, having awakened skills dormant, to Emily's knowledge, since she'd left secondary school.

'Flag recovered,' Kathy said triumphantly, if prematurely, into her boom mike. 'Max is out. I'll get this back to base. Continue the assault, Rory.' With that, she made her way towards Liz, turning her back on Emily, her business partner of six years and friend of over a decade, who with a tangible, rippling frisson of delight, stood up and shot her in the back. Five times.

Stealth wasn't really much of an option when you were carrying a two-foot-square, bright-red flag on a four-foot wooden pole while simultaneously trying to retain hold of your paintgun and your balance. Speed was, at least, worth striving for, though only marginally more attainable for precisely the same reasons. With this in mind, she had opted for short bursts of pace between trees; she wasn't exactly slipping silently and invisibly on elven feet, but at least she could put some wood between herself and any incoming paintballs as she got her breath back and scoped the next stretch.

'The base is secure,' Joanna said in her earpiece. 'But Rory

Glen's creeping about somewhere. He had a go earlier but I warned him off with a few volleys. He'll be back, though, so keep a sharp eye.'

After the chaos of the skirmish that had left her with the flag and four players out of the game, Emily had become a little disorientated, but she told herself this was no bad thing, because if she didn't know where she was headed, then it would be harder for her opponents to intercept her. That said, wandering ever-deeper into the woods in the wrong direction and all alone would be neither tactically astute nor remotely sensible. She was relieved, then, to look up and catch a glimpse of the turret from which the UML pair were monitoring the contest. That gave her a fix on her destination and a means of avoiding the most direct route.

She felt the tension grow again as she got closer to the base, something exacerbated coincidentally by the silence in her earpiece. Baxter had reminded the fallen that they were not allowed to relay any relevant information to their still-active team-mates other than that they'd been hit and were thus out of the game. Nobody, to her knowledge, had broken this rule, but their on-going chatter was still clogging the channels, so Baxter had instructed them to avert their mikes. It had been a couple of minutes since she'd heard anything at all: no contact from her own surviving team-mates (no news being good news), and no eavesdropped communiqués from the enemy.

The tennis court was in sight, barely, through the last screen of foliage. After those final trees there was a wide arc of exposed, open ground to be traversed: beds of gravel between lines of paving stones, bark pathways intersecting rough grass and kempt lawn, and, rather strangely, two glass panels cut into the flowerbeds. She could see Joanna, patrolling back and forth inside the court between the exits, at first glance boxed in, but in terms of the game, formidably protected by wooden (and thus paint-proof) boards, four feet high on all sides beneath the tall wire mesh. The tree line meant the rear entrance to the court offered a shorter dash without cover, but being thus the more attractive option, she reckoned it also the more likely to be staked out. Figuring blundering recklessness had served her well so far, she took a deep breath and made an all-or-nothing charge for glory.

'Joanna!' she called, shouting, near-hysterical with giggling excitement as she ran. Joanna caught sight of her and came forward to the front entrance to offer cover fire as Rory came hurtling from the bushes thirty yards and forty degrees away.

'Don't look back,' Joanna shouted, but Emily couldn't help turning her head as Joanna crouched and fired past her. Rory, however, wasn't running towards her, but zig-zagging in minor fluctuations of a near-perpendicular tangent of her path. She understood why about a quarter of a second later when he unleashed his cascade of shots and took out both of them. Joanna's tactical calls had given them a near-decisive advantage, but her big mistake had been the one Parlabane of all people warned against. By going to the entrance, she'd put them both in the same line of fire, making one big target that was all too easy for Rory to daub in predatory purple.

'Fuck piss bollocks,' Joanna mourned, while behind her, Emily could hear Rory chuckle in self-satisfied delight as he jogged towards the base.

'Jack. This is Joanna. Are you on this channel?'

'Sure am.'

'We're at the base, Emily and I are both hit. Rory's gonna have both flags in about ten seconds. It's down to you, I'm afraid.'

'This is Liz,' said a second remote voice, defying UML's imposed silence. 'Trust me, Jack, however inconsequential you might believe this game to be, you still don't want to

91

be sharing a planet with that bastard if he wins it. You do everything in your power. I'll give you money. Sexual favours. Whatever it takes.'

'Hey, pile on the pressure, why don't you,' Parlabane replied.

'Much obliged, ladies,' Rory said as he bent down to pick up the red flag. '*All* of you,' he added pointedly for Liz's benefit, then headed into the court to seize the blue standard.

'Avert microphones please, dead people,' Campbell appealed.

Emily removed her headset altogether as she got up and helped Joanna to her feet.

'Look,' Joanna said excitedly, flipping the boom away from her mouth and pointing towards the trees. 'It's . . . shit, just Liz on her way back. Thought it was Jack.'

'What's the difference? One's out of the game and the other couldn't hit water if he fell out of a boat. Rory's as good as home.'

'I wouldn't be so sure,' Joanna said, a mock-stern but definitely coy admonishment in her expression.

'No, believe me, I was with him. He was tactically pretty smart, but he painted half that forest purple. Our best bet is if Rory impales himself on one of the flags.'

'He missed every shot at the target practice over there, didn't he?' Joanna asked rhetorically, pointing to the lamp-post near the carpark where they'd had their cursory weapons training. 'From twenty feet, yeah?'

'Every shot. Yes.'

'Right. Now follow the angle from where we were standing.'

Emily did.

'You've got to be kidding.'

'Nope.'

A good thirty yards past the lamp-post, well back in an otherwise near-empty carpark (and partially obscured from where they had been standing by a short hedge), there sat the liveried yellow minibus with a UML logo on the bonnet. A cruder design was picked out in purple down the flank.

'I don't get the significance of the letter, though. Is it W for wanker?'

'It's not supposed to be a letter. It's supposed to be an arse.'

It was an appropriate moment for Parlabane to make his reappearance, the bushel hiding his light having been discarded. He stepped furtively from the tree line close to where Emily had made her own final, doomed dash for home.

'Get the bastard,' Liz shouted to him, pointing at Rory as he emerged from the base bearing both flags. He was exiting by the rear, which would leave him with more distance to cover overall, but less of it across open ground. Once he made it to the trees, he was as good as gone. Parlabane had only a few seconds to make the difference. At this point, Emily knew she would have been blazing away with her weapon, getting as much paint into the air as the mechanism would allow and putting her faith in the law of averages over her own accuracy. Parlabane, though, dropped to one knee and held the gun steadily in both hands, eyes fixed on his running target. He rolled his head around his neck, blinked once and levelled his weapon, the barrel minutely following Rory's trajectory towards the safety of the woods, which were two seconds, one second away. Parlabane's finger left the trigger-guard and moved to the trigger itself.

Then his protective goggles turned purple and he fell over.

Rory disappeared into the woods a moment before Vale emerged from them, forty yards down the tree line.

'You know,' said Parlabane as Vale ambled towards him, 'deep down I just knew you were going to do that.'

'Then I'd hate to disappoint you.'

'What about Rory?' Emily asked. 'We'd better tell him he's won.'

'Nah, fuck it,' Liz replied. 'Let the bastard run. Wouldn't want to deprive him of his heroic moment bringing the flag to base – even if it is the best part of a mile away. Who's hungry?'

Buggery and Aperitifs

Rory's phone went off as he made his way down the grand staircase to the lobby. He felt the vibration against his chest and heard only the accompanying buzz, having disabled the ringtone before sliding the thing into his inside breast pocket. This action had become a *de rigueur* matter of etiquette in recent times, people making such an eye-rolling scene if your mobile happened to ring while they were in the process of eating – even if they weren't at your bloody table. Sometimes they'd act like you'd got your dick out and started having a chug in front of your fellow diners. It was a conversation, for God's sake: what did it matter whether it was to someone at your table or someone on the other end of the line? Well, clearly it mattered to some. The amount of tutting that could accompany a ringtone in a restaurant could be far louder than the electronic jingle itself, to say nothing of the germ-disseminating phlegm-spray all those clicking tongues generated. And how many bloody times did you hear the shrewish mantra of the mobile-phobic: 'Do they think they're *that* important that they have to be in touch at all times? It's not as though it's a million-pound deal or a matter of life and death they're talking about.'

Rory *had* taken calls on this mobile that were entirely and crucially pertinent to million-pound business matters. Unfortunately, they had so far been in airports or hands-free at the wheel of his car; unfortunately because he'd dearly love to take one in a busy restaurant, just so that he could go up to one of these snivelling wankers and say:

95

'Actually, I *am* that important and I *was* talking about a million-pound deal.'

The done thing now though, especially in company, was to kill the sound, switch to vibrate and then excuse yourself so that you could take the call out of the room without anyone knowing that's what you were up to. Phone call as excretory function. Lovely. As Liz had advised him, this was doubly polite because not only did it prevent the noisy interruption and awkwardness of taking a call at the table, but it avoided the implication towards your fellow diners that there was someone more important or more interesting whom you'd rather talk to than sit listening to them bumping their gums. Rory took her point on this one, but didn't think how it looked reflected how it was. Taking a call at dinner was no disrespect to the merits of your company. You could be having dinner with Keith Richards, Robert De Niro, Heidi Fleiss and the Dalai Lama, but if you didn't recognise the incoming number you'd still want to take that call, because it was new, because it was full of possibilities, because it was the next, unwritten page.

Rory, not having engaged any company yet, didn't have to make his excuses this time, though he knew he'd have to keep it brief. He intended to make a good impression on his fellow guests, and knew that those with mobile-phobic tendencies would regard it as outrageous attention-seeking to be having a cellular-conveyed conversation in a public place while there was a dedicated, functioning landline at his personal disposal in his bedroom upstairs. Besides, even he would concede that to walk into a social gathering of relatively new faces while yours was clamped to your phone made you look like a complete wanker.

He slid the phone into his palm and opened it, always a pleasure. Petty, juvenile and admittedly quite sad, but a pleasure nonetheless. It was a Mazienen M-Kard, a silver sliver about the size of three stacked credit cards when dormant, but with two aluminium wafers extending its length top and bottom when activated. The extension at the top housed the LCD panel and speaker, while the strip at the bottom bore the mic. Rory had been through dozens of mobile phones, upgrading with each generation of technology or even the latest non-essential but gadget-tastic feature, whether it be photo-messaging or voice-recognition-dialling-and-commands, but the M-Kard remained his favourite despite being almost nine months old. It was a comparatively ascetic piece of hardware, waterproof, necessarily light on extras, a slender and elegant exemplar of spatially economic design. Its sound quality was unremarkable, it didn't take pictures, it didn't play MP3s and its minuscule keypad was a bugger to write text messages on, but it looked beautiful, weighed nothing and made Rory feel like Captain Kirk every time he used it.

The only drawback about the M-Kard was that it looked like the kind of natty receptacle a flash bastard such as himself might plausibly port his Charlie around in, which was something you unfortunately had to consider when observing this nascent twenty-first-century dining protocol. If you were constantly excusing yourself before 'just nipping out to the bathroom', and they clocked you wheeching this suspicious silver number from your pocket as you went, then they could have you down as a cokehead before the coffee and mints were served. Add to that the fact that he worked in advertising and people would regard it as a given.

This particularly pissed Rory off, because he didn't do cocaine but was nonetheless widely assumed to and scowlingly disapproved of accordingly. As far as he understood, it was a drug that made people feel hyperconfident, unselfconscious, dynamic, visionary and empowered, while causing them to riff tirelessly and energetically upon thoughts and ideas that came pouring forth like a Vegas slot machine paying out the jackpot. Given that this was how

Rory felt and behaved most of the time anyway, there was little incentive for him to be sniffing up Johnson's Baby Powder cut with a minute quantity of something that had previously spent time inside a condom shoved up a Colombian farmhand's arse. But try telling that to the people who thought he had the portrait of Dorian Glen in his attic just because he had a creative gift and didn't go around with his face tripping him the whole time.

He recognised the number on the LCD. Finlay, his younger brother. Now there was someone who *did* do a lot of drugs. Mostly hash, recreationally (or rather for 'rest enhancement' as Finlay put it), but no stranger to posh or whizz when he needed an eighteen- or even twenty-four-hour session at the computer in order to get a piece of code into operable shape. Finlay, however, was shy, modest, geeky and reclusive, so on the rare occasions when his scrawny pale frame was dragged, squinting, into the daylight, those who met him would find it hard to imagine him even fronting up at the off-licence to ask for a can of Top Deck shandy. 'What an adorable little computer-geek,' they'd be thinking. 'Let's adopt him. He'll be easy to look after, I've read about them: they live on phone-out pizzas and Pepsi Max, and as long as he's got access to Sky One for *Buffy* and *Star Trek*, that'll be all his appetites catered for.' Unlike that nasty cokehead brother of his, natch.

There was one appetite that Rory and Finlay did share, with equal voracity, allowing them to enthuse openly with each other about something even less acceptable in polite company than smoking, cocaine or mobile phones at the dinner table. It was even-money that was precisely what he was calling about, which was why Rory was not remotely tempted to hit Divert.

'Finlay, how's it going, bro'?'

'Cool. Where are you?'

'Middle of nowhere. That thing I told you about.'

'Oh yeah. Is it good?'

'Look, I can't talk. About to do some meet and greet.'

'Shake and fake.'

'Exactly. So cut to. What is it?'

'Two words: Dawn Yuill.'

'Whoah, whoah, don't tease me. Seriously?'

'Seriously.'

'Real skin, or more cheesecake?'

'Nip-slip. Getting out of a limo at some awards do. More than a nip-slip, in fact. The way she's leaning forward, it's a lot more than just your usual blurry down-blouse.'

'Confirmed visible nipple?'

'In colour. And uploading now. You got net access there?'

'Nah. Have to wait until I get back. Something to look forward to. Where'd you get it?'

'My source at *HotGoss*. They'll have it on Thursday, unless she finds out and her lawyers try to get an injunction.'

'No chance. It was a public place, no case to make. Besides, she needs the exposure. Is it colour?'

'Oh yes.'

'You don't let me down. You are my ambassador to pr0n, man.'

'Later.'

Kirk out.

Dawn Yuill. Wow. Falling out of her party frock with verified nipple-in-shot. Something to look forward to indeed. And from a source image, too, rather than scanned in from newsprint with the next page's inverse headline buggering up the contrast and obscuring the merchandise.

The former *Scotland Tonight* frontwoman was not exactly a knock-'em-dead beauty, but the prurient interest/titillation factor was paradoxically amplified by her sheer ordinariness, even that hint of frump about her. Since moving to the bigger playing field of the London media, she had thrown her lot in with the clean-up-TV shower, playing the role of high-profile prude when she wasn't fronting 'lifestyle' shows or, Lord help us, her Sunday morning 'let's pretend religion still has a role in popular culture' pseudo-current-affairs sham. None of these higher purposes, however, had placed her above whoring this same schoolmarmish image in the most hypocritical fashion, when she did that profile-boosting photo-shoot, ostensibly for the *Radio Times* but liberally distributed in advance to the red-tops. It depicted her as a classroom disciplinarian with more black leather than blackboard, calculated to fuel the secret fantasies harboured by Disgusted of Tunbridge Wells when he wasn't tuning into her Sunday show or reaching for the Basildon Bond.

For all of that, a stolen paparazzi shot of her inadvertently displaying one breast was worth far more, for example, than last week's candid, topless-on-holiday pics of nubile young thing Karen Lewis, because you knew Karen was going to deliver the goods at some point: if not thanks to a telephoto lens in the Caribbean then when the script demanded it in whatever low-budget Brit-flick she thought was a career step-up from soapland and her failed singing career. But Dawn Yuill, well, it was more than a matter of exposed flesh. It felt like a victory.

It was a privilege of living in this media-saturated era that there was a camera standing by on fast-repeat shutter to capture the moment should any female of even micro-scopic celebrity happen to fall out of her dress, slip her bikini top off or venture out at night in a frock and underwear combo that underestimated the near X-ray properties of modern professional flash photography. And thanks to the internet, or 'Satan's switchboard' as Finlay approvingly referred to it, these images could be instantly and endlessly shared, like an exchange of infinite bubblegum cards in the great playground of pr0n.

(Not all images could be shared, it had to be said, and

not for purposes of exclusivity or selfishness. There were only three people in this world, as far as he knew, who had seen the full-frontal nude digital pics of June Shelley *without* a four-foot tube of Natraline lip-balm protecting the sitcom actress's modesty. Those three were Tom Kerr, the photographer who had conducted the shoot (and quietly shot more than June Shelley noticed), Rory, who came up with the campaign ('Your lips feel naked without it'), and Finlay, who was allowed to view them only on Rory's machine but most definitely not allowed copies. If they ever surfaced anywhere public, in fact if they were even known to exist, June Shelley would very quickly become the least seen but highest earning nude model in British history. But that, in itself, was half the thrill.)

Rory was a collector. All boys were collectors, to a greater or lesser degree, and of sicker or healthier things. There was probably a valid, anthropological explanation for it, this male compulsion to hoard and catalogue, from diesel locomotive serial numbers, to Hawkwind off-shoot backlists, to body-part trophies. In the grand scale of these things, Rory didn't reckon he scored particularly high on the sad or harmful indices, but it did sometimes bother him that he couldn't really say why he was doing it or what exactly he thought he was collecting. What was it about these images, posed and knowing or stolen and intrusively voyeuristic, that drove him not just to look but to retain? Was it that by glimpsing the hidden parts of the body he was capturing part of the soul, as was the mythic aboriginal superstition? He didn't know; he only knew that he was compelled to collect. If there was a manifest benefit beyond the immediate gratification upon first view, it was in the curious feeling of comfort and reassurance he felt when he saw on TV – or even more so, met in the flesh – a woman of whom he owned such an image. It diluted the threat, the mystery, the power that they otherwise held, defused whatever inexplicable force made him feel, well, *impotent*, if that was still the right word to describe a condition so chronically marked by raging hard-ons.

The bar was satisfactorily populated as Rory made his entrance. He cringed any time someone used the phrase 'fashionably late' (mandatorily followed by gratingly self-congratulatory laughter), but there was something to be said for getting one's timing right for even the most modest of gatherings. The first person there always looked a little sad and desperate, whether for alcohol or company; and if you got there too soon after, you'd be one-on-one with the loser, with later arrivals unable to distinguish who'd got there after whom. Nightmare.

More satisfactory was the informal – but importantly not uniform – dress code, as it was always a pleasure to see how the female company scrubbed up. He understood the practical and levelling considerations of those fleeces, but they had an unforgivingly obscuring effect on the eye candy. If any woman had nipples capable of making a visible indent in those things, then he didn't *want* to see them.

He checked his watch. With dinner eight for eight-thirty, he wasn't 'fashionably late', and was relieved, noting a couple of absentees, not to be 'ostentatiously last' either. Not that his entrance went unheralded in any case.

'Here comes the man of the moment,' called out Grieg Rossi, still hearty in his congratulations, which suggested an ongoing insecurity about having been the first man to fall. Nobody had blamed him for losing the base – that was down to inexperienced tactics and Jack Parlabane's admirably deft duplicity – but he was still behaving like the OG-scoring defender towards the striker who's bailed him out with an equaliser. Oh, and a late winner too, not to sell himself short.

Rory stopped in the doorway and placed his hand on his

heart. 'I only did what any one of us would have done in the same circumstances,' he said.

'Hear, hear,' applauded erstwhile team-mate Kathy McKenna, in a dress that made up for lack of cleavage with some quality pokiosity, both rasps making a dainty but divine impression in the blue cloth. 'Well said. So now you can reprise the sentiment when we tell you it's traditional for the flag-capper to buy the drinks.'

'Absolutely,' he replied, a round being a small price to pay for the opportunity to be simultaneously magnanimous and victorious in company. It was therefore a modest disappointment to be reminded that UML were picking up the tab for everything. Besides, he was the only one without a glass anyway.

Everyone was a lot more chatty and relaxed than might have been expected, so chalk one up to UML for the ice-breaking properties of the afternoon's hostilities. More than vindicating Rory's stance against the professional cynicism of Jack the Hack, it had been not only a morale-boosting exercise, but definitely a team-building one too. As well as the obvious unifying aspects shared on one's own team, there had been an irresistible instilling of respect for the other side, too. Tactical move and counter-move, skill, stealth and audacious gunplay, these were the things being discussed and dissected, with compliments towards one's opponents being the principal thrust of conversation.

'I loved the way you . . .'

'I thought I had you until you . . .'

'You played it dead right with that move . . .'

Pride of place in the small but cosy, whisky-lined bar was a UML-inscribed laptop sitting on a table next to Tim Vale's camera, to which it was linked by a USB cable. On screen was a repeating slideshow of brilliantly lively pictures from the game; pictures, it should be mentioned, that no-one had any idea he was taking at the time, as no-one had even seen

103

him between the first and last moments of the match. Given his decisive late intervention, it would be churlish to say it had limited his contribution to the red team's success, but it was clear that he had spent the majority of his time silently and invisibly sniping for images rather than opponents. Consequently, the shots had that natural and kinetic, heart-of-the-moment look that you only saw in pictures when the subjects weren't self-consciously aware of being photographed. He had captured their expressions wonderfully, and email addresses were being hurriedly scribbled down for the receipt of copies. UML were bound to be delighted, as would be Kathy and her partner. Whatever Parlabane contrived to write about the experience, the camera didn't lie about what a good time everyone was having. Rory made a mental note to ask for a look at the guy's portfolio when they got back down the road. He seemed a little long in the tooth not to have made a name for himself with snaps like that. Maybe he'd come late to it, or had a pedigree in another field. No matter, he had something Rory could definitely use when the right campaign came along.

Parlabane, to be fair, was not being the cooler-than-thou spoilsport smart-arse Rory had feared, but it was worth remembering that journalists took a professional pride in being duplicitous, two-faced bastards, so his instinct remained one of caution while in his midst. He was chatting to Toby Seaton, the other source of minor unease and discomfort on this trip. It had always been a finite possibility that Rory and Toby would run into each other again, though not a possibility he'd ever enjoyed contemplating. The longer it had gone on without happening, the more he'd believed that meant it never would, on the grounds that if they hadn't bumped into each other already, then their circles must be comfortably distant. But there Toby had been, outside the minibus, looking even more nervous and apologetic than ever; different, changed in many ways but still unmistakable. They'd acknowledged each other through tentative eye-contact, and an awkward exchange of where-life-has-taken-us info would be required at some point, but, fortunately, in all probability that would be it. Neither would be wanting to stick on a *Now That's What I Call Eighties* CD and go ambling down memory lane.

Rory was handed a second glass of champagne by Liz, who'd had her back to him prior to that as she chatted to Joanna, the podgy IT type who'd apparently compensated for presenting the biggest target by providing the sharpest strategic advice. Grieg, her colleague from Catalyst Solutions, had provided no such nous, as being in Human Resources he wasn't party to the late-night geek fests that had honed Joanna's tactical awareness. Liz revealed herself (though that was hardly the right word) to be wearing a rather stiff-looking tartan frock that circled her neck just above the collarbone and described her chest in only the most elliptical terms. It wasn't unattractive by any means – let's face it, Liz seldom was – but it was a rather disappointingly starchy number nonetheless. For business, Liz always dressed sharply, even elegantly, but she never wore anything that betrayed any information about what lay beneath. Nothing sheer, nothing clinging, no lycra, and not even a hint of peanut bumps on a winter's morning: it left so much to the imagination that it was practically a blank canvas. In frustration he sometimes wondered whether her dress sense factored in the consideration of denying his prurient gaze, and in his more paranoid moments whether this was in response to his being conspicuously leery. If so, then at least she hadn't circular-emailed the entire sisterhood. If Fiona from Accounts started turning up in black polonecks and Arran sweaters, that was the time to worry.

Earlier in the week, Finlay had made a crack about this weekend being Rory's big chance to 'get a few drinks into her and see what happens when she lets her hair down and you're both away from prying eyes'. Rory had been horrified, not least by the thought of her suspecting this to be his motive. The letting-her-hair-down part he'd hold his hand up to, but anything further sounded like a nightmare. They had a company to run, a business relationship and important responsibilities that would all still be waiting for them next week. Besides, never mind a few drinks, a woman like Liz would need GHB before she let Rory near her. He wasn't too proud to say he considered her out of his league. She had a good ten years on him, and that wouldn't, shouldn't matter, but the age gap seemed far more pronounced simply because she made him feel very immature. That was in fact an important dynamic in their relationship, something they both played off creatively, but the notion of it having a sexual manifestation was like a fourteen-year-old making a pass at a maturely sophisticated auntie.

All he'd really hoped for with regard to the trip was for the informal atmosphere to reveal what she dressed like in less buttoned-down mode, and maybe to be thrown a few titbits to fill in a little of that canvas. Some hope. The tartan dress was letting on even less than the yellow fleece, with only a glimpse of tantalisingly black bra-strap on offer beneath the shoulder seams.

There was compensation to be had elsewhere, though. The waitresses he'd seen flitting around were kitted in crisp white blouses without obscuring frills or (disaster!) pinafores. One was buxom, just the right side of plump, the other delicately petite, and both featured discernible lace beneath translucent cotton. Just as well, really, given that the guest side so far only had Kathy's contribution to commend it, with her business partner Emily Bell yet to make her appearance.

'The hero of the hour,' Liz said. 'Joanna here was telling

me how you took out her and Emily before your victorious flag run.'

'What can I say, I've always been a natural ladykiller.'

Liz rolled her eyes, but at least she was smiling as she did so.

'You must make certain allowances for Rory. He has to channel so much of his creative gift into his work that there's not always much left for other areas of expression.'

'That's Liz's roundabout way of saying she thinks my patter's rotten.'

'It's advertising you're in, isn't it?' asked Max Redman, seamlessly joining from a different conversation to his left with little more than a swivel of the hips and a moment's eye-contact. It was the kind of thing you could get away with without anyone taking the huff in a gathering of this size, with the company just too big for one conversation and just too small for the full roam-and-mingle game. It made for an easy and unpressured vibe, but the disadvantage was that you could begin a sentence addressing four people and find that two of them had been replaced by the time you ended it.

'Yes. We're based in Leith,' Rory replied.

'TV ads? Print? Billboards.'

'All of the above. Depends on the campaign. These days we can be doing anything from beauty products to government information.'

'Anything on telly at the moment that we'd recognise?' Joanna asked.

'Well,' Rory prevaricated, trying to think of something that was both comparatively recent and acceptably cool to own up to. His hesitation was fatal, Liz steamrolling over the top of his pause and gleefully bringing up the very thing he'd been intending to avoid.

'Beechtree Finance,' she announced. 'It's on the satellite channels all day, housewives and unemployed target market.'

107

'I think I've seen it at the gym,' Max said. 'Only time I see TV, to be honest. That's the one with the woman looking like she's waiting for the other shoe to drop.'

'That's it.'

'But by the end she looks like the weight of the world's been lifted. Yeah, I know the one.'

'Except it wasn't just the weight of the world that was lifted, was it, Rory?' Liz chided.

Rory braced himself. It was at times like this that he rather resentfully felt as though he was the subject of a morality tale. He'd had his say, got his way, got results, cashed the cheque and taken the plaudits, but there was an outstanding bill to be paid, and Liz was ensuring it be met in full.

'What?' Max asked, intrigued and insistent.

'Well, did you notice anything different about the actress between her "saddled with debt" appearance and her "weight off my shoulders" look?'

'She seemed sunnier. Younger, almost. But I thought that was the point.'

'I've got to hand it to you, Rory,' Liz said. 'You were right about one thing: nobody is going to admit to noticing it, even if they can't miss it.'

'What?' It was Joanna's turn to become impatient for the juicy revelation.

'Max is right. She seemed sunnier and younger. But what he's too polite or bashful to mention is that her tits got tighter and higher after she made the call to Beechtree Finance.'

Max blushed, red beyond the point of denial.

'Rory directed the ad himself, and he had the actress wear two different bras for the Before and After effect.'

Rory could feel himself redden, as much in anger as embarrassment. Robert Aldrich had a constant supply of ice on-set to keep Susannah York's nipples erect when they were shooting *The Killing of Sister George*. It flattered no-one to dissect whatever behind-the-scenes tricks were required to

108

have a sometimes subliminal effect on the viewer. He didn't feel like he ought to be apologising for it, but he was definitely on the backfoot under these circumstances.

'You should have read the shooting notes,' Liz went on. 'She was supposed to go from looking "bovine, saggy and past it" to "busty, full-figured and desirable". The effect was achieved by putting her in a wireless bra that was actually two sizes too big and giving bugger-all support, then changing to Gossard's finest. The weight wasn't entirely off her shoulders, but it did have some serious uplift.'

Max nodded equivocally. 'All right, I did notice that, but I thought it was either my imagination or the fact that she went from slumped to sitting up straight. I never imagined something like that was, you know, a creative decision.'

'Got your attention, though, didn't it?' Rory countered. 'I mean, how many other loan outfit ads could you reel off, any of you? Liz rails me about this kind of thing all the time, but she's just shooting the messenger. Guys respond to these things, sometimes in ways they're not even aware of. It's my job to get people's attention and make them remember the information. What does it matter whether I do it with a cute catchphrase or a curvy actress? Why does everybody have to get so precious about it?'

'But you're using sex to sell personal loans,' argued Joanna. Her tone wasn't aggressive, but he could tell she wasn't just playing devil's advocate either.

'And Scott's are using it to sell porridge oats, but nobody's getting morally indignant about them parading a six-pack in a kilt, are they? Sex sells, sex gets people's attention. What's the point of pretending it ain't so? Would we be a better society if none of our ads exploited sexual attraction to sell their products? 'Twas ever thus. People have been selling sex or using sex for ulterior purposes since civilisation began. That's why we talk about the oldest profession.'

Joanna looked away distastefully, the conversation having

become uncomfortable though he hadn't meant it to sound aggressive.

'So you're basically saying you're a whore?' asked a voice, which turned out to belong to Kathy, having insinuated herself into the group. She was sporting a welcome smile to dispel the confrontational edge the discussion had threatened to take.

'Absolutely not. I'm saying I'm a pimp. Other people sell their sexuality – I just find ways to market and exploit it. Assisted by Ms Ford, here, I might add.'

'No, no, Rory. You're the one going to hell. I'm only watching.'

'Save it for the judge.'

'No, I'm saving the Helen Lindstrom story for the judge.'

'Don't you dare,' warned Rory, who really didn't think she would dare, but was utterly chilled by the prospect. A bit of ribbing and point-scoring was one thing, but that would be low, that would be below the belt, that would be . . . another invoice in respect of that overdue morality bill. He felt his guts turn to stone, and took a sip of his champagne just to keep his hand busy and thus hide his nervousness should it encourage Liz further.

'Who's Helen Lindstrom?' asked Max.

Oh God.

'A model,' Kathy informed. 'Mid-ranking. Lads-mag cover status – where do they all come from, by the way, and why do we know their names? – and about eleven minutes into her fifteen.'

'Yeah, they just sort of appear from nowhere, don't they,' Rory said, hoping to re-route the discussion. 'There used to be your supermodels, your page-three girls and your young TV and pop starlets, but now there's this indeterminate tier of sorta-celeb models, isn't there? Your Catalinas, your Jordans, your Jacintas. *Her* real name's Mabel, by the way.'

110

This raised a laugh, Rory garnering as much eye-contact as he could in a quick sweep of the gathering.

'Jacinta, she's the one who made her name doing the muesli commercial?' asked Joanna, providing an out. Rory could have kissed her. Well, hugged her, maybe.

'Yeah, that's the one,' he confirmed. 'Sex to sell cereal, I'm afraid. And a springboard to the lads-mag circuit for the lucky lady.'

'I don't see why,' Joanna said with a shrug. 'It was hardly a memorable ad, and she was barely distinct from any number of other models cavorting around in swimming costumes. Why did she particularly catch anyone's eye?'

'And why do women in the ads always eat breakfast cereal in their swimming cozzies?' Kathy asked.

Rory was faced with a choice of paths, neither of which appeared to be leading directly away from uncomfortable and hazardous ground.

'You're asking the wrong guy,' he replied, repaying Joanna's unwitting assistance with utter disingenuousness. Nothing personal, he just needed a route out of the woods and reckoned this might be it. 'I might use certain models because they're recognisable, but the arbiters of which ones *get* recognised are the lads-mag editors, presumably anticipating the tastes of their readers. Maybe if you could find a fourteen-year-old male, he could shed more light on it.'

'Bollocks,' Liz said, stepping from the metaphorical trees to block his exit. 'Jacinta made her name from the muesli ad because you could have hung the proverbial wet duffle coat on her nipples. Never mind catching the eye – she was practically poking it out.'

At this, Kathy glanced down then lifted her champagne glass so that her forearm was covering her chest. Nightmare. He hated it when women became self-conscious like that. Made him feel like they were about to start with that 'all men are potential rapists' stuff. Unfair, too: it was Liz's fault

111

for blowing a cold wind through the conversation, but at least she seemed to have forgotten how they got on to the topic.

'So what's the Helen Lindstrom story?' asked Max.

Bastard.

'Helen Lindstrom? Do tell,' said another voice. It was Emily, recently arrived at the bar or recently departed from another conversation. In fact, it appeared that most of the room was looking this way, first-hand celeb gossip naturally winning out over 'so what does your company do' blethers now that the paintballing post-mortem was complete. He thought he'd made a passable impression on Emily so far, taking her side against Parlabane on the bus, and she'd seemed pretty sporting about it when he gunned her down towards the end of the game. She seemed a little serious and stressed earlier, but now she looked far more comfortable with a drink in her hand and a roomful of fellow guests, it being more the natural territory of the PR creature. She was wearing a fine black dress with a drawn collar and a split down the front. Her hands were clasped in almost prayer position around her champagne flute, so it was not yet apparent how much the split might reveal and whether she was standing up for herself, so to speak. Also obscured at this stage was what she thought of Rory, but he couldn't envisage his stock doing anything but plummet in the next few moments.

'Why don't you tell it, Rory?' Liz said, finding a way to make it worse. It felt like she was handing him a revolver. He couldn't refuse because it would further flag up his embarrassment, and he couldn't soft-soap it either. Liz was getting her revenge for some of the, ahem, creative decisions about which she had objected but been over-ruled, and there was to be no wriggling out. Best to take it like a man.

'Okay,' he began, trying to strike an impossible balance between wittily shameless and humorously apologetic. 'Just remember, I didn't make advertising such a sleazy place –

but I do have to work there. We used Helen Lindstrom for a poster and print-media campaign we did for Kreem Soda. I personally thought we showed admirable constraint in eschewing all the sperm gags we could have worked with.'

That got a few laughs, but mainly from the guys.

'Anyway, don't know if you saw it, but we went for a spoof aphrodisiac theme, kind of trying to out-Lynx "the Lynx Effect". Sort of "beware what you're unleashing when you open this stuff – can you handle what all these women are going to do to you once you've become irresistible".'

'By drinking Kreem Soda,' Kathy said sardonically.

'Exactly. We were playing the so-naff-it's-cool card, which is actually a tricky one to pull off. Look at those Pot Noodle abominations if you want to see the carnage when it goes wrong.'

'So that was Helen Lindstrom? I thought it was Mira Neeson,' Emily asked. Put the house on it: outside of four-teen-year-old males and middle-aged lads-mag editors, the one constituency guaranteed to know their sorta-celeb models was female PR consultants.

'Yeah, we were just saying they're all interchangeable,' Joanna told her.

'It *was* Mira Neeson,' Rory continued. 'Because Helen Lindstrom walked off the set during the shoot and we had to get a replacement.'

'Why?' asked, well, just about everyone other than Liz. They didn't all vocalise it, but they didn't all need to.

'I was trying to get a certain look from her that she wasn't comfortable with,' he ventured, eyeing Liz to see if the empress's thumb would go up or down. Her look said up, but in the correct sense of the gesture: down actually meant sheath your sword and spare the fallen. Her own feelings were by this point barely material, though: the empress knew the crowd's desires, and their desire was to know what that look was.

113

'Okay, bear in mind we were going for exaggerated sexuality, intimidating aggression. Well, she was managing "come over here, big boy", but it wasn't quite lascivious enough.' Rory took a gulp of champagne. The crowd thought he was teasing out the moment, but he really needed the alcohol. 'So I told her, em, basically, that she should look like, well, no way of cushioning this one . . .'

'Get on with it, Rory,' Liz commanded.

'Okay, I told her to look at the camera like she wanted it up the arse.'

There was a divisive mixture of embarrassed chuckles, amused guffaws (amused at the tale or Rory's discomfort, it was impossible to know) and, mainly, bemused sighs. Rory felt about three inches tall, all of it dick. He tried to avoid eye-contact without making it obvious he was avoiding eye-contact, but couldn't help catch a glimpse of Emily turning her head, as though shrinking from his loathsome presence.

Then Liz steamed in with the punchline, but one that was unlikely to redeem the real butt of this joke.

'What Rory didn't know at this point was that Helen's ex-boyfriend had just done a kiss and tell with a Sunday tabloid in which he revealed, well, do I have to say?'

Evidently not. There was more laughter this time, partly in relief that the point of the tale wasn't merely to illustrate what a cynical, sexist twat Rory was. No, instead it was a sheer belter because it illustrated that as well as being a cynical, sexist twat, Rory could also be a blundering numpty.

The petite waitress appeared in the doorway. She looked a little flushed and flustered, though the heat in the kitchen wasn't dampening that Robert Aldrich effect.

'Ladies and gentlemen, dinner is served,' she announced, at least five minutes too late. Rory no longer had an appetite.

114

Best Kept Secret

If it was true that food could become suffused with the atmosphere of the kitchen in which it was prepared, then Alison hoped the diners' tastes ran towards the tart. To the usual cocktail of heat, insufficient ventilation, unchecked egotism, petty animosities, lack of space and pressure of time had been added a form of performance anxiety resulting from the all-round raised stakes of the debut UML weekend. Mathieson was like an entity composed only of nervous energy and knives, pinballing around the stations all afternoon, interfering and interjecting compulsively, whether it be over the desired width of julienned courgettes (margin of error in millimetres, apparently) or the colour of the double cream (almost magnolia, he claimed, and this down to sabotage, he was sure, oblivious in his paranoia to the blown lightbulb directly above the fridge). And all this without Lady Jane being within three hundred miles of the place.

His salvos of indistinct instruction and abuse were punctuated by mutterings about him being the one who was 'saving all you useless fuckers' jobs', to remind them of his selfless motivation in harnessing his genius to their common cause, only for it to be impeded at every turn by their worthlessness and incompetence. 'If it wasn't for me, what fucking chance do you think we'd have making an impression here today, and yet here you all are trying to drag me down with you.' Etcetera. Mutter mutter mutter. But what passion, what commitment, what perfectionism. And none of it at all related to him having heard there was a journalist from *The*

Saltire in the house and therefore a chance of British cuisine's best-kept secret, unsung hero and star of the future finally getting his name in the paper.

She felt a little disloyal admitting it, but her ally Ger had been less than blameless in ratcheting up the tension, doing his bit to quietly stoke the flames then stepping back to watch the growing insanity from behind his personal force-field. It seemed that he hadn't been entirely kidding about avenging himself once the chef had nothing left to teach him, as there could be no other explanation for actions, on this most sensitive of days, that seemed likely and intended to induce spontaneous combustion before dessert. Though Alison could appreciate that Ger had been tactically judicious in choosing this vulnerable time to strike, she was more than a little peeved at his lack of concern over collateral damage and civilian casualties.

His choice of weapons had been music. Music had often been an area of strife in the kitchen; perhaps not itself the cause of war, but a frequent site of battles. When Mathieson was in his domain, he literally called the tunes, exercising the right of rank as much for its own sake as for what it delivered. This was of course merely Alison's impression, but it was backed up by her belief that he didn't have any real enthusiasm for music, and even occasionally insisted on none being played rather than let anyone else have a shout. In fact, she suspected that he not only had little enthusiasm for music, but was strangely wary of those who did, and found it comforting – even gratifying – to deny them.

Alison naturally expected older guys' musical tastes to make her feel frivolously youthful. Mathieson's made her feel like she ought to be subscribing to *Mojo*. She'd never considered herself someone who took music in any way seriously (she was two testicles short for that), but half an hour of his compilation CDs was usually enough to convince her she belonged among the cognoscenti by comparison. His

116

taste wasn't just naff; it was passé naff. (Had nobody the heart to tell him how long it had been since Boyzone were a going concern?) Unless, of course, he was simply ahead of the game for when all this dreck had retro-ironic-cool status conferred upon it a few years hence.

But his playlists aside, Alison's suspicion was mainly borne of the unsolicited pronouncements he tended to make, as though in defence of his selections. These were never offered in reply to anything anyone had said, but to what he obviously believed them to be thinking.

'I think it's pathetic when All Saints get lumped in with so-called girl bands. They're what you used to call a female vocal group. Nobody would lump The Supremes in with Atomic Kitten, would they? And All Saints are more than that, because the Appletons are songwriters in their own right. Their music's a lot more sophisticated than the cynics give them credit for. This is the stuff that's going to endure, too, not all that obscure, self-indulgent weird-for-the-sake-of-it crap.'

Meaning music that made him feel intellectually inadequate, like Sum 41.

Or try this:

'It's like the emperor's new clothes. People just make out they're into certain music in order to seem cool or "alternative". But they don't really like it – how could they? It's like saying you'd rather eat a raw skinned rabbit you caught in a rusty snare than sit down to a Michelin-starred meal. It's just a pose. Nobody wants to admit they like Robbie Williams because it's not *cooool*. But they're just posturing. Who wouldn't rather listen to *Angels* and *Millennium* and all those songs than some clever-clever arty-farty racket.' Meaning anything with lyrics that weren't about girls/boys or dancing.

'They said Robbie had no talent, he was just a boy-band dancer. Well, now he's playing stadiums. Shows how much they know.'

117

Ger, throughout these rants, never said a word, nor was it easy to even catch his eye at such moments, mainly because both parties knew it would provoke mutual bouts of hard-to-suppress sniggering. Alison initially thought this was down to a shared scorn for Mathieson's conspicuously insecure opinionating, but that was before Ger decided to avail her of all the facts.

Their beloved chef, she learned, had been in a prototype boy band himself, back in the late Eighties, around the time of Big Fun and Brother Beyond. Just too early, in other words. It was pre-Take That, pre-East Seventeen, when the anonymous conspiracy of music-hating evil geniuses was still trying to perfect its formula for production-line teen-pop Frankensteins that would stomp in synchronised choreography across the face of the charts throughout the Nineties and relentlessly beyond. They were called Three-D, the gimmick being that D was what each of their first names started with, Mathieson pretending to be named 'Danny' for the short-lived duration of the enterprise. They released two singles. The first, *(You Make Me Feel) So Funky!*, got them to number twenty-eight in the charts and earned them an appearance on *Top of the Pops*. The second Ger didn't know the title of, 'because it sank with nary a splash and took all hands down with it, leaving only three identical triple-D-embossed baseball caps bobbing on the waves'.

This revelation, in tandem with Spinmeister Mathieson's hot selections, confirmed Alison's suspicion that you really had to have no taste or respect for music to be in a 'male vocal group' as the chef referred to them. It was difficult (and rather horrifying) to imagine that there was an entire generation of teen males in their bedrooms right now pretending to be doing choreographed dance routines on *SMTV* instead of fiery axe-licks at Donnington.

With all of this in mind, Ger had lit a slow-burning fuse and watched in quiet amusement as it smouldered throughout the afternoon, edging nearer to the pile of ACME dynamite it was ultimately intended to detonate. Mathieson's dinner preparations having begun from just south of high doh, it did nothing to restore his composure that each of his chosen CDs kept jumping, skating and repeating until he was forced to switch off the machine in frustration. This minor and far from serendipitous technical hitch was more than tangentially connected to Ger having smeared pork fat liberally around the CD player's laser lens earlier in the morning, ensuring that only random, staccato snatches of the chef's music were played. It would be the first time that anything by Craig David sounded avant-garde.

With the chef's stereo out of commission, Ger had taken the 'opportunity' to play his own, normally only switched on when the boss wasn't present. At first, Mathieson was too distracted by his own efforts to achieve perfection/acclaim/meltdown to even notice that Ger's machine was playing, and had sufficient other outlets for his inner toddler that he didn't feel the need to demand silence or attempt to commandeer his assistant's stereo (which on any other day Alison would have loved to see). Instead he seemed to forget that it was an aspect of his environment that he normally controlled, and restricted his reactions to the occasional scornful rant about whatever happened to be playing.

It was almost disturbing to see such transparent hang-ups made manifest in an adult human being, especially one who was otherwise on the way to making a decent success of himself. Perhaps it was a kind of transference: haunted by his previous failed bid for the limelight, he had to convince himself he had been robbed by wrong and unjust forces in order to bolster his belief in his own worth. Or maybe he was just a wank.

'Listen to that nonsense. You're telling me [who's telling you, Peter?] *that*'s supposed to be "intelligent" music? It's

119

about a guy plugging in an electric heater, for fuck's sake. How banal is that?'

Ger just carried on with his work, silently smiling that little smile that suggested other people's tantrums were a paradoxical source of his own inner calm.

As ever, with twilight bringing dining time closer, the temperature in the kitchen rose, literally as well as figuratively. The ovens and burners drove up the heat while Mathieson, as conductor, cranked up the tempo. In seamless (but hardly unobtrusive) synthesis, Ger's soundtrack matched the growing pace, volume and overall discordance. System Of A Down was not music to soothe the savage beast, and nor, did she suspect, was that Ger's intention.

Alison was roughly one Armenian-speed-metal-polka beat away from hitting the Stop button herself when Mathieson finally cracked and commanded Ger to 'turn that fucking shit off before I take that stereo and beat somebody to death with it'.

'Nae bother,' Ger said, cutting the cacophony. 'Sorry, got a bit caught up in myself. Need somethin' a bit cheerier, eh?' he asked, reaching for a blank CD-R case.

Alison heard a burst of primitive beatbox snare followed by a few bars of era-distinct, sub-Stock-Aitken-and-Waterman synthesised brass and 'same beat suits all' syncopation. The chef looked up accusingly, automatically suspecting Ger to be taking the piss by putting on what he considered Mathieson's kind of music, but as the intro could have been any one of a hundred identical singles of its time, he failed to recognise it – and therefore the *true* extent to which Ger was taking the piss.

> *Well, we're movin' to the beat,*
> *And the word is on the street,*
> *That there's somethin' crazy happenin' toni–ight.*
> *All the boys are on the town,*

And the girls are gettin' down,
And the way you move is makin' me feel right, right,
    right – oooooh
Baybay! You make me feel so funkay!
I wanna take it to the—'

Click.

There was a Wild West bar-room kind of silence after Mathieson hit the Stop button, just the sound of a few bubbling pots and the hum of the labouring extractors to be heard. Charlotte, who had just come in the door, stood stock still, instantly detecting that the tension was far greater than usual. Ger looked up from the saucepan he was stirring towards where Mathieson stood next to the CD player, near catatonic with sheer, incredulous dismay.

It was safe to assume he hadn't been aware that anyone present knew of his place in the annals of rock 'n' roll, but what was really going to sauté his ego was not knowing how many or for how long.

The silence drew on, Mathieson eyeing the three of them in turn, trying to read how much they knew, almost willing a reaction. The situation – and indeed the tension generally – could be instantly defused if he chose to laugh it off, but only in the same way the Arab-Israeli conflict could be averted if both sides chose to accept their share of the blame and attempt to see the other's point of view.

'Sorry,' Ger eventually said. 'Did you want System Of A Down back on?'

Mathieson remained silent for a moment longer, then a shudder visibly ran through him, heralding the moment when the fuse reached that pile of ACME dynamite. He grabbed the CD player, yanking it from the worktop, leaving the lead still plugged into the wall, then jammed it into the dishwasher and rotated the dial to On with an angry flick of the wrist.

Ger shook his head and grinned, then got back to stirring his pot. This did little to douse Mathieson's ire. He wanted to say something, shout something, scream something, but seemed so backed up with competing furious emotions that nothing could get through the bottleneck. In his frustration, he rounded on Alison, who had stalled en route from the crockery cupboard when the Three-D song got hooked.

'What you fucking looking at?' he demanded, shoving her away with both hands. She toppled back and thumped into the wall, but retained her grip on the half-dozen plates she'd been carrying.

'Cool the jets, man,' Ger said quietly, a note of intent warning in his voice. 'If there's a problem, talk tae me.'

'Yeah, you're all right, Alison,' Mathieson spat. 'Your big, brave knight in shining prison fatigues is coming to the rescue. Question is, what's he getting from you, eh? Protection's not cheap from the criminal fraternity, but then maybe you're paying in kind, eh?'

'Leave it,' Ger warned again.

Mathieson put his hands up. 'Leave it? I wouldn't touch it. Frigid little bitch. You go ahead if you fancy your chances, Papillon. But I'd warn you, you've got some competition. You all know she's a lezza, don't you: Lady Jane, I mean? Her and Sir Lachlan is just one of those upper-crust marriage of convenience things. She's a muff-muncher, mark my words.' He turned to Alison again, looking her up and down, eyes blazing with rage. 'You better watch out, girl. She likes you for those perky little tits of yours, and your yes-ma'am, no-ma'am routine. Fuels her sordid *Upstairs Downstairs* S and M sex fantasies. She'll be trying it on soon enough. And when that happens, you're either gonna be eating pussy or out of a job.'

Alison was, she understood, supposed to be insulted, disgusted and coweringly intimidated by this, and thus rendered tearful, trembling and crushed. She was insulted and disgusted, but other than the perky tits remark (in conjunction with that UML guest whose eyes popped out on stalks when she'd entered the bar) making her think she should ditch the camisole for a bra tomorrow night, that was it. Unfortunately for Mathieson, two out of three didn't cut it. She hurled the plates down at the floor, causing him to spread his feet to avoid being hit, and thus exposing his crotch in advance of the foot she was already sending in. He jumped back, enough to cushion the impact but not enough that the message failed to register. However, he had a reply ready and prepared.

'Right. She's out of here. Assault. You're fucking fired, and you won't work anywhere my name is known again.'

'Bollocks she is,' Ger interjected, walking over and looking Mathieson in the face. 'You hit her first. But tell you what, why don't we run it by Sir Lachlan? How do you reckon he'd feel about us being another person short on the crew this weekend?'

Mathieson said nothing, but clearly knew the answer.

'Aye,' Ger confirmed. 'And bear in mind he won't want to fire me before Monday either if *I* boot your baws.'

Night of the Eighties Undead
(Parental discretion advised)

It had all been going far too well. He really should have seen this coming. Parlabane hadn't been so much lulled into a false sense of security as effectively distracted from the potential horrors at hand, and this, he'd have to admit, was a testament to UML's success in achieving part of their stated objective. From the shared-adversity/mutual humiliation ordeal of the 'identity affirmation exercise', through the uncomfortable but necessary coalescing and cooperation, to the surprisingly enjoyable mayhem of stalk and splat, the effect had indeed been to mould them into a functioning unit and thereby suppress the individual traits that might otherwise prevent them getting along. It was plausible UML had picked up the principle from an ant colony. It didn't matter who you were, you all had a shared objective and your contribution to achieving that made you valuable to your colleagues irrespective of blah blah blah. Yeah, magic. Group hugs and high-fives all round.

But now they were all having dinner together.

That was when he remembered that he had been less apprehensive about whatever indignities UML might visit upon him this weekend than about the type of people he would be having to put up with: viz, the type of people who thought this kind of carry-on was a great idea.

The important thing was to keep reminding himself that it was good copy. Contrary to what Emily Bell believed, he had not come here to bury UML: he'd guessed his fellow guests would do that for him, just by being themselves. He only had to write it down. It wasn't exactly a scoop, for instance, that the endlessly self-congratulatory advertising industry believed image, design, wit, humour, concept and vision to be no substitute for a nice pair of tits, but it was rare to have such a candid admission to quote.

Poor bastard. Parlabane had almost felt sorry for Rory, seeing the guy stitched up like that by a colleague whose high-minded principles were nonetheless not forcing her to seek employment where she wouldn't be party to the whole-sale exploitation of etcetera, etcetera, etcetera. He could read the script pretty clearly: it wasn't just a spot of boss-baiting, it was conscience therapy. Even if the guy had it coming, doing it in front of a group of near-strangers he'd be stuck with at close-quarters for two days had made Liz look as cynical and ruthless as Rory. Everybody had laughed, but as much to dispel the tension as out of genuine humour.

For a guy who struck Parlabane as having skin so thick you couldn't cut it with one of those two-handed broad-swords adorning the staircase, Rory's response was surpris-ingly subdued. He'd done a bit of playing the incorrigible rogue, pretending to take it on the chin, but his reticence around the dinner table seemed conspicuously out of char-acter, especially when the vino began eliciting more veritas than Parlabane wanted to hear from everyone else.

It was Toby who started it, albeit inadvertently.

'A coup d'état,' he suddenly said, during a lull in conver-sation over generous digestifs. Prior to that, discussion had been polite but dull, with Campbell as UML Master of Cere-monies inviting a bit of oral CV circulation from each of his guests. Baxter hadn't joined them for dinner, having 'prep-arations for tomorrow' to attend, according to his china. They were all seated around one large oval table in a book-lined conference room, commandeered for their dining purposes because of its intimacy. It lent a more relaxed, dinner-party air to the proceedings (initially at least), which would have been lacking had they taken their places in the conspicuously under-capacity main restaurant. It also facilitated Campbell's desire to encourage large-scale single discussion rather than private little chats between those closest by, which was no doubt intended to bond the greater unit, but felt in practice like an inadvisedly awkward game of spin-the-bottle. Rory Glen was about the only person Parlabane imagined being naturally comfortable holding the floor like that, but between his sudden attack of bashfulness and the fact that everybody now knew more than they cared to about how he made his living, he had little to contribute, leaving the spotlight to rightly reluctant others.

Normally when surrounded by those who would describe themselves as 'business people' jawing about their jobs, Parlabane felt like Charlie Brown in those scenes where adults were talking, their speech rendered as meaningless 'waah-waah-waah' noises, the speakers oblivious to the listener's incomprehension. On this occasion, however, the empathetic dread and cringing he felt watching each of them stumble and flounder meant he was unable to zone out so much as usual of what they said.

In addition to what he already knew about the Reflected Gleam and Seventh Chime delegations, he learned the following:

Max Redman was Something In The City. Parlabane may have been listening more closely than he particularly cared to, but the string of titles and positions Max had held defeated his ability to comprehend what exactly the guy did. It had long been Parlabane's belief that the more complicated your job title, the less tangible the contribution you made to society in return for your wage packet (or stock options).

'I'm a plumber. Call me in late September when the weather turns Baltic and your central heating system throws a seven after deciding it can't face another winter.' Any problems there?

'I'm an electrician. Call me when you flip a lightswitch and end up looking like Don King.' Clear enough?

'I'm a Strategic Coordination Supervisor in charge of Investment Risk Assessment in Nascent Technology Markets. No, I'm not sure what the fuck I do either, but I'm pulling down six figures, so it must be pretty important, wouldn't you say?'

Max recounted umpteen such bafflingly nebulous posts, but to further muddy the waters, while failing to adequately describe what it was, on any given day at the office, that he actually *did*, he was now doing it on a freelance consultative basis and currently held no title whatsoever. He confessed a little surprise as to why, therefore, he had been invited on the junket. Campbell wasn't forthcoming in response. He threw the question back to Max in an attemptedly coy fashion, prompting the mutually satisfactory musing that, as someone moving among several companies, he'd be well placed to spread the word.

Max had neglected to fill the 'plus one' place offered on the weekend, citing a desire to 'throw myself in without a lifebelt' because now that he was freelance, it was his day-to-day job to 'drop into the midst of strangers and make myself an indispensable part of the machine'. Parlabane suspected this was a circuitous way of saying 'I have no mates', which might be an embarrassing admission, but would at least have made him sound less of a ham shank.

Another person confused, if flattered, by her invitation was Joanna Wiggins. Although these days working long-term for Catalyst IT Solutions in Liverpool, she was also an independent contractor, and not one particularly high up the Catalyst food chain either, by the sound of it. This time Campbell did volunteer that 'it's part of UML's philosophy in making people feel part of something, that the impetus should not always have to come from the top'. He neglected to add the proviso that the top was nonetheless where the decision and the outlay would have to come from, no matter how many eager employees sang in praise of what UML had to offer, but that would have spoiled the faux-egalitarian New Labour cuddliness of the sentiment.

Joanna had opted to bring a companion in the shape of the singularly gormless Grieg Rossi, who in his role as a Human Resources apparatchik at an IT outfit was in the pitiful position of being someone computer geeks actually looked down on. As such, he was utterly made for the job, as his combination of physical clumsiness, verbal ineptitude and unwaveringly glaikit expression must have made even the most gauche and pallid code-cruncher feel like a cock-sure sophisticate.

Finally, there was Toby Seaton, on the face of it another unlikely invitee given that he was in charge of a local charity in Newcastle, and such organisations tended not to have much green to throw around on upscale morale-boosting exercises, staff's motivations generally coming from less capricious sources. Toby's organisation collected furniture, household appliances and generally anything of practical value from those who no longer wanted them, and then redistributed the goods among householders currently in no position to upgrade. They specialised in house clearances, coming in after the removal firm had taken all the treasured belongings and offering practical catharsis to those left wondering what to do with the orphaned sofa that doesn't match their new living room. Parlabane sensed something incongruous about the man and his job, there being a distinct whiff of the upper orders about him. Sure, there were plenty of aristos at the head of charities – where would the lunch and party circuits be without our good causes, darling? – but this was small-scale, unheralded and very much down-and-dirty. From the sound of it, Toby spent his days driving vans and lugging fridges, not glad-handing dignitaries and managing photo-ops. There was a tale of a toff laid low here, and Parlabane intended to hear it. If nothing else, perhaps it would explain what UML hoped to gain from his endorsement. Connections to big money and big influence were a far more plausible motive than any more of the phoney reaching-out-to-all-levels mince Campbell was hawking.

Toby had come alone too, though this turned out to be because his assistant had gone down with appendicitis the night before, leaving him with no time to seek a replacement before setting off from Tyneside at dawn. When he heard this, Parlabane expressed his sympathy for both of them. Within an hour, he was wishing he'd subsisted the past week on a diet of clipped toenails.

'A coup d'état.' Really pretty much out of nowhere, conversationally. The last signpost sighted on the road of discussion had been pointing to the paintball post-mortem rehash exit ramp, Vale having prematurely concluded the careers version of you-show-me-yours-and-I'll-show-you-mine by judiciously – and not entirely dishonestly – stating that he was 'a former civil servant'. Not even Campbell wanted to coax forth any elaboration on that.

'What did you say?' Campbell asked Toby.

'Oh, sorry. Just thought of something we were talking about this afternoon. Before the game got going, Liz and Joanna were discussing whether there were any other circumstances in which you could shoot your boss and still keep your job.'

There was laughter, mainly from those who'd been on the red team, though it was unclear whether this was because they hadn't heard the remark the first time or because they had spent the match teamed up with Liz's boss. Rory cracked a thin smile, but appeared to have moved on from cowed and reflective to borderline huffy. Unaccustomed as he was to public not-speaking, he had been keeping his mouth busy by filling it with wine, and one could measure the distance between feeling sorry for himself and inevitable belligerence in fluid ounces.

'No,' Vale interjected. 'Strictly speaking, in a coup d'état, if you shoot your boss, the point of the exercise is that you end up in *his* job.'

'Good point,' Toby conceded. 'If a pedantic one. The thing is, though, you could shoot your boss but not get fired, like Liz here today.'

'I don't think she did actually shoot her boss, to be fair,' Max pointed out.

'Might not stop her getting fired, though,' growled Rory. His tone and timing were comically perfect, but Parlabane clocked a look in his eye that didn't entirely suggest he was joking.

It wouldn't normally fall to Parlabane to play peacemaker in any kind of situation, being someone who had built if not a career then at least a reputation upon an irresistible tendency to pour kerosene on smouldering timber just so he could stand back and write about the flames. However, jail had taught him a whole new respect for the need to calm the herd, so the thought of someone getting pissed and volatile in such already awkward and socially confined circumstances was something he literally didn't have the stomach for these days. Consequently, he intended to cap the growing aggro. The results demonstrated why the opposite was more his forte, but he did at least try.

'What do you call a heifer in a number-seven football jersey carrying an M-16 assault rifle?' he asked the assembly, pitching a gag he'd heard on *Off The Ball*.

Every head turned his way expectantly, in anticipation of some moment of comedy genius that could justify such a peremptory derailing of the conversation and impudent requisition of the floor.

'A right-wing military coo,' he informed them, to blank looks almost all round. It perhaps understandably whipped

130

over the heads of some of the English contingent, and the football reference evidently sidelined a further constituency in the Scottish females, leaving only Rory, who was buggered if he was going to cheer up for anybody; Campbell, who had displayed no evidence to suggest he could ever be successfully prosecuted for possession of a sense of humour and was anyway still peeved at having lost control of the discussion; and Vale, who'd laughed the first time he heard it but was determined to enjoy the spectacle of Parlabane dying on his arse.

'They can't all be gems,' he apologised with a shrug, which got more chuckles than the gag.

'We could do with one here,' Rory grizzled, almost but not sufficiently under his breath. 'Get rid of that shower we've got at the moment,' he added, louder.

'Hear, hear,' said Max, in the moment that heralded the evening's imminent, hurtling descent into becoming the dinner party from hell. 'Only way to shift them, I reckon. It's not as if there's a viable opposition, more's the pity.'

'What?' asked Kathy. 'You reckon we could get a more right-wing government than is already in power?'

'We can but dream,' Rory said.

'It would never happen,' ventured Liz. 'A coup I mean. We don't really do extremism in this country, not in large enough numbers anyway. Salman Rushdie wrote in *The Satanic Verses* that it was because of the weather.'

'The weather?' asked Joanna, laughing.

'Yes. Miserable summers, mild winters. No droughts, no hurricanes, no extremes. It's never that cold and, crucially, it's never that hot, so we don't lose our heads and we don't like things to go too far in one direction.'

'Sweet moderation and all that,' agreed Toby.

'I don't know,' Kathy said. 'We went pretty far in one direction during the Eighties. There wasn't much sweet moderation in evidence when Thatcher was in power. If you

131

weren't "one of us" you could fuck off, as far as she was concerned.'

'Well, somebody had to draw a line and force people to choose which side of it they wanted to stand,' Max argued. 'There were too many subversive types trying to undermine this country back then, and Margaret Thatcher had the steel to expose them for what they were and make a stand against them.'

'The "enemy within",' agreed Rory.

'By what measure did disagreeing with Thatcher become equated with undermining the country?' Emily joined in. 'It's called opposition. It's called democracy.'

'Oh, come on,' Rory said. 'The left was full of nutters in those days. I was a student back then, and I remember the types. They were spoiling for a fight all the time, didn't matter the issue. The issue was just that week's excuse. Same agitators, same nutters. One week it was the miners, the next it was Apartheid, then gay rights, then the week after that it would be, I don't know, save the fucking whale.'

'Exactly, Rory,' Max resumed, buoyed by this show of solidarity. 'There's a difference between democratic protest and concerted, organised troublemaking.'

'Yeah,' said Emily. 'Democratic protest is a protest you agree with. Organised troublemaking is one you don't. I've got a two-inch scar on my skull courtesy of a police baton during an anti-Apartheid demonstration. Do you think I got it because I was troublemaking, or do you think I was exercising my democratic right to protest?'

'I'm not saying there weren't important issues at stake,' Rory said, sounding a little cowed and conciliatory in the face of Emily's onslaught. 'I can understand folk getting hot under the collar about certain issues, but not bloody everything. There was an orthodoxy about you lot: here's a list of the things we support and the things we oppose. This month's boycotts and demonstrations are as follows. One minute you were wanting sexually explicit material banned – even page three – and the next you were campaigning *against* a law that would ban sexually explicit material in schools.'

'Only *homo*sexual material,' Kathy corrected. 'Clause 28 was minority bashing for the sake of it, the playground hard-man beating up the unpopular kid because it made him look good in front of his mates. Damn right I protested about it. I'd say the question is why didn't you?'

Kathy's eyes were bulging, Emily merely sighing. The latter looked like she had less appetite for the fight, but more through fatigue than a lack of conviction. She'd heard both sides of the arguments too many times before, he guessed, as had Parlabane, and both knew the likelihood of anyone's minds being changed about much, even twenty years later.

'Actually, I think you'll find there was a bit more to it than that,' Max weighed in, his tone imprudently patron-ising. 'If you knew what those loony-left councillors were doing in London with public money . . . Makes me mad to this day just thinking about it. Bah bah green sheep, remember that? Changing the words because it might offend ethnic minorities. Early days of political correctness running mad.'

And there it was, the line he'd known would be along soon enough: 'Political correctness gone mad.' Parlabane had referred to it recently in a column as 'the distress call of the thwarted bigot'. Any time he heard it, he felt he ought to rejoice, because somewhere, something must be being done right. In that respect it was the opposite of 'a victory for common sense', which invariably hailed some act or decision that satisfied the base and brutal instincts human civilisation had spent the past ten thousand years evolving away from.

It should have been his cue to join the fray. In these days of anodyne debate and somnolent apathy, Parlabane had been longing for a return to such impassioned, even entrenched political anger. However, this exchange only had the heat and the bitterness, being merely a remnant of an old, stale but evidently still festering divide. It was like the night he and Sarah, vainly defying the approach of their forties and despairing of modern nightclub music, attended an Eighties Alternative retro night. After the initial hit of nostalgia at a few forgotten classics and emotion-memory carnal stirrings in response to the contemporary goth-wear, it all seemed very tawdry and sad, devoid of the dynamism that had made the music, the clothes and the culture exciting at the time. It was devoid of that dynamism because it couldn't move forward, couldn't develop, couldn't evolve. It was no more than a snapshot, a compilation album. You couldn't go back, and, what was worse, it taught you nothing to try.

This was old news, an eternal echo of a dead debate: still reverberating, but unable to progress. He no more felt like joining in than he'd felt like moshing around to *She Sells Sanctuary*.

Still, he did owe the combatants a point of clarification.

'Bah bah green sheep never happened. The *Sun* made it up. They admitted it later. In fact, they and their counterparts made up most of the loony-left GLC stories. It was a concerted propaganda campaign, in cahoots with Tory Central Office, to rubbish the GLC so that they could abolish it.'

'Says you,' Max insisted.

'Says the journalists who wrote it. They were all pretty up-front about it once the GLC was gone and the job was done.'

'You can't expect me to believe that. If they weren't true, why weren't these stories challenged? Why weren't they sued?' Max demanded.

'Pointless. It was a smear campaign. A *Sun* or *Mail* reader's mind isn't going to be changed by a rebuttal in some other paper they don't read.'

'That's if they could find a paper to print their side of the story,' Kathy added. 'The Tories had the press sewn up in those days. There were so few mainstream outlets for dissent it was like living in a fascist state.'

'I was waiting for that one,' Rory muttered disdainfully. 'The Lefty's Lament. Anyone who disagrees with them is always a fascist. The country was like a fascist state in the Eighties because you were in the minority. Is it only democracy when you get your own way?'

'It was like a fascist state because—'

'To be fair, Kathy,' interrupted a voice, 'that kind of intemperate language doesn't help anyone.' Parlabane looked down the table to confirm that it had come from the previously silent – and still very softly spoken – Toby. 'If I recall, it was your own Denis Healey who spoke out against those calling Margaret Thatcher a fascist because it devalued the term and meant they wouldn't recognise the real thing if it came along. I lost count of how many times I got called a fascist just because I was a Tory. It didn't make me examine my conscience and re-evaluate my politics – and it didn't give me much respect for your lot either.'

'Mmm,' approved Grieg, nodding, his first contribution since 'Could you pass the white wine?' about an hour back. 'I voted for Thatcher, first time I could vote: '87. Didn't mean I was some kind of extremist. I didn't pay much attention to politics, to be honest. I voted Labour in '97. It's all about choice, isn't it?'

Sadly, thus spoke the voice of the constituency that really decided British elections: the uninformed and barely interested wavering numpty.

'Quite,' agreed Campbell, who had looked a little shell-shocked throughout the preceding exchanges. 'I've always voted Conservative because I'm basically a business-minded person and they've always, to me, been the business-minded party. But I've never been any kind of extremist, and yes, like the others, I'd resent the implication.'

Liz was nodding too. 'It could even be argued that being so intolerant of your political opponents is fascistic in itself.'

'Well, bloody hell, isn't that just typical,' Emily exclaimed. 'You don't see a Tory for ages, then half a dozen come along all at once. Okay, you want to talk about political intolerance? Margaret Thatcher turned conference debate into Stalinist rallies and witch-hunted the so-called Wets – and that was just how she dealt with dissent on *her* side. She seemed offended by the very idea of anyone disagreeing with her, and she cracked down hard to try and stop it. Her regime had MI5 spying on law-abiding British citizens because they were "potential subversives". If you were a member of CND, they were tapping your phone. Does that sound free and democratic to you?'

'The intelligence services have to spread a wide net to catch big fish,' Campbell stated. 'It's a necessary evil that they'll end up spying on people who are innocent, but you're just as likely to be monitored if they think you're an extremist of the right. It's the only way to catch the dangerous ones before they do serious damage. Basically, if you're doing nothing wrong, what's the harm?'

'You mean aside from gross invasion of privacy and violation of your civil rights?' Emily retorted. 'Anyway, I'm not talking about extremists plotting to blow up parliament. MI5 were infiltrating trades unions, political groups: legal, democratic organisations. That's how they broke the miners' strike: they had agents close to Scargill, passing on information to the state. What was Arthur planning to blow up, do you think, Max?'

'It's no wonder Thatcher was such an admirer of Pinochet,' Kathy added. 'Every time she was at Wembley

Stadium for the FA Cup Final, she must have been eyeing the place up with a wistful sigh and thinking: "If only".'

'Sounds like we're back to calling people fascists,' said Liz. 'I take it you're being facetious.'

'I'm entirely serious,' Kathy insisted. 'She knew what Pinochet was doing, and it didn't stop her inviting him round for fireside chats. I've very little doubt that woman would have had subversives eliminated if she thought she could get away with it. In fact, she did, in Gibraltar. The SAS shot dead three IRA members, unarmed and in broad daylight. The order came from the top, and her own sources don't dispute that. Thatcher wanted to give the IRA "a bloody nose", their words, after Brighton.'

'And quite bloody right,' said Max. 'They were there to massacre British soldiers and citizens in a bomb attack, not abducted from their beds by snatch squads. They weren't political opponents, they were terrorists.'

'They were murderous scum,' Kathy stated vehemently. 'But according to the laws of the country those SAS operatives were supposedly protecting, even murderous scum have a right to be tried in a court before sentence is passed, and that sentence is no longer allowed to be death.'

'Sure. They should have been apprehended, at the risk of killing or injuring British soldiers in the process, put on trial and then, on the off-chance they actually *were* convicted, they would call themselves political prisoners and be out by now as part of the so-called Peace Process. In fact, they would probably have cabinet posts in the Northern Irish Assembly. Is that what you'd prefer? Gibraltar wasn't an act of fascism, it was self-defence against fascism, for what else could you call blowing people up because you can't get your way in a democracy?'

'Live by the sword, die by the sword,' Grieg added, in another essential contribution. 'They got what they were planning to dish out. I've no sympathy for terrorists.'

'Neither have I,' replied Kathy, 'but the point is we're supposed to be better than them.'

'Fight fire with fire, I say,' Grieg observed, going all out for that clichés-to-words-spoken record ratio.

'I don't imagine Red Adair's with you on that one,' Parlabane mused, unable to resist in the face of such unthinking vapidity.

'It's just a metaphor,' he replied testily.

'Or an analogy, even,' Parlabane corrected.

'Yeah, well, the point is, the world wouldn't miss a few more dead terrorists.'

'And would we kill them after they'd carried out an attack or pre-emptively?'

'Preferably before. Either way, it's no great loss.'

'How long before?' Parlabane asked. 'When they're poised to strike? When they're on reconnaissance? When they're hatching their plot? When they join a proscribed organisation?'

'No, we should wait until they've killed as many people as possible, as usual, before we do anything that might have hand-wringers like Philip Young bleating about civil rights,' said, inevitably, Max. Philip Young was the spokesman for Taking Liberty, not an organisation Parlabane imagined Max having a direct-debit subscription to. 'You know, I really do wonder how many people would still be alive today if we *had* been fighting fire with fire.'

'Absolutely,' Grieg agreed. Campbell nodded also. Max was looking around for further assent. Liz wore an impatient frown, as those overemotional female creatures were wont to whenever men started talking about killing each other. Rory, who had grown quiet during the latter stages of the argument, didn't meet Max's eyes. Instead he looked across at Toby, rather furtively and not for the first time. Parlabane couldn't see Toby's face to read what, if any, response he had for either man.

Whatever support he had received was enough for Max to persist.

'If you ask me, we should have given the IRA a few more bloody noses.'

'Yeah, because they really eased off after Gibraltar,' Parlabane responded.

Max ignored this. 'No, instead we spend a hundred and fifty million pounds of British taxpayers' money on an inquiry into Bloody Sunday, putting on public trial the very service men and women who *defend* our country. What about an inquiry into Omagh, into Enniskillen, into the *thousands* of deaths dealt out by the IRA since?'

'Oh for Christ's sake, I've heard enough.' It was Vale who'd spoken, his intervention commanding the room with its severity in conjunction with surprise, given that he had up until that point listened to the debate politely but silently. Parlabane was more taken aback than any of them. He'd known the guy for more than a decade, and this was about the closest he'd heard him come to raising his voice. Vale was the kind of person who took pleasure in his own political inscrutability, amused by the assumptions and extrapolations of those foolish enough to attempt to get inside his head. It had been no surprise that he'd sat wordlessly throughout this bout of dead-horse flogging, or that he'd be wearing a wry smile while the intelligence services were being both lionised and burnt in effigy. He wasn't a man easily offended, and Parlabane had little idea what would do the trick, not being ever quite sure what Vale took seriously or what he held dear. Well, he knew now.

'First of all, we don't need an inquiry into what terrorists did because the whole point of terrorism is that it's unaccountable. Our security forces must be supremely accountable, because whatever they do, they do in the name of this country and it's a name some of us want to remain proud of.'

139

'Look, mate,' Max said, pitching at conciliatory but inevitably hitting patronising. 'Those are high ideals, and we ought to be proud of them, but it's easy for you to say, when you've spent all your working life in the civil service pushing pens. I was in the TA, I know a lot of soldiers, and it's not as easy as you think to practise what you're preaching. Those guys are the ones putting themselves in the firing line to defend us, so I think we should cut them some slack.'

'Yes, those servicemen are there, as you say, to defend our country, and *when* they are defending our country, they are defending a way of life in which soldiers don't gun down civilians. You say we should cut our soldiers some slack. In my experience, people are happy to cut soldiers and policemen plenty of slack, see them dish out some "instant justice" – as long as it's people they disagree with on the receiving end.

'We've all got that nasty little streak inside us, that secret desire to just silence the person saying what we don't want to hear. And that nasty streak embraces force because when force is on your side, reason, logic and morality don't have to be. You're talking about fighting fire with fire. Well, who here hasn't fantasised about putting a bullet in the head of some scumbag the world could do without: Bin Laden, Le Pen, Nick Griffin?'

'Alan Titchmarsh,' suggested Rory.

'Quite,' Vale continued. 'You tell yourself the world would be a better place without them, but would it? Sure the world wouldn't miss another bloodthirsty extremist or racist hate-monger, but the moment they were gone, the world would then be a place where we kill people because we don't like what they're thinking. I don't know about the rest of you, but I'm proud of my country because my country isn't in that world, despite what those on the left might fear and those on the right might wish.'

Vale sat back in his chair and took up his malt, signalling the end of his contribution and, from the reaction, the end of the debate. There was silence, apart from the sound of other glasses being lifted to mouth or refilled from bottles. Suddenly everybody was thirsty and nobody had anything to say. It was like school dinners after the headmaster had just told everybody off.

'So,' Parlabane said, interrupting the awkward hush. 'Who's up for charades?'

Troubled Sleep

Rory was lying awake, despite the quantities of food and alcohol that would normally have seen off consciousness within moments of curling up in the customary coma position. Tonight, though, there was no getting comfortable, so he was on his back, trying to empty his head of its unwelcome and noisily rancorous guests. As always, the best way was to think about more pleasant, relaxing and appropriately nocturnal things, but it was like trying to watch a DVD while those same guests were still hanging round the living room. It was impossible to retreat into sexual fantasy because even his fantasies needed a minimum of plausibility to hang their titillation on, and right then it felt like there couldn't be a woman in the world who didn't despise him.

When he was in his early teens, and his schoolmates were giving thanks to Sanyo for their Betamax pirate-hardcore delivery system, his VCR enthusiasm had been for capturing nude scenes from late-night movies – but only those featuring actresses he already knew from other roles. He remembered sitting up into the wee hours, through endless ad breaks and false promises, for the possible bounty of glimpsing hitherto unseen breasts beneath a well-ken't face. And when he found it, it was gold, with soft-focus footage of the erstwhile Bionic Woman or Lois Lane taking their tops off far more of a thrill than the full-on stuff his mates were whacking off to. To Rory, it was like the difference between seeing a stripper in a nightclub and seeing the girl next door take her bra off at the window. There had to be a relationship, if you like, a point of reference, otherwise it was just another pretty face (pretty tits, pretty bum, double pene-tration and multiple cum shots if that was your thang; the point was, no depth of depravity was a match for extant familiarity).

Was it a fetish? Unquestionably, but that wasn't all it was. Was it perverse? Only in accordance with the eternal rule that 'what turns *me* on is erotic but what turns *you* on is perverse'. Was it sad, pathetic and embarrassing? Well, so far he hadn't met any girls he imagined would be impressed if he told them all about it, so it was definitely well down the list of Interesting Things About Me to reel off over first-date dinner. And was it on the wane? Hell, no.

He'd once thought this voyeuristic streak, his 2-D love, as he came to think of it in his youth, would end or at least dissipate when he started getting some first-hand experience. That maybe once you'd got your paws on your first pair of naked funbags, you'd be less inclined to strain the limits of your eyesight as you tried to detect the outline of aureoles through blouse and bra beneath that bank teller's namebadge. *Wrong!* That getting fully naked and doing everything you'd ever heard of, read about, imagined and fantasised would dim the allure of at least the next tight skirt or lycra-restrained embonpoint that bobbed into view the next morning. *Wrong!* In retrospect, he'd deduced that his naïve theory had been comparable to thinking you'd never want to watch another football match just because you'd got a game for the local Sunday amateurs. It just didn't work that way.

At least Finlay had a viable excuse: he was a *bona fide* computer geek who didn't get out much and very seldom got laid. It was expected of him that he'd be thus retarded in the sexual area of his emotional development. Rory, with his success, his money, his social sphere and his sex life, lacked any comparable mitigation, beyond the enduring personal philosophy that self-indulgent id-stroking was its own justification.

And he knew what people would think, what assumptions they'd be likely to make, with the words 'sexist', 'misogynist' and 'wanker' featuring large and liberally; but they were dead wrong. Real life, real psychology didn't work like the flowchart on some right-on feminazi student pamphlet. He wasn't sexist in his dealings with women; he'd appointed more of them than he had men, and not because of any preference about what he'd rather be looking at from behind his desk. Jeez, you only had to get an eyeful of Theresa Graham of a Monday morning to nail that one. He wasn't some feminist's voodoo-doll fantasy boss who gave the job to the girl with the biggest tits or the shortest skirt; not unless she was also the candidate who could do the job best. He'd hired them in every instance because he recognised and required what they could bring to the table. Rory respected women in each and every way even the feminazis could wish for. He just couldn't help what the sight of them did to his brain.

He could be introduced to a Nobel-prize-winning female scientist who had eradicated an endemic disease in between senior government ministerial posts and publishing works of acclaimed poetry. He would cower before her intellect, be humbled by her achievements, be shamed by his comparative insignificance. But none of that would prevent him trying to picture what she looked like under her clothes, or cause him to avert his gaze if she turned just the right way to afford a glimpse between those second and third buttons. This didn't diminish her standing in his eyes, did not detract from his awe, and did not mean he was reducing her to a sexual object. It was just that he couldn't pretend she wasn't – as well as all those other things – a sexual object as identified somewhere deep and primal inside every straight male.

He knew some guys were better at filtering it out, numbing it or censoring it, but suspected also that he was more sensitive to this primal instinct than most. It was as

144

though he was a kind of sexual empath, born with some carnal higher awareness, a more acute and sensitive means of tuning into the signals. If it was a crime, it was its own punishment, because there was no rest from it throughout the waking day. And truth be told, while it had at times threatened to drive him crazy, professionally it had served him well.

Sex sells. Yeah. Everybody knew that. Everybody knew petrol was combustible, too, but that didn't mean anybody could design a Porsche.

The Helen Lindstrom story had been bad enough, but that business after dinner . . . It had just been so ugly. What was that about? All that nonsense was over, long over. He didn't even vote any more, and if he did it wouldn't be for the Tories. But as soon as that Eighties vault was wedged open, the anger and hatred had come spilling out and it was like he was back there again; like they were *all* back there again, for there'd been no quarter given by the lefties either.

When he tried to picture women, he thought about Liz and her ambush; Emily and Kathy and their looks of disgust. It was hopeless. So, inevitably, something else started playing – once again – on the internal widescreen plasma. He was back once more to another Friday night: two weeks ago now but still vividly fresh and undiminished in its recurrence. He'd been driving home, towards the end of the rush-hour, the traffic lightening but the roads still slow because of the rain. It was absolutely tanking down, that way where the drops seemed to be bouncing back up when they hit the pavement. It was dark, really dark, earlier than it was due, and not earlier as in hours, but months. This was December dark, headlights and streetlights swallowed by the rain like they may as well have been torch flames. He was grateful for the comfort of his BMW, but it was no pleasure to be driving. Pedestrians trotted alongside, more holding up newspapers and plastic bags than brollies, testament to the

145

suddenness of the downpour. They were only visible for any length of time when he was stationary at red signals, otherwise they just appeared in blinks and flashes, picked out by another car's lights as it turned, or briefly silhouetted against windows. It felt uneasy that they should be so difficult to see, one of those moments when he became uncomfortably aware he was in control of a potential killing machine.

It was a great night to be inside, whether that was at home in front of the home cinema set-up or in a pub with a real fire going and a crowd of familiar faces determined to be there till the last. That was what he'd been deciding when he saw them. He pulled up, about ten or twelve cars back from the lights, little chance of getting through in just one change, which was why he put the machine in neutral and stuck on the handbrake. They were three or four yards away on the pavement, in front of a garden gate: teenagers going by their dress, a guy and a girl, kissing under a hopelessly insufficient umbrella, which she was holding with one hand, her other locked around the guy's waist. The rain was running off the brolly on to one of his shoulders, water pouring off both their coats on to their shins, necessitating a jeans-over-the-radiator scenario whenever they both got home. Well, one of them presumably was home, just about, but wasn't in a hurry to get inside, where parents and other complications dwelt.

They didn't care. Not about the rain, not about the cold, not about the hundred commuters passing by in their insulated metal boxes. If this was where that kiss was happening, then that was all that mattered about the location and the prevailing conditions.

His first thought had been, how miserable. Not the night and the weather, but the restrictions of being that age: not having the freedoms you needed, your own place, independence, privacy, the money that bought all of the above.

It had been years since he'd been caught in the rain longer than it took to get from the car to the door, or in the worst instance to hail a passing Hackney. There was no need to be out there in the rain, never mind that being the only place he could kiss a girl.

Then, as the lights changed and he had to move on, he realised it had been even longer since there'd been a girl he wanted to kiss so much that he'd settle for doing it outside on a freezing night in the pouring rain in front of a hundred passing commuters. That's when he knew it wasn't miserable at all. That's when he knew they were happier than he was, because in that moment they had everything they wanted in the world.

Parlabane held his breath as he stood against the wall, balanced on the balls of his feet, watching his door very slowly swing open. A shaft of light fell across the foot of the double bed, picking out a tangle of sheets and the trousers he couldn't be arsed hanging up before he crashed out. The intruder stepped silently and delicately through the door, across the shaft and swiftly into shadow, approaching the head of the bed.

'Bang you're dead,' Parlabane said, flipping the lightswitch to reveal Vale, who was already pointing his fingers towards him in the shape of a gun.

'Call that one a draw, shall we?' Vale asked.

'What are you up to, Tim?' Parlabane replied, climbing back under the covers. 'Have you ever heard of knocking? Or what about that dashed handy contraption on the bedside table? Allows room-to-room conversation. Amazing thing. Dreamt up by a Scottish chappie, you know.'

'I've been knocking – softly, I admit – for two minutes. Didn't want to hammer the door because it might waken someone. Not *you*, clearly. It never ceases to amaze me, Jack, that you can sleep through any amount of loud noise, but the minute sound of someone picking a lock brings you instantly to consciousness.'

'It's not that amazing. Somebody knocking my door represents an unnecessary interruption to my sleep. My mind knows I'd like them to fuck off, so takes no action. Attempted intrusion, on the other hand, sets off all the emergency alarms, which are on an extra-sensitive setting in my subconscious when I know *you*'re in the building.'

'Well, I'm probably not your first uninvited guest tonight,' he said, taking a seat by the bureau-cum-dressing table.

'How so?'

'Have you tried your mobile since dinner?'

'No.'

Vale tossed it across. It landed in Parlabane's lap, bouncing a little on the sheets stretched over his crossed legs. He pressed the On button a couple of times to no response.

'What gives?'

'SIM card's been removed. Mine too. And probably anybody else's who didn't bring their mobile with them to dinner.'

'That's probably just me and you, then. To these business types, it's like a security blanket. They want you to think they're expecting a call on a million-dollar deal any minute. Anyway, UML hi-jinks?'

'I expect that's what Mr Baxter was up to that he couldn't attend dinner. Preparation indeed. They'll mop up what they missed at some point between now and tomorrow's activities. Tricks in store, I'd wager. Thought you'd want a heads-up.'

'Cheers. But why didn't you phone?'

'I'd be surprised if Baxter or Campbell aren't listening in. They're here to play games with us, and as far as I can see they've got complete control of the environment. I noticed my room had been entered when I came back upstairs, and not by a turning-down service, either.'

'How did you know?'

'Trade secret, old boy. There are signs you can't help but read once you've learned to recognise them.'

'You must have loved it when Max talked about you pushing pens in the civil service. I was surprised to see you wading into that particular mire.'

'As was I that you weren't wallower-in-chief. I can only listen to so much ignorance when I'm on my own time. Men like Max are just immature, if you ask me: military fetishists in awe of real soldiers and seduced by the idea of simple solutions. Kill all the bad guys and hey presto: perfect world. That said, Kathy and Emily got my dander up too with their pseudo-totalitarian nonsense. I really have to say that conspiracy theorists assume far too much competence, unity and organisation on the part of their imaginary enemies. If our security forces were anything like as synergised as those pair believed them to be, I'd sleep a lot easier at night.'

'Unless some git broke into your bedroom.'

'Petulant and self-important persecution fantasies,' Vale continued, ignoring the jibe. 'Just a political version of blaming the umpire because your team keeps losing.'

'To be fair, the umpire wasn't as impartial as he should have been in those days.'

'Maybe not, but he wasn't killing anybody. That's the offensive part of the persecution fantasy. It didn't happen and it wouldn't happen. Otherwise what's the point of what I was up to all those years? I've never been a "My country, right or wrong" type. I did some pretty distasteful things, and I did them because I believed in the ways in which we were better than the enemy. Safe to say a pretty bloody big one was that we don't kill our own citizens.'

'Except we did, in Gibraltar. Well, I suppose the point was the targets no longer wanted to be British citizens, or subjects rather, and in that much they certainly got their wish.'

'Flavius was an aberration. One that pissed me off, in fact.

No sympathy for the IRA pond-life, but it sent out a very nasty and very irresponsible signal that everyone knew came from the top.'

'So, just between you and me, do you think it's possible that certain official elements might have been tempted to kill in seeking that simple solution you talked about? I mean, look what's coming out in the wash about Pat Finucane.'

'You have to understand, Jack, the army mentality over there, despite the official line, was that they were at war, battling a merciless and deceitful enemy, same as if they were overseas. That's the pity of it: they adopted attitudes and did things there that they'd never dream on the mainland. Nobody's ever opened fire on a bunch of white, middle-class British demonstrators, have they?'

'The wogs start at Belfast, then?'

'I'm not excusing it, just saying it generally isn't security services policy to assassinate people.'

'Yeah, but what about Alastair Dalgleish and his enforcer George Knight, for God's sake. They left a long trail of corpses and tried to add plenty more to the list, including yours truly.'

'Knight's lot were a private dirty-tricks department, not a government assassination unit. Granted they were a very well-connected bunch and they called in a lot of high-level, ask-no-questions favours, but it wasn't a state conspiracy, was it, Jack? Even you'd have to admit that.'

'I would. But given that there were people involved so close to government, and that there were security forces personnel – even just ex-personnel – prepared to do those things, it leaves open some scary possibilities.'

'Rogue elements, rogue individuals are always a possibility. But the point is that they *would be* rogue, and rogue is all they'd ever be. The infrastructure makes it very hard and very risky to find co-conspirators for something like that, never mind multi-level complicity and approval. I'm not saying it couldn't happen, though it would have to be on a very small scale, but to be honest, like time travel, if it was ever going to, it would have happened by now.'

'How so?'

'What I mean is, the kind of political climate that might have nurtured such a notion is long gone.'

'The Eighties, you mean? Thatcher?'

Vale chuckled.

'Good God, no. That's what was most farcical about tonight's discussion. They all thought the Eighties was some kind of defining era in the polarisation of British politics, when it was really just the era in which they started paying attention. The late Sixties and Seventies was when Kathy and Emily would really have had something to be paranoid about. Never mind MI5 bugging Arthur Scargill – what about MI6 bugging Harold Wilson? Around the time of the three-day week, there was genuine fear in certain circles – and lip-licking anticipation in others – that we were going to have a military coup; that the army was going to have to move in because the government couldn't control unchecked subversion from the unions.'

'Really? I don't remember much about that.'

'Of course you don't, and neither do that lot we just had dinner with, because while all this was going on, you shower were riding Chopper bikes and watching *Mary, Mungo and Midge*. It's like we were talking about on the road up here: the politics of the Eighties felt extreme to you, and to the others, because you were at an age when *all* your feelings were extreme.'

'Aye, true enough. I'd admit age has had a mellowing effect even on me. The downside is that I can no longer blame everything on a bunch of homicidal right-wing nutters out to kill all the lefties and silence the dissidents.'

'God forbid you should have to work for a living, Jack.'

*   *   *

151

Red Bull had nothing on embarrassment. If clubbers wanted a little extra help to lever up those heavy eyelids, there was no need to hold their noses and swallow back a concoction that looked and tasted like some nocturnal mammal's piss. Instead, they should crack open some quality Australian Shiraz and let their tongues make twats of them: sustained wakefulness guaranteed.

UML would sure have their work cut out creating a sense of unity and togetherness in the morning, though at least they'd know how the red team and the blue team should really line up. What a mess. Emily knew she wouldn't be the only one feeling it (or at least hoped she wasn't the only one feeling it), but given her and Kathy's PR role, it was all the more embarrassing to have been such major combatants. Ironically, it had been the success of the proceedings up until that point that had caused everyone to let their guards down and be less circumspect than was normal or wise at a table of comparative strangers. In her case, this was far less forgivable, but in mitigation, with everyone getting along so well and displaying such open enthusiasm, it had made her lose focus of her already indistinct role. Yes, she and Kathy were there because they had responsibility for UML's PR, but they were also there as guests and to take in the whole experience from a client's point of view. If there had been no such blurring, she'd have been there as a professional: watched what she drank, watched closer what she said, bitten her lip when she heard something she didn't like and deftly redirected discussions into more comfortable territory.

Instead she had brought too much of her real self to the table – they all had – and the results had been horrible. She winced when she recalled her 'you don't see a Tory for ages' remark, especially in the light of her having claimed Thatcher fostered division. How much more 'them and us' could she have made it? Liz had looked more insulted and alienated by that line than the 'fascist state' stuff, and she'd been right when she pointed out how intolerant it was. But if she felt regret for her downright rudeness – even in the face of a provocative blowhard like Max – then what Vale had said just made her feel like an idiot. He sounded like a man who knew what he was talking about and a lot more besides, his position given further weight by his measured words and lack of any apparent agenda. He made her accusations sound like what they really were: self-important histrionics and ignorant, self-pitying conjecture.

Vale hadn't elaborated on what his former civil service job had entailed and he therefore had no verifiable authority about what he said. He could, like Max suggested, have been the lowliest pen-pusher in the dullest department, with access to no more and no different sources of information than the rest of them on the subject at hand. But she still knew he was right. He'd made her feel like a rebellious but stupid teenager, which stung all the more because it pointed to a hard lesson still not fully learnt.

God, all that invective flying around, all those unfounded assertions and accusations, moral outrage a quick-fix substitute for knowledge. Old habits that had never died. Despite everything that had passed, there were clearly still vast seams of anger unmined, and not too far below the surface, either.

Though it was no consolation, she hadn't been the worst, and not even the worst on the left. That distinction went to Kathy, who had weighed in with unrestrained and unwary enthusiasm, loyally tying her colours to Emily's mast in the perhaps guilty knowledge that her partner had been the one more actively involved way back when. That made her feel bad too, because Kathy didn't know all she ought to about Emily's political past. It wasn't a time she liked to dwell upon, but she knew it would be hard keeping it out of her stubbornly wakeful head after the time-tunnel they'd all been peering through tonight.

And flash! That was when it hit her: the answer to the question she'd thought might keep her awake before the dinner-party debacle unfolded.

Mirror, mirror on the wall: who's the leftiest of them all?

Motivational Oratory (ii)

'You've got what it takes, otherwise you wouldn't be here.'

Shiach walked back and forth across the floor, the men standing to attention in two rows, heads high, eagerly awaiting what he had to say. It was late, but they wouldn't sleep tonight anyway, he knew, much as they might need it before such an occasion. It would be worse than the night before Christmas when they were kids. In fact, for most of them it was maybe more like the young player before his big debut: nervous anticipation keeping him awake, all the time aware that the lack of shut-eye wasn't going to help his sharpness when the time finally came to step on to the pitch. And, naturally, the more you worried about things like that, the harder it was to relax and get even close to nodding off.

They knew you didn't get two chances at something like this. Only Marko and Bruce were the genuine article, as well as himself, of course; and not forgetting Fotheringham, though his professionalism was less martially manifest. The rest were what Fotheringham had disparaged as 'trialists and tourists': eager for the chance to practice the abilities and aptitudes some knew – and some merely thought they knew – they had.

Selby's people had never flushed out those closest and most loyal to him, contenting themselves with merely cutting off the head, but it hadn't killed the body. All these years on, he still had some valuable and eager contacts, allowing him to recruit the personnel he needed to relaunch his enterprise. Right now, he'd concede that collectively they

155

didn't make the most impressive bunch, but nor would he have expected them to be. It wasn't the men who began this operation who should be judged as a unit, but the ones who ended it.

You've got what it takes, otherwise you wouldn't be here. That was a joke, in as much as it didn't refer to their mettle but the non-returnable bonds they had lodged in order to prove how much they wanted this chance. Savings had been cashed, homes remortgaged, prized possessions sold off to get on board this once-in-a-lifetime opportunity. Some of them would have what it took, some would manage pass-marks and no more, and others would inevitably fail. The first test would be when they saw what they were being armed with. The looks in their eyes then would tell him plenty about who really had the stomach for this and who just wanted to play at soldiers.

At thirty grand, it was an expensive game, but an under-taking such as this needed substantial seed money. The first Ministry of Vigilance had been built on no more than patri-otism and duty, and look how that had ended. This time, as he had explained to Fotheringham, like any other concern of worth these days, it would be a privatised, profit-making venture. Fotheringham had seemed a little petulant about this at first, muttering about not having broken him out of jail so that he could strike out on his own, but Shiach assured him that his bidding would still be done. Government contracts would be tendered, of course, but having rotted in jail for over a decade, protecting said government by keeping his mouth shut, it was time to look after number one. The real money was in the corporate world: that was who really ran countries these days, and they required just the same vigilance with regard to threatening and seditious individuals as any government did. Besides, Fotheringham had a bloody cheek playing the ingratitude card considering the time it had taken the bastard to come to the rescue.

156

'I was just too small a fish,' he'd said by way of apology. 'I had to bide my time, same as you. Play my hand too early and we'd both have been fucked. And we both know Selby was keeping an eye on you. If I'd engineered a stunt like your supposed suicide while he was alive, he wouldn't have bought it unless he actually saw a corpse. Williams was less fussy: he just needed to know it was done.'

Shiach had to hand it to Fotheringham: he didn't just owe him his freedom, he probably owed him his life too. As soon as Selby was gone, Fotheringham guessed Williams would prefer to have Shiach simply wiped out than the worry of him still rattling around the prison system. It had been therefore typical of the Architect's talents to place himself in Williams's path and get himself nominated for the job. He'd always been a genius at being what people wanted him to be, and understood that people trusted you more if they thought they had come to you, that your actions were their idea.

It was no surprise that Fotheringham had risen like he had; more so that he'd held on to his principles in doing so. That said, he did confess he had thought for a while that Shiach was something best left in the past.

'It all looked like it was working out,' Fotheringham said. 'The Cold War ended, and we'd won it. Thatcher was gone, but the important thing was there was no way back for the hard left. The advent of New Labour confirmed that. Some of it still hurt, though. The Roland Voss debacle, for instance. Hateful, deceitful, nasty little man, deserved exactly what Dalgleish and Co did to him, but some friends of mine went down with that ship.'

'George Knight, I heard. Can't you get him out too?'

'I wish I could, but he's a prisoner who *does* officially exist. I have promised him a consolation, though.'

But it wasn't petty score-settling that had made Fotheringham realise the MoV's time had come again, for

157

its purpose had never been anything personal, nor even truly political. It had always been about protecting this country from threats that its own laws – and political squeamishness – left it vulnerable to, and since September 2001 that vulnerability had taken on a whole new scale.

'What I resent most about them,' Fotheringham told him, 'is that they can exploit the freedoms and processes we stand for, while despising and condemning us for holding them. They're using the liberties our country allows them in order to plan attacks on us, and what can we do? Snoop, intercept, maybe make a few arrests, after which they regroup and try again. Like the IRA said, we have to be lucky every time: they only have to be lucky once, and slapped wrists aren't going to deter them from rolling the dice again.'

Looking at the recruits assembled before him, it didn't look like the MoV were ready to take on Al Qaeda quite yet, but you had to start somewhere. In their case, you had to start by clearing obstacles from the immediate path, and that was what this initial exercise was about. Innocent people would have to die, but the way Shiach saw it, the state owed him a few.

Fotheringham had been sceptical about quite what some of the recruits could bring to the table, other than thirty thousand a head, but Shiach's answer was simple. The last time, they had made the mistake of recruiting guys out of an ideological motivation, and things had fallen apart because they weren't up to practising what they preached. This time, he had gone for men who wanted to kill first and foremost, and would be happy to let other people worry about the reason. Again, some of them would fail to walk the walk like they'd talked the talk, but they would be few and they were expendable.

They were hungry for action, already electrified by anticipation. The rush of a lifetime? In retrospect, no doubt, but in the moment it would be no surprise if they felt nothing.

That's how it tended to be in the extremes of existence. Processes took over that were older than the civilised soul, that pre-dated the way the mind made sense of things. Serial killers, it was said, felt nothing at the time, but got their juice in the anticipation and the remembering thereafter. Crash survivors often had no recollection of what they'd gone through, not even of the fear.

'We're about to leave for our destination,' he told the assembly, his voice reverberating around the girders above. 'This is your last chance to walk out if you have any doubts about your wishes or abilities to go through with this. After we leave here, however, there will be no desertion. We will kill you, that's a promise, because once this begins, if we cannot trust you, we cannot let you live. If you leave now, no questions will be asked, no recrimination will follow, though we will expect your discretion, and you do not wish to imagine the lengths to which we will go if that discretion is not observed. So I say again, this is your last chance to leave.'

He stopped and looked at the floor, hands behind his back, in a gesture intended to convey to anyone bailing out that they would not have to face him should they wish to do so. No-one moved.

He waited a few moments in silence, giving everyone a lingering opportunity to confront their own doubts and allowing any ditherers to do themselves a favour. Still the company remained strong.

'Everything in your lives so far has just been a warm-up,' he told them. 'Tomorrow is when you will really become yourselves. Tomorrow is when you'll be getting your money's worth in what is inarguably the ultimate experience of its kind. Any divisions among you will be forgotten. The people you were outside, already half erased, will be forgotten by yourselves, not just each other. Presumptions, prejudices and conceits will be discarded like worthless

159

wrapping paper as you find out what each of you is truly made of. Weakness will be exposed, in arm, in head and in heart, and it will bring failure, humiliation and ostracism upon itself. Not everyone is going to go home happy with what he's learned about himself. But a team will be built, each member as aware as he is reliant upon what the others are worth.

'It will be a team united by that most ancient human commonality of purpose, older than war, blade and even flame: the hunt. Since men first combined their efforts to bring down some less savage beast, there has been no stronger bond than between those who united in the kill. For they knew that together they were lords over their foe, kings of men. And blood would ever anoint them.'

Saturday, October 26, 2002

Torture

He could see nothing, whether his eyes were open or not. His clothes felt like they were swallowing him: pressing, pulling, dragging, some enveloping parasite determined to squeeze the fight from his limbs until he drowned there in the darkness. He had no idea how long he'd held his breath, how much further there was to go or whether the figures overlapped in favour of survival. Only the thought of a mammoth corporate-killing lawsuit assured him that it felt a lot scarier than it actually was.

Okay. Parlabane really had to chalk one up to Baxter: *this* was what you called a trust exercise.

There had been a drysuit and a pair of heavy-duty walking boots (both his size, in accordance with details supplied on his RSVP) lying on his bed when he returned from breakfast. The former had been the most worrying sight of the weekend so far. There were two portents that truly depressed Parlabane in this world, and one was anything that suggested deep water – unheated, unchlorinated and unattached to a changing suite and a lounge bar – would be featuring on the day's agenda. (The other was Christian fish logos on cars parked outside any house where he was about to have dinner.) Heights were no problem, as many of the more noteworthy episodes in his career would testify. Neither exertion nor exposure could summon any dread, not even when combined with the prospect of it being in the company of Thatcherite recidivists and unreconstructed Trots. But water, *outdoors*, why? There was just no need at this point in mankind's evolution to be in it or on it. We had

163

invented other, superior ways of traversing the stuff that involved far less risk of coming into direct contact with it. It was dangerous. It denoted the parts of the planet that we were unable to inhabit, a very big heads-up being the fact that we couldn't fucking breathe in there. But most of all he hated it because, this being Scotland, it was always freezing and he was an unrepentant Big Jessie.

They had all been shepherded aboard the minibus with no indication of their destination or intended activities, beyond the odd teasing remark from the UML pair. This had made for a quiet journey, as the prevailing climate among the rest was simmering suspicion with intermittent outbreaks of mutual embarrassment. Parlabane started whistling *We Are Family* at one point, which inexplicably failed to usher in a new mood of laughter, forgiveness and reconciliation.

There was a light drizzle falling as they climbed on to the minibus, turning to misty smir by the time they got off. The cold and damp had steamed up the windows with the breath of twelve drysuited, befleeced and lightly sweating adults, which had made it difficult to follow where the road was taking them. They found themselves at the foot of a ridge, the river at their backs and the hotel absent from the visible horizon as Campbell drove off. There were a few anxious pairs of eyes watching the departure of their transport, no doubt roughly calculating the time of their trip against approximate speed and its ramifications for what lay between this valley and their next hot meal. With no idea how they might have looped and doubled back, Parlabane knew it was a pointless exercise. He guessed they could as easily be ten miles out from base or less than two. Still worrying about the implications of the drysuit, he had actually been grateful to see the minibus leave, as it would spare him the concentrated 'wet dog' assault on his nostrils during the return trip that would have been the result of a

164

dozen damp fleeces in a confined and unventilated space.

Baxter led them up the side of the ridge, rising in a diagonal that made the climb tolerably gentle for those who had failed to resist the black pudding and potato scone options on the breakfast menu. At the top, instead of a plateau as expected, there was a long U-shaped trench, running like a gigantic rain gutter along the ridge. It began shallow-sided but steep, tight and narrow about a quarter of a mile west, and broadened, widened and deepened towards a small corrie-loch a further couple of hundred yards east. From above, the body of water would have resembled a giant teardrop, much like the one Parlabane felt like shedding when they began making their way down and Baxter pointed out what lay in store ahead. The tail of the 'tear' had a break in it shortly before it widened dramatically to fill the horseshoe corrie at the east end of the ridge. The land rose at the break just enough to lie above the water-level, which made it difficult to imagine what geological quirk could have accounted for it. Gravity argued none: water ran downhill, and yet there was water either side of a dry platform in the middle of a slope. There was only one possible explanation, and Parlabane's scrotum was already going into pickled-walnut mode in anticipation of it.

'A lot of the area around here used to belong to the army,' Baxter explained. 'Some of it still does. It's okay, I don't think it's one of the spots they used to blow the shit out of, so you shouldn't need to worry about stumbling on any unused artillery shells. They used it for training exercises because of the variety of the terrain, I'm told. Forests, moorland, swamps, hills, cliffs and, as you can see here, water. Now, if any of you are wondering about that implausibly convenient stretch of ground across the tail of the corrie loch, it may clarify things to inform you that beneath the sparse covering of weeds and scattered gravel are several tons of concrete. And the reason the water doesn't simply flow

165

around this partial dam is that just beneath the surface are four tunnels. This, I should emphasise, is not evidence of worryingly daft design and engineering on the part of army bridge-builders, because the purpose of the construction was not to get the squaddies *over* the drink . . .'

Baxter left it at that for the moment, a chorus of groans confirming that no further clarification was required.

'Tunneltastic,' Rory remarked with dark relish, proving that the chorus was not unanimous and that he for one was lapping up their discomfiture. Parlabane might normally have respected such gleeful misanthropy, but at that moment he would have happily slapped on a 'Hypocrite' baseball cap above his 'Big Jessie All-Star XI' baseball jersey while energetically lamping Rory with a 'Shut Up You Smug Tory Twat' baseball bat.

'But don't worry,' Baxter resumed, unslinging his back-pack and laying it on the ground. 'I'm not going to shove you all down there on your lonesome. I understand from my colleague Francis that last night's post-prandial delib-erations were, shall we say, full and frank. Well, now's the perfect time to kiss and make up. Kind of a hands-across-the-water initiative, you could say.'

Baxter produced a heavy coil of climbing cord from his backpack and dropped it to the ground. It was very fine stuff, identified by Parlabane's informed (and covetous) eye as 5.5mm Spectra Cord, claimed by its manufacturer to be ten times stronger than steel. Its minuscule diameter meant Baxter had been able to fit a good fifteen, maybe twenty yards worth into his backpack. Parlabane couldn't work out how it was likely to factor into the imminent sub-aquatic low-jinks, but was pretty confident he wasn't going to like it.

'The good news is that I'll be going first, as somebody has to thread the needle. Then you'll be coming through one at a time, attached to the rope, so that the person ahead can speed your progress by giving you a tow. The bad news is the running order, which will be as follows: Tim, then Grieg, then Kathy, Max, Emily, Rory, Jack, Toby and finally Joanna.'

Each of them cast a glance at the person mentioned before their own. Bracketed by the peace-making Vale and the neutral or abstaining Joanna, the rest were being forced to rely upon last night's foes. Cute.

Grieg put a hand up, the eejit evidently regressing to schoolboyhood perhaps in response to the class-trip vibe generated by steamy-windowed transport and the forced company of people you couldn't stand.

'I can't do this. I get really claustrophobic. I'm sorry.'

Baxter just smiled and bent down to his backpack again, from which he pulled a sheaf of photocopied papers. He flicked through them until he found the one he was looking for, holding it out to Grieg.

'Your acceptance form. Clothing and shoe sizes, special dietary requirements (unticked), medical information. According to this, you are not pregnant, not on prescribed medication and do *not* suffer from claustrophobia. Get in line.'

There was a burst of cruelly delighted laughter at this from Rory. Anyone else who might otherwise have enjoyed Grieg's humiliation had their pleasure curtailed by the knowledge that the same emergency exit had just been slammed in all their faces.

Grieg shrugged, muttering something about 'worth a try'. Rory slapped him on the back, still laughing.

'Always read the small print,' he told him. 'Come on then, let's do this,' he added, booming to the whole assembly with deliberately overplayed enthusiasm as he began removing his fleece.

'Eh, not so fast, Rory,' Baxter cautioned. 'Who said anything about getting undressed?'

'But we've got suits on,' Rory protested, confused.

'The suits are to stop you getting hypothermia from wandering around in wet clothes.'

'And what's the point of that?'

'Two points. One, a degree of realism: you wouldn't be leaving your clothes behind if you really had to negotiate a hazard like this. And two, it'll flush out anyone here who ignored the instruction at breakfast to leave your mobile phones behind.'

'Bollocks,' Rory grunted. He zipped his fleece back up and removed a small metallic rectangle from an inside pocket, handing it to the waiting Baxter.

'There's next to no signal out here,' Baxter reiterated. He had previously mentioned it when he instructed them not to bring their mobiles, at which juncture it became apparent the others hadn't yet discovered that their phones had been disabled. 'Ironically, due to the hills, just about the only place you can get a signal round here is in the vicinity of the hotel, where there's landlines anyway.'

He popped the phone into his trouser pocket and, grinning at Rory, proceeded to strip down to his drysuit, placing his clothes and boots next to his backpack near the edge of the bridge.

'I'm not here to play – I'm just the ref,' he explained, taking hold of the rope and slipping carefully into the water. It came up to just below his chest. He tossed one end of the rope to Vale, took a breath then disappeared below the surface, gently submerging himself rather than diving. Parlabane began counting the seconds.

'Let's chuck the bastard's clothes in while he's under,' Grieg suggested.

'Not with my moby in his pocket,' Rory replied.

Baxter emerged at the other end, breaking the surface as unhurriedly as he'd disappeared. It may have been in order to assure them that the journey didn't require haste or flailing desperation, but his pace was equally likely to be down to cautious footing, minus the protection of his boots.

Parlabane had lost count due to the distraction of Grieg's suggestion. The figure wouldn't have mattered anyway. It was going to feel like forever, no matter what.

Vale got the ball rolling after carefully placing his digital camera on the far side of the bridge, jumping in with a loud splash and markedly less concern for what was underfoot. Baxter ordered Grieg to get in too, to help pay out the rope and to pull it back when his own turn came. He waded in reluctantly from the side, hissing breathy curses at the temperature of what flooded his boots.

Spontaneous hugging, high-fiving and vocal whooping were, in Parlabane's book, just not acceptable between sober adults enjoying the privilege of having been born east of the Atlantic. It was a foul, phoney and nauseating thing to behold, deserving of all the scorn and cynicism one felt compelled to pour upon it. Parlabane, however, felt little such compulsion even as he watched all of the above unfold, knowing he would not be in a position to pass judgement until he was on the other side of that tunnel. He watched Vale bashfully tolerate Grieg's grateful embrace and Kathy grasp the singularly unhuggable Grieg in much the same way. Max burst forth from the water yelling in relief and self-salutation, laughing as he offered a two-handed shake in thanks to Kathy, then sharing a double high-five with Emily after she enjoyed the benefits of his speedy and enthusiastic tugging. Emily in turn gigglingly endured a sustained bear-hug from the bellowingly exhilarated Rory.

That was when the scorn and cynicism started to creep back, and indeed became the thing that sustained him during those endless seconds in the miniature abyss. It was cold, dark, lonely and scary, as he travelled a distance that was impossible to measure at a pace that was impossible to gauge. The weight of his clothes made it feel like he was swimming through treacle, the exertion a further strain on his bursting lungs, and every pull on that rope was a divine act of succour for which he greatly owed its source. But in spite of it all, he knew there was still no fucking way he was going to hug Rory Glen.

'Wooh! Way to go, Jack, welcome to the other side,' Rory said, one hand helping Parlabane to his feet, his other arm poised to initiate an embrace.

'Aye, very good, whatever,' Parlabane replied, withdrawing his right hand to wipe his hair from his eyes, at the same time raising his left to deflect any unsolicited manly affection. Rory looked a little put out at this show of bad grace, and Parlabane surprised himself by feeling bad about this. 'Nae offence, big yin,' he added, by way of reparation. 'It's just that the last time I came out a tunnel like that, a nurse skelped my arse and it all kind of went downhill from there.'

Parlabane called the go-ahead to Toby and began pulling when he felt resistance on the rope. Thinking of the dead weight of even just his own clothes, he felt that bit more churlish about his failure to show Rory more gratitude. Rory's powerful shoulders must have shaved a good few seconds off his time submerged, a favour he wasn't sure he'd be able to pass on to Toby. He was giving it his utmost, and since recovering from what happened in prison, he was in arguably the best shape of his life. Unfortunately for Toby, that best shape was still short, light and sinewy. Mother nature and father heredity had bestowed upon Parlabane a low centre of gravity and a blessed middle ear. Stealth, agility, balance and aim came with unearned ease. To that, he had added enough muscle to haul himself around vertically, with or without the aid of ropes and pulleys, but not enough to change the fact that Toby had drawn the short straw. Doubly so, given that if he did make it through alive he'd then have the task of assisting the heaviest member of the party. After a few full-blooded heaves, Parlabane had only managed to haul through a paltry length of rope, and

170

was beginning to wonder whether the guy had forgotten that he was allowed to propel *himself* to some degree. This prompted an urgent consideration that, given a bump on the head going under, this could actually be the case.

'Rory, gimme a hand here,' Parlabane asked. 'I think something's wrong.' Baxter stepped forward to offer a third pair of arms as a cold note of concern rippled around the pool. The rope progressed at speed until all the resistance was suddenly lost, dumping the three of them in the soup like tumbling dominoes. They all got to their feet as quickly as they could, Parlabane the nearest and first to approach the bridge. As he did, a figure erupted from the water, spitting a mouthful accurately into his face, standing upright, opening its arms and singing: 'Ta-raa!'

Wiping the water from his eyes, he saw, amidst gales of laughter, that it was Joanna, which while being itself a relief, still begged a pertinent question. Rory gave it voice.

'Where the hell is Toby?'

A number of necks strained to look over the bridge, but he was not to be seen on the other side.

'There's more than one tunnel down there,' Toby announced, revealing himself to be standing behind the group, watching the fun unfold.

'As the actress said to the bishop,' Rory added, clearly feeling less self-conscious about yesterday's little moment of chastisement.

There ensued more whooping, back-slapping and general subsumation of all into one single unified consciousness. Parlabane was starting to wish he'd drowned.

What's Under Your Feet

The kitchen had an air of unaccustomed, almost unnerving quiet despite all hands being present and busy. Dinner preparations were under way early, given a welcome head-start because lunch had been taken care of immediately after breakfast, in the form of a hamper to be eaten on the move. It didn't look much of a day for al fresco dining, but having humped themselves around the hills for a few hours, the UML guests would no doubt find that hunger, as well as making the best sauce, could also make a restaurant of a rainy outcrop.

There was an undoubted manifestation of calm after the storm, following the hot-blooded antics of the night before. Part of it was inevitably the process of simply getting on with the UML weekend, now that it was in flow, dissipating the tension built up by so long waiting and worrying about it. In happy accordance with the swan's feet principle, from the guests' point of view, the hotel appeared to be running itself with all grace and efficiency. What it had taken to achieve that was futile to dwell upon.

Right enough, it wasn't only the hotel staff's frantic activities that were concealed beneath the surface. According to Julia the housekeeper, she'd had to grant one of the UML blokes access to another guest's bedroom before breakfast while the occupant was upstairs in the fitness room. Under orders to comply, Julia had nonetheless insisted on witnessing what he got up to, which turned out to be tampering with a mobile phone. Silly games. It was like *Big Brother* without the beachwear.

Naturally, the biggest factor in the kitchen's newfound cordiality was Mathieson, who had barely said a word the whole morning and had failed to even make eye-contact with Alison or Ger. Apart from a few grunted one-word answers, the only thing she'd heard him say (or more accurately overheard him say when he didn't know anyone else was nearby) was when he asked Charlotte whether the journalist had mentioned anything about the food last night. Charlotte replied that she didn't even know which one the journalist was, prompting the slightly desperate enquiry as to whether *any* of them had commented on the quality of the meal. Charlotte gave a diplomatic, but for that, transparently platitudinous answer: 'They all said it was nice.'

Alison loved that. Charlotte didn't have the devilment to be deliberately offending him, but she couldn't have said anything less satisfying to his hungry ego.

Mathieson was noticeably less full of himself even before this inadvertent put-down, though this took the form of quietly seething as opposed to any genuine humility or penitence. Ger had fairly clipped his wings, and it wasn't like him to handle anything with good grace. Still, the tangible benefit was that he kept his mouth shut and Alison was able to enjoy some music on Mathieson's now de-greased CD player while she worked, without the usual accompaniment of unsolicited comment and monomaniac whining.

It wasn't her music, but it was one of Ger's albums that she had developed a liking for, and that she already knew would make her think of this place whenever she heard it in the future. This music had occasioned one of the first things Ger said to her that could be construed as in any way solicitous, in as much as it was evidence that he must have been paying her attention even when he didn't appear to be listening.

'There's one for you,' he'd muttered, indicating the CD player as a bassline picked its way ominously across the intro.

'How so?' she asked warily, listening to the lyrics. It was, as Mathieson was to frequently and scornfully point out, about an electric heater. She was waiting for the punchline.

'This is the first time you've been away from home, isn't it?' he asked. 'Away from Inversneck and the family hearth.'

'Yeah.'

'I'm no' sayin' you're a wee lassie or anythin', just . . . Bet it feels a bit of a leap. A bit scary, a bit exciting, a bit sad.'

'All of the above,' she admitted. 'But you've got to do it sometime.'

'That's what the song's about. The first thing you buy for your newly independent digs, maybe a heater or a kettle or whatever. It represents that big leap, from which there's no goin' back, into a wider, deeper, scarier, *older* world.'

Alison listened.

I won't melt your precious wings, so come on and plug me in.

She nodded. It was Ger's way of saying he understood she might be feeling a little vulnerable. He didn't strike her as the type to be eagerly on the lookout for damsels in distress, but it let her know she had a friend.

She hadn't bought a heater (lack of ventilation in her room other than a postage-stamp-sized, grimy and cracked window made this unnecessary), or indeed a kettle, but she had been thinking a lot about the significance of this time. So long spent dreaming of spreading those precious wings, it was still daunting to do so, even when her maiden flight had only taken her to McKinley Hall. It wasn't much, but for the time being it was her new world, and another song on the same CD echoed the need she felt to find out whatever she could about this place she had, for the time being, thrown in her lot with.

Look over there you used to say
The shape of the land beneath the street
Ridges and valleys and underground streams
You have to know what's under your feet

She had grown up in a Seventies-built estate, watching the town expand slowly outwards in clumps of new housing until there was little left of it that felt old, that spoke of stories and secrets, other than the harsh, open expanse of bleakness and ankle-traps that was Culloden Moor. She'd lived in a low-rise modern house, gone to low-rise modern schools, hung out in a low-rise modern shopping mall and fended off spotty chancers (until the less than crazee hour of one in the morning, thanks to a determined preponderance of Wee Frees on the Licensing Board) in low-rise modern nightclubs. None of these places had tales to tell that were much older than the ones you could read wrapped around your chips. McKinley Hall, in that respect, was a compendium, an anthology – and not one ever likely to appear on the children's bedtime story shelf.

She'd ironically found out more about the place during her brief trips home to Sneck – via the library and the net – than could be reliably discovered in situ. Sir Lachlan, though garrulous when caught at the right moment, preferred to expand upon his family's ties to the place and upon its physical attributes than tread anywhere near the episodes that history's prurient tastes would more likely focus upon. As witnessed by his pep talk, even the word 'history' was uncomfortable for Sir Lachlan, due to its unavoidable inherent allusion to all that had happened here. Lady Jane, having married into the family, did not appear quite so burdened by it, but was sufficiently defensive of what she was now a guiding part of that her staff knew there was a word they must never utter if either of the couple was even potentially in earshot.

175

The word was (whisper it): cursed.

There was no legend of *a* curse, of vengeful necromancers nor of any primary episode of mythical mumbo-jumbo. The locals along in Auchterbuie didn't speak of 'the curse of McKinley Hall', and nor did the writings that made mention of the place. But the word cursed was used, and it meant cursed as in plagued, as in despised, as in wicked, as in doomed. And allowing that sober, rational, objective analysis was forgiving of the odd coincidence, it was fair to say that the evidence bore this out.

The McKinleys themselves could not complain of having been personally afflicted or of this misfortune having been suddenly precipitated upon them. Death was here first. They should have scoped out the neighbours before moving in. The land – this otherwise hospitable and accommodating cradle among the hills, both served and confined by the coils of a river – had been known both as Cairncalb and Cruaidh-calb since long before anyone built upon it, names that still appeared on maps of the area the estate lands covered. Cairn denoted a place of burial, not exactly a rarity on any map or a cue to play string crescendos in your head. The 'cruaidh' part, Alison learned, had been assumed to mean rocky or harsh; 'calb' a gushing of water. However, the etymologies of both words were coincidentally ambiguous; or *un*coincidentally ambiguous, as far as she was concerned. 'Cruaidh', according to some, had come to mean harsh, but quite liter-ally meant 'blood raw'; while water was not exclusive in being the gushing liquid 'calb' had always referred to.

Legend, myth, oral history, whatever you wanted to call it, was not particularly exercised by the fact that people had been buried on the site. It just wasn't too convinced that they were dead when they got there. Some traditions claimed it a place of execution, others of pre-Christian human sacrifice. Still others spoke of massacre, a word that was worryingly non-unique in the accounts of the place's history (though admittedly in the self-reflexive process of such things, it would have been tempting to the more hysterical of compilers to allow their speculations to become coloured by subsequent events). What was documented for definite was that there had been two incidences of mass murder on the site – if not the very building – where Alison now resided. The first had been in 1467, back when the first great hall of the McKinleys had stood for less than half a century. Accounts predictably varied as to motive and blame, depending on which clan history's particular spin you were reading. Clans were constantly at each other's throats in those days, few of them distinguishing themselves with displays of tolerance or magnanimity. Often they settled their differences by arranged engagement on some windblown moor, Pyrrhic victors enjoying bragging rights but little more in reward for suffering a lesser cull. Occasionally, however, they went for the risky but more decisive pre-emptive strike to the heart, which at the earlier McKinley keep took the form of stealing in at night and slaughtering whole families in their beds before burning the place down.

Understandably, history had been bequeathed little evidence of how the McKinley defences were so catastrophically breached. Some form of betrayal was generally accepted to have been crucial, but naturally nobody had ever been inclined to offer personal corroboration of the theory.

By chance, the laird and his youngest son survived, due to having been delayed overnight on a hunting expedition. Nonetheless, it was more than two centuries before their descendants' fortunes waxed strong enough to fully rebuild their seat, a construction that formed the basis of what still stood today.

By the early Eighteenth Century, the McKinleys were back to playing kings of the castle, but the true laird of Cruaidhcalb was still picking up his fealty. Douglas McKinley, the main man in those days, by all accounts lacked the benefit of modern insight into man-management, to put it mildly. Paranoia and a ruthlessly self-defensive streak were both understandably bred into his lineage, but Douglas's tyrannical brutality and abject lack of compassion put him in a very extreme percentile. Local judiciary power in such hands contributed largely to the horrific incidence of capital punishment at the time, and the ever more trivial offences for which it was meted out. His gallows never empty, he generated sufficient ill-will among his subservients that eventually some of them tried to kill him. It was a desperate and amateurish plot, ironically reliant upon repeating history in recruiting the complicity of the laird's own guards, who were not assumed to be particularly loyal to their increasingly psychotic master. However, history only repeats itself when people fail to learn from it, and that could not be said of the McKinleys. Whether through fear or finance, Douglas had made sure those entrusted with his protection knew what side their bread was buttered. The plot was foiled, its perpetrators exposed, and Douglas's revenge was truly terrible, for it did not stop at the principals.

He hanged entire families, ruling complicity in the conspiracy by whatever merest connection would suit. Fathers, brothers, wives, children. One boy went to the gallows at eleven years.

Ah, the upper classes. How we look to them for enlightenment and example.

Douglas may have spared no effort (or lives) in the family's defence, but as steward of its fortunes he failed to appreciate that there was more to the job, and as such failed the McKinleys dreadfully. As well as damning the name in local regard, his neglect and lack of judgement oversaw a decline in the family's enterprises that his successors struggled in vain to arrest. The hall passed from the McKinleys' hands in 1823, and was not to return to their ownership until Sir Lachlan bought it more than a century and a half later.

It did not prove a happy investment – certainly not a long-term one – for many of its owners in the intervening time. The place changed hands repeatedly until the 1930s, when the next long shadow fell upon the place in the shape of Magnus Willcraft: aristocrat, composer, former opera-singer, occultist and one-time Aleister Crowley acolyte.

Willcraft made no secret that he had sought the place because of its past, though it was questionable whether he considered this more conducive to his dark dabblings or to the enhancement of his personal notoriety. To either end, he had entertained a genuine fascination with the more ancient purposes of the site, and brought in archaeological assistance, excavating both in the grounds and in the foundations. He built down there too, bringing in help from the continent rather than entrust the work – or more pertinently, knowledge of it – to the locals. Nobody in current employ had any idea where these chambers were accessed, far less the inclination to look, given that they were known to have been the venue for Willcraft's occult rites. What his excavations uncovered, he chose not to share, though those scornful of Willcraft's cultivated self-image suggested this meant the answer was nothing. Others were less cynical. Willcraft did revel in his infamy, but was also very private about his personal affairs, particularly what he referred to as his religion. You don't buy a house in the middle of nowhere if you really want to attract attention to yourself, and Willcraft's fiercely guarded privacy provoked much rumour and speculation among the locals.

National curiosity about McKinley Hall took off in the late Sixties due to betrayed loyalties of another kind when, following Willcraft's death, a former lover-cum-disciple sold her tales of subterranean ritual and orgy to a Sunday tabloid. This inevitably opened the rest of the place's squalid past to ghoulish scrutiny, leading to its subsequent purchase in the early Seventies by the rock band Stormcrow, who recorded an album there but didn't survive to see its release, all four of them dying in a tour-bus crash in 1975. This was further proof of the Hall's doomed luck, according to Ger, because it would have been better fortune had their bus crashed *before* they recorded the album. 'Total pish,' he said. 'Pseudo-Satanic claptrap that wouldnae frighten your granny. It was wankers like that who forced the Sex Pistols into being.'

Alison hadn't knowingly heard any of Stormcrow's music, but knew enough to concur with Ger's judgement that they were wankers, as was Willcraft before them. What was it that drew them? Stormcrow, whatever their professed mysticism, were just a bunch of middle-class Oxbridge dropouts, but they must have believed there was something they could tap into here, other than marketing potential. Willcraft before them was not so different: another musician seeking a form of inspiration, tasteless as it was. Did they think there was some lingering spoor to catch scent of, some enduring entity that could guide them in unlocking the secrets of man's darkest inclinations?

She didn't believe there could be something inherently evil about a place. It was bricks and mortar, a point on a map. Evil things had happened here, but that didn't mean any force was compelling them to do so again. Something, however, compelled evil men (and mere wankers) to the scenes of evil deeds. Perhaps it was simply that which caused one horror to be piled upon another on these grounds though they were centuries apart.

Poor Sir Lachlan certainly had his work cut out when he got his hands on the place and stated his intention to rehabilitate more than just the building. Down in the local village of Auchterbuie, they referred to the restored enterprise as McKinley Revival. There was a heavily ironic tone to it, the sentiment not intended to be encouraging. They clearly didn't fancy Sir Lachlan's chances, given the family's track record with the place, and the story so far wasn't exactly encouraging. It was at least to his credit that despite seeking the tourist's coin, he was determined to blot out the very aspects that might be most likely to attract them. Never mind chasing humps and ripples around a conveniently enormous and opaque loch: this was real Scottish horror, something we did pretty well without having to make up monsters.

For all its 'wha's like us' keech, Scotland was actually a country that liked to think it had been spared extremes. While refilling wine glasses, Alison had overheard one of the guests say as much of the UK as a whole: that it had been spared extreme weather and extreme governments. But what, she had wanted to ask, about extreme drinking and extreme ill-health? What about extreme landscape? And what about the extremes of our past: extremes of brutality, of judicial cruelty and torture? What about the obsessions of Jamie the Saxt, the sadistic persecution and retribution in the name of religion? Who was to say there hadn't been other extremes of slaughter, disappeared from history by the convenience of lost ages, like the convenience of miracles and self-resurrecting sons of gods being in a time before reliable documentation.

Alison had heard her fellow Scots proudly disavow Britishness in distaste at its connotations of imperialism, conquest and any other national characteristic they'd like to attribute conveniently to the English, but it was a deluded cop-out. The Scots had brought as much brutality to the table as any of its union partners. There was a joke they told each other but didn't like to share with visitors: what is the definition of a Scottish homosexual? A bloke who's more interested in women than drinking and fighting.

Blood spattered the history of McKinley Hall, stained even the ancient names of the land. The place needed to be exorcised, and if it took the form of silly corporate head-games, then who could complain about that?

Mathieson had been going back and forth from the kitchen for a few minutes, returning each time with crockery that Alison recognised from one of the big display cabinets in the restaurant. She'd never seen it put to use in all the time she'd been here, even on the night there'd been a McKinley family gathering and a celebration menu for Sir Lachlan's birthday. She was grateful for his absences, brief as they were, as she kept catching his eye. Despite his muted conduct, he still seemed to be simmering as the day went on, and she got the feeling that he'd hit boiling point before it was over. She'd spotted him eyeing Ger intently too, but with more wariness than anger, now that the sous-chef had threatened to take himself off the leash.

The chef returned once again with another antique dish, placing it on a worktop with the rest, then seemed to be hanging around, doing not much of anything but stare at his two perceived dissidents.

'I'm away for a slash,' Ger announced, as men were inexplicably wont to do.

Mathieson watched him leave, then a few moments later, rather nervously broke his silence.

'Alison, c'mere a second.'

She glanced across. He wore a shaky smile, reminiscent of any number of trembling wee shavers standing before her as they mustered the bottle to ask for a dance.

'It's okay,' he said, though she wasn't convinced it was herself that needed assurance. She took a few steps across the floor, but kept a noticeable distance between them. 'I've been thinking about last night,' he continued. 'It wasn't pleasant, was it?'

'No.'

'It occurred to me I've never shown you anything. I've

182

left all that to Ger. It's hard when you're running the show, believe me. But we're ahead of the game today, so let me teach you something now. Stand there, just where you are.'

He picked up a stack of the display crockery, four wide serving plates, and placed it on her left palm. 'Have you got that?' he checked. 'Okay in one hand? Not too heavy?'

'It's fine. They're lighter than they look.'

'The weight is all in their value,' he said, placing another stack in her right hand. 'These have been in the McKinley family since the Eighteenth Century.'

'You're making me nervous,' she said truthfully, and not just because of what she was holding. There was a sleekit, underhand nastiness creeping across his face.

'They're utterly irreplaceable,' he went on. 'You, on the other hand, are not. So if you drop them, you'll be out of a job. Bear that in mind during the next few seconds.'

With a hateful smirk, Mathieson reached out with both hands and grabbed Alison's breasts. She began drawing her arms in as a reflex, but the weight of the plates, in her mind at least, prevented her from being able to fend him off. Instead she stepped backwards, but found her path blocked by the fridge. Mathieson looked her in the eye, his hands still mashing and fondling.

'See, the lesson is, if you want to get on, you need to know your own worth. And if that isn't much, then sometimes you just have to put up with things you don't like and keep your fucking mouth shut.'

'What the fuck do you think you're doing?' demanded a voice. They both looked around to see Ger in the doorway to the hall.

'Alison and I are just enjoying a wee lesson in kitchen hierarchy.'

'You'll be enjoying a wee lesson in bollock removal if you don't back off.'

'No, Gerard, you don't understand. I wanted you to see

183

this, to remind you as well what the score is round here. See, what you said last night got me thinking. The pair of you can go running to Sir Lachlan if you like, but apart from it being your word against mine, what's the chances of him firing his chef in the middle of *this* weekend?'

'Let's find out,' Ger replied.

It was worse than if she'd just let him away with it. The humiliation of even saying it to Sir Lachlan was almost as bad as the deed itself, to say nothing of standing in a small room with three men at the time. Mathieson must have been loving it. He kept glancing at her chest. She felt like she wanted to be wearing the world's thickest, baggiest jumper, not this flimsy little blouse.

Sir Lachlan was looking about as comfortable as Alison felt. She could see where it was going. The guy was marooned, his wife out of the picture and so many of his eggs in this basket. All those centuries of grief and one last chance to turn it around in the name of his ancestors. Was he going to throw it all away just because a minor member of staff got her tits felt?

Mathieson was playing it perfectly, too. He was calm, relaxed, even slightly apologetic, not denying anything happened but seeking to trivialise it instead, the perfect out for Sir Lachlan in the circumstances. Kitchens are different places, blah blah blah. Intense working environment, a lot of physical familiarity, misread signals, things can get out of hand, everybody needs to calm down, job to be done at the end of the day.

Sir Lachlan was nodding along rather impatiently with every word, his decision clearly made. Alison felt sick. She was wishing she'd just dropped the priceless crockery and nutted the bastard.

'We all have to put up with indignities sometimes, in order to get the job done,' Sir Lachlan agreed, looking at his desk,

184

not making eye-contact with anyone. 'There's few of us can afford to be so proud that we can't tolerate a degree of unpleasantness when our livelihoods are at stake. I know I can't.'

He looked up at last, eyeing Mathieson. 'That's why I've tolerated having you around this long, Peter. You're a turd. You insult my wife, you abuse my staff and you act like this is some career bus-stop where you're killing time waiting for your lift to turn up. Pride, as I've said, is a luxury, but self-respect is a right. It would cost Alison her self-respect to have to continue working under you, but not as much as it would cost mine if I kept you in my employ. Get out. Now. I want you out of the building in fifteen minutes.'

Ger balled both hands into fists as the chef stared at Sir Lachlan in incomprehension. 'You heard the man,' he said.

Mathieson left the room without a word, let alone a parting retort, rendered speechless by sheer disbelief.

'Thank you, sir,' Alison said quietly, frightened her voice would break.

'Not at all,' Sir Lachlan replied. 'My apologies for what you had to put up with. Just don't sue, please.'

'But what are we going to do?' she asked, feeling suddenly guilty about the consequences. 'We're short as it is.'

'I'm sure my new head chef and his assistant can manage dinner for twelve. And in keeping with what I just said, I'm not above pouring drinks and waiting on tables if that's what's needed to keep the show on the road.'

He stood up and bent down to a nearby cupboard, producing a bottle of single malt and three pewter quaichs.

'I don't know if a toast is appropriate under such circumstances, but I do reckon we're all going to need a drink,' he said.

There were no dissenters.

They sipped their malts and discussed the evening's menu, watching at the window as Mathieson stuffed a holdall and some plastic bags into the back of his Peugeot convertible.

'Good riddance to bad rubbish,' Sir Lachlan said.

'It was almost worth it for the look on his face when you fired him,' Alison said. 'Rendered catatonic.'

'Yeah, it wasn't like him not to get the last word,' Ger agreed.

Ger finished his whisky then did a double-take as Mathieson climbed into the car and closed the door.

'What?' Alison asked.

But he was gone, running from the room, and so was Mathieson, with a huffy squeal of tyres down the drive.

Ger returned a couple of minutes later.

'He did get the last word. He's fucked off with all the meat.'

Running Up That Hill

Emily had seldom been so grateful for the simple delights of a sandwich. This one, to give it its due, was not all that simple – pesto, roasted peppers, fontina, Parma ham and rocket between two wedges of focaccia – but it could have been Dairylea on two slices of white pan and been equally welcome. According to her watch, only three hours had passed since a very hearty breakfast, but between that and this hillside lunch there had been the trials of the tunnel and a long ensuing trudge in wet clothes.

The hamper had appeared like a desert mirage, suddenly in sight but seemingly so far out of reach that it felt as though they might never get there. The hideous yellow fleeces at least had the mercy of being comparatively quick-drying, but said comparison being only with denim, which in conjunction with their uniformly squelching footwear had made their progress like wading through an endless swamp. Unquestionably, after that the sandwich was a feast, but Emily would have traded a twelve-course tasting menu at a Michelin-starred eatery for dry boots and a change of socks.

Rory was not alone in querying the purpose of tackling the tunnel fully dressed. Baxter's point was true enough with regard to the 'reality' of negotiating such a hazard, but in reality there was no actual need to go through the bloody tunnel in the first place, so why drench everyone when there's miles of hillside trekking ahead? Their guide wasn't saying, but Emily suspected that this wasn't because he lacked an answer. There had been no oversights so far, nothing undertaken without a tangible pay-off later.

The purpose of tackling the tunnel in itself only became clear from the other side. She'd never have believed that the distance between wanting to strangle Rory Glen and wanting to hug him could be measured in a few metres. Toby had impressed her too, and not by his swimming skills. Emily had caught a few glimpses of Joanna as they all stood waiting for their turn to take the plunge. Yesterday, Joanna had been happy to make jokes about her comparative immobility, but Emily had yet to meet an overweight woman who couldn't be reduced to crippling self-consciousness under the wrong circumstances. Joanna looked more scared with each turn that brought her own moment closer, but Emily suspected she was even more scared of bottling out or asking for extra assistance for fear of drawing too much attention to the reason why. Toby, under the auspices of playing a prank, had engineered a way of speeding her passage without even acknowledging to her that he was doing so. Of course, it was possible that he was actually a selfish bastard who neither trusted Parlabane's towing abilities nor fancied his own solo task of hauling the big fat bird, but Emily doubted it. There was something humbly solicitous about Toby, which made his contemporary political allegiances all the more surprising. Or maybe it just made her own political prejudices more conceited.

The hamper was waiting for them at the edge of some woodland, close to where a narrow track, wide enough for one vehicle, emerged briefly from the trees before bending back on itself. They approached along a gently climbing valley floor, a long spur rising to their left, truncated maybe a quarter, a third of a mile past their goal. It was the professionally sharp-eyed Parlabane who spotted it, Baxter having told them only that lunch would be waiting for them. Rather oddly, Baxter needed Parlabane to point out what he was talking about, the hamper evidently somehow not matching his expectations. He'd glanced at his watch and muttered

188

something about there being still time, then relayed the incentive of Parlabane's discovery to the damp and tiring horde.

While the rest sat down to eat, Baxter stayed on his feet, frequently checking the time and pacing around close to the bend in the track so that he could see both approaches. That was when Emily decided to make her move, both the sandwich-assisted waxing of her courage and the opportunity of getting him alone finally coinciding. On the march, he'd usually been buttonholed by another guest, and when he wasn't, she'd lacked the nerve to broach the issue. Her trepidation existed on a number of levels, one of which being that neither of them would be comfortable if what she had to discuss was overheard. The main one, of course, was the possibility that she'd got it totally wrong and he wouldn't have an earthly what she was on about.

She was pretty sure, though. The more she looked at him throughout the morning, in light of what had come to her last night, the more it explained not only why he was so familiar, but why he hadn't reciprocally recognised her. Or rather, why he wasn't letting on as much.

She wandered over, putting a good dozen yards of privacy between the pair of them and the group.

'Something up?' she asked, bottling it a little and opting to procrastinate. He turned around. She looked in his face for some clue to whether her presence provoked any unease, bearing in mind that he might not want this.

'It's Francis. He was meant to be here with the minibus.'

'We're getting a lift home? Why eat out here, then?'

'Not a lift home, just a precaution in case anybody was struggling or turned an ankle or whatever.'

'Do cold, wet tootsies count?'

''Fraid not. He must have had to deal with something back at the hotel. At least he left lunch.'

She swallowed. Time to nibble the muzzle, if not fully bite the bullet.

'He told you all about dinner, then. It got pretty heated, and not just the flambé dessert.'

'Yeah. But there's nothing like cold water to douse the flames.'

Ooh, fleet little sidestep.

'Could have done with you there to even up the teams, *Daniel*.'

He fixed her with an intense, indignant look for a moment, then melted with a sigh and a smile.

'I was bound to get my cover blown eventually. I didn't see the need to blow it myself. That's why I never said anything to you. Couldn't be sure if you'd recognised me, and, just as important, couldn't be sure you wouldn't pretend you hadn't anyway.'

'Why would I do that?'

'Because it would be easier,' he said. 'For both of us.'

'I'm sorry,' she replied, realising what he was saying. 'I wasn't trying to out you or anything. I just needed to know it was you. It was driving me crazy. It's been what, fifteen, sixteen years? You changed your name?'

'I changed a lot of things. I had to make a clean break from the past. Danny Brown no more.'

'I'm sorry, I didn't mean to intrude. I should have sussed why you weren't playing happy reunions. I'll leave it, okay?'

'No, don't be daft. I was just a bit wary; didn't want you calling me a bourgeois traitor for where I've ended up.'

'Oh come on, look where I am. He who fucks nuns, eh? I guess when the revolution never came, we all had to pay the rent.'

'Insane times. Best forgotten, if you ask me.'

'After last night's dinner, I'd second that. But if you're on the lam, so to speak, why did you come to Seventh Chime for PR?'

'That was Francis's call, not mine. Someone recommended Seventh Chime to him. Bloke at a party gave him a card –

Kathy's card, as it turned out. By the time I found out you were her partner, things were already too far along.'

'That explains the brevity of your phone calls.'

'To be honest, I wasn't sure how much you'd want to dredge up the past either. But in fact we really do, as a matter of policy, stick to email wherever possible. It means you've a ready-made transcript of everything for reference and clarification. It makes for an efficient, dynamic and undistracted business relationship. Lacks the scope for personal rapport, admittedly, but we find places for that elsewhere, like this weekend, for example.'

'Efficient, dynamic business relationships. Smash the state, huh?'

'And you wonder why I'm lying low. I voted for the Lib Dems. Do you want to get your dig in for that too, get it over with?'

'At least they're to the left of New Labour.'

'Splitters!' he said, causing them both to laugh.

'Your face is different,' Emily told him, recognising the changes now that she was close enough to see what was still the same. It wasn't just the years, the tidy crop and the absence of a badge-burdened green raincoat that had made him hard to place.

'Car crash, '93. I looked like a panda for six months. Nose has never been the same. You look a bit different yourself. Hair especially.'

She ran a hand through it automatically, something she'd never have managed way back when. 'Yeah, ideological reasons. I reckoned I was personally responsible for about half the hole in the ozone layer just through hairspray CFCs.'

He laughed, but it sounded a little forced: polite but uncomfortable. He really wasn't quite ready for this.

'So what do I call you?' she asked.

'Donald, please. It's easier. Less confusing, for me most of all.'

'Okay.'

'Oh, and I'd appreciate it if you didn't tell the rest of them.'

'Of course.'

'Especially Parlabane. It would be manna from heaven for him to find out what's in my past.'

'I wouldn't dream of it, though on evidence so far I don't think he's as bad as he's painted. Even if he did find out, I think he'd probably cut you some slack for being on the side of the angels.'

'Were we?' he asked, in a way that did not invite an answer.

Baxter gestured with a nod of the head that she should follow him back to the group, where he said nothing to the others about the lack of an expected minibus and driver. With nobody having pulled up lame and the atmosphere notably chirpy now that the sugar was hitting everyone's bloodstreams, he announced that it was time to press on, and pointed to the top of the spur.

'Only if we don't have to do any swimming at the top of it,' Parlabane said.

'No,' Baxter assured him. 'But mouthy journalists might have to do some flying at the top of it. And you can quote me on that.'

'I left my Dictaphone in my other drysuit. If I can't remember your quote exactly, is it okay if I paraphrase? Something along the lines of: "You're all mine now, mine, you hear? And you're going to die on this hillside. Muaha-hahaha!" That cool?'

'Die horribly,' Baxter advised.

'Horribly. Got it.'

The climb was far steeper than any of their ramblings so far. It was nothing Emily couldn't manage, but she was aware of the greater effort registering upon her body temperature. For the first time in more than an hour, instead of damp, cold and clammy, she felt damp, hot and sweaty.

'Horses sweat,' she remembered a particularly prissy schoolteacher correcting her. 'Gentlemen perspire. Ladies *glow*.'

She couldn't get that Kate Bush number out of her head, though running was a rather flattering description of their collective progress. 'Trudging with a hand on each knee to assist with the climb because your thighs are aching like buggery up that hill' was more accurate, but didn't really scan, and it would have been hard to fit the 'yay-yay-yow's in around it too. She wasn't sure quite what had popped the song in there, though; whether she'd have thought of it on the ascent anyway, or whether it had been sparked by contemporary contemplations. It was said that smell was the sense most closely connected to memory, but pop music had formidable mnemonic properties too, and not necessarily the songs you liked. She'd never owned a Kate Bush record in her puff, but that song had been part of the arbitrarily selected soundtrack to that period of her life. She couldn't hear it, couldn't think of it without thinking of back then; same as she couldn't think of back then without hearing that song. A sniff of 'skin-coloured' Clearasil (actually only skin-coloured for those with beige skin, to whom acne was presumably the least of their dermatological problems) was the only thing more capable of rewinding the decades to that time when the world was just waiting for her to sort it out with her Doc Marten's and delusions of maturity.

She expected to feel more breathless, more tired, but the further she climbed, the less she felt the strain, and if anyone had suggested stopping for a rest, she'd have shouted them down. There was a compulsion to reach the top, not just in her, but palpably in the looks and strides of the whole group. Emily wasn't exactly a Munro-bagger, but any time she'd climbed a hill, it had been the same: an irresistible drive overriding considerations of comfort, fatigue, hunger or blistered heels. It felt ancient, instinctive, and wasn't some macho because-it's-there crap. Perhaps it was psychologically very simple: from the top, you could see what lay ahead. You could see what was next.

She was among the first to afford herself that perspective, getting there just behind Baxter and Rory. They could see along the top of the ridge, and that it wasn't truncated quite where it had appeared from below. It dog-legged, or dog-stumped might be closer, cut off shortly after the point where it turned. 'Glowing' quite profusely, Emily calculated that it might have been quicker to go around the spur rather than over it, but tingling with the endorphin rush released by having done so, she applauded Baxter's choice. The sense of achievement was amplified when their guide, after waiting for the last of them to catch up, told them to turn around and pointed out a tiny Saltire fluttering in the distance, elevated above the greenery by the tower at McKinley Hall.

The view ahead had no such icon to indicate civilised settlement, nor any landmark to suggest (to her untrained eye, at least) what their route forward would be. More hills, more woodland, and a stretch of coarse moor spread before it like an Unwelcome mat.

'Where to now?' someone asked, thinking along similar and foot-sore lines.

'We wait here for a helicopter to take us home,' Kathy replied. 'It's in the UML brochure.'

'Like hell it is,' said Baxter.

'Hey, we're the PR firm. I'm writing the brochure copy, and if I say there's gonna be a helicopter, you bastards better deliver.'

'I'd settle for a beer scooter,' Max said.

'Amen,' agreed Rory.

'Well, I'll have to slip an erratum notice into the brochure,' Baxter told them. 'Page twelve, paragraph three. Due to a

194

typesetting error, the word "helicopter" appeared in place of "Shanks's pony".'

'Are we going back the way we came?' Rory asked, his tone suggesting the affirmative would be met with disapproval. It seemed unlikely he'd be feeling the pace (or admitting it anyway), just voicing the disappointment everyone would feel if there weren't new sights to distract them on the journey home.

'Would I do that to you?' Baxter replied. 'No, everybody just catch your breath, then it's onwards and downwards.'

'Down there? Further away?' Liz asked. 'Have you got a tent stashed somewhere?'

'The lie of the land is quite deceptive,' he assured her. 'Believe me, you'll be back in half the time it took you to get here. So everybody catch your breath and enjoy the view, then you can let your feet earn your stomach an indulgence.'

'Speaking of the view,' said Parlabane. 'Is there any kind of boundary that denotes what part is still army land?'

'There's fences, if that's what you mean, but we're still a good way away from it. Why?'

'Just wondering what that pair are up to.'

Baxter looked down and ahead, as did Emily. There were indeed two men in military fatigues now visible on the coarse apron of moor before the woods. They must only have emerged a moment ago, while the group were looking towards the hotel. They had begun digging with heavy spades, oblivious to their audience on the spur above in a way that suggested they understandably assumed themselves to be the only living souls in a considerable radius.

'They're digging,' Grieg observed, proving that last night's display of wit and incisiveness was no fluke.

'Probably a mass grave,' Baxter said dryly, sounding a little intolerant of the portentous tone Grieg had adopted.

Rory laughed. 'Let's ask them. HAW!' he shouted. 'Room for one more inside?'

Both of the diggers stopped and looked up. The one nearer the woods dropped his spade and ran towards the trees, where he turned his back and bent to pick something up. He wheeled back around, the thing he'd retrieved held in two hands at his shoulder.

'Christ, that's a rifle,' Max said.

Five shots rang out, the sound tarrying a moment behind the muzzle flare.

There were screams, cries and many swearies as the group hit the ground, burying themselves face-down in the grass. Emily couldn't believe how much had turned in a moment. It made her reversal of sentiments towards Rory in that watery tunnel an aeon of meditation by comparison. There was no double-take, no slow-motion piecing together of the evidence, no purgatorial pause of incredulity, no top-down view of herself as she inquired: is this real? She was standing on a hilltop sharing a joke, her body flushed but tingling with exertion. Bang bang bang bang bang, and she was on her face, trembling, her stomach threatening to empty itself, the people around her uniformly prostrate and equally alarmed. When she dared to raise her head, the very same sight looked different, as though she was suddenly viewing it all in black and white. Parts of it were instantly less vivid, blurred out of focus as though the image had been pared down to only the most necessary details, stripped of anything peripheral, irrelevant or distracting.

One of the men was pointing at the other, the distant and indistinct sound of his angry words carrying on the breeze a second or so later. The one who had fired lowered his gun, but only so that he could pick up a second rifle and hold it out to his companion, who was on his way towards him. With both of them now thus armed, Emily flattened her head to the grass again, but no further shots were heard. She looked up once more, and saw that the pair of them were jogging away in different directions: one dead ahead towards the slope, the other making for the end of the spur.

'Is this a fucking stunt?' Rory demanded furiously of Baxter. 'Because it's in pretty poor taste if it is.'

'Everybody just keep the head,' Baxter responded. 'Pull it together, okay?'

'Why are they shooting at us?' Grieg asked.

'How the fuck should I know?' Baxter retorted. 'Believe me, the point at which I was in complete control of the day's activities has passed.'

'Did they think we saw something?' Grieg persisted, thinking aloud.

'Maybe it's the fact that we saw them there at all,' Max opined.

'Christ, does it matter?' said Liz. 'They're not gonna tell us, even if we ask really politely. So let's get a move on.'

'Where to?'

'Down the hill, for a start,' Baxter advised. 'Quickly but carefully. Watch your footing. Then we make for the woods. We've a decent start on them, so we can make it count.'

'What good's a head start against a bullet?' Grieg enquired.

'Good enough if the shooter can't see you through two hundred yards of trees,' Toby answered.

Toby and Baxter looked at each other, Baxter giving him a nod of acknowledgement for his support. Emily looked around the other faces: some helpless, awaiting guidance; some expectant, awaiting leadership; some determined, awaiting only the assurance that the rest were ready for the flight. She didn't see Parlabane's expression. His face was turned away towards his friend Vale, the two of them having some kind of wordless summit.

'Make for the track,' Baxter advised as they began their descent. 'Veer right where it bends – that'll take us away from the spur. And don't look back.'

'We'll never outrun them,' Emily heard Liz say.

Their progress felt like running in a dream, fear stretching the distance in spite of their haste.

'They're carrying full-size, semi-automatic rifles,' Max told her. 'If you've ever felt the weight in one of those things, you'd put your money on us. Just concentrate on your footing.'

It was heavy on the calves, almost as heavy as the ascent had been on the thighs, but this way, the strain was all in the impact and balance. Gravity was an ally, but only if harnessed with cautious restraint. Emily's heart was telling her to charge forward, her middle-ear arguing against, the latter just about holding its own.

Baxter had advised against looking back, but Emily couldn't help stealing glances not only behind, but towards the end of the spur also. All logic – arithmetical and geographical – told her there would be no threat to see, but she needed the reassurance that their efforts weren't about to be brought to an abrupt end. There were no soldiers, only conspicuously yellow fugitives, randomly spread but almost identical in their posture: knees bent, arms out, palms down, fingers stretched. From a distanced perspective – both phys-ical and emotional – it would have looked like a costumed performance by the official UML Synchronised Shitebag Troupe. Kathy and Rory were making the quickest progress, Kathy reaping unanticipated benefits from her morning jogs around Inverleith Park, as much from its practice in rut-negotiation as physical fitness.

Baxter was no slouch either, but he was trailing the leaders due to stopping and turning around every few seconds to check that nobody had got into difficulties. He wasn't the only one. Toby was keeping pace with Joanna at the rear, holding an arm out now and then to offer extra balance, while Parlabane and Vale had drifted to either flank, their eyes as often on the people between them as the ground under their feet.

198

With the group spreading out according to pace, they automatically began following the progress of those in the vanguard, irrespective of how they had each envisaged their path down. Rory and Kathy were angling their route sharply towards the bend in the track leading into the forest, which took them down a steeper incline than they had negotiated on the way up. Gradient wasn't the only reason the group had previously avoided it.

Baxter called after them, but their momentum meant it was too late for them to stop themselves. The grass thinned out with very little warning and gave way to yards of treacherously intractable scree. Rory hit it first, barely a second before Kathy. Emily stopped as she saw the results. Rory scrambled a few paces, still attempting to find purchase, like Wile E Coyote in mid-air before realising he's run off the cliff. Kathy had enjoyed a moment's more notice to brake, so didn't hit the scree with quite as much pace, but this only meant that she was able to cushion her inevitable fall. She still ended up the same as Rory: flat on her back, skidding down the slope like it was a flume in a waterpark.

Grieg had been entranced by this spectacle too, but not enough to stop. Emily knew this because he clattered into her back and sent the pair of them tumbling forward. She turned a full somersault but was unable to get any kind of grip when her feet came back around into contact with the grass, and found herself rolling ever faster, the hillside and sky spinning in her view like she was inside a washing machine. The only thing more sickening than the sensation was the thought of the rock that might be waiting for her skull or spine. She grabbed at tufts of grass, her bodyweight jerking her wrists painfully when her fingers found anything to grip. It did the trick, however, by virtue of turning her spin the necessary eighty or so degrees in order that she was rolling along the slope rather than down it. This brought her to a stop, but it was a few seconds before her eyes caught up, the world still slewing off in one direction whenever she tried to focus.

She lay still until the effect dissipated a little, then sat up slowly, assessing her condition and regaining her coordination. There was the beginning of an ache in her right buttock and thigh that she knew was going to have a lot more to say for itself in a couple of hours, but for now it would be tolerable. It would have to be.

To her relieved surprise, she saw that the Human Snowball technique had taken her almost to the valley floor. There were only a few more yards before the slope flattened out, the cover of the trees beckoning ahead across one last gauntlet-run of exposed moor. She glanced to her left and saw that Rory and Kathy were on ground-level too, though instead of sprinting for the woods, they were standing at the foot of the scree, beckoning the others to board the express and readying themselves to assist at the terminus. Emily presumed their route down had been more tolerable than her own. The only person she'd have wished a similar descent upon would have been the gormless clown who'd precipitated her own, a needless sentiment as he was stumbling around a few yards to her right, dizzy from having stood up too soon.

Kathy and Rory assisted the skidding yellow descendants as necessary, helping them to their feet and, in the case of Max, arresting a dangerous spin-cum-tumble. Baxter was yelling at the rest to keep running, accepting the unspoken wisdom that this proven fastest pair were best equipped to recover ground once they'd made sure everyone got down safely. Vale and Parlabane fell in last above the scree, the former holding something in his left hand as he watched his predecessors. Emily realised with a degree of outrage that it was his camera. It seemed as negligently frivolous as it did tasteless, but then what kind of photographer would Jack Parlabane insist upon? Maybe he was dedicated to the bitter end and was recording what he could in order to bequeath some sort of *Blair-Witch*-style future scoop.

Remembering her own responsibility, Emily put an arm around Grieg's waist and guided him in a steady jog until he was stable enough to continue alone.

A few seconds later, she glanced back to see how far this hindmost duo were lagging, and nearly fell over again at the sight of the pair skidding down almost upright, as though on invisible snowboards, both urging their unnecessary helpers to get moving. She was sure she'd heard somewhere that Parlabane was into climbing, so maybe this was no great shakes to him. Possibly that was how he and Vale had met.

Rory and Kathy caught up just as Emily reached the track. There was still a distance of about fifty or sixty yards to go before cover.

'Are we having fun yet?' Rory asked, panting.

'No,' Emily replied, 'but if I ever need a cheap exfoliation treatment for my arse-cheeks, I'll know where to come.'

She looked back, Rory too. The still and silent landscape appeared as indifferently deserted as when they had first set eyes upon it. It felt difficult to believe that there was anyone else out there, never mind what they had witnessed on the other side; a difficulty that was proving rapidly contagious.

'No sign,' Rory said. 'Maybe they were just putting the wind up us.'

'They fired shots,' Kathy reminded him.

Parlabane and Vale were approaching at the rear, stealing the odd glance behind themselves.

'Could have just been to chase us off,' Rory persisted. 'Maybe Donald's map-reading isn't quite on the money and we *were* trespassing. A volley over our heads to get us to bugger off sharpish. Did the trick, didn't it?'

'They came after us too,' Kathy added.

'Did they, though? That's how big boys chase off wee boys: a few angry paces and the wee ones get off their marks. They don't hang around, so they don't know the big boys have stayed where they were, pissing themselves.'

'What do you think?' Kathy asked Parlabane, who was now trotting alongside.

'I like Rory's odds, but I don't like the stake.'

'Point taken,' Rory conceded.

They caught up with the rest under the trees, the group stopping to catch their breath at a judicious spot affording both a view of the spur and a quick escape into cover if needed.

'This is when Donald tells us congratulations on completing the latest UML test,' said Liz. She sounded sardonic, but it was hard to tell whether she was being scornful should this turn out to be the case, or despairing of her own wishes that it would. The possibility had flashed across Emily's mind, though it had been hard to evaluate amid other, threateningly mortal concerns. It seemed like a desperate hope in the 'Maybe I'll wake up and it'll all have been a dream' category, but with the added plausibility of 'surprises' and 'challenges' being on the UML agenda. The thought of enormous legal vulnerability argued against the company engaging in reckless stunts, but, on the other hand, waivers and disclaimers had been signed in respect of 'strenuous and physically demanding outdoor activities'.

Baxter ignored both the remark and the expectant looks awaiting his response. Instead he looked into the trees, away from the track, comparing the limited view with what was on his map.

'We should get off the road, take the less obvious path,' he said. 'And we should do it before they get line of sight.'

'Line of sight?' Rory muttered, evidently still fancying those odds enough to be less concerned than the rest about the stake. 'They're hardly going to get that, sitting smoking a fag a mile back on the other side of that hill, are they?'

Emily looked behind once again, a near-superstitious compulsion in response to Rory so blatantly dropping his drawers and mooning fate. Parlabane was looking back too, in time to see fate drop its own drawers in response, only fate was facing forwards. One of the soldiers was visible, jogging over the brow of the hill. Spotting his quarry, he dropped to one knee and fired. Emily heard something explode from a trunk a few yards away, at almost the same time as the report reached her ears.

Everyone ran deeper under the trees.

'That's what I meant by line of sight,' Baxter shouted angrily. 'The other one could be even closer. Let's move it out.'

'We'll just call you Archie MacPherson, shall we?' Parlabane said to Rory.

'Eh?'

'It's Andy Ritchie on the ball, very disappointing, he hasn't really contributed much in this ga— oh he's scored! Great goal from Andy Ritchie!'

'Fuck you.'

As Baxter began leading the group off the track, Emily noticed Vale take a few steps to one side in order to look up at the trees, searching for and examining the bullet hole. Max spotted this and came over too.

'Looks heavy-calibre,' Max said. 'Army issue, I'd wager.'

'I'll take your word for it,' Vale replied.

'I know a bit about these things,' Max assured him.

'What are you two after, a fucking souvenir?' Baxter shouted. 'Come on.'

'Where are we headed?' Rory asked.

'I think I know a short cut.'

'You *think*?'

'You got any better ideas? Actually, it's not so much a

short cut as a way of putting greater distance between us and them.'

'How so?'

'You'll see, but only if you shut up and keep moving.'

'No, keep talking, Rory,' Kathy said. 'Tell us again about the soldiers staying where they were.'

'Kathy,' Emily chided. 'Knock it off.'

'Sorry. Just wishing he was right, that's all.'

They proceeded Indian file, which discouraged Emily from constantly looking behind, as all she'd have seen was Rory. As far as she was aware, it was Parlabane who was rearmost, and therefore first in the queue for a bullet should the soldiers catch up. It occurred to her that Parlabane was probably first in a lot of people's queue for a bullet, though she wasn't sure if his presence here was therefore a talisman or a curse: whether his survival of previous murder attempts meant he was a smart guy to have around, or whether it skewed the law of averages to their disadvantage.

She let a couple of people pass her until only Parlabane was at her back.

'I'm not being funny here,' she said, 'but this isn't the first time you've been shot at, is it?'

'Actually, come to think of it, I believe it is.'

'But I'm sure someone told me there'd been attempts on your life.'

'Oh, yeah, but nobody actually popped one off before. Probably why I'm still here. As far as I remember, I think only one of them was planning to use a gun. Alastair Dalgleish's hired help brought a knife, and Ian Beadie's errand boy used a more improvised implement.'

'So how did you come through all of these unscathed?'

'I didn't. I lost a length of intestine in jail. Feel free to make a remark about me being no less full of shit as a result.'

'I'm sorry.'

'Don't sweat it.'

'How did you survive the others?'

'You looking for tips?'

'You could say that.'

'Can't help you. Not today. I survived most of those attempts through two things I haven't got right now.'

'And what were they?'

'A gun of my own and the drop on the bad guy.'

'Shit.'

'Best keep running.'

She did. The pace was disquietingly undemanding. She couldn't say she'd prefer it if every sinew was screaming, her vision blurred or her lungs threatening to implode and prolapse through her windpipe, but at least it would make her feel the distance between the fugitives and their pursuers was not narrowing with every footfall. Bound to each other as they were, the group could only be as fast as its slowest member, which was making her think extremely uncharitable and politically unacceptable thoughts connecting her personal survival with Joanna's dietary discipline. She'd never articulate such notions, but when there were gunmen on her trail, it was difficult to prevent the more ruthlessly pragmatic parts of her mind from protesting that *she* shouldn't die just because someone else couldn't say no to a cream cake.

Making it worse, she was sure she could hear footsteps close by that didn't belong to Parlabane.

'Did you hear that?' she asked him.

'What?'

'Footsteps?'

'Just me, my dear, sorry to alarm you,' said a voice. It was Vale, appearing at her side as though he'd been teleported there. She realised she hadn't passed him when she dropped back.

'Where were you?'

'Call of nature,' Parlabane answered for him. 'It's a

205

problem at his age. He went for a slash, which probably made him the only one not shitting himself.'

'Charming, as ever, Mr P.'

Perhaps provoked by this little exchange, Emily began to think she could hear running water. It was hard to be sure with the wind picking up now and again, rippling the leaves and masking more distant sounds. After another fifty yards or so, there was no question: not only was the rushing noise clear and consistent, but the surface of the water could be glimpsed to her left through gaps in the wood. It got closer the further they proceeded: their route remained straight, but the river was bending to meet them, and unless it bent back upon itself, it was going to drive them away from the direction of the hotel.

Moments later, they were on the edge of a steep bank, several yards of fast-flowing water blocking their path three feet below.

'Looks like the short cut's fucked,' said Max.

'This *is* the short cut,' Baxter replied.

'How the hell are we supposed to get across that?' Grieg demanded, horrified. 'Look at the speed of the current.'

'As a team,' Baxter insisted. 'You don't think we can get across this? Good, because hopefully they won't think we can either. Which means they'll still be searching this side while we're hightailing it on the other.'

He took off his backpack and uncoiled the rope they had used back at the tunnel. For a moment, due to the way he was dangling it from his wrist, Emily thought he was planning to cast it across the flow and lasso something on the other side. Possibly the notion had sprung from her reluctance to contemplate a plan that involved actually getting into the water. It was moving steadily, a calmness upon the broad surface denoting that it was far from shallow beneath. It appeared to be unseasonally in spate, unseasonally in as much as it was, theoretically at least, not meant to have pissed down all through June, July, August and September as it had done this 'summer'.

'I need a volunteer to go first. I'll be going last to make sure we all make it.'

Toby put a hand up, just ahead of Rory and Max.

'Thanks, Toby, but you're a little light on your feet.'

'I'm not,' declared Joanna, stepping in front of the other would-be volunteers. A contrite voice in Emily's head acknowledged the possibility that her survival chances might well now be improved because someone else couldn't say no to a cream cake.

Joanna passed the rope through two belt-loops on her trousers and allowed Baxter to tie off one end. He, Rory and Max then took hold of the slack and paid it out gradually to ease her reverse climb down the bank into the flow. She wobbled a little as her legs went under, but regained her balance before turning so that the current was hitting her side-on. The water came up to just above her waist. Rory went next, coiling the rope around his forearm and wrist as Joanna edged her way forward to make room. Emily could now see how it was going to work: the more of them were in the water, the greater weight secured them against the current, something their two-man pursuers would be unable to match. That was what Baxter meant when he said it was a way of putting greater distance between them.

Max followed, then Toby and Grieg before it was Emily's turn. For the second time that day, she was enormously grateful for the drysuit, her feet telling her what temperature the rest of her body was being spared. She attempted to ease her way into the flow but felt her boots slide downwards outwith any control she might exert. It plunged quicker than she'd anticipated, no gradual slope towards the centre, just a sudden drop until she was waist-deep, the tug of the current powerful and relentless. She could feel the strain at the sole of her boots, as well as the constant force her legs had to push against. All things considered, it was a bugger of a moment for Rory to lose his footing. He stumbled and fell backwards, his head briefly submerged, the jolt enough to tumble Joanna ahead of him too. The three remaining on the bank secured the line one behind the other, heaving to like a tug-of-war team, the eight in the water held in an arc until the fallen pair recovered themselves.

Emily looked from bank to bank. Joanna wasn't going to reach the other side before the last of them entered the flow, at which point their fates truly were bound together.

The next couple of minutes were like her time in the tunnel intensified and infinitely elongated. As looking back required her to compromise the comparative stability of a sideways stance, she resolved to blot out what was going on behind and focus upon Joanna's progress. That way, also, she wouldn't know the point at which Baxter left dry land.

If some of the previous legs of their journey had felt worryingly slow, this was a helpless agony, suspended between wishing it was over and hoping Joanna didn't move too quickly or too suddenly lest the lot of them get whipped off downstream. Eventually, Joanna did reach the other side, but it was only when she was in touching distance of the near-vertical bank that Emily's perspective could confirm her newest fear: that Joanna was too short to make the climb. The news was relayed across in the form of a warning that the whole line would have to move upstream a few paces to where the bank was shallower. They moved not exactly as one, but there was enough slack between each to allow them to measure their paces individually. Unfortunately there wasn't sufficient slack for Rory to give Joanna a punt-up without letting go of the rope himself, but there were no further mishaps and in a comparative twinkling, the pair of them were on terra firma. Joanna untied herself and secured the end of the rope around a tree while Rory crouched down to help Max from the water. With the line now secure at the other end, Emily felt confident enough to look behind, and was glad she hadn't before. There might have been slack elsewhere in the rope, but it had ended with Vale, leaving Baxter to hold only the older man's hand.

Once a few of them were safely on the other side, it felt even more excruciating that those left in the water were still necessarily moving so slowly, an effect multiplied when Emily joined them on the bank. Her moment of personal relief was merely a transient blink before she was once again tortured by the sight of those still to emerge.

Distraction came in the form of news.

'I can see the minibus,' Joanna called out. 'It's parked on the track not far ahead.'

'Campbell?' Baxter shouted.

'Don't see anyone on board.'

'Christ, where is he?' he muttered, before more audibly advising them to make for it ASAFP.

Despite Baxter's impassioned entreaty, Rory and Max stayed in place to continue helping the arrivals up the bank, while Emily remained because her eternally hypercharged conscience wouldn't leave until she'd seen them all across.

Kathy emerged, then Liz, the latter bellyflopping like a landed salmon after sliding from the increasingly nervous Max's grip and almost slipping back down the bank.

'On you go, Max,' Rory told him. 'I've got this.'

'Sure?' Max asked apologetically.

'Go. You too, Emily.'

She watched Rory grip Parlabane's forearm. After that there were only two left. This was silly, she told herself. Even sillier if she ended up the slowest runner once the last of them were clear. She allowed herself one last look behind before planning to set off, which was when she saw the soldier. He was on the far bank, not directly across, but a distance back, just on the cusp of where the river bent into her sightline.

'Look out!' she shouted, pointing to where the soldier was now taking aim.

All of their heads turned in response. Rory hauled at Parlabane's arm with sudden desperate haste, successfully landing the reporter but toppling himself to his backside in the process. Down in the water, Baxter pushed at Vale as if trying to launch him ashore, with disastrous effect. His efforts did send Vale more quickly against the bank, but once Vale's bodyweight had swung from his path, Baxter's momentum carried him forward and sideways, off-balance into the current. Emily saw his head go under, then reappear amid a thrash of hands, by which time he was already yards downstream.

'The bus!' he yelled, spluttering, his feet finding enough purchase to slow but not stop him. 'Run!'

A rifle round was better than any starter's pistol. Emily got off her mark without looking back, finally running flat out along a track with no obstacles and a tangible goal at the end.

As she approached, she could see fumes escaping from the exhaust: glorious, blessed, merciful pollution. When she got there, she found Toby in the driver's seat, the others aboard and gazing anxiously out of the rear window.

'No sign of Campbell,' he confirmed. 'Keys were in the ignition.'

'Did you hear the shot?'

'Sure did.'

'We lost Baxter.'

'He was hit?'

'No, swept away.'

'Shit. Who we waiting for then?'

His question was answered as Rory, Vale and finally Parlabane arrived at the door and clambered quickly aboard the minibus. Emily shifted along her double seat to make room for Rory, Vale taking a spare seat next to Liz as Parlabane slid in alongside the driver.

Toby was eyeing the door, as if expecting Baxter to appear at any second.

'Drive, for fuck's sake,' Rory ordered.

Toby put the vehicle into gear and released the handbrake. As he did so, a figure clad in camouflage fatigues stepped from the trees about twenty yards ahead up the track, rifle held at his waist.

'Jesus,' Toby yelped, looking back to the rear window like he was planning on reversing.

Parlabane stretched a foot across Toby's legs and stamped the driver's sopping boot hard against the accelerator.

'Just go,' he said firmly. 'Drive at the bastard.'

The minibus leapt forward as Toby released the clutch. He bowed his head towards the steering wheel, as low as he could without losing sight of the track ahead, and then a little lower than that. Everyone else ducked too; everyone, that is, but Parlabane, who grabbed hold of the wheel and corrected the vehicle's course as it threatened to slew off the track towards the river. Emily raised her head in time to see the soldier dive out of the way as the bus bore down on him, the engine shrieking a kamikaze war cry, still in first gear.

Toby sat up and changed gear, checking his rear-view mirror for what everyone else was looking for out of the back window. The soldier reappeared on the track after a few seconds, shouldering his weapon and firing at will. There were screams and gasps, but no impacts. The bus accelerated, taking the first bend so fast that the rear wheels slid off the track, the vehicle threatening to topple until its diversion was corrected by a sturdy tree. Toby changed down and accelerated again, heading fast along a straight stretch, putting cover and distance between them and their pursuers.

Parlabane was applauding, hands in the air. He turned around, a look of delighted devilment on his face that was incongruous to the point of offensive. 'Again, again,' he said loudly, laughing.

'What?' several voices demanded.

'You've really got to hand it to these UML guys: that was a rush. Wouldn't you agree?'

'A rush?' Kathy retorted, furious. 'There's two people missing, we almost got killed and we're still, quite literally, not out of the woods. Is this your way of telling us you're finally flipping out?'

'Oh, come on . . . Toby, slow down,' he advised quietly, putting a hand on Toby's arm. 'I think we can all breathe out now.'

'Didn't you hear me? There's two people missing. They could be dead.'

'Two people missing, both UML people. That doesn't strike you as a coincidence? Listen, I didn't want to be the prick at the cinema who keeps telling you he can see the boom in shot, but I think we can all knock off the suspension of disbelief bit now that the fun's over.'

'Suspension of—?' Kathy cut herself off, taking a moment to mull it over. Emily, it seemed, wasn't the only one who had been wondering whether it was all a set-up, but she hadn't been ready to conclude as much when doing so could prove suicidally negligent if she was wrong.

'Take a step back and examine the evidence,' Parlabane said. 'We just happen to stumble across the scene of something highly secret and dangerous at the exact moment it's taking place, amid miles and miles and miles of absolutely fuck-all? What is this, *The Secret Seven*? We just happen to have a grandstand view of whatever it is from a hilltop which conveniently affords us a major headstart when these guys, who don't know what – if anything – we might have seen, come bombing after us? And to get us running, they start taking pot-shots from a distance of about half a mile, maybe more? Oh, and let me rewind. Campbell and the

212

minibus are missing, having failed to make the rendezvous. Subsequent events hint that the guy may have had to do a runner or even been abducted to some grisly end, but he bravely fought off the evil baddies long enough to make sure he dropped off our lunch?

'Then to make our escape, we have to cross the river, but it's okay, because Baxter just happens to have rope and we just happen to be wearing drysuits, all of which we thought had already played their part due to a very deft curve-ball the man threw us earlier in the day. Baxter just happens to go last across the water, just happens to be still in there when the soldier appears, and just happens to get swept away when the last of his corporate guests are ashore, heading for a minibus that just happens to be waiting with the keys conveniently in the ignition. Finally, a third soldier just happens to appear as we drive away, to give us that last fright as we fashion our escape as a newly bonded team unit.'

'Third soldier?' Toby enquired.

'Didn't you notice he was bone-dry? He couldn't have crossed the river.'

'All I was looking at was the gun.'

'What about the bullet hole in the tree?' Joanna asked. Emily looked at Max, who was gazing down uncomfortably, trying not to catch anyone's eye. She suspected he knew he was about to be, in the local tongue, 'fun' oot' regarding his professed ballistics knowledge.

'Remote-control pyrotechnics,' Vale stated almost apologetically, not wanting to humiliate the guy any more than was unavoidable. 'Detonated by Baxter. He was holding something under his map. The damage to the tree was from an outwards impact.'

Rory was the first to start laughing. Within about twenty seconds, even Max had joined in.

Mysteries of the Flesh

'I think we should just give everybody the vegetarian option,' said Ger. 'Tell them it's a team-building thing for them all to have the same menu.'

'There's not enough to go around. Well, I suppose if we change the starter we can use the aubergine and a few more peppers, but it's still going to look a little stretched, a little, I don't know . . .'

'Like a plate of side dishes missing the meat?'

'Guess so.'

'Aye. Actually, that's what all vegetarian dishes look like to me, but that's neither here nor there. I suppose if we forget about the soufflé, then we can re-route the cheese and make some individual tartlets. At least pastry's got a bit of bite. No, I cannae fuckin' believe I'm sayin' this. My first ever menu in charge and I'm talkin' aboot servin' up glorified quiche? Against the alternative of goin' with this . . . *stuff* of unknown and as far as I'm concerned dubious provenance.'

Alison and Ger looked again at the meat sitting on the worktop, blood and juices running along dozens of tiny crevices in the polythene bags it had arrived in. Its vendor had appeared at the kitchen's outside door a couple of hours after the dual departures of Mathieson and his intended main course, an unlikely messiah figure in a green full-length cagoule, mud and bloodstains on his boots. It wasn't unusual to get opportunistic hunter-cum-hawkers at the back door, looking for a quick sale (and often a swift no-questions disposal) for what they had bagged. However,

214

what they were flogging tended to be more reliably identi-fiable, usually because it still had skin, bone, fur or feathers attached.

Ger had spent a while trying to retrieve the situation by telephone, ringing other hotels in an initial radius of a ninety-minute round trip and then expanding this to three hours as he failed to get a result. The odds, he admitted, had been against him. This was for dinner on Saturday night, busiest of the week, and even if Sundays weren't as hot, nobody wanted to take any chances of going short before the week's first deliveries on Monday morning. Yes, some-body could probably have spared something, but not for some no-name sous-chef they'd never met. Some of them might have heard of Mathieson, but Ger couldn't drop the name because the chances were either: A, that they'd hate the bastard and not want to help his establishment; or B, be pals of his and want to know why he wasn't the one on the line, leading to the same result as A.

In true desperation, he'd resorted to calling the nearest 'supermarket', which was the statutory rural Spar in Auchterbuie, to enquire what they might have in their three-foot-square refrigerated section. It turned out they had just sold the last of their meat – a shrink-wrapped gammon joint – which was a bitter shame because the kitchen had both cheddar *and* tinned pineapple rings.

Sir Lachlan had proposed his own remedy for the situ-ation by announcing his intention to take to the hills and shoot something for dinner, even if it was only a few bunnies. 'At least they'll be organic,' he had joked.

However, ninety minutes later he still hadn't left the building, due to having failed to locate any shotgun cartridges. This, Alison reckoned, did not augur well for his abilities to locate anything worth shooting either. 'It's been a while since I used the old blunderbuss,' he admitted, 'but you never lose the knack.' The same, evidently, couldn't be said about the cartridges. He popped his head around the door every half hour or so by way of a lack-of-progress report, muttering about whatever possible hidey-hole he was next about to investigate.

Ger was confidently pessimistic about Sir Lachlan's chances, theorising that there weren't actually any cartridges to find.

'Lady Jane'll have binned them yonks ago. If you knew him as well as she does, do you reckon you'd allow him access to live ammunition?'

It was a very plausible point, and one that pointed all the more stiffly towards a meat-free repast.

Then this chancer had appeared with his poly bags, his agitated body language screaming out POACHER, or so they thought until they saw what he was punting.

'It's pork,' he'd insisted, though he wouldn't elaborate how he'd come by it. His offering already butchered, Alison revised poacher to simply 'thief'. Without any guarantee – nor even clue – of source, and no use-by date to go with, Ger was not quite ready to let desperation override his professional judgement.

'Okay,' the guy said, sensing that Ger's deliberations were ultimately tipping against him, 'I'll give you it for a round thirty quid. Come on, we can help each other out here. We both know I could still flog this tomorrow, but it sounds to me like you need something for the table tonight.'

'I'm not trying to drive the price down, mate. I'm just not quite ready to take your word for the freshness of this meat. I'm not even convinced what kind of meat it is. It doesn't look like pork to me. Where did you get it?'

'Fuck's sake,' the guy sighed. 'Okay, I stole it. I think we both fucking know that. And it's not pork, but as far as your guests are concerned it could be.'

'What is it?'

The guy swallowed, sighing again. 'Ostrich,' he admitted.

'Ostrich?'

'There's a farm just outside Blairhaugh. They do the slaughtering on-site but package it down in Perth. It's the in-thing in London restaurants,' he offered winningly.

'My baws it is,' Ger replied.

'Everybody'll be eating this stuff soon, mark my words. Sainsbury's are already stocking it.'

'Brilliant. So we can look forward to seeing that wee mockney prick riding aboot on wan in an advert next year?'

'Dunno aboot that pal, I'm just tryin' tae make a few bar.'

'Twenty.'

'Twenty-five.'

'Done.'

'So what are we going to call it?' Alison asked, once the purchase was made, the chancer departed and the meat transferred to the fridge. 'Or do we just come clean?'

'Bollocks to that. I mean, we can't lie about what it is, but we need to be a wee bit coy. That's usually the cue to resort to French.'

'How about *Icare d'Afrique*?'

'Icarus?'

'Yeah. His wings were useless too.'

Ger grinned. '*Ça plane pour moi*,' he confirmed.

A Matter of Taste

A loud rumbling boom from outside cut through every conversation and silenced the room at a stroke. There was a moment's pause before people began laughing at their own startlement, sudden frights being something that had already been an understandably pervasive theme of discussion. The curtains were closed in the bar, rain-lashed windows not making for a decorative view, so Parlabane hadn't noticed any lightning flash, but the encroaching low-sky gloom of the late afternoon had made it no surprise. That said, given the engineered thrills of the preceding hours, there was something about the thunder's very portentousness that was bordering on camp.

He wasn't the only one to think it.

'So, Donald,' Rory asked loudly, 'was that an actual clap of thunder, do you reckon, or a UML-generated, artificial, scare-the-pants-off-you clap of thunder?'

'No point asking him,' Toby replied. 'Neither he nor Francis are going to tell us the truth about what is and isn't their doing, are you?'

'Granted,' Campbell admitted. 'But I think you might be paying us an undeserved compliment if you think we can control the weather.'

'My point still stands, though,' Toby went on. 'The pair of you are now officially unreliable sources of information. Anything you deny responsibility for remains suspect, given your vested interest in things appearing to be beyond your control.'

'Including the weather?' Baxter asked.

'We'll give you the benefit of the doubt over that,' Toby conceded. 'Mind you, they used to say the Scots blamed Margaret Thatcher for the rain, so I wouldn't be the first to be so paranoid.'

'Oh God, let's not go there again tonight,' Campbell said, laughing nervously in the transparent hope that overt – even affected – good humour would encourage everyone to maintain the day's hard-forged esprit de corps.

'We didn't really believe that,' Kathy assured Toby. 'We knew fine that if she really could make it rain on Scotland, there'd never have been a dry day.'

'Touché.'

'Well, anyway,' Campbell said, cutting through any possible further contributions, 'I think now would be an appropriate time to issue you all with your first UML campaign medals.'

He stepped away from the table he'd been leaning against and drew their attention to the aluminium box sitting in the centre of it. With a magician's-lovely-assistant arm-waving flourish, he flipped open the lid and revealed ten metal badges snuggling amidst a bed of dark-grey protective foam. Then he called the guests forward one by one and pinned the badges to appropriate places on their evening attire, a cheer and a round of applause greeting each mini-ceremony.

Parlabane examined his. It was a surprisingly heavy and substantial wee number for such a pointless trinket, but here in the world of corporate stupidity, it was bad for the image of both parties if anything came across as cheap. Things like the UML gig were aimed at suits, whose self-importance had to be stroked on a regular basis, and needless expense was a guaranteed way of achieving that. Economies were what those on the shop floor had to worry about.

Talk predictably returned to how they had 'earned' their medals, lots of perspective comparisons and not a little revisionism on certain parts. Rory was happy enough to admit

219

buying the whole scam at face value, his only tilt at its plausibility having been his off-the-mark claims that the soldiers were feigning pursuit. Others were allowing retrospect to skew the extent to which they were willing dupes, not least Max as he attempted to back-pedal from his ballistics beamer; and then there was Grieg. The word 'twat' could have been invented for him, its role as a pejorative gynaecological reference and thus crude term of lazily bandied abuse merely groundwork in preparing itself for its one true and destined application to this glaikit bawbag. With every sentence he was appropriating more and more of Parlabane's evidence as things he'd noticed himself, and if he kept on at this rate, within the hour he'd be recalling sauntering down the hillside puffing on a stogie while all the fools rushed obliviously around his centre of unhurried calm. Parlabane would have put the house on his Y-fronts telling a different story.

'So where are the other UML guys,' Rory was asking Baxter. 'Or are you not introducing us so that we can't ID them too early in your next stunt?'

'There will be no more stunts,' Baxter said with gleefully open dishonesty. 'You have my word. But to answer your question, the villains today weren't UML personnel. Just some locals, blokes from the village down the way. We bung them a few quid, they get to dress up, shoot replica rifles and play soldiers of a Saturday afternoon.'

'They earned their pay today,' Rory said, smiling. 'So did you. A fine performance, Mr Baxter. *The point at which I was in complete control of the day's activities has passed,*' he mimicked. 'If you ever fancy turning your hand to acting, I know a few directors. One question that eludes me, though: You told everybody to leave their mobiles because you obviously didn't want us trying to call the cops, but I was a naughty boy and took mine anyway, until you confiscated it; and by the way, good thing for you it's waterproof. What would you have done if I'd asked you to dial 999?'

'Why didn't you?'

'Dunno, it didn't really occur to me. Panic, I suppose, and I didn't think anybody would be able to get there in time to make any difference. Plus you said there was no signal.'

'There you go, then.'

'Ah, come on, you couldn't rely on that. What would you have said, what was the contingency? Go on, it's over now – or might I be anticipating something in tomorrow's scenario?'

'Not at all. Try calling the cops now. There's a signal here.'

Rory whipped out his ostentatiously tiny M-Kard mobile and snapped it into operation with affected nonchalance, hopelessly failing to disguise the delighted nine-year-old who thought the gadget made him the coolest kid in base-ball boots. The nonchalance turned quickly to consternation and brow-furrowed scrutiny as the device failed to come to life.

'Works better with the SIM card in,' Baxter said.

Rory nodded, remembering. 'At the tunnel.'

'No, while you were in the gym this morning, actually. Courtesy of the light-fingered Francis.'

'Sneaky bastard. So do I get it back now, or . . .?'

'Oh sure, don't worry. It's your property and we're not school prefects. You're the paying customers, after all, or would be, theoretically. Francis has them planked some-where safe. I'll get him to sort you out in a minute.'

'Them?'

'He removed everybody's. It was to add that moment of the-car-won't-start panic if anyone did manage to sneak a phone out on to the hike. Not that anybody seems to have noticed. Francis,' he called theatrically, to attract everyone's attention. 'When you've got a moment, could you retrieve and distribute our valued guests' SIM cards?'

This provoked widespread patting of pockets and con-firmatory pressing of keys, Joanna and Liz distinct in

221

mentioning that they'd each discovered the faults that morning but assumed their phones to be on the blink, and useless here besides.

Baxter produced his own mobile and displayed the inactive screen for Rory's benefit. 'In case you assumed your guide had one and demanded he dial 999 with it when yours failed.'

'But what if there'd been a genuine emergency?'

'I had mine,' said Campbell. 'And despite appearances, I was never very far away, believe me.'

Baxter followed Campbell to the door, the pair of them flagrantly conspiratorial in their quiet chat, clearly lapping up the curiosity.

'Well, they didn't get *my* SIM card,' Grieg was telling anyone in earshot, 'because I left my phone back in the car.' He announced this with inexplicable pride, as though it would be interpreted as a demonstration of uncanny prescience in addition to his already established ice-cool composure, rather than merely proof that he was a gormless twat who'd forgotten to lift his mobile from the hands-free dock.

With his colleague gone, Baxter returned to the bar and signalled to Parlabane to join him near the door. He grabbed a handful of peanuts and obliged, dangling a bottle of Beck's between two fingers.

'I just wanted to say,' Baxter began quietly, 'I've heard all the accounts of the day and I appreciate your cooperation in keeping your mouth shut when you could have easily blown the gaff.'

'I'd like my not mentioning the SIM cards over breakfast this morning taken into consideration too. Does it get me a room upgrade?'

'Only if you don't mind sharing a four-poster with Sir Lachlan,' Baxter replied, nodding towards the loudly be-tartaned patron who was tonight cheerfully and energetically

222

manning the bar. 'His is the only one bigger than the guest accommodations.'

'Nah. If that's what he's wearing, I seriously don't want to see the bedclothes. And I don't want to *think* about the pyjamas.'

'Seriously,' Baxter resumed. 'I know you don't owe us anything and I can't even ask that you be fair in what you write, but I do ask, humbly, that you don't give away our secrets. We'll be asking everybody to be circumspect, but you're the one in a position to really spoil the surprise. I mean, we've got other tricks up our sleeves for when that one's worn thin, but if you give away the principle . . .'

Parlabane shook his head. 'It's one thing being the smart-arsed critic who takes the piss out of a movie he didn't like: it's all about opinions and that's his prerogative. But the type who gives away the ending is a fascist, because he wants to put you off going so you won't *have* an opinion.'

'I think we understand each other.'

'Well, not entirely. A bottle of Cragganmore would pretty much guarantee nothing inadvertently slips out when I'm at the keyboard writing the final draft.'

'Jack Parlabane in bribery and corruption shocker. Now that would be a headline.'

'I only expose the ones who don't pay me off.'

A couple more rounds were downed throughout the throng, dispatched with a surprisingly unflustered efficiency by Sir Lachlan, who Parlabane would have to admit had struck him initially as of the bumbling aristo genus, choco-late-teapot subspecies. Last night it had been a champagne-or-orange-juice, help-yourself affair, down possibly to a lack of staff, as suggested by the flustered and rarely sighted waitresses, in likely combination with UML's wise reluc-tance to allow this drouthy shower unfettered access to the single malts. Tonight, however, though the waitresses were all but invisible, the bar was in full service, capably staffed

223

by a man whose title, Parlabane appreciated, was unlikely to have been conferred in recognition of pouring drinks. Not that a knighthood was in any way intrinsic proof of being much cop at anything, given that if your aristo family successfully retained its wealth throughout your lifetime and you could sit through a civic reception without spitting food at other guests, it was pretty much impossible to avoid getting some kind of honour from the establishment. However, there weren't many aristos comfortable at the sharp end of the service industry, so if Sir Lachlan was being forced to slum it, then he was wearing it well (though the odd fly snifter he was helping himself to was no doubt playing its part in easing his dignity).

With the atmosphere thus augmented, it was a while before people started to notice that the passing of time had not brought the three magic words they'd been waiting for (and increasingly feared never hearing) since finishing their sandwiches at the foot of the spur. Eventually, though, insistent stomachs prompted the checking of watches and the odd baleful glance at the thoroughly looted-looking lazy Susan, now bereft of olives, peanuts and Bombay mix.

'Yes, I must apologise,' Sir Lachlan said, noticing the rising incidence of anxious glances towards the door. 'We've had some problems with staff, and they're running a little short-handed in the kitchen. I'm sure it won't be long now.'

Baxter was looking to the door too, but it seemed that it wasn't just his appetite that was prompting him. Campbell hadn't returned from his SIM-retrieving errand, which presumably hadn't required a round trip of this duration, and with Rory staring expectantly at him every few minutes, M-Kard in hand, his patience was clearly draining faster than any glass in the room. Rory had been fidgeting since he learned of the sabotage, presumably unable to function properly without the assurance of knowing his digital-age thumb was there to be sucked if he needed it.

224

'I'm going to see where the hell he's got to,' Baxter said irritably. 'If they shout for dinner, don't wait for the bugger.'

'We won't,' volleyed several earnest replies.

'You could say it's a matter of taste. They're playing on our values as well as our expectations, particularly our expectations of *them*, in terms of what we deem acceptable.'

It was Kathy who was talking, in between mouthfuls of broccoli soufflé, which looked even less substantial or satisfying than last night's vegetarian option. Liz was the only other herbivore of the group, Parlabane being grateful that there weren't enough of them to merit any divisive ideological confrontations over the issue. Kathy struck him as plausibly tending towards the militant in her vegetarianism as in the rest of her political make-up, but with her biz partner and principal ally numbered among the bloodthirsty, it was unlikely she'd be getting in anyone's face over the issue, unless provoked. He really, really hoped that didn't happen. It had been a long day and he couldn't face another night of pointless, entrenched squabbling, especially over that issue. Having been through tunnels, under water, across rivers, up hills and down slopes, burdened throughout by a weight of wet clothes and the inhumane unpleasantness of squelching socks, he felt he'd earned the right to tuck into a hot meal without morally justifying its content.

In common with the rest of them, he'd no idea what *Icare d'Afrique* was, but by the time it was finally sitting in front of him he'd have eaten a farmer's arse through a hedge, and so wasn't asking any questions. It was coated in beaten egg and parmesan then shallow fried, which to Parlabane made it taste like veal. Fact was, to Parlabane, anything coated in beaten egg and parmesan then shallow fried would taste like veal, including the aforementioned farmer's arse. As such, it was hearty and welcome, but tended a little towards the bland if he was being picky.

Discussion took a while to commence, and not because Campbell wasn't there to play pass-the-conch. Starters were devoured with undignified haste, the etiquette of waiting for all to be served before commencing feeling like a Herculean test of will power, especially with Sir Lachlan alone providing both waiter and sommelier service. Neither of last night's waitresses had put in an appearance, and the sweat on their host's brow belied the calm smile he presented while ferrying plates from kitchen to table.

'I can only apologise again,' he said sincerely, noticing the ravenous looks that greeted his eventual appearance with the first of the main courses. 'Our staffing crisis has actually worsened since you had your aperitifs. One of our wait-resses is helping the chef and the other one has chosen a singularly inopportune moment to disappear on us.'

'Maybe she's been kidnapped by Baxter and Campbell, wherever they've got to,' Rory suggested. 'And our next mission is to rescue the help so that we get dessert before midnight.'

It was this, together with the relief of rapidly filling bellies, that finally sparked a conversation more elaborate than a few grunts in acknowledgement of the fare. Even these had been offered grudgingly in some quarters because 'yes, it's lovely' used up a good second and a half that could other-wise be spent shovelling food into their mouths. The onset of a degree of contentment and hence relaxation was conducive to a more detached discussion of what they had experienced earlier in the day, the pre-prandial reconstruc-tions having provided a less insightful commentary than even Jonathan Pearce could have offered. Nor did it hurt that their deliberations were conducted in the absence of Grieg, who, having finished his main course, had borrowed the minibus keys from Toby in order to retrieve his mobile from across the river where they'd left their cars.

'We assumed certain givens,' Emily continued, a forkful

of *Icare d'Afrique* dancing in her right hand. 'And that's what predisposed us to believing the scenario. I assumed, for instance, that UML wouldn't countenance a situation in which panic might lead to injury, such as having us all running for our lives down a steep hill. It was the belief in something as simple as that which made me think things must be outwith UML's control.'

'What if we had injured ourselves?' Joanna asked. 'A twisted ankle or a broken wrist wouldn't have been a million-to-one shot out there.'

'We all signed waivers,' Liz reminded her. 'We assumed it was to cover activities like yesterday's or the tunnel thing, but we didn't really do anything more risky or strenuous on the chase. It went through my mind, like it must have gone through everyone's at first, that it couldn't be for real. Personally, the reason I bought into it was that I couldn't believe they would do something that people might say amounted to a sick joke. From a corporate point of view, I thought they'd be on very dodgy ground. It worked, though. I can't see many people coming on this weekend then taking the huff and complaining about it, even if they did think it was in poor taste at the time. The end justified the means.'

'Exactly,' agreed Emily. 'Taste was how they messed with our heads. We assume certain givens, so if the test you're facing – such as the tunnel – is still comfortably PC in terms of those assumed values, there's a psychological safety net. Something happens outwith those values and you're genuinely scared because you assume UML wouldn't cross those lines.'

'Disneyland for adults,' Liz agreed. 'Like a rollercoaster, it's the illusion of a loss of control that makes it exciting. Except at Disneyland, you know it's an illusion. We didn't out there today.'

'Jeez,' Rory said, chuckling. 'That's a head-job, isn't it? And it means that pretty much anything goes from now on.

Because given what we already know – and what they know we know – they'll really have to push the envelope if they're going to scare us again.'

'I'm not sure they would try,' countered Liz. 'For that very reason. No matter what stunts they might pull, everybody knows now that it's part of the "experience". The novelty was in blurring what we believed was under their control. You can't do that twice.'

'Fair point,' Rory conceded. 'But it doesn't mean now that the game is afoot they won't be trying to put the wind up us *some* way. I mean, doesn't anyone else think it's ominous that both Baxter and Campbell are absent right now?'

There was both wicked and nervous laughter from around the table, the sort of mixed anticipation you heard just before the aforementioned rollercoaster reached the downturn.

'And those SIM cards never came back, did they?' Rory continued, clearly relishing the ramifications. Rory was the loud guy in the car behind you on the rollercoaster, who held his arms up while yours gripped the bar, and bellowed his exhilaration throughout. Even an extended period of separation from a functioning mobile failed to dampen his excitement.

Joanna gave it a go, though. 'Nah, too late tonight. They'll be off preparing tomorrow's tricks or something. We've all had a knackering day. If we were paying corporate clients, we'd be expecting a degree of pampering to balance the action. Nobody's going to recommend the UML experience if it involves sleep-deprivation, are they?'

'Depends whether the end justifies the means,' Emily reminded her. 'What are you doing but making more assumptions about where the comfort zone begins and ends?'

'My comfort zone begins in my bed,' Joanna replied. 'And it'll take more than kid-on soldiers to keep me from it tonight.'

'It'll take whatever UML decides, if that's their agenda,'

Rory argued. 'We can take nothing for granted. The hotel staff could be in on it too, for all we know. Disappearing waitresses, what's that about? Even the so-called staff shortage and slow service could be part of the wind-up. We're assuming the hotel wouldn't intentionally be running a slow service with Sir Heedrum Hodrum roped in to pour the drinks, but how do we know for sure?'

'It's insane,' Emily said, laughing. 'Brilliantly insane. We can't rely on the veracity of anything here, even each other. How do we know everyone at this table is really who they say, or that one or more of us isn't a UML plant?'

'Oh no, please, make this stop,' Parlabane appealed. 'I feel an Escheresque nightmare coming on.' He was therefore enormously grateful for the interruption of Sir Lachlan and – belatedly proving they weren't extinct – a waitress, come to clear away the main-course dishes.

'Once again, apologies for the amateurish service,' Sir Lachlan said. 'And by that, of course, I mean myself. Alison here is a shining professional. Believe me, she and our chef Gerard have worked miracles in the kitchen tonight.'

'And before any of you panic,' the waitress added, 'I'd just like to say that me escaping from the kitchen doesn't mean there's no dessert. It's all in hand.'

The girl looked post-flustered, her face flushed and her hair a little damp from the heat, but with a certain glow about her from knowing the hard part was over. She and Sir Lachlan set about gathering the mostly empty plates, asking everyone in turn how they found their meals and being answered in all but one instance by the usual politely appreciative platitudes. The exception was Max, who had a left a small chunk of his meat at the edge of his plate.

'It was quite unlike anything I've had before,' he said. 'But would you pardon my ignorance – all our collective ignorance, I believe – and put us out of our misery as to what African *Icare* actually is?'

229

Sir Lachlan took an exaggeratedly deferential step back to allow Alison to answer. She blushed a little at being put under the spotlight, smiling nervously and clearing her throat before she answered.

'Ostrich.'

Parlabane took it to be a sign of Britain's recently embraced gourmet ethic that nobody reacted with any display of distaste at this revelation; not that this was an accurate indicator of their true feelings. In these days of food being the new sex, its countless magazines the equivalent porn, nobody wanted to be the food-prude Mary Whitehouse.

'Ah, I'd never have guessed,' Max admitted. 'It seemed closer to red meat than fowl, but I was put off track by the markings. I didn't know they branded them like cattle.'

The waitress looked confused. Max lifted his knife and uncovered the uneaten piece of meat. 'It still had a bit of skin on it, which I found a little tough so I left it.'

The girl looked at the plate for a moment, her eyes focused in steady scrutiny before widening as the colour drained visibly from her face. She let the pile of plates she was holding drop the couple of inches to the table with a loud clatter, and stumbled against Vale's chair. He reacted with those inhuman reflexes of his, vacating his seat and spinning it to catch her falling weight in one flawless movement.

Rory and Emily exchanged knowing looks, the pair of them having been conspicuously pleased with each other's company all evening and acting like the self-styled naughtiest kids in the class.

'Give her space,' Vale said, ushering Max and Toby away from their chairs.

'What is it, Alison?' her boss asked.

'It's nothing. I just got a bit light-headed. I'm okay now, honestly.'

She waved away all ministrations and lifted the plates

again, exiting the room in a hurry. Sir Lachlan followed, clearly still concerned despite her insistences.

'Poor girl must be exhausted,' he muttered.

With staff levels already at critical, it wouldn't look too impressive to the guests or the HSE if those remaining started dropping from overwork.

'What was that about?' asked Joanna.

'She didn't like the cattle-mark thingy,' Max explained.

'Well, it's maybe just my natural meat-revulsion talking,' Kathy mused, 'but I thought the mark looked more like a tattoo.'

'Oh don't,' said Joanna, wincing.

'Fuck off,' laughed Emily.

'You know, it did a little,' agreed Liz conspiratorially.

Fucking vegetarians, Parlabane thought. If they couldn't make you feel guilty for eating meat, they'd try to put you off it. It was good humoured, but with no lack of malice. They knew that if food was the new sex, then there had to be somewhere even the most liberal and adventurous drew the line, and what they were suggesting constituted the equivalent of incest.

The others weren't taking the bait, but Max, the mark having been on his meat, looked decidedly queasy. 'The waitress was certainly spooked by it,' he said. 'And she got it out of here in a hurry.'

Rory laughed approvingly and began clapping his hands. 'Very good. I thought her wee funny turn looked pretty staged, but you've got to hand it to them. We said they'd have to push the envelope, and *that* is definitely pushing the envelope.'

'It's disgusting, is what it is,' said Joanna. 'What on earth would be the point of making us think we've been eating . . . you know? Especially as they know we're on to them and aren't likely to believe it.'

'It's like a knowing wink, if you ask me,' said Rory.

'Playing with our taste and assumptions again, setting the scene with something a bit nasty, so we won't have a clue what to expect next – other than the fact that it's liable to be pretty macabre if this is the overture. Ah, and note again that neither Baxter nor Campbell are here to be grilled.'

'Oh, are we eating them too?' asked Liz dryly.

Rory laughed, quite delighted by Max and Joanna's discomfiture. 'You will taste *man* flesh,' he boomed, in imitation of Christopher Lee in *The Fellowship of the Ring*.

Parlabane's constitution wasn't easily disturbed, and certainly not by mere imagination, but he knew it might be a while before any more farmers' arses featured on his metaphorical menu.

Joanna got up from the table, drawing her eyes off Rory with undisguised loathing. 'I'm sorry, everybody, but this isn't my idea of a joke. I'm going to bed.'

'What about puds?' asked Liz.

'Do you think I've any appetite after that?' she retorted accusingly.

Liz made a less then penitent Oops! expression once Joanna's eyes were averted, a few shared smirks defying the awkwardness of the moment.

'I'm off too,' said Max, with restrained but discernible indignation. 'Not to bed, but you'll forgive me if I don't want to hang around the dining table. I'll be in the snooker room later if anyone fancies a game,' he added, trailing a late olive branch.

'Yeah, we'll have a few frames,' Rory called after him. 'Just as soon as we've finished our chilled monkey-brain desserts.'

The Mark of a Man

'Are you sure you're all right?' Sir Lachlan was asking, hirpling along behind Alison as she hurried for the kitchen, its atmosphere of heat and pressure promising a sanctuary of the familiar as her heart thumped. She felt inexplicably cold in the corridor, and needed the embrace of that sometimes stifling warmth like a lost toddler needed a hug from her mummy. She'd never understood what people meant when they said they felt like someone had walked over their grave, until she'd seen that man's dinner plate. It was daft. She didn't believe in any sixth-sense nonsense, but she knew that events and circumstances could conspire – no, coincide – to give the most rational person the shivers, and such a confluence had washed over her in that dining room. Overheated, dehydrated and running on empty, she was well primed to let her imagination off the leash when she glimpsed those leftovers.

'I'm fine,' she told him as he nipped in front and held the door open for her. 'Just gave myself a fright. It's silly. Ger'll laugh, wait and see.'

'Ger'll laugh at what?' the new head chef asked, pouring whisky into individual steel measures for warming prior to combustion atop dessert.

Alison put the pile of plates down on the worktop above the dishwasher, the branded meat on top, surrounded by scraped-away parmesan and uneaten veg. 'That doesn't mean anything to you, does it?' she asked. 'I mean, I've only heard you describe . . .'

Ger's gaze locked upon the plate as though it might rise

233

up and strike if he took his eyes off it. The 'cattle-mark' the guest had referred to was a small logo, blackened on the skin by the heat but still legible. It was in the shape of three interlinked capital Ds.

Sir Lachlan had taken hold of the whisky bottle as soon as Ger put it down, and was poking around in the wrong cupboard for some glasses.

'Well, if you're feeling better, Alison,' Sir Lachlan said, 'I think a wee dram might be in order in recognition of both your efforts, and in recognition particularly of the creative talents of this man here. It won't be the last time you hear this, Gerard, I'm certain, and I'm sure it counts more if it comes from the guests rather than the proprietor, but bugger it, I'd like to heartily propose that we toast the chef.'

Ger looked up at last from the plate, his face a picture of ashen disbelief. It wasn't the reaction Alison was hoping for, and it didn't look very likely that he'd laugh.

'No, you can't,' he said, his voice hollow, throat dry. He gulped, his eyes returning to the uneaten meat.

'Oh, don't be so modest. Why ever not?'

'Because it looks like I've already shallow-fried him.'

'What?'

'The chef. Mathieson. I think that's his tattoo.'

'What the devil are you talking about?' Sir Lachlan asked.

Ger remained still, breathing deeply in a demanding effort to retain calm.

'Mathieson was in a boy band in the late Eighties.'

'A boy band?'

'You know, like a pop group. One-hit wonders. They were called Three-D. This was their logo.'

'Hang on,' Alison interrupted, relief hitting her like a cooling breeze. 'Okay, I get it. Panic over: this was the bastard's revenge. He took the meat then got someone – a mate probably – to turn up at the door and sell us this stuff. *He* marked it with the logo for a sick joke.'

234

Ger shook his head, slowly and solemnly. 'I didn't even know he had a tattoo, so how could he assume anyone would recognise it? Fair enough, I wound him up yesterday by playing his song, but he'd no way of knowing I'd seen their logo or would remember what it looked like.'

'Wait a minute,' Sir Lachlan said, screwing up his eyes in confused consternation. 'Are you saying . . . You're *not* saying . . .'

'That we've just cooked the fuckin' chef, yes.'

'So how come you didn't spot this tattoo when you were preparing the meat? How come it only came to light on a dinner plate?'

'I don't know. I washed the meat and coated it. Yes, I'd have expected to notice something like that, but . . .'

'But what, man?'

'A few pieces had a membrane above the meat. Tattoos can penetrate well beneath the top layers of the dermis. Underneath, the marking would be faint, but would show up if . . .' Ger swallowed. 'Would show up if heated.'

'No,' said Sir Lachlan. 'I don't . . . I mean, I can't . . . You can't . . . No. Where did it come from, for God's sake? No, I simply don't believe it. There must be a more reasonable explanation.'

'Look. A man turned up at the back door and sold us some unidentified meat that he claimed was ostrich. I bought it because we were desperate, and we were desperate because our chef got binned and cleared oot the fridge. A piece of skin on that meat bears a mark with, shall we say, a significance regardin' the personal history of our departed head chef. Those are the facts. If you can combine them to produce a conclusion that *doesnae* involve me offering Long Pig as my debut dish, I'd be delighted to hear it.'

Sir Lachlan gripped the whisky bottle by the neck and put it to his lips, swigging it back straight. 'God almighty, how the hell could this have happened?' he asked no-one in particular. 'It just can't be true. After everything that's gone on here and everything I've worked to overcome, I refuse to believe that when we finally look like turning the corner, we feed the bloody head chef to our guests as an entrée.' He took another swig and looked imploringly at his employees. 'I mean, what the bloody hell else can go wrong here? Is one of the guests going to reveal himself as an Egon Ronay researcher? "Charming location, atmospheric establishment, menu ideal for South American plane-crash survivors. Avoid March as hotel is booked out by the annual Sawney Bean ancestral family gathering."'

Alison took the bottle from him and placed it down away from his grasp.

'With respect, sir, I don't think the hotel's reputation is the issue right now.'

'She's right,' agreed Ger. 'What we fed the guests is a secondary consideration. The primary one is how it got to the kitchen. If this is how it looks, then Mathieson was murdered here today; in fact, murdered, skinned, butchered and sold back to his place of erstwhile employment within a couple of hours of leaving.'

'By someone whose face Ger and I have both seen,' Alison remembered with a chill. 'Oh, God, he even had bloodstains on his boots. I thought he was a poacher. What kind of sick bastard would butcher somebody and sell him for meat? And what kind of nutter would do it at the expense of letting us see his face? We could identify him.'

'The kind of nutter who doesn't expect you to tell anybody,' Ger said, quiet and cold.

'Why the hell wouldn't we . . .' Her words tailed off, the answer sinking in before she could finish her question.

After-Dinner Games

Vale appropriated the role of sommelier after what was unanimously deemed to be an irredeemable lapse in service, opening and distributing the bottle of Shiraz that had lain on the sideboard since Sir Lachlan's hurried departure. He had a lithe elegance about him as he moved around the table filling glasses, a mercurial alertness about his features, neither of these properties tallying with Emily's notions of long-serving civil-service desk-jockeys. Perhaps his late career-change to photography had truly liberated the guy's spirit. She would like to think so.

'I don't think Sir Lachlan will mind,' Vale assured them. 'Though we'd probably best lay off making free with the optics in the lounge.'

'At least for another half-hour,' added Rory.

There were four of them remaining around the table, following a slew of exits in the wake of Joanna and Max. Emily wasn't sure whether it was the wine, the fatigue or merely the perspective afforded by having been briefly in fear for her life earlier on, but she couldn't motivate herself to empathise with Joanna's indignation nor feel any disapproval of those making light of her and Max's discomfiture. Perhaps, just perhaps, with her PR hat definitely lying crumpled and discarded in a corner somewhere and her guilt-driven leftist reflexes dampened by last night's rancour, she was learning to lighten up a little.

Kathy and Liz had both expressed their regret at opting to forego dessert, but cited a combination of exhaustion and grave doubt as to whether they'd be seeing it before dawn,

237

given the speed of service thus far. The ever-conciliatory Toby had gone off to join Max in his mooted game of snooker, an act of amelioration perhaps intended to prevent the latter from thinking he'd painted himself into a huffy corner. Rory had made his own gesture of solidarity by suggesting that Toby take the open bottle from the table plus a couple of glasses, though he might not have been so generous had he known their host wouldn't be back to replace it.

They heard the distinctive slam of the heavy front doors from down the corridor.

'Sounds like Grieg's back,' Rory observed.

'Could be Baxter,' Emily suggested.

'Nah. Him and Campbell are hiding in a cupboard some-where, waiting for us to go and investigate. Major tactical misjudgement, if you ask me. After dinner, a few bevs and a hard day's yomping in yellow, they've seriously miscal-culated if they think we can be arsed playing hide and seek. Actually, maybe it's Sardines they're playing, and that explains why all the bloody staff have disappeared.'

But Rory was wrong. It was Baxter who emerged from the corridor, hair and clothes damp from the rain.

'Campbell show up?' he asked, a little breathless from running.

'No, not that we're aware,' Parlabane replied.

'Shit.'

'Where have you been?' Emily inquired. 'You've been ages. You missed dinner, and that's saying something, the time it took.'

'Sorry. What did you have?' he asked distractedly, as though from automatic politeness.

'*Man* flesh,' boomed Rory, looking around for a response, but nobody was laughing. Baxter's face, in conjunction with the duration of his absence, suggested all was not well.

'Look, I'm sorry to be a party-pooper, but I think we might have a wee problem.' His voice was low and a little too

238

controlled, hinting at great efforts to constrain a less sober delivery. The phrase 'wee problem' sounded anything but.

'What's up?' Parlabane asked.

'More a matter of what's down. As in the bridge.'

'The bridge? Down how?'

'Down as in one end is bent and mangled and the other is dangling into the ravine. You remember that clap of thunder earlier? Well, I don't think that's what it was.'

'You've just come from there?' Parlabane asked. 'On foot?'

'Yeah. The road's longer than it seems because of the loops, but on foot you can take a few short cuts. I went out that way looking for Francis. We had something planned for tomorrow involving a hidden shelter in the woods. I'll come clean, he wasn't going to retrieve the SIM cards – he was going to hide them there and tell you all they'd gone missing. Then we were all going to "discover" them tomorrow, big Abracadabra moment. But there was no sign of him anywhere. I think something might be going very wrong.'

'Nah, nice try, Donald, but we're not biting,' said Rory. 'We're too tired. Have a seat. There's still some wine left.'

'Rory, this is not part of the UML Experience, all right? My colleague is missing and I need you all to be serious for a minute. The fucking bridge is down. The *bridge*! You know, the thing connecting this place with the only road out of here? It's wrecked. Do you think our budget stretches to shit like that? It certainly wouldn't stretch to repairing it.'

'Whereas fibs and porkies cost nothing,' said Parlabane. 'Why don't you take a seat and wait for Grieg. He'll be able to verify things one way or the other, unless he's driven the minibus into the ravine, of which he strikes me as being entirely capable.'

'The fucking minibus is right outside,' Baxter stated angrily. 'He hasn't driven it anywhere.'

'It's what?'

'It's at the front door, where it's been since this afternoon. Go and look, for God's sake. Jesus Christ, we've got a serious situation on our hands and I'm stuck in some kind of boy-who-cried-wolf nightmare.'

'So where's Grieg?' Emily asked, checking her watch and doing some disturbing arithmetic regarding the time since Joanna's singularly gormless companion had left.

'Having a beer somewhere with Campbell and all the missing staff members who're in on this nonsense,' scoffed Rory.

'Missing staff?' asked Baxter.

'One of the waitresses is AWOL, according to Sir Lachlan,' said Parlabane. 'And we've not seen him or any other staff for a wee while either.'

'Does this not tell you anything?' Baxter challenged Rory. 'I mean, you aren't noticing a pattern here at all?'

Rory stood up and handed Baxter a glass of wine, which he initially made to bat away, but thought better of it and downed the lot like it was water. If this was merely his latest in-character performance, then it was one Stanislavsky would have approved of.

'Look, there's a simple way to get to the bottom of this,' Rory said. 'We phone the cops, tell them about the bridge. If you're shitting us, you won't allow that to happen, like earlier today. Sorry if having your bluff called buggers up your plans, but better the flaws get ironed out during this dry run, eh?'

'Calling the police sounds like a very good idea,' Baxter replied. 'There's a phone on the wall behind you. Do it now, because the sooner you appreciate the gravity of this situation, the sooner we can do something about it.'

Rory turned around and lifted the slim, black handset hugging the wall next to the doorframe. 'What do I dial for an outside line?' he asked.

'Nine,' said Baxter.

Rory hit nine and held the handset to his ear, then pressed the cradle up and down before hitting nine again.

'No outside line. Very funny. Now what do I really dial?'

'You really dial nine,' Emily said, having made a call from her room that morning.

Baxter tried to grab the handset from Rory, but he was fobbed off as Rory dialled zero instead. They all heard a phone ring down the hall at reception.

'Maybe it's just this extension,' Rory suggested, hanging up and heading out into the corridor. They all followed, looks being traded as they left the table and moved for the door. Parlabane and Vale, she had already observed, were schooled in an unspoken communication that suggested they knew each other from more than just a few shared assignments. They were both checking Baxter for the sincerity of his expression, he expectantly examining theirs for signs that they believed him. He looked Emily fully in the eye for perhaps the first time since that awkward, pseudo-clandestine reunion by the hill, and she saw genuine, restless anxiety, an appeal that said: 'You know me and I need your help.' It wasn't a card he'd ever play if his game was a bluff.

Rory was holding out one of the receivers from the phones on the reception desk, a blank expression on his face. He was less cocky but he wasn't ready to admit he was worried yet.

'It's dead as well.'

'The switchboard's blank,' observed Vale.

Parlabane hopped behind the desk and gripped the mouse on the desktop PC, clearing the screen-saver. Its monitor displayed a dial-up networking dialogue box informing the user: Unable to establish connection. 'The phones really are dead,' he confirmed. 'Internet access, everything.'

'This proves nothing,' Rory insisted. 'In fact, what did I just say? If you're shitting us, you won't allow me to phone.

241

Voila, I can't. Same as earlier, you'd already disabled the phones. Back then it was the SIMs, now it's the landlines.'

Baxter put his hands to either side of his head in frustration.

'Take the fucking minibus, then,' he said. 'Check it out for yourself. I just hope you don't run into whoever out there is responsible for demolishing the only direct means of escape.'

'Check it out for ourselves? Great idea, like phoning was a great idea. Except that Grieg's got the keys to the minibus and he's conveniently out of the picture. Remember what Toby said? You are an unreliable source of information. You have a vested interest in things appearing to be beyond your control. Christ, I wish I'd gone to my bed like the others, I'd be missing all this shit.'

'Okay, how's this for control?' Baxter asked, holding up a set of keys.

'You've got a spare?'

'Of course I've got a spare. You don't think I'd entrust a spanner like Francis with the only set?'

Rory took them. 'Let's go for a ride.'

'We've got to warn the others,' Baxter entreated.

'No, no, you're coming along where we can keep our eyes on you. And when we get back, the Milky Bars are on you.'

'Fifty-year-old Springbank,' Baxter said as Rory pulled open one of the front doors.

'Eh?'

'Fifty-year-old Springbank. It's in a locked cabinet behind the bar. If it turns out I'm lying, it's yours.'

'And what's my stake if you're not?'

'The least of your worries.'

Rory trotted out into the wet night and hopped into the minibus driver's seat, Baxter clambering into the row behind him. Vale, Parlabane and Emily remained beneath the stone pagoda that extended from the front wall above the storm doors, deliberating the necessity and wisdom of them all taking the trip.

'Do you reckon this is straight up?' Emily asked. 'Or is us going off on a night-time trek in the minibus actually part of Baxter's plan? He seems genuinely anxious to me.'

'See above, re Escheresque nightmare,' Parlabane replied. 'No point thinking about it. That way madness lies.'

'I'm staying put,' said Vale, resting his back against one of the two stone pillars that supported the stone canopy. 'If somebody has dynamited the bridge, then driving down a road with no exit strikes me as extremely foolish. And if all is well, it's a waste of time. My instincts are towards the latter. Like this afternoon, why would some anonymous ne'er-do-wells just happen to be targeting our merry little group?'

To Emily's surprise, Rory climbed back out of the minibus again and walked around to its front.

'Engine's dead,' he reported. 'Conveniently. Or inconveniently, if you believe we're under threat from evil forces. I'll just reconnect the sparkplug or whatever neatly reversible damage Donald here got up to while we were eating.'

He popped open the bonnet, Baxter standing at his back.

'Shit,' Rory gasped.

'Doesn't look too fucking reversible to me,' Baxter observed bitterly.

Emily stepped out into the rain, while Parlabane pulled the front doors wide open to shed more light on the minibus. There wasn't a cable left uncut, and the light spilling out of the doorway illuminated a black patch of fluid oozing from beneath the vehicle, the rainwater nudging the slick into tributaries and rivulets but unable to wash it fully away. Vale walked across the monobloc to the Range Rover Emily assumed to belong to Sir Lachlan. He knelt down next to the vehicle and patted the underside as well as the ground next to it.

243

'Brake line has been cut,' he reported. Vale walked briskly to the VW Golf a little further along the concourse and repeated the drill. 'This one too. Can I suggest we get inside? I might be getting a little too caught up in the spirit of the UML Experience, but I do rather think we might be in some danger.'

Parlabane held open the door as they filed quickly inside; all but Rory, who ambled at the back in a deliberate demonstration of ongoing scepticism.

'Yeah, yeah,' he said. 'So the staff cars have been tampered with. UML wouldn't cross that line, would they? Except that the whole hotel is in UML's pocket for the duration of this weekend. Look at yourselves. What are we doing right now that we didn't do already today? Running around in a panic thinking something scary's going on. Donald here even mentioned what he called "that car-won't-start moment" to me earlier.'

'"Only the true messiah would deny it",' quoted Baxter.

'Eh?'

'Meaning there comes a point where you have to listen to what you're actually being told as opposed to what you want to believe. Do you know what sub-dom is, Rory?'

'Yeah. It's the politically correct term for S&M. Is that what we're playing tonight?'

'In sub-dom sex, the partners establish a codeword between themselves so that if the sub wants the dom to lay off, he or she'll know it's for real – as opposed to all the "no, no, please stop I beg you" stuff that gets both their rocks off. I realise I'm trapped in this cry-wolf shit of my own making, but will you please, please, please listen to me when I say that if we *had* established a codeword, then right now I would be screaming it at the top of my fucking lungs. This is not a joke, it's not a stunt and it's not a fucking team-building exercise.'

Rory shrugged.

'Yeah, but you would say that.'

Baxter lunged at Rory, Vale and Parlabane diving to intervene before an event elsewhere served as sufficient distraction to cool their passions. The sound of a seven-foot window being panned in can have that effect.

'What the fuck was that?' asked Rory.

'Came from down the hall,' Vale said. 'Sounded like our little private dining room.'

They ventured forward cautiously, the need to know pushing them on against the resistance of what they might find out. Rory took the lead, bolstered by scepticism more than bravery. Vale gestured to Emily to stay back, but she only complied as much as remaining a few paces behind. She was equally compelled by the desire to know what was really going on as by an outright reluctance to be standing near the front doors on her own.

Rory reached the open doorway first, followed by Parlabane and Baxter a long second later.

A door swung open further down the corridor, sparking a new wave of minor myocardial distress before Sir Lachlan, the waitress and the chef emerged into view. For three people out of the loop on recent developments, they looked disproportionately concerned about investigating a sound of breaking glass.

'It's Grieg,' Parlabane reported, while Rory stood and stared, gaping like a goldfish on Quaaludes.

Emily swallowed, feeling a dryness in her throat as she made to speak. 'How is he?' she managed to ask, though she feared they all knew the answer.

'Shorter,' said Parlabane.

Emily made to move forward but Parlabane blocked her path. 'You don't want to see this,' he told her.

'Now, Rory, you're the expert,' Baxter stated acidly. 'So tell us, do you reckon that's an official UML mock-up headless corpse, or what?'

The remark at least shook Rory from his catatonia. His eyes lost their glazed stare and instead focused disbelievingly upon Baxter, like he was blaming him for the reality that had come literally crashing down. If so, he was only shooting the messenger.

'That is the single most revolting thing I've ever seen,' Rory observed, his words flowing slow and deep.

'I'd be surprised if it retains that distinction over the next few hours,' Parlabane predicted.

'We're in a lot of trouble,' said Rory, speaking barely above a whisper.

'*Oh* yeah,' confirmed the hack.

Sunday, October 27, 2002

Much to Digest

Parlabane stepped aside to let Sir Lachlan and the chef look for themselves. The girl wisely declined, and didn't look like she needed any such bludgeoning visual cues in order to appreciate the gravity of the situation. All three of them, in fact, had appeared to be already fearing the worst before they had any idea of what was lying front-down (he couldn't accurately say 'face-down') on the dining table.

'I'm with your man Rory,' said the chef. 'That's the most mingin' thing I've ever seen as well.'

Parlabane suspected that the sight was not without competition in the chef's experience. He was a sinewy-looking hardcase with facial scarring unlikely to have resulted from overuse of the same Bic disposable, and upon first glance Parlabane was fantasising about the guy kicking Gary Rhodes's spiky little head in.

'We need to call the police,' Sir Lachlan said.

'Your phones are out,' Vale told him.

'Well, one of you must have a mobile.'

'S'awright, I've got mine,' said the chef. 'It's in my jacket, hangin' up.' He disappeared to the kitchen and emerged a few seconds later with a depressing expression of concern as it failed to respond. 'What the fuck?'

'SIM card's gone,' said Rory. 'Ours too.'

'How could it have . . . Fucking Mathieson,' he said, answering his own question. Wrongly, Parlabane would guess.

'Who's Mathieson?' Vale asked.

'Ex-head chef,' Sir Lachlan said. 'He was dismissed today. Ger here took over his duties.'

249

'Dismissed?' asked Baxter. 'Just like that? What for?'

'Does it matter?'

'Well, I'd bloody well say so if it could explain anything that's happening around here tonight. How was his mental state, would you say?'

'It doesn't matter,' insisted the chef, weighing in on his boss's behalf.

'If he's a nutter and he's gone postal, I'd say—'

'It doesn't matter,' Ger repeated, with a certainty that Parlabane didn't fancy one bit. 'He left in the huff and he thieved all the meat en route, but he hasnae "gone postal" and he's no' responsible for that poor bugger on the dining-room table.'

'How do you know?'

Ger sighed. He, Sir Lachlan and the girl, Alison, traded looks.

'One moment, Gerard,' Sir Lachlan said, before stepping into the dining room. He returned a few moments later carrying the brass ice-bucket that had earlier been chilling Liz and Kathy's Chardonnay. 'Okay, go ahead,' he instructed, emptying the melting ice on to the carpet.

It was another Kodak moment, truly: Rory and Emily engaged in Freestyle Synchronised Boak, each miraculously getting their heads clear of the receptacle between heaves to allow the other a shot. Sir Lachlan stood between them, holding the cooler on his outstretched palms like he was doling out the salver of Ferrero Rocher. *Wiz zis spew-bucket you are really spoiling us.*

Parlabane closed his eyes for a moment, waiting for – and in truth expecting – nature to take its course. It didn't, but that wasn't to say it wouldn't any time soon. He felt saliva rising around his gums and tongue, as though the cursed meat was still in his mouth, but then that was always the sensation after eating something he regretted, no different from a pudding supper without first consuming six pints of Heavy.

250

Vale simply shook his head. It would take a lot to turn that bastard's stomach, and Parlabane very much doubted the Headless HR Officer would even make the top-ten most revolting things the ex-spook had ever seen.

'How could you be sure?' Parlabane asked Ger.

'A tattoo. It made unmistakably specific reference to a previous career.'

'He didn't used to be a farmer, by any chance?'

'No, he was in a boy band. Why?'

'Nothing.'

They moved back to the reception hall, away from the dining room given what it now contained and what had earlier been consumed there. Emily and Rory sat at the foot of the grand staircase, a Y-shaped affair that split on the first landing and doubled back on itself to reach an overlooking gallery above. Alison and Ger stood leaning against the reception desk with its useless phones, Sir Lachlan to one side of the front doors he'd just locked. Vale stood next to the seated pair, Parlabane opposite, as directed by a private gesture no-one else noticed. Between the two of them they had a view of all possible points of entry, if not much means of defending themselves in the case of incursion, which was where the reassurance of being with Vale broke down. The more you realised he knew what he was doing, the plainer it became that you didn't have a clue.

'So that's two dead and two missing,' Vale summed up, once everyone had regained some approximation of composure.

'Not to mention no way of phoning for help,' Rory added.

'Never mind phoning,' said Ger. 'Let's get the fuck ootta here and we can tell the polis at Auchterbuie.'

'You can't,' Rory informed him. 'All the vehicles have been sabotaged and there's no way of crossing the river anyway because the bridge has been destroyed.' Rory looked at Baxter by way of acknowledgement, or maybe even

251

apology. Baxter was neutral in response. It was no time for I-told-you-so. 'So not only can't we escape or call for help, help would be a long time getting here.'

'How long before anyone's likely to notice the bridge and raise the alarm?' Parlabane asked.

'Julia the housekeeper and the other domestics live in Auchterbuie,' said Alison. 'They're usually in by seven.'

'Shit. So whoever's out there has at least until then to do what they came here for.'

'They?'

'Well, I hardly think this is the work of one person, however deranged,' said Parlabane. 'If it was, he wouldnae be announcing his intentions by lobbing corpses through the window and feeding us *chef parmigiana*. He'd be picking us off one by one with maximum stealth. Besides, what's going on here must have taken planning and coordination. Your average psycho doesn't wake up one morning and say to himself, I think I'll lay lone siege to a Highland mansion tonight.'

'Jack's right,' said Vale. 'We're looking at above-average psychos, plural, but psychos nonetheless. Whoever it is took out transport and communications, then let us know most blatantly that we were under siege. The first part demonstrates tactical efficiency, which is worrying, but it's the second part that's really bothering me.'

'How so?' asked Rory.

'The second part is a luxury afforded by the first. They know we can't go anywhere, so they're willingly giving up the element of surprise, giving us a chance to dig in.'

'And why's that scarier than them just coming in and killing us all without warning?'

'Because, one, it suggests they're confident nothing we do will make a difference, but more terrifyingly, two, it means they *want* resistance. They're not here to shoot fish in a barrel. These bastards want some sport.'

'Why don't we kill our*selves* then,' Parlabane suggested. 'That would fucking show them.'

'Yes, thank you for that, Jack. Always good to know you can be relied upon for constructive suggestions.'

'Sport?' Emily asked, as disgusted as she was incredulous. 'Are you serious?'

'I'm not saying it's the purpose of the exercise, just a by-product. The purpose of the exercise can be seen on the dining-room table.'

'But why?' she asked, then turned to look at Parlabane, who didn't believe he was being paranoid in thinking there was a hint of accusation about it.

'Jesus, why is it that whenever there's homicidal psychopaths on the loose, people automatically assume it must have something to do with me?'

'I'm sorry, I wasn't . . .'

'It could be as much to do with the place,' suggested Alison quietly, eyeing Sir Lachlan with what looked like apology.

'This place?' Emily asked.

'It's been a nutter magnet for centuries.'

'Alison,' Sir Lachlan protested.

'I'm sorry, sir, but there's things these people ought to know. Even the ancient names for the area refer to blood-letting. It's been host to massacres, human sacrifices, summary executions and occult rites.'

'To say nothing of very dodgy Seventies prog-rock,' Ger added. 'Stormcrow.'

'Stormcrow?' asked Parlabane. 'That was *this* place? Jeez, it really has witnessed some atrocities. And Magnus Will-craft, then, too? The Crowley wannabe?'

'That's right,' Alison said.

'It doesn't mean there's any kind of bloody—' Sir Lachlan began explosively, then bit his lip and swallowed, calming himself. 'There's no curse,' he said, almost in a whisper. 'And I don't believe in such things.'

253

'Me neither,' Alison told him. 'But there's obviously something that draws headbangers to this place more consistently than it draws tourists. I'm just saying if a bunch of people were to get slaughtered here, it wouldn't be the first time.'

'I don't think history's going to help us, however we interpret it,' interrupted Vale. 'First things first. We need to inform the others of the situation – significantly poor Joanna – and get everyone together. Then we need to secure this place to whatever extent we can. Sir Lachlan, what do you have in the way of weapons?'

'I've got two vertical-barrel shotguns, but I can't for the life of me find any ammo. Been looking all afternoon.'

'With respect, sir,' said Ger, 'would it be possible Lady Jane's hidden it? 'Cause if you can think where she might have stashed it . . .'

'My wife?' Sir Lachlan almost laughed. 'You think she wouldn't trust me with a gun. Little you know us, Gerard, little you know us.'

'I don't doubt the ammo's been removed,' said Vale, 'but not by your wife. Any other weapons?'

'Just the swords.'

'What swords?'

'On the walls. The rapiers and the claymores up the . . .' Sir Lachlan took a few steps forward, staring up the staircase. Every head turned to follow his line of sight. The claymores that had hung criss-crossed on the walls around the reception hall were absent, only the single painted targe in the centre remaining. 'How could I not notice they were gone? I've been buzzing about like a blue-arsed fly, serving drinks and waiting tables while some interloper's . . . Oh no.' Sir Lachlan's gaze finally settled on the glass cabinet at head-height on the half-landing, ominously empty. Parlabane vaguely remembered noticing that there was nothing in it when he passed on his way down to dinner, but couldn't recall for sure what had been in it the last time, and assumed whatever it was must be away for cleaning.

'Oh good God,' Sir Lachlan said.

'What was in the case?'

'Rapiers. Kept behind glass because if you leaned on one it would cut you to the bone before you even felt the pain of it breaking the skin. The claymores were the real thing too, but these were what you'd call battle-ready. Stone-sharpened once a year to keep them that way. A family tradition, dating back to times when the McKinleys had to be ready to defend themselves.'

'Is the targe serviceable?' Vale asked.

'Couldn't tell you. It's a reproduction. Wood doesn't keep like steel.'

'Probably why they left it. Still, better than nothing. Do we have knives?' he enquired of Ger, who nodded and took off for the kitchen, Alison following. Hers looked less a gesture of faithful comradeship than a belief that alongside him was the safest place to be. Outside of Vale, Parlabane reckoned she was probably right.

'Jack, you and Sir Lachlan go down to the snooker room.'

'Just Lachlan, please. I hardly think it's the time to observe formalities.'

'As you wish. Donald, you and I will go and break the bad news to Joanna. Emily, Rory, you two go and get Kathy and Elizabeth. Together. Nobody goes anywhere alone. Then we all meet back here ASAP, got it?'

'That Vale chap knows what he's about, doesn't he?' Sir Lachlan said, leading Parlabane down an enclosed stairwell at the south-west end of the main ground-floor corridor. 'Do you know much about him, or have you just met on the weekend?'

'We go way back. It's a long story.'

'Did I hear someone in the bar say he was a photographer?' he asked, with open surprise.

'That's right. Why?'

'He hasn't always been, surely.'

'Not vocationally, no.'

'I don't mean to pry. It's just, I'd have said he has a look of the services about him.'

Parlabane said nothing. No matter what the circumstances, it was Vale's call whether he wanted to divulge anything about his past, and on this trip it would have posed awkward questions had anyone found out that these days he made his money as a security consultant.

'It's something I'm seldom wrong about. I was in the army myself, you see. That's why I laughed at Ger thinking my wife wouldn't trust me with a gun.'

'You saw active service?'

'The Falklands.' He stopped on the stairs and pulled up his shirt and waistcoat to reveal a scarred indentation on the right side of his midriff. 'Argie bullet took the ends off two ribs. I still get the odd . . . well, it's not a twinge, just a sort of memory of the pain. Never felt pain like it. Comes back every time I see that woman,' he added with a bitter smile.

'Long as we're having that *Jaws* moment,' Parlabane said, and pulled up his own shirt to show Sir Lachlan the three-inch scar above his navel. 'Assassin's blade. And I sure felt the pain again when you started talking about those rapiers. This was just a sharpened steel ruler.'

'Goodness, how . . . vulgar. What kind of thug uses something so crude?'

'The kind who isn't allowed access to proper knives.'

'A prisoner? What were you doing there, an interview?'

'Six months.'

Sir Lachlan held open the fire-door at the bottom of the stairs. As soon as he did so, Parlabane could hear the clack of snooker balls being racked and the low bass of a quiet remark followed by laughter. It was a testament to the steadfast structure that no sound from above could penetrate down here, not even the crash of a seven-foot window having a decapitated corpse hurled through it. Such insulation made his perspective right then like looking through a window in time, even if the aperture only looked out upon the world of half an hour ago. They had no idea. Here were two men having a post-prandial game of snooker, probably finishing off that bottle Rory had suggested Toby take with him, a pleasant end to a memorably diverting day. This was how it should have been. Parlabane wished he could join them in their time-bubble, adrift from the main flow of the continuum, but instead he had to pop it, wake them from their dream lest they be murdered in their slumber.

Oh well, at least coming from him there'd be no repeat of Rory and Baxter's back-and-forth shite as to whether it was another elaborate hoax. He was the last person anyone would believe to be complicit in any UML-sponsored shenanigans. The matter of how to broach the issue was nonetheless problematic, to say the least. He'd never forget telling the then greenhorned lawyer, Nicole Carrow, over an otherwise civil cup of tea (and after apologising for necessarily breaking into her flat), that a failed attempt had already been made on her life and that a team of professional killers were outside waiting to get it right next time. It felt worse than telling an entire orphanage of under-sevens that there was no Santa Claus.

Tact and sensitivity were considerations, certainly, but time was of the essence. Hmm. All those who didn't indulge in inadvertent cannibalism this evening take a step forward. Max, Toby, not so fast.

Maybe not.

'You know, this part of the building dates back to the Fifteenth Century,' Sir Lachlan said, tapping a white wall affectionately with his knuckles. 'It's basement level now, because of the way the hall and the gardens have been built up, but there used to be grand rooms with windows to the

257

south. You still get natural light in the games room, though. The landscaper and the architect I hired for the renovation worked wonders, and now there's these marvellous skylights that sit in between flower beds at ground level.'

The older man clearly wished he was back in the world of half an hour ago too, filling in a visitor on the history of this place he was so proud of. The only history Parlabane could think about was Alison's allusions to the multiple acts of slaughter that had taken place here, and whatever essence a vicarious connoisseur of human evil such as Willcraft had sought to distil from it. Like Alison, Parlabane didn't believe in curses, but he didn't much believe in coincidence either.

As they ventured along the corridor, he could see further into the games room. Toby was bent over the table, spotting the black, then gave the frame of reds a shake before lifting the triangle, which was when he noticed the new arrivals. He placed the frame upright behind the reds, presumably a signal for Max not to break yet, and stepped away from the table.

'Jack, Sir Lachlan. Just in time for a game of doubles. You can toss a coin and the loser gets me for a team-mate. How was dessert?'

'Dessert's off,' Parlabane said.

'Is something up?'

Parlabane stood in the doorway, surveying the games room, this sanctuary of innocence, appropriately festooned with playthings. The full-size snooker table dominated, but there was room also to accommodate a tennis table, bookcases and a sideboard bearing chess sets and board games. He'd have expected to see a hooded light suspended above the baize, but instead the room was illuminated by wall-lamps and a few ceiling spots, the ceiling itself being distinguished by the two huge latticed-glass panels Sir Lachlan had modestly described as skylights. With near-midnight darkness above, they appeared merely as black rectangles, and Parlabane reckoned he might not have noticed them at all but for Sir Lachlan having made mention of them and for the fact that a man came crashing through the one above the snooker table just as they were about to enter the room.

Max stepped back in reflex and caught the edge of the tennis table around the top of his thighs, which sent him tumbling backwards upon the blue-painted wood. Toby also managed to trip himself in fright, having been in the process of turning away from the table when his attention was rapidly dragged back there. Tripping over his feet, he landed on his bottom on the floor in a squatting position, looking up at the figure who had landed, upright, on the green baize.

He was dressed in dark grey, streaked-camouflage battle fatigues, heavy boots on his feet, his face an intense snarl of aggression. He looked late thirties, maybe early forties: tall, muscular, fit, formidable. And in either hand he held glinting swords that Parlabane now recognised as having been in the glass cabinet that morning.

'Fuck me,' he gasped.

The man gave a roar in response, and began whirling the swords in his hands with an expertise that appeared as spectacular as its ramifications were dreadful. His wrists rotated like they were servo-assisted ball-joints, his fingers flashing like a speed-metal guitarist's as they altered their grip, interchanged, compensated. Parlabane felt a spasm in his guts as he thought of the damage one malnourished halfwit junkie had done him with a flimsy, planed-down measuring implement. He thought of Sir Lachlan's words about stone-sharpened blades, cutting to the bone through the mere weight of being leaned against; he thought of poor, glaikit, shite-talking, gormless Grieg's head, wherever the hell it was; and he thought of a dozen scared eejits trying to fight this off with a few Kitchen Devils and a reproduction targe from Ikea.

The invader ended the display of flailing steel with the

259

swords crossed in front of his camouflage-jacketed chest.

'Right, come on,' the man growled, stepping forward along the snooker table, eyes focused on Toby, who was paralysed by shock and disbelief.

If Parlabane felt time had stood still during the swordsman's display, then it seemed to accelerate in that moment as the intruder lifted his foot to advance. He too had been transfixed by the sight, this terrifying demonstration of portentous proficiency, and the spell seemed only to be broken in that micro-second when the swordsman made to move towards his victim, at which point it was too late to intervene, even if there had been any way of doing so. Toby was isolated, closer to the table than to Parlabane. There was no way of getting to him before this assassin, whose first, decisive step signalled death as surely as any signed order of execution.

It was over in less than a second.

The intruder's eyes fixing on Toby, his black-booted right foot came down on the blue as his other foot left the table. His momentum brought the ball of his left foot down on the pink and the first of the reds, which rolled away instantly and whipped his leg out backwards from under him. He fell forward, his hands thrust out, still gripping the crossed swords as his considerable bodyweight fell towards them. The hilts landed simultaneously on the baize about half a metre apart, either side of the upright wooden triangle. Acting as a fulcrum, the frame forced the ends together in a scissor effect and most efficiently cut off his head. It bounced once and doubled against the black, knocking it off the jaws of the corner pocket as the head came to rest against the bottom cushion.

There was a moment of total stillness, no words, no breathing, just the whir of a convection heater and in Parlabane's head the repeated sound of metal on metal together with the snicking noise that had accompanied it.

260

He stared at the body on the baize, the head lying a foot or so distant, the image of how it got there looping in his mind. It had been so spectacular, he was half expecting the corpse to kneel up, arms out and the head to go: 'Ta-daaaaa! Ayyy thangew!'

Toby looked to Parlabane and then to Max, glances traded all around as though seeking confirmation from an independent source that what they'd just seen *did* actually happen. Parlabane, realising time was still a major factor, decided to provide it.

'Well, are you not going to give the man a round of applause?' he asked. 'I mean, that was fucking amazing, didn't you think? Honestly, if you'd asked me ten minutes ago, hypothetically, if it was possible to cut your own head off, I'd have said unequivocally no. You've really got to hand it to the bloke – though it's fair to say luck was involved. I mean, there's no way he could do it again.'

Max looked at Parlabane as though he'd grown a second head, perhaps in compensation for their visitor losing his. 'What in the name of God is going on?'

'We're in a lot of trouble, guys, that's what's going on. We're two men down already, though I suppose you could say we've now pulled one back; not that it was down to our efforts. I haven't seen an own goal of that calibre since Terry Butcher retired.'

Repulsion

What a mess, what a bloody mess. It was just plain wrong, like the editor of his personal biopic had accidentally spliced in footage from the life of some poor fucker in Somalia or Rwanda. 'Nightmare' was the word everyone else seemed to be muttering to express their mixture of horror and violently enforced credulity, but that didn't cover it for Rory. A nightmare was some girl you'd brought home browsing on your PC and accidentally opening your history folder. A nightmare was his candidly snapped nude pictures of June Shelley finding their way on to the internet. A nightmare was your business partner telling a room full of near strangers how you'd asked a B-list model to feign a desire to be anally penetrated. Besides, actual nightmares were unreal terrors in your sleeping state. The sleeping state tonight had been where they were all safe and comfortable, two days into a jolly where the only fears were a controlled part of the entertainment and the only danger was that the wine might run out. No, this was not a nightmare. This was waking up to find your sheets soaking wet and realising you'd only *dreamt* you'd got up and gone for a slash.

He was supposed to be back in the lounge bar at this point, sipping single malts and trading tales, maybe even catching that one extra smile, that sly, shared secret one, from Emily, with whom he'd begun to build up some quality rapport. Not that he'd have been in with a shout of anything like *that*, nor even necessarily looking for it. They'd been getting on kind of like . . . well, like he'd have expected to get on with one of the blokes on this trip, just somebody you sparked it

262

off and wanted to jaw with. Somebody whose take on things you wanted to listen to, whom you most wanted to hear laugh when you told a story, whose face you looked to for a shared reaction when someone did or said something you both knew the other would find entertainingly stupid. What had been most surprising was that there was no hangover from the previous night's hostilities, as though neither felt there was anything to forgive or even get hung up about. He'd expected that, between the politics and Liz's revelations, he'd be doing well to get a civil word out of her, as in his experience lefties bore grudges and did not consort with the enemy lest it be interpreted as tacitly condoning their atrocities. Instead, she'd seemed to find him funny, and any digs she made had been either good-natured or almost daring him to transgress her perceived lines of political acceptability. She'd been taking the piss, and he liked that. The banter should have been flowing along with the wine and the whisky, but instead . . .

Fucking hell.

Rory had had it good in life so far. He knew that; in fact considered it important to acknowledge. You've got to appreciate when you're having a good time *at* the time, so that you didn't end up a miserable old sod in an armchair wishing for days that weren't coming back. He'd been dealt a good hand, been given plenty, and taken more than was rightly offered at times (his personal Christmas morning ritual of earlier years being a case in point). He saw that as a mark of character rather than a flaw. Life was for living, and it was the people who were prepared to reach out and take more than their allotted portion who drove civilisation forward. Not all progress was down to altruistic motives, however we liked to romanticise ourselves. Truth was, if we weren't greedy, selfish and hedonistic, we'd be without most of the things that made life worth living. However, somewhere in his mind there had always lurked a fear that one day the bill was going to arrive. This wasn't a sign of a guilty conscience – Rory didn't spend many nights awake weeping for the little children – but just a symptom of realising that what you've taken for yourself can be taken back. One day, he'd always worried, life might find its way of exacting dues and exerting a kind of balance. Bereavement, injury, disease, June Shelley's pics going public and the bitch suing him for every penny he had. That kind of thing.

Not this. No chance. For one thing, that bill was to be marked for the exclusive attention of Rory Glen, Esq, and no karmic sin he'd committed could possibly justify what was being exacted from all these people.

They were assembled around the grand staircase, a ragged and sorry bunch. Joanna was sitting on a sofa adjacent to the front desk, Baxter next to her with an arm around her shoulders. Her eyes were red but she looked too shocked to really cry, too numb to feel the things that would course through her when she was able to let go. She wasn't the only one to look numb, though if the others were like Rory, it had to be a defence mechanism: the mind anaesthetising itself against the effects of the single, dominant emotion that might otherwise paralyse them or turn them into quivering wrecks.

Toby was a sight to behold, his white shirt soaked with blood, his face smeared, hair stuck by it where he'd run his fingers through. He'd been 'hosed', according to his own description, being caught right in the firing line of the intruder's secondary but non-lethal weapon: carotid arterial spray. Sir Lachlan had a few dark, damp patches too, sustained while retrieving two of his heirlooms from the gatecrasher's still-twitching hands.

Emily and Kathy sat together on the stairs, the latter sporting some quality pokiosity that now seemed so irrelevant as to be barely worth noticing. Having been called from her bed, she'd grabbed a pair of jeans and her shoes, leaving herself braless under the grey sweatshirt she'd been wearing as a nightie. Actually, there'd been plenty of visual goodies on offer when it meant nothing and he was in no position to enjoy it. He'd accompanied Emily to rouse their respective colleagues, and though he'd stayed at their bedroom doors, the hour of the night and the urgency of the situation had afforded glimpses that would otherwise have been treasured. Tonight they felt like the nude scenes in *Schindler's List*. Liz had hurriedly answered the door in a towelling dressing-gown that she hadn't quite pulled across, and seemed thereafter less concerned about her modesty than by haste to pull on some clothes. Hadn't it been one of his admitted wishes for the weekend to see Liz in something more revealing? Wish granted. Whoop-dee-doo. Next time wish for a fucking machine gun, you tool.

Standing in the centre, of course, all eyes upon him, was Vale. That quiet little man, fading into the shadows for two days, but decisive whenever he stepped out from cover. Rory had all but forgotten he was on their team during the CTF match, as he'd been anonymous, invisible, until emerging to make the crucial contribution of taking out Parlabane when it was all or nothing. Politely enduring their half-cut bluster like he was too shy to speak, then cutting through the posturing and histrionics to the inalienable truth. Nothing to look at on the surface but a nimble elegance and modest charm, hinting at no greater hidden qualities than the old guy at the wedding who has the ladies queuing for a dance because he still cuts a rug better than the young bucks could ever hope to.

Talk about keeping your powder dry. Throughout all the phoney wars and team-building charades, where leadership, character and other such qualities were supposed to emerge, he'd kept his head down and let everyone else get on with it, clearly aware it was all just a game. Then the minute it became real, he had been the one to stand up, hold the centre

265

and tell the others what to do. Nor had Rory missed the significance of Parlabane's conduct, looking to Vale for instruction with implicit trust. Parlabane was the type of guy who instantly derided pretensions towards authority, as well as someone who'd come through plenty of scrapes himself, and yet he was regarding Vale like he was his commanding officer. Photographer? Yeah maybe, if it was a hobby in semi-retirement. But civil servant? Your arse. There was more to know than Vale was owning up to. In that respect he wasn't alone, though at least Vale's secrets were likely to be of use and of relevance.

The bloody Toby kept sending meaningful glances Rory's way, as he had done once or twice the night before, when Rory had been crapping it that the wet and woolly bastard would decide he needed to unburden himself before the gathering. It would have been far worse than anything Liz could contrive to reveal. He knew Toby was just seeking an unnecessary acknowledgement of the perspective their shared past afforded upon the excesses of the discussion, but at least last night it would have been pertinent. Right now it had fuck-all to do with anything, and opting to blurt it out would contribute nothing to their situation apart from perhaps making everybody else hate the pair of them. To avert that end, Rory had returned Toby's glances with a look that said: 'Keep it shut.'

Vale recapped the situation for the newly arrived and newly bereaved.

'We are isolated with no means of communication or transport. There is no way of crossing the river other than how we did so earlier today, which I would file under "suicide" as it would involve going out there into the darkness on foot. It would also be pointless, as it strikes me as unlikely that the cars on the other side of the river would have escaped the same attentions suffered by those outside the front door, and it's fourteen miles from that car park to

Auchterbuie. Our adversaries, having engineered this situation and having thus flaunted their deeds so far, can only be assumed to intend the same fate for all of us.'

'Killing every witness means never having to say you're sorry,' offered Parlabane.

'Or indeed having to explain your actions and motivations, never mind being caught,' Vale resumed. 'Happily, one of them has fallen on his sword, though not, it would have to be said, out of honour or conscience. We can assume that there are more – many more, given the confidence implied by their actions and by their choice of weapons. Men with the wherewithal to blow up a bridge could be reasonably expected to lay hands on firearms if required, and yet they come at us with blades: butcher one and decapitate another. As to why, my only guess is sadistic pleasure. It doesn't matter. What does is that until or unless we can find a way of raising the alarm, we have to do whatever is in our power to fend off further incursions.'

'And that's going to involve killing the bastards,' said Max tetchily. 'Just in case any of the bleeding hearts among us thought we'd manage it with a peace protest.' He didn't sound as angry or defiant as his words suggested, merely a scared man short of someone to blame.

'Actually,' Vale told him, 'for the time being it's going to involve preventing conflict by keeping solid stone between us and them. But if it comes to hand-to-hand fighting, I don't want bodies, I want prisoners.'

'I'll get you prisoners,' said Joanna, her voice weak and croaky but her tone gravely sincere. 'As long as you pull me off the bastards in time.'

'Prisoners?' Max asked, appalled. 'What, are you worried about the Geneva Convention?'

'No,' interjected Parlabane. 'That would suggest we'd be concerned for the welfare of any prisoners we took. We need information.'

'What are they going to tell you? *Why* they're doing it? Knowing the motive, if there is a fucking motive, isn't going to make me feel any better about getting run through. We're under siege and *you* want to ask them questions? Believe me, mate, violence is the only language they'll understand.'

'Can I ask a question?' It was Liz who spoke, putting her hand up as though to apologise for the interruption. 'It's kind of a communications issue, and apologies if I've missed something and we're going over old ground.'

'No, by all means, please,' invited Vale.

'Well, you said they took out the bridge, cut off the land-lines and disabled the cars. What about the mobiles?'

Rory was swallowing back a sarcastic enquiry as to just how much she had missed, and whether she'd even caught the part about headless corpses in the dining room and base-ment, when he realised what she was saying and that he was the stupid one for missing it. To be fair to himself, Liz's perspective had the clarity of her being starkly confronted with all the facts and details, compared to the muddier view of those who'd been in the centre as those facts and details emerged and developed around them. Nonetheless, he still couldn't believe they'd missed it.

'I mean, the other stuff some intruder could pull off, sure,' she continued, 'but how could they know all the SIM cards had already been removed from our mobiles?'

As the implications sank in, all eyes turned to Baxter, who sat up straight, a startled rabbit in twelve pairs of headlights.

'We told no-one,' he said, shaking his head. 'I swear. No-one. Why would we? The UML Experience, everything we were building, none of it would have worked if we let the details slip. The only people who knew anything were the guys who played the soldiers, and they only knew their parts, not ours.'

'Which leaves only you and Campbell,' Parlabane pointed out.

'Francis? Come on, you've met him. Did he strike you as someone complicit in a conspiracy to mass murder?' He looked imploringly at several faces, alighting last and longest on Emily's, Rory noticed. It was odd, as if he expected her more than anyone to believe him.

'No, but if he did strike us as such, he wouldn't be much use in said conspiracy, would he?' Parlabane said.

'Sounds like we're back to "only the true messiah would deny it".'

'Yeah, except this time it's you who's being asked to accept what the facts are telling you. Campbell was the first to disappear. He was also the only person with a functioning mobile phone. His SIM was never removed, was it?'

'That's true,' Baxter conceded. 'But that's just the way we split the tasks. It could as easily have been me who had the shadowing role today, and him accompanying you on the trek.'

'Could it?' Parlabane asked. 'Was he the architect of those games? Did he decide those roles, and therefore who would and wouldn't have a phone by tonight, Donald?'

This time it was Rory who looked to Toby when the word 'architect' was mentioned. He wasn't seeking a response, rather hoping not to see one. He got his wish, Toby still intent upon Baxter.

'He did,' Baxter conceded quietly, his voice burdened with defeat. 'Mind you, if . . . no,' he decided, shaking his head.

'What?' asked Vale.

'Ach, I was thinking if he wasn't part of this, there's a chance his mobile could be in his room, but who am I kidding?'

'We'll search his room anyway,' said Vale. 'See if there's anything in there that can give us a few pointers.'

'I'll come with you,' Baxter volunteered.

'All in good time. First priority is defence. They could be

269

coming through the windows any minute. We've got work to do.'

Baxter and Campbell couldn't have dreamt up a more effective bonding exercise than this one, Rory reckoned, as the unlucky thirteen set about barricading themselves inside. History offered encouragement. As Sir Lachlan pointed out, it wouldn't be the first time the McKinleys had turned their home into a fortress, and the first McKinley construction had been precisely that. Less encouraging was Rory's assumption that the first McKinley construction probably didn't have quite so many invitingly pregnable windows, and that its defenders were not only better armed but better trained in fending off invaders. The only thing he considered himself adept at fending off was Jehovah's Witnesses.

Nonetheless, the admission that he'd done a bit of fencing at school and uni had been enough for Vale to assign Rory one of the bloodstained rapiers and the targe. Vale had been coaxing anyone who had – or even thought they had – any kind of potentially useful skills or abilities to sound off, on the grounds that they had to make the best of whatever they had, no matter how modest. Toby owned up to his student time in the Officers Training Corps, Max to a spell in the TA, and Sir Lachlan to having been an officer in the full-on, nae-kiddin' army. It would have meant more if they actually had a gun between them, but there you go: it was better than nothing, and that was Vale's point. Once again, Baxter might have been looking on jealously at this spontaneous pooling of resources and burgeoning one-for-all spirit if he wasn't simply bricking it like the rest of them. Vale didn't mention specifically what *he* was bringing to the table, or where he'd learnt it, but nobody was sufficiently distracted from the impending danger to ask.

'The twenty-first century,' Rory had muttered as Sir Lachlan handed over a blade and Vale fetched the targe down from the wall. 'And we're looking at hand-to-hand fighting with . . . *these*. If we could muster a bow and arrow, it would constitute an arms race.'

'Meantime,' said Parlabane, 'heart and hand and sword and shield, we'll guard McKinley Hall.'

'Aye, very good.'

Rory stood by in case of attack while Toby opened the front door in order to bolt the heavy double storm doors in the vestibule. Once secured, with the front doors locked once again, four of them put their backs into shifting the reception desk across the entrance as a further brace. The polished floorboards were never going to look the same again, but as this was a far smaller aesthetic deterrent to potential guests than a blood-strewn pile of corpses, Rory didn't imagine Sir Lachlan having a hissy fit about it. Meanwhile, Emily, Kathy, Liz and Joanna, having collected everyone's keys, were raiding bedrooms for double mattresses, carrying one at a time between each pair, then chucking them over the gallery banister. From there, they were dragged to either side of the front door and leaned against the windowframes atop tables taken from the main restaurant. They were then secured, if that was the word, by bedsheets and lengths of torn-down curtain material nailed to the wall at either side.

'It won't hold them out for long,' Vale said, 'but nobody's going to come bursting through at speed either, and they'll be on their faces when they do.'

Further mattresses were ordered to be taken, along with bookcases and an antique bureau, to block the enclosed stairways each leading up to the first floor and down to the basement level, where the snooker room had already been breached. These stairways were at the far ends of the two main corridors extending from the reception area, the extremities obscured from the centre by S-bends in either hallway. Alison and Ger were working their way around the interior doors, Alison locking them while Ger stood by with

271

the kind of kitchen knife that Rory associated more with Jason Voorhees than Jamie Oliver. They had started with the makeshift dining room, primarily because it had already been established as a point of entry, but also to close off any view Joanna might have caught of Grieg's body as she helped hump furniture along the corridor.

Rory, with his absurdly anachronistic armaments, was assigned to assist and escort Liz, Kathy and Joanna in barricading the eastern stairwell. They took two mattresses there first, then two tall bookcases from the lounge bar, roping in the assistance of Ger and Alison to unlock the door again and ditch the contents. Meanwhile Sir Lachlan led Emily, Max and Toby at the western stairwell. They put their backs into shifting a bureau from the drawing room as a foundation for their barricade, a task that seemed to be testing the strength and coordination of all four of them.

Rory looked at the two mattresses buckled between the wall and the banister on the landing. They didn't so much comprise a barricade as a handy cushion to protect invaders should they trip on their way up to kill everybody.

'We need to take these out and start with the bookcases,' he said, standing the rapier on its point outside the door and resting the targe against the foot of the second stair going up. The others nodded their agreement. Unsurprisingly, nobody had been feeling particularly chatty, and anybody who gave an indication of having some kind of plan in any given situation was unlikely to meet with dissent.

Quietly, wordlessly, they got on with pulling the mattresses back into the corridor, then manoeuvred the first of the bookcases through the narrow fire-door. Awkward as it was, Rory was still grateful he wasn't at the other stairwell attempting the same negotiation with the bureau.

He and Liz first tried wedging the bookcase the way they had the mattresses, but it was too wide, and whatever force they could use to jam it in at a diagonal, if matched by their adversaries would simply dislodge it again.

'I reckon the best bet is to turn both of them on their sides at an angle across the landing,' Liz suggested. 'Then have bookcase, mattress, bookcase, mattress.'

Rory pictured it. There'd still be a gap at the top, but the barrier would be four widths thick, meaning anyone climbing over it from below would be prostrate to the point of lying flat as he did so. If Rory was waiting with a sword, it would be like sticking their heads through the guillotine.

'Why can't we just pile them up this side of the fire-door?' asked Kathy through the glass, the door having been closed to give them more room to manoeuvre. 'Then get some tables from—'

Her question was answered by a figure in combat fatigues lunging down the stairwell from the landing above. He was already in mid-air as Rory turned to see him, proving their barrier was too late even if they could decide how to erect it, the invader having presumably entered through the snooker room and ventured upstairs while they were deliberating in the hall. He bore a claymore above his head in two hands as he leapt, the hilt facing forward, the blade ready to be brought down with all murderous weight upon Liz and Rory, pinned on the landing between the closed door and the bookcase.

Rory heard a tinkle of metal as he reached for his shield, and saw that the intended arc of the claymore was at least a foot greater than the sloping ceiling would allow. The steel bit hard into plaster, killing its momentum and twisting the hilt in the intruder's grip. His feet came down a few stairs short of the landing as he attempted to arrest his lunge, his momentum sapped by the unintended blow struck above his head, but not enough for him to stop. Rory grabbed the targe as the intruder toppled forward, the claymore loose again. Its movement remained restricted in the narrow passage so that it could not be swung, only thrust, but between bodyweight and gravity it was still enough to meet Rory's shield with shuddering impact.

Muted screams rang out from the corridor as Kathy witnessed the attack from through the fire-door's thin, wire-latticed window. The tip of the claymore and the first six inches behind it passed through the wood of the targe, but the collision deflected its course just past Rory's side before the intruder's body slammed into his and drove him against the wall. Unfortunately, the first thing in the blade's deflected path was Liz, who was sent sprawling over the side-turned bookcase. The attacker recoiled a few inches and pulled back his sword, which Rory noticed from the tugging against his fingers to be stuck in the targe. His eyes locked on those of his adversary, Rory tightened his grip and pushed forward with the shield, trying to prevent the intruder from dislodging his weapon.

'Rory!' Liz warned as she spotted the intruder loose his left hand to unsheathe a knife, with which he slashed out in a narrow arc. Rory stepped back against the wall and let go of the targe as the knife whipped across his chest, tearing at least three hundred quid's worth of jacket. The intruder rocked on his heels at the sudden absence of resistance, his broadsword now awkwardly encumbered at one end. He gave it a wiggle, as if trying to flip it away, or maybe testing whether he could just club Rory with this new combined implement. Evidently deciding against both, he dipped the targe to the floor and placed his foot on it, as a second swordsman appeared on the upper landing, also bearing a claymore. Rory knew this was his only chance, but before he could hurl himself, the fire-door flew open like a grenade had gone off behind it. The edge of the door caught the intruder a glancing blow to the head that spun him against the banister and tangled his legs around the embedded clay-more as he fell.

He turned around to discover what had hit him, but it was questionable whether he would have had time to fully focus upon what would be the last thing he ever saw: Joanna stepping through the doorway, swinging Rory's rapier with both hands in merciless, like-for-like vengeance.

'God almighty,' gasped Liz.

'There can be only one,' Rory added.

'Eh?'

'Nothing.'

Someone who did have time to focus was the second swordsman, who watched his comrade's head bounce and roll to the lower landing like it was on the end of a hypnotist's chain. He stopped in his tracks, frozen a couple of steps down from the landing, until he caught sight of whatever was in Joanna's eyes, at which point he uttered 'fuck this', turned on one heel and took off.

Rory looked to Liz, as much surprise as horror reflected in her face, which meant she was thinking the same as him.

'These guys are shite,' Rory exclaimed.

The erstwhile force of vengeance stood, trembling, her knuckles white and every sinew stretched as she gripped the sword. Kathy put an arm out slowly and gently to touch her, the sound of several footsteps thumping along the corridor outside the fire door. Joanna almost jumped at Kathy's contact, suddenly shaken from her trance. She stared at what lay before her then at Rory, as if asking him how it happened. The rage that had seized her was exhausted, leaving her merely its spent and bewildered vessel. She dropped the rapier and burst into sobs as Kathy led her away.

Rory helped Liz over the bookcase, noticing with concern that she had a patch of blood on the sleeve of her sweatshirt.

'You're cut,' he said.

'Barely broke the skin,' she said. 'Bigger bruise than a cut, the point was so dull. Get after the bastard.'

Rory lifted the rapier and began climbing the stairs as Parlabane and Vale arrived at the fire-door, further footsteps behind them announcing more tardy reinforcements.

'Jeez,' Parlabane remarked. 'Store janitor to the ketchup aisle.'

'They were already inside, upstairs,' Liz said. 'Two of them. There could be more.'

'Finish the barriers, both of them,' Rory heard Vale order, his voice cut off as the upper-level fire-door swung shut behind him. He thought he heard screaming too, but it might just have been Kathy's echo inside his head.

Emily recognised Kathy's scream instantly. She'd heard it a hundred times, usually at around eleven o'clock on a busy Monday when her mid-morning caffeine hit coincided with the second post or when Carol the secretary told her their accountant was on the other line. This was louder, even from the other end of the building, and didn't descend into self-conscious giggling at the end.

'That's Kathy,' she informed the others, all of whom had reacted to the sound.

Max and Toby immediately let go their end of the mattress they'd just lifted and went haring down the corridor in response. Emily was inside the stairwell, standing on the bureau, her role more about guidance than muscle, which meant the loss of their hands left her stranded for a moment as she prevented the mattress from toppling down the flight below. She stretched a hand out to Sir Lachlan, seeking assistance in getting down so that she could follow the others, but instead he stepped around the desk and shouldered the burden they'd just abandoned.

'Stick to your task,' he said, in a tone that told her this was not a suggestion. 'Whatever's going on up there, it's out of your hands. We need to get this barricade up.'

Emily bit her lip and nodded. She didn't like it, but she

276

understood. Not knowing was the hardest part of fear. So far there had been several horrible developments, but they had come in the form of reports and revelations. This was the first time there was something going on live that she was aware of, something she had an invaluable stake in, and yet she just had to ignore it, do her job and wait for news.

They had lodged a mattress beneath the front legs of the bureau, pinning one end of it at the top of the flight so that intruders would have to walk up it, rather than the more conducively tractable stairs, in order to approach the barrier. The second mattress, they were planning to wedge upright between the desk and the corner of the banister, presenting a six-foot vertical obstacle in front of the bureau. The weak point was that it could only be pinned in place on one side, creating a hinge effect allowing the enemy to pull it open like a door. However, the weight securing the pinned end would mean it wouldn't be a very easy door to open, and after they squeezed through it, they'd still have to get over the bureau, all the time vulnerable to defenders' blades.

Between them, Emily and Sir Lachlan edged the mattress over the bureau and into the waiting slot, then she stepped back to the floor. They both crouched down to put their shoulders against the desk in readiness to pin the second mattress in place.

'After three,' said Sir Lachlan. 'One—'

'Wait,' warned Emily, sure she could hear heavy footfalls on the stairs above. She and Sir Lachlan got to their feet in time to see two men, one with a broadsword, the other with a machete, come charging down the upper flight towards them. Sir Lachlan grabbed a fistful of Emily's dress with one hand and his rapier from the floor with the other, pushing her towards the door as he lunged forward on to the stairs to meet them. She screamed and heard a clash of metal as she pulled the handle, the door only swinging in a few feet before jamming against one end of the bureau. On the stairs, Sir Lachlan was parrying the broadsword to force back one opponent, but the other was shaping to launch himself through the gap between them and the wall. Sir Lachlan spotted this intention and called to Emily to run as he launched a kick into the second attacker's path. She saw his right leg buckle as the left made contact, the assault on the second man disrupting his balance in fending off the first, and she had to dive through the narrow gap between door and frame before the three toppling bodies came down on top of her.

She heard thumps and cries as she rolled into the corridor, then the sound of the fire-door swinging open and once again finding resistance. Emily looked back. The man with the machete emerged through the gap, his face blacked out with camouflage paint but his eyes burning with eminently readable intent. There was movement behind him, a thrust-out leg slamming the door closed while he was halfway through it. The impact whacked his head against the frame, but he merely shrugged it off as the door rebounded from his burly figure. He raised the machete and began moving forward.

Emily turned and scrambled to her feet, finding herself facing down a long corridor, at the end of which Alison was locking a door, Ger standing over her protectively with a knife.

'Get down,' Ger called, but Emily could feel, not just hear, the heavy paces behind her, and her legs refused to cease taking her away from the imagined down-swing of that machete.

'I SAID GET FUCKIN' DOWN,' Ger shouted, stepping across her path and altering his grip on the enormous knife he was carrying.

Emily heard something whip just over her head as she hit the deck, turning on to her back instinctively to face her pursuer.

278

He was no longer pursuing, knocked clean off his feet like he'd run into an overhanging branch. Emily heard a truly revolting thud as his head hit the thinly carpeted wooden floor, but any neurological damage was rendered moot by the fact that Ger's knife had already diverted his brain's blood supply on to the walls and carpet.

'Sir Lachlan,' she remembered. 'There's another one in there with him.'

Ger walked past her and knelt down to remove the knife from the intruder's neck, also prising the machete from his grip.

As he stood up, the fire-door swung open and a claymore was tossed through it, landing on the lacquered wood that flanked the carpet with a ringing clang. Sir Lachlan stepped awkwardly through the gap, wincing as he did so. There was blood seeping from his right thigh and his left hand, his fingers clenched over his palm.

'Bugger got away. Took a dive into the mattress and disappeared through the gap.'

'What happened to you?'

'Oh, the bastard with the machete had a swipe at me on his way past to get to you. And I got this on my hand from my own bloody sword. I whipped his claymore – I should say *my* claymore – from his grip and he let it go more easily than I was expecting. He was more interested in getting out of there than standing up for a fight. I could see it in his eyes. Who the hell are these people?'

'Not exactly the musketeers, are they?' observed Ger.

Sir Lachlan surveyed the mess on the floor of the corridor.

'Not exactly, no. Mr Vale wanted a prisoner to interrogate. D'Artagnan here isn't going to tell him much, is he?'

'I hope I'm wrong, but I expect there'll be others.'

'Me too. There's no way the clowns we've just seen off were running the show.'

*   *   *

279

Rory charged after the sound of footsteps, urged on by an adrenaline surge that he hoped would continue to provide such an imperative drive if and when he caught up with his quarry. He could see no-one in the first-floor corridor, but estimated the fugitive to be only a few yards ahead. Once around the S-bend, the bastard came into his view, pounding towards the next fire-door, through which lay the gallery overlooking the grand staircase and reception hall.

'Come back and fight, you useless fucking shitebag,' Rory called after him, hardly a compelling invitation, he'd have to admit. That said, it felt good to watch him run, felt like the tide had turned after the hopeless, numbing dread that had descended since Grieg came crashing through the window sans under-used head. He braced his shoulder for impact and powered through the fire-door as the escapee kept going headlong, not even checking over the banister to the lower floor as he passed. The guy wasn't looking for options: he knew exactly where he was headed.

'We've four people on the far stairway,' Rory shouted, 'and they've all got swords as sharp as the one that cut your pal's visit short.'

The logic seemed impeccable at the time, until the runner did the arithmetic and came to the conclusion Rory intended, at which point it didn't seem such bright thinking. He stopped short of the next fire-door as though Rory's words had locked it, and turned to face what was now the only obstacle between him and, if not escape, then at least temporarily keeping his options open. Rory now realised he hadn't exactly been expecting the guy to lay down his weapon and say 'it's a fair cop'; in truth, he hadn't been expecting *anything* in particular, as he hadn't been thinking any further ahead than getting the bugger to stop running.

He had a desperate look in his eyes, as much fear and horror as Rory himself had been feeling before, mixed with the same leavening of sheer survival instinct. Doubling his grip on the claymore, he charged towards Rory, shouting a wordless, inarticulate war cry as he did so.

The world slowed, like Rory was in bullet-time, or, more accurately, claymore time.

Shit. He was four yards away.

Okay, moment of truth. Own up: how many fencing classes did he go to? Quite a few back at school, all of twenty years ago, then a few in early student days before the pursuit of a different swordcraft laid claim to his enthusiasms. You scuttled back and forth along a line, dressed like an anorexic bee-keeper, facing a similarly prancing tit with his similarly pathetic-looking foil, and you got points for touching. *Touching, for fuck's sake.* 'Stand back lest I touch you, ye filthy blackguard.'

Nope, touching wasn't going to do it, and even if he had his face-mask, he couldn't quite picture the claymore reverberating off it and giving the guy pins and needles in his finger.

Three yards away, the claymore held to one side, ready to be swung in towards him.

So, to recap, touching and white outfits. Those were the main memories. Any principles still lingering in there, dormant, ready to be awakened by something like, ooh, let's see, a crazed and desperate assassin now two yards from cutting him in half?

Rory's head still drew a blank, but his legs had total recall. Balance and timing, they reminded him, as his knees bent automatically and his feet took him a short half-yard to the left, outside the path of the unstoppably swinging claymore. His torso turned as if on ballbearings, affording him a view of his attacker stumbling against the banister, his feet unable to compensate for the absence of impact as he swung the heavy sword at a target who was no longer there. The war cry spent and a dollop of doubt diluting the blind confidence of his desperate purpose, he righted himself and lunged again. This time, Rory's arms got in on the act too, bringing the rapier up with no great power, but more than enough to deflect the attack as his feet had already angled him away from its focus. He wouldn't exactly say it was all coming back now, but clearly what basics his body had retained were more than this chump ever had the benefit of. The guy was sapping his own strength, allowing Rory to use his momentum against him with minimum effort on his part. On the third lunge, Rory dropped his centre of gravity and moved in before the attack could advance, bringing his rapier up so that his opponent stepped forward on to its point. Rory stopped the blade at the man's sternum, the tip already through a layer of camouflaged material.

'Drop it,' Rory said.

He did.

Rory kicked the sword away and stepped back, still levelling the rapier at his opponent's chest, as Vale emerged from the fire-door bearing a claymore of his own.

'Your prisoner, Mr Vale.'

'Sterling stuff, Mr Glen. Now you'd better get downstairs and have that looked at.'

'Have what looked at?' Rory asked, glancing down at himself like someone had told him his fly was open. There was a damp red patch visible on his shirt where his jacket flapped open. He put his hand to it instinctively and felt the sting that adrenaline had been suppressing since he'd been slashed across his chest on the stairwell. It felt like getting a speeding ticket through the post. 'Bollocks,' he said.

'It looks superficial, but it's going to need some antiseptic and dressing,' Vale advised. 'Go get yourself a seat. Donald and I will handle our new guest.'

'I'll tell you nothing,' the man said, sounding more scared than defiant.

'Want to bet?'

'You can't threaten me because I'm dead anyway. They'll kill me if I talk.'

'See?' said Vale. 'Bet lost. You're telling us things already.'

Recoil

'Only one made it back out. No response from the rest.'

'Yes, I do have eyes and ears myself.'

'First wave was a wipe-out. And they've got a prisoner. Brian, I think. I'm not confident he won't talk.'

'Let him. He can't say anything that can possibly be of practical use. And whatever else they learn won't matter. They'll be too dead to tell anybody.'

'Not if we don't raise our game, they won't. Face facts, we just got a kicking in there. Let's get the second wave in before this shitstorm gets any worse.'

'Calm down, for God's sake. Neither of us came here for a turkey shoot. What would that tell us about anybody? We planned for losses, you know that.'

'Yeah, a few of the fucking try-outs, but we lost Marko, for fuck's sake. He was one of our best.'

Indeed he was, Shiach reflected. Battle permitted no quarter for mourning, but he was acutely aware of what had just been lost, not only to him personally as a friend, but to their undertaking. Marko was a man of initiative, an invaluably distinguishing quality when so many thought that following orders was the most that was expected of them. Marko understood the practical principles of what they were about and could adapt accordingly in the moment. This had been typified earlier in the day when he'd encountered that bloke in the Peugeot, who happened to be driving by when two of them were disabling the vehicles in the carpark at the gates to the estate. Your average grunt would need to be told that the guy had to die. Your above-average one would take it upon himself instinctively. But it took a man of Marko's calibre to interpret the implications of the man's clothing and his car being full of butcher-meat, and thus come up with such a use for the body. If the cops weren't baffled enough by what they would find tomorrow, then the coroner's revelations about the condemned's last meal would put the tin lid on it.

It was a bloody shame. He had sent Marko in to lead the first group because he wanted to get things off to a good start and thus encourage the recruits. Shiach had watched events unfold on his laptop, white icons denoting the guests and black his men within the wireframe model. Moments after Marko went in, the three white ones were on the move, while Marko's black one remained motionless. In its topological simplicity, it was a stark way to watch a friend die. But now was not the time to dwell upon it.

'Keep the head, man,' Shiach told him. 'Marko's a hell of a loss, one we'll feel all the more after the dust's settled, but don't lose perspective. It was bad luck, that's all. He had an accident, and they ended up with a few weapons. We'll deal with it.'

'And you sent in the four try-outs right behind him regardless, so now they've got more weapons.'

'We had to find out what we were up against. Now we know.'

'Yeah, and so do they: idiots, that's what they'll be thinking. Which is why we should go in heavy right now and put them straight.'

'No, it's why we should hold our ground and remember that we control this whole situation. They aren't going anywhere, you know that.'

'Sure, but they're fortifying their positions and working on how they're going to keep us out.'

'Let them. And let time work for us. Right now they're flush with victory, high on relief and endorphins. They got lucky, and at the moment they might even believe this is a fight they can win. Go in now and they'll still be psyched. We've got all the time we need, not to mention a few secret weapons. Let's let the excitement wear off and the self-doubt wash in, give them a while to simmer in their own fears. Then we'll show them what we're really made of.'

Information

'We're not seriously going to torture this guy, are we?'
Parlabane asked.

Vale's face lacked its customary mercurial levity, even the
signs that were sometimes presented in wider company for
only confidants such as Parlabane to read.

They were standing in the central reception hall again,
rapidly established as their base of operations, and, increasingly, as a makeshift field hospital. The small roll of band-
ages in the reception desk's first aid kit was accounted for
by Liz's arm and Sir Lachlan's hand, enforcing a resort to
bedsheets for the latter's thigh and Rory's chest. The Dettol
hadn't gone very far either, which meant a bottle of Glen-
fiddich had to be cracked open for a less than celebratory
early-hours toast.

Rory, having apparently endured his injury obliviously
while pursuing and apprehending their prisoner, must have
come close to expelling his own larynx when the single-malt
antiseptic was applied. He'd protested resentfully about the
cure being worse than the disease, until Vale described the
symptoms of a few wound infections he'd witnessed in his
time.

Sir Lachlan was more stoical, perhaps assisted by having
had the foresight to take some of the antiseptic internally
before allowing it to be applied. Kathy affixed all bandaging.
She was the only one with a first-aid qualification more
recent than a Boy Scout or Girl Guide merit badge, having
done a six-month voluntary stint in Sonzola a few years
back. She'd gone there, she explained, to help dole out food

parcels but ended up, like all her fellow volunteers, helping treat the endless civilian casualties in a state that resumed its ongoing civil war any time it took a break from fighting with its neighbours.

'See, these lefty pacifist types can be quite handy to have around sometimes,' Emily had said to Rory.

'Yeah, it's all the practice you get, patching up bleeding hearts,' he replied. It could have been a nasty and inappropriate echo of the night before, but it sounded more like laughter in the dark than point-scoring.

Sir Lachlan insisted on returning to man one of the stairwell barricades, despite the encumbrance of his injuries and Kathy's concern that what she had done would merely stem the blood loss.

'You need to get to a hospital,' she told him.

'All the more urgent that we see off these scoundrels, then, isn't it?'

Two guards were posted to man the barricades at either stairwell, Sir Lachlan partnering Toby while Joanna insisted upon doing her bit by joining Max. If anyone was inclined to be old-fashioned or even merely chivalrous regarding traditional gender roles, then Joanna's earlier contribution held their comments in check. Nor was she deterred by sharing a post with the remains of her act of rage, refusing suggestions that they drag the constituent parts out of sight with a stated intention to use the head as a missile if it came down to it.

Their prisoner was seated cross-legged on the floor, his hands tied at the wrist behind his back with ripped bedlinen. Vale had retrieved a wet bar-towel from the lounge and used it to wipe away the camouflage paint from the man's face. Without the streaked markings and the scary-macho signals they sent out, he appeared ordinary to the point of frumpy, and the main thing the paint had been camouflaging was fear. He looked early forties, losing it on top, fairly well built but a bit of a pot belly suggesting the pub might be winning out over the outdoors recently. Not exactly a killing machine, as had been adequately demonstrated.

Vale was eyeing him with curious intent, a weighing-up going on inside his head that made Parlabane very apprehensive. He'd known Tim a long time, but he'd never have felt confident about saying he knew him well, or even believing that there was anyone who did. Much like himself, it had been Vale's life to know about other people, particularly the parts they didn't want anyone else finding out; but while Parlabane had merely negotiated whatever obstacles lay between him and what he needed to know, Vale had been engaged with the very science of secrecy. As such, he was far better equipped, and definitely far more inclined, to protect what he wanted to keep back about himself.

They had frequently joked about Vale's past: mainly, Parlabane thought, as a means of two otherwise close friends skirting around an area that one of them was not prepared to open up about; even as a means of skirting around the acknowledgement of that. Parlabane knew very little for certain, but there had been hints enough to understand that Vale had been in some very serious situations and had doubtless done some horrible things in the name of survival. The most he'd ever said about it was to confess he had 'done things I wish I hadn't had to; wished it had been someone else doing them; wished they hadn't been necessary'.

The sole such circumstance he'd discussed at any length was his involvement with the disaster aboard that Floating Paradise oil-rig place, whatever it was called. Vale had taken out a number of hijackers in what was a pretty morally straightforward kill-or-be-killed scenario. Parlabane had once killed a man himself in similarly non-negotiable circumstances, and knew he wouldn't flinch tonight if he had to do it again. He too wished it hadn't been necessary, and he too knew that horrible things sometimes had to be

289

done in the name of survival. But looking at Vale as he surveyed their captive wretch with intent, he couldn't help doubting whether this poor clown could tell them something that was so valuable as to be worth tainting their collective conscience with something the self-defence stain remover couldn't be applied to.

That said, the guy *was* only here because he wanted to play his part in killing everyone in the room. It could be argued that he owed them a reason more than they owed him any mercy. It could be argued, but Parlabane wasn't sure he wanted to.

'Rory,' Vale said. 'Give me your sword, I need one that's razor-sharp. In fact, I need more than one. Take this claymore to Lachlan and tell him I need a loan of the other rapier.'

'You got it,' Rory said.

Emily stepped into Rory's path and put a hand out to stop him.

'Hang on,' she said, looking at Vale as well as casting appealing glances towards Kathy and Baxter. 'Are you sure about this? I mean, defending ourselves is one thing, but . . . Christ, what can he tell us that'll make a difference?'

'We won't know until we ask.'

'I know, but . . . Jesus. You're not going to torture him, surely.'

'Of course I'm not going to torture him,' Vale replied, sounding hurt, which Parlabane knew to be bollocks: if you wanted to hurt Vale, you'd need more than words. 'I'm not even going to touch him. I'm simply going to engineer a circumstance in which cooperation would serve his best interests.'

Parlabane guessed their prisoner wouldn't have been the first person to consider a Life Fitness FlexDeck treadmill as an instrument of torture, nor was he the first to persevere against the complaints of his tired limbs out of a desire to keep his body in optimum shape. His predecessors, however, would have been more concerned about love handles, cellulite and general cardiovascular well-being than the avoidance of impalement. So far, it was proving a far more fertile means of tapping into those deepest stamina reserves than the prospect of being able to fit into that once-favoured frock or in penitence for that sinful second helping of tiramisu.

Vale had nominated himself the fitness instructor from hell by lashing the two rapiers, at head- and stomach height, to the vertical steel support-bars of some weight-resistance apparatus, then manoeuvring the contraption until the twin blades overlapped the rear of the treadmill, upon which their prisoner was standing. With his hands tied behind his back, he had no way of climbing out or interfering with the settings, especially not once Vale had set the thing running, starting at twelve kilometres per hour.

'It's entirely in our visitor's gift to extricate himself from this predicament,' Vale explained, as if the poor sod wasn't there. 'He talks, I stick the brakes on. So, let's start with an easy one. How many?'

Baxter had joined them in the fitness room, though fortunately not in the proxy Amnesty observer role requested by the squeamish Emily. Parlabane hadn't been entirely comfortable with what they were up to either, but he had confidence enough in Vale's scheme that he could do without someone else's Jiminy Cricket act. He had therefore suggested that Baxter might prefer to join Ger and Alison in searching Campbell's room, but Baxter put him straight regarding his real reason for being in on the interrogation.

'I don't want to know what's in his bedroom: I want to know who the fuck Campbell really is. Six months I've been working with this prick, eating with him, drinking with him, looking him in the eye, and all that time he's actually been planning to kill me. I've got some fucking questions of my own.'

The prisoner was jogging fairly comfortably, probably feeling like he could hold out for a while at that speed, but his face betrayed his awareness that Vale only had to press that circle with the upwards-pointing triangle to accelerate the pace. Nonetheless, he said nothing, a look of compelled determination setting his features. Parlabane read it and so did Vale: he really was more scared of his comrades than he was of them.

Vale upped the speed to fourteen kilometres per hour. The whine of the treadmill got higher, the footfalls quicker, the sharp exhalations more frequent. He still looked compelled and still looked scared, but every footfall was one nearer the point when he'd start thinking of the more immediate danger and the simple way he could avert it. Vale studied his face, looking for a sign, a cue. It came with a grimace, a tell-tale that he was feeling the effort, and Vale responded to it by upping the speed to fifteen. It wasn't a huge increment, but it must have felt like enough. There was a moment of panic in the man's eyes at the initial increase, followed by relief that it wasn't as much as he'd feared, followed in turn by despair in the realisation that this wasn't going to get any slower and there might not be much left in his tank. He looked to Baxter and Parlabane imploringly, hoping one of them would play dove to Vale's hawk. Going by Vale's cold determination and Baxter's seething anger, Parlabane reckoned he was the closest thing present, so merely looked away. Baxter and Vale simply gazed back imperviously, which was when he decided to answer.

'Maybe twenty,' he said, breathing harder. Talking wasn't going to make the running easier, he knew. 'Minus the dead. Don't know exact. Around twenty.'

'Who are they?'

'Don't know. Nobody . . . knows surnames. First names

only, false ones at that.' He exhaled sharply again, his face showing the strain in repeated grimaces of effort. There'd be no resistance now, only thoughts of the growing pain in his legs and chest, and the swords they were working to keep him away from. 'No identifying . . . materials,' he added.

'I wasn't expecting names. I meant, are they all as good as you, or do we have something to worry about?'

'Don't know. There's pros at the top.'

'Is one of them Campbell?' Baxter asked.

The prisoner stared blankly back at him, genuinely confused. Chances were the name Campbell meant nothing to him. Baxter belatedly realised this.

'Who's the guy on the inside?' he demanded angrily.

The guy looked around his three interrogators, alighting last on Baxter with an expression that suggested his last question had been in Chinese.

'All right, an easier one,' Vale resumed. 'Who are these pros?'

'Soldiers, mostly, I think. They set the stage. Then we got . . . got greenlight.'

'Was the greenlight throwing our decapitated fellow guest through the window?'

He looked surprised. 'I guess. Only told us . . . you'd know we were coming.'

'How many of these pros?'

'Four. Three now. One of them . . . first man in. Snooker room.'

'Armed? Guns?'

'Not sure.'

'Bollocks you're not,' Vale said, reaching for that upwards triangle again. He didn't have to press it.

'I mean . . . they're not . . . planning to use guns. Only blades, that's the order. I heard something about . . . about darts. But we were told . . . only blades.'

'Why?'

'Same reason as . . . they told you we were coming. A test. Anybody . . . can kill with a gun.'

'A test? Of whom? For what?'

'I can't . . . keep this up,' the prisoner breathed.

'Then you'd better answer all my questions quickly.'

'I've got one too,' Parlabane ventured, impatient that Vale's understandably pragmatic line of inquiry wasn't addressing his own greatest curiosity. 'Why? Why us, why here?'

'Don't know. Told nothing . . . about targets.'

'What are you, auditioning for hit men?' Parlabane asked. 'You didn't ask any fucking questions about who you'd be killing or why?'

He swallowed, looked to the ceiling, his expression contorted by the strain of more than effort. They were definitely into the territory of what he was still scared to reveal, but the bastard definitely had something to say. Vale saw it too, and upped the speed to sixteen.

'Threats and witnesses,' he blurted immediately. 'Please turn the speed down, I'll talk. Please.' Vale instead crossed his arms and took a step away. 'Okay. That's . . . what he said. Here to eliminate threats. But once it starts . . . everybody's a witness. Every witness is a threat.'

'And what's your end?' Parlabane asked. 'Money, or just kicks?'

'Thirty K,' he said, the heavy exhalations now coming every three or four breaths.

'Thirty K per head? Fuck off. You wouldn't even be getting that if you were any good.'

'Thirty K. That's the bond.'

Vale and Parlabane's eyes met, one of those 'did he really say that?' mutual exchanges.

'You're paying them?' Vale asked rhetorically.

'Non-returnable security. Proof you're serious. Same

bond, whether trialists or tourists. Tourists . . . just paying for . . . safari. Chance to kill . . . no strings, no comeback.'

'And what are the trialists aiming for?'

'Make the team.'

'What team? A team to do what?'

'Only find out . . . if you make the team.'

'Bloody hell,' said Vale, exasperated.

'How did you get the trial?' Parlabane asked. 'An ad in a shop window?'

The prisoner's eyes narrowed in strain. He was channelling more of his concentration into maintaining the pace than into thinking of his answers. Parlabane now fully understood the method in Vale's apparent barbarity: the guy wouldn't have the spare energy to dream up any lies. However, that finite energy would only keep him away from those blades for a limited time, and it appeared to be fast running out.

'I think we should slow him down a bit,' said Baxter, evidently having noticed the same thing. 'Come on, he's talking now.'

'Yes,' Vale retorted, 'and he'll shut up again if we cut him any slack. Keep it coming,' he told the prisoner. 'Who the hell are you? How'd you get the gig?'

'A guy in . . . the TA. He's one of the . . . soldiers. Chance to . . . join the elite.'

'Is he the man in charge?'

He shook his head, saving some breath.

'Who is?'

'Is it the insider?' Baxter asked. 'Is it Campbell?'

'Told you. Don't know . . . names. Don't know . . . anything . . . 'bout him.'

His face was reddening, sweat pouring off his head and into his eyes, his hands unable to wipe it away. The heavy exhalations were now coming every breath.

'Oh God, please,' he appealed, looking to Baxter, the UML

man having recently identified himself as the closest thing to a voice of clemency as he was likely to hear.

Vale stared at the prisoner. 'If you don't have his name, you better give me something else. A description, age, accent, anything.'

'A tattoo,' he wheezed. 'On his arm. Please, the speed. I can't . . . I can't keep up.'

'Come on, Vale,' Baxter appealed. 'He's tiring, and he's no use to us dead.'

Parlabane shared Baxter's anxiety, but remained silent. Whether this was because he trusted Vale or merely feared crossing him was something his conscience did not wish to contemplate.

'And if he doesn't talk, he's no use to us alive.' Vale took a further step back, arms still folded. 'You were saying, about a tattoo.'

'A tattoo,' the prisoner repeated, as though having to work hard merely to refocus his brain. The footfalls were duller, heavier, and from the colour of his face he looked as much at threat from imminent cardiac arrest as from the rapiers.

With a frustrated sigh, Baxter leaned forward and stabbed a finger at the control pad, pressing down before Vale could intercede. 'He can't tell us anything if he hasn't the breath to fucking speak,' he muttered.

'Tattoo,' the prisoner gasped in a desperate whisper, a look of sudden terror on his face contrasting with the mildly indignant petulance on Baxter's as he calmly held the button. That was when Parlabane looked at the speed readout and saw it flash up 17 18 19 20. The fucking idiot was looking at the control arrows upside down.

'Ferry-aaaah,' the prisoner yelled as one of his flailing boots caught his other ankle and he stumbled, prompting an effect like he'd been running against the resistance of a bungee cord. He was thrown backwards as though yanked, driving his body upon the waiting swords: one point jutting through his neck and the lower through his abdomen.

The upper blade must have severed his spinal cord, because he was dead in the blink of an eye.

'Oh my God,' Baxter yelped, holding his hands either side of his face, staring in horrified disbelief. 'Oh my God.'

'You fucking idiot,' Vale shouted. 'What the hell were you doing?'

'I was trying to slow him down. I pressed the thing, I . . . oh my God, I pressed the . . . but I was on the opposite . . . oh my God. I think I've killed him.'

'Ach, no, he's just winded,' said Parlabane. 'Christ almighty, Baxter.'

'I'm sorry. Oh my God.'

'Just promise you won't try and help *me* if I'm in danger.'

'I won't. I will. I mean . . .'

'Get him out of here, Jack,' Vale said with laboured calm as he began to unlash the rapiers.

Medieval Bastards

Baxter wandered down the stairs in a disconsolate daze, requiring no further urging to exit the fitness room. Vale emerged a few moments later bearing both of the blood-smeared swords. Down below the grand staircase, Parlabane could see Alison and Ger seated on the floor against a wall, the girl's head rested against the chef's shoulder, her eyes red with crying.

'What happened to the prisoner?' Rory asked.

'Assisted suicide,' Vale replied. 'Ask Jack Kevorkian over there,' he added, indicating Baxter.

'He's dead?'

'Only in the sense that the oxygen supply to his brain has been cut off and he's been partially disembowelled.'

'That would do it,' Rory agreed. 'He tell you anything?'

'More than nothing, less than enough. I'll bring you all up to speed in a tick. What of the search?' Vale asked Ger, an almost hushed gentility to his tone anticipating stark news in response.

'We found Charlotte,' Ger reported, the mention of the name eliciting a sob from Alison. 'She was in the bath.' Ger made a tiny gesture across his throat, little more than an outstretched finger and a flick of the wrist. It was enough, and they knew he didn't just mean she'd had her throat cut.

'It's official,' Ger went on. 'Campbell is with the bad guys. The SIM cards were in his bin, ground into pieces.'

'Did you find anything else?'

'Didn't exactly use a fine-toothed comb. You'll understand if we didn't feel like staying long.'

'Quite,' Parlabane agreed. 'The fine print doesn't matter. We've seen the headline. Campbell's with the bad guys, and as this isn't the kind of undertaking you can exactly be recruited to from management consultancy, we can assume he's been with the bad guys from the beginning. We can only guess at how far back that beginning might have been.'

'But what I don't get is that it was me who brought in *him*,' Baxter stated. '*I* came to *him*.'

'That might have been how it looked to you,' Parlabane told him, 'but you'll never know what lengths he could have gone to to put himself in your path. If you didn't bite, he'd have had others in mind. By this stage, you probably don't know which aspects of UML were your idea and which he only made you *think* were your idea.'

'It's possible,' Baxter conceded, looking like he couldn't remember which way was up. 'We met at an exhibition. I was still working for, well, it doesn't matter. I had this idea and he was very encouraging of it, so when I decided to take the plunge and fly solo, I had his card.'

'And don't tell me, when you ran the idea past him, he said he could raise the investment.'

'Yes.'

'Well, now we know how,' Vale said. 'Around fifteen people paying a thirty-grand fee to take part in a human safari.'

'You're fucking kidding me,' Rory said.

'Not-so-cheap thrills, and a chance to try out for some other undisclosed undertaking,' Vale went on. 'Seems Campbell was dedicated to an all-action team-building exercise after all, but we aren't the candidates. We're the obstacle course.'

'The poker-faced bastard,' said Rory. 'He was there amongst us all the time, observing us, acting the shepherd when he's really the fucking gamekeeper. Watching us from his tower yesterday, tracking us in the woods today, sounding us out during dinner last night. Dresses us in luminous yellow so we're easier to keep an eye on. Sends us on a big long trek up hill and down dale, in wet clothes, running from an imaginary enemy, all the while he's spying. And to top it all, the whole UML is-it-real shenanigans lull us into a false sense of security, you could say a false sense of *in*-security, where we ignore all the danger signs and become incredulous of what we should be wary until it's too late.'

'But this took months to set up,' Baxter protested. 'Have you any idea how much work and planning went into it? Business plans, research, tenders, the kit we laid out for, PR . . . and it was all a front just for one night of carnage?'

'In my experience,' Parlabane said, 'people are prepared to dedicate extraordinary time and effort in order to get away with *one* murder. Now multiply that time and effort by tonight's intended body-count. Besides, the preparation wasn't all about providing a front. Look what else it provided: an isolated location, an environment they could control, the conditions Rory's just described. Plus, it didn't only supply the victims – it allowed them to be hand-picked. This isn't just a safari or just a test. This is a hit.'

'But I thought you both chose the guests,' Kathy said to Baxter. 'Mind you, it was Campbell who told me that.'

'No,' he replied. 'The guests were all his choices. I suggested plenty, but there was always a reason why they were unsuitable, according to him.'

'And some weird reasons why his choices *were* suitable,' Emily suggested.

'Seventh Chime and Reflected Gleam were both approached at his suggestion,' Baxter added. 'Oh God, that means . . .'

'What?' Parlabane asked, clocking Baxter shooting a panicked look towards Emily, not the first time he'd spotted such an unspoken exchange.

'Never mind, there isn't time. But you're right. The only

people here at random are the staff and the "plus ones".'

'Who are the plus ones?' Liz asked.

'Grieg, Tim and yourself,' Emily told her. 'Rory was named on the invite.'

'He wanted Jack Parlabane,' said Kathy, 'no question, despite you being the worst journalist to possibly invite on this kind of junket. He wanted Max and Joanna, despite neither being in a position to directly bring UML any future business. Toby too, despite working for a charity that doesn't have a pot to piss in.'

'Our prisoner talked about threats and witnesses,' Parlabane said.

'Who the hell can we be a threat to?' Kathy asked. 'I work in PR, for Christ's sake.'

'Well, speaking as a plus one,' Vale observed, 'I think that matters less right now than the fact that they're definitely here to kill everybody, named invitee or not. They got a panelling in round one. They wanted resistance, but they won't have been expecting *that*. They'd cleared the place of all decent weapons, which should have made it safe for them to send in their B or C team. We got a lucky break with the incredible self-decapitating man. But just because we fought them off doesn't mean they're going to call it a night. Once it begins, everyone's a witness, that's what the prisoner told us, and all witnesses are to be eliminated. They've fallen back to regroup. When they come in again, they'll come in with everything they've got. We need to be ready.'

'How many, did you say?' Emily asked.

'Three who know what they're doing and maybe a dozen would-be warriors.'

'And would coming in with everything entail more than swords?' enquired Rory darkly. 'I mean, if they're not taking any chances . . .'

'That's the doomsday scenario, yes,' Vale conceded.

'Wouldn't they have used guns already if they had them?'

Emily asked, sounding desperate rather than optimistic.

'The prisoner claimed it was part of the trial,' Parlabane informed her. 'It doesn't mean they don't have any. But on the other hand . . .'

Vale looked at him with genuine puzzlement. He seemed surprised not to know where Parlabane was going with this, but he shouldn't have been. Vale might be the one who understood tactics, combat and subterfuge, but when it came to comprehending outright deviousness, Parlabane was the ranking officer.

'The trial is a secondary consideration,' Parlabane explained. 'Number one is the hit, and getting away with it. They might be testing recruits and giving some psycho-tourists the trip of a lifetime, but what's the gain to balance the added risk factor of blades over guns? It makes the hit harder than it needs to be, as we've amply demonstrated. Why the hell wouldn't they properly arm these guys? They've got the resources, so there has to be another reason, and I reckon it's that they've got an interest in making this look like something primitive, something utterly fucking medieval.'

'Why?' asked Emily, but Parlabane could see Vale was catching up.

'To disguise the motive,' Vale said, an answer that seemed to strike a disturbing chord with Rory.

'Confusion in the aftermath,' he said in apparent disbelief.

'Bullets make it a hit,' Parlabane went on. 'It's clinical, precise, calculated, so the intention is clear. Cops start asking the who and why, looking for links, connections; normal, *rational* fucking reasons for why someone wanted all these people dead. This way, instead there's a macabre mystery in a place with a blood-drenched past, carved-up corpses in a spooky house, murdered using swords pulled from the walls and display cabinets. No witnesses, no suspects, and no motive because it's clearly an act of insanity. Jesus, think about this: post-mortems would reveal that several of the guests had undigested human flesh in their stomachs. Mathieson's skeletal remains will no doubt turn up, proving that we ate the fucking chef. The attention of the whole country gets focused on the murders, but everyone is asking why the gothic bloodbath in the gothic mansion.'

'Instead of why us,' Emily observed.

'Precisely.'

'Yeah, well, even if you're right and they don't use guns,' Rory said, looking more rattled than the rest, 'there's still more of them than there are of us, and I doubt the swords they took from here are the only blades they've got.'

'True,' conceded Vale, 'but swords aren't the only weapons we've got.'

'Eh?' Rory asked. 'Am I forgetting something?'

'Yes. Who we're up against. They might have fancied themselves as assassins, some of them might even believe they've got what it takes to pass this so-called test, but there's no way these wannabes coughed up thirty grand for a fair fight. They paid for the chance to live out their sickest fantasies with minimal risk and no comeback. Well, let's find out what kind of appetite for horror they've really got. If violence is indeed the only language they understand, I'd like to show them who's got the wider vocabulary.'

'Fuck yeah,' agreed Ger, lifting his bloodstained kitchen knife from the floor and getting to his feet. 'Vale's right: their trialists have been pish. I havenae seen a less promising line-up since Barnes and Dalglish. Enough aboot team-building. These bastards killed Charlotte. I'm up for some team-demolition.'

Vale doled out the duties to anxious but willing volunteers, some sent on specific tasks, others on errands of information, replacing and reassigning those previously posted to the barricades. Parlabane remained without a stated purpose as this ferment got underway, an oversight he was not inclined to believe meant Vale needed him for tactical consultation or as a personal bodyguard.

Vale glanced at him and then at the half-landing, by way of requesting a quiet word, and Parlabane suspected he knew what it was about. He responded with a nod and swiftly made his way up.

'You did well at rummelling up the troops, Tim,' he said, the pair of them sitting down together on a stair like it was a bench in a quiet pub. 'But what you didn't say was probably better for their morale than what you did.'

'Yes, well, I wasn't the only one holding back. We both know these guys will have a last resort.'

'No shit. And they're bound to engage it pretty soon seeing as their trialists didn't get on the scoresheet.'

'Maybe not right away, though.'

'Why the hell not? There's going to come a point when the job needs done and they need to get out.'

'Yes, but if you ask me, they budgeted for losing at least one of their own. They bet on it, arguably. We've even saved them the bother of lopping the head off.'

'Bet on it?'

'Fixed odds on the final score. They need an extra headless body for that aftermath you described.'

Parlabane got it. 'For Campbell.'

'Bit of a giveaway if everybody's dead and he's missing. Francis Campbell won't be his real name, but the non-resident staff could give a detailed description.'

'Plus a hunt for him points the investigation straight at UML,' Parlabane agreed.

'And that's why they decapitated the girl too. Leave some corpses headless and some not, and the cops are going to wonder why, and check that bit closer to confirm identities.

But if all the corpses are headless and the heads never found . . .'

'Lovely thought.'

'And here's another, regarding that last resort. If they're planning to take our heads and the fight gets too tough, they could just put a bullet in each of our skulls and still leave your mystery horror show.'

'The prisoner mentioned darts.'

'Could be tranquillisers. Same principle, same result: they put their target down from a safe distance, then it's heads you lose.'

'Safer from their point of view, too,' Parlabane observed. 'They can make as much mess as they want, but one tell-tale stray bullet, one overlooked shell-case even, and the charade is blown. Plus it's less risky if a weapon should fall into enemy hands.'

'Indeed. And the bad news is, darts or bullets, that's not the only part worrying me. Look at the kit bought just for UML's sham: clothes, paintguns, radios, badges. What's the chances their budget didn't stretch to a few pairs of night-vision goggles?'

'Pretty slim,' Parlabane answered. Vale didn't have to explain: when the pros in charge decided it was time to mop up, they'd cut the power, leaving everyone else blind.

'If the lights go out, we're finished,' Vale confirmed

'Do you reckon there's a back-up?'

'I'm betting my life on it.'

'Yours, mine and everybody else's. Where's Sir L?'

'On his way. I sent Rory to relieve him.'

Sir Lachlan was indeed limping down the corridor when they descended the stairs. He had good news, bad news and, for Parlabane in particular, extremely bad news.

'There is a generator, yes. The bad news is it's down in the basement level. It's oil-fired, a bit of a relic.'

'But serviceable?' Vale asked.

305

'I couldn't honestly say. We've only had one power outage since I bought the place, and the electricity was restored before we managed to put it to the test.'

'That doesn't sound promising,' Parlabane observed.

'No, no, I mean we didn't get as far as turning it on. There was no fuel for it; I mean, none handy.'

'None handy? And is there any handy now?'

'It was one of those things that should have been done at the time, but, well, once the crisis was averted, you know, there's always something more pressing . . .'

'We'll take that as a no,' Vale said.

'There is fuel, though. There's cans of petrol in the outbuilding: it's where we keep the gardening machinery.'

'That outbuilding has to be seventy yards from the nearest outside door,' Parlabane said grimly.

'More like fifty,' Vale estimated. 'But might as well be a mile.'

'I don't suppose there's a secret tunnel known only to the keepers of the ancestral family home?' Parlabane asked dryly.

'Not that the ancestral family thought to impart to me, no. Plenty of chambers and passages down below, but no way out except the way you go in. I suppose there is always . . . no.'

'What? Tell us anyway.'

'Well, the telephone cable passes over the outbuilding, but you'd need to be Spiderman to get up and down from there.'

Vale smiled. 'I know just the chap.'

Improvisation

Alison looked at her watch. It had been an hour and a half since the attacks at the stairwells, and the longer they went without a reprise, the more the tension grew. Nobody was about to start kidding themselves that the bloodied enemy might have run off with their tails between their legs; the growing delay just meant that they were regathering their forces and choosing their moment to strike. She remembered the unforgiving time-scale as calculated by the earliest possible discovery of the downed bridge. It was two fifteen, and these bastards had all night.

Waiting was the worst of it. Okay, obviously it wasn't worse than when they had been actually under attack, but that at least passed in a blur of reflex, panic and shock, over before she really knew what the hell was going on. When she looked back upon events, they played out in slow motion, certain moments stretched and suspended, whereas at the time, they had unfolded so quickly that she'd felt no more able to react and respond than she was able to dodge bullets. In retrospect, she could see Emily crouch, scrambling an eternity on the floor as the man with the machete loomed behind her, then her running, as though through knee-deep tar, before Ger told her to get down and launched his knife. Live, in real time, it had just been a staccato of snapshots, glimpsed in about two seconds: Emily, bad guy, Emily running, *zing*, bad guy dead. Not enough time even to take a deep breath, never mind a decision, but time enough for Ger to heft his knife, pick his spot on a moving target and bring the guy down.

I was a bit mental when I was younger.

'What *were* you inside for, Ger?' she asked him, when at last he looked her in the eye after the mutual shock of the kill.

'It wasnae tax evasion,' was all he would say.

He'd reacted very swiftly in Campbell's bedroom too. Alison only caught a glimpse of Charlotte's feet sticking over the edge of the bath before he'd grabbed her shoulders and wheeled her around.

Poor Charlotte. She was only eighteen, younger than Alison. She'd been planning to travel too: she was saving up to go to Australia. Her big sister had spent a year there and knew a few places in Cairns she could find work. They'd talked about it some nights, when the two of them weren't both so knackered that they coveted even minutes of sleep-time. Charlotte had been trying to sell Alison the idea, intoxicated by her own enthusiasm to the point where she already had the two of them sharing a beach-front apartment. Cairns hadn't sounded like Alison's thing, but it had been fun to ride shotgun on someone else's dream. Now it would never be more than that.

Ger's was a solid shoulder to cry on, but while she leant on it for comfort, the tears didn't gush the way she felt they ought. True cathartic grief took time and abandonment. Alison could afford neither.

She was grateful to have a task, grateful further that it hadn't involved lugging corpses up the stairs to the windows at the front of the gallery. She was assigned to the kitchen for her contribution, though it didn't completely spare her an eyeful of gore. Vale had warned her to wait outside for a few minutes while he and Ger took the body of the man Ger had killed and laid it on the island worktop in the centre of the kitchen. They emerged shortly afterwards, Ger with the body over his shoulder and Vale carrying something in a canvas bag. She'd expected the stainless-steel worktop to be more bloodstained when she went back in, but there were only a few smears, the corpse having bled all he was going to on the corridor floor. The smell, however, was revolting, causing her to gag and run to the sinks. She expected to throw up but didn't, which was when she remembered that she hadn't eaten anything since lunchtime.

Having something to physically get on with was a welcome distraction, but it wasn't as though she could exactly lose herself in her work. The possibility that they could come crashing through the windows any second was a hard one to lose sight of, and every time the wind gave the back door an otherwise familiar rattle, she was halfway to the corridor.

It could come any time, that was the truly horrible part. There were moments when she could almost – almost – concentrate so hard on the task in hand that she almost – almost – forgot what the task in hand was in aid of, and then the bigger picture would return to central focus. This was a temporary lull; the storm could resume at literally any second, and when it did, its rage would be terrible. She busied herself on the far side of the room from the windows as a precaution, gathering what she needed and performing the requested preparation with trembling haste, the sooner to get herself back out to the central reception area. Oven-cleaner, hob-cleaner, caustic soda, anything that bore the legend 'Avoid contact with eyes and skin' was bundled into a cardboard box, then she took every chilli in the cupboard and whizzed them in a blender with wasabi powder and vinegar.

The crashes of breaking windows shuddered through her, reverberating unmistakably into the kitchen despite the sound of the blender. Alison ran from the room, forgetting even to lock the kitchen door behind her, the very act she'd been rehearsing in her head every few seconds as she prepared herself for sudden flight. Not only had panic erased her awareness of vital procedure, but it caused her to run directly towards the source of danger, simply because that's where other people were.

It wasn't what she'd feared. Under the circumstances, there was hardly such a thing as a false alarm, but it was, this time at least, not the bad guys who were lobbing dead bodies through the windows. Vale, Ger and Sir Lachlan stood at the front platform of the gallery, above the main doors and their flanking windows, each before a now pane-less frame.

She understood. This was what Vale had meant about wannabe-warriors and their appetite for horror. All of the enemy's attention would surely now be focused upon the front of the house, where three of their own had been thrown down to the monobloc: hacked, skewered, headless, dead. How's your stomach for the fight now, boys?

The message was clear: come and have a go if you think you're hard enough. She just hoped it wasn't equally clear that they were bluffing. As many as sixteen left, Vale had said: homicidal, pissed off and already committed to a task they now could not afford to leave unfinished. A besieging force, superior in number, tightening its grip on a less-than-impregnable fortress, while inside they were scrabbling to furnish means of resistance from anything that came to hand. The grand piano had been disembowelled and its wires were being fastened by Baxter at neck-height across every inwards-opening ground-floor doorway. The resistance machines had been carried down from the fitness room and were having their cables restrung by Toby, more piano wire attached to their weight pegs. Emily was sharpening the end of a broomhandle with a kitchen knife. Crockery and cutlery were being stockpiled at those now glassless upstairs windows. Sir Lachlan was soaking bedsheet rags with spirits from the bar then twisting them into the necks of the bottles to furnish extremely upmarket Molotov cocktails. And Alison was bottling 'ocular marinade' for Vale. It was *Zulu* against *Home Alone*.

Vale knew it, too. He was readying them for resistance, nothing more. When battle came, he did not expect victory. He had asked Sir Lachlan whether, when it came to it, there was somewhere to which they could fall back, some place where they could make a final stand. The only options Sir Lachlan could offer were barricading themselves in the tower, behind its heavy oak door, which carried the risk of the invaders simply burning the place down around them; or to descend into the chambers and passageways beneath the building. This had the advantage of its entrance being concealed and therefore buying some time before the enemy discovered them, but Alison liked the sound of hiding out down there even less than the tower. Those chambers were the places excavated by Willcraft for the remnants of past slaughter, site of his own evil dabblings. With death beckoning them to come on down and join the party, it would be like sealing themselves inside their own tomb.

The sound of synchronised freestyle deid-bampot window-plummeting was Parlabane's cue. It would draw maximum attention to the front of the building and thus lessen the chances of his being spotted scrambling above the rafters at the rear, where he was reaping the whirlwind sown by a lifetime of misspent agility. He kept telling himself that Vale wouldn't have sent him out to do this if they had any alternative, which was undeniably true, but there was no way the swine hadn't enjoyed landing Parlabane with this just a tiny little bit.

Access to the roof was via a window halfway up the tower, above which was the turret from where Campbell and Baxter had observed their game of Capture the Flag. There wouldn't be much to observe tonight without the aid of infrared, which made him further regret that his wife Sarah had made him ceremonially dispose of his Jaguar Nightscope a few years back, amid other accoutrements of his less orthodox journalistic methods. (The explained monetary value of the device had almost won it a temporary reprieve until she had a peep through it at a less than serendipitous moment and saw the couple in the ground-floor flat across the street having a shag on their settee, behind the normally reliable cover of closed Venetian blinds. Copulating blurry white blobs weren't exactly hand-shandy material, but the damage was done.)

Down below, there was blackness beyond the short reach of the hotel's exterior lamps, no moon or starlight above due to the cloud cover. He could picture how black it would be if the power went out, which concentrated his efforts on picking his way across the roof to where the telephone cable was terminated. The rain had stopped at least, but the tiles were still slippy, and his balance had to compensate for the canvas bag on his back, the handstraps encircling his shoulders schoolboy-fashion.

If he moved too sharply, he could feel the weight in the bag shift in a revoltingly languid way. It didn't smell quite so strong now he was outside, but still the slightest whiff prompted his sensory memory to fill in the rest.

There was no rope. Ordinarily, that wouldn't have been a major concern, as it would be accurate to say that scaling rockfaces and man-made edifices with his bare hands *was* Parlabane's idea of a good time. Climbing along an inch-thick cable thirty feet above the ground was not a daunting prospect, nor would have been shinning down and then back up a telephone pole, even with a tin of petrol in a bag on his back. The problem was that the said telephone pole was close to a hundred yards past the targeted outbuilding, and the avoidance of traipsing across sword-wielding-nutter-infested territory was the very reason he was taking the elevated route. He needed a means of getting down and up again at the point where the cable overhung his destination. Unfortunately, the piece of kit he'd spied some hours back that was ideal, indeed designed for just such a purpose, was probably several miles downstream by now, having been swept away during Baxter's fake demise.

Bedclothes were out, despite being in abundant supply. A figure dressed in black, his face darkened with beef-stock powder that the chef only reluctantly owned up to being in possession of, could plausibly make his way across the moonless night sky without being detected. Start hanging white sheets down from the phone-line and you might as well be banging cymbals and playing a kazoo.

That was when Vale came up with a solution. Parlabane supposed it was in keeping with the group's necessary efforts to make use of whatever was to hand, but you never saw shit like this on *MacGyver*. The only practical resource they had passed up was the headsets from yesterday's headgames, on the grounds that Campbell had been monitoring then and so would plausibly be monitoring now. The chance to eavesdrop might even be why he hadn't removed or destroyed them.

'Yeah, but can't we use them to mislead, the way we did in the game?' Parlabane asked.

'Not if he knows we know he's listening. Betting on a bluff is dangerous enough, but betting on a double-bluff is like playing Russian Roulette with three chambers loaded.'

Parlabane conceded the point, but mourned the passing of the principle. It had been encouraging to briefly imagine making the bad guys look one way while they snuck out the other, but it failed to address the next, larger question of where the bloody hell he thought they could sneak out to. Defending the house at least gave them somewhere to make a stand – as long as the lights stayed on.

'Still bored, Jack?' Vale had asked, as Parlabane prepared

to embark on his mission. 'Or is the day job looking a bit more attractive right now?'

'Jury's still out, Tim. I mean, do you know how many times I've sat in a press conference and heard Nicola Sturgeon say the minister should resign? I think she must say it in her sleep.'

'Still, a fine mess old chap, eh? Gives a rather vivid perspective regarding what Kipling was on about.'

'Kipling?

'Yes. If you can keep your head when all about you are losing theirs . . .'

'Indeed. And I'd have to say that between them, Campbell and Baxter have really dropped us—'

'We've been friends a long time, Jack,' Vale interrupted. 'I adore your wife and I know what you mean to her, so I have to warn you that if you attempt to finish that sentence I shall feel compelled and justified in killing you.'

'Come on, I let the "heads you lose" remark go. And the Kipling.'

'Get busy, Jack. And remember . . .'

'Yeah, yeah. No guts, no glory. Very fucking funny.'

The cable was terminated a foot or so below the eaves at the westernmost end of the building. It was damp and therefore a little slick, but consisted of a reassuringly thick interwoven spiral, supplying the two dozen or so connections the hotel employed. Parlabane reached down with his left leg and hooked his foot around the line, giving it a tug to make sure it wasn't going to rip from the wall when he applied his weight. He leaned out to grip it with his left hand, but couldn't reach without committing his balance beyond the point where he could still keep hold of the eaves. Breathing in, he loosed the fingers of his right hand and let himself drop that last few degrees, crossing both feet around the cable. It held. Gripping with both hands, he pulled himself tight against it, the weight in the bag shifting to the centre, tugging at his oxters.

He felt a sharp pain in the left side of his chest, but knew despite the multiplicity of anxieties and physical demands being brought to bear upon it that it couldn't be a heart attack, as the said organ was still pounding away like the bass inside a ned-driven Fiesta at traffic lights. Before an exploratory hand could reach the spot, he realised that the pain was being caused by the cable pressing upon the stupid UML 'campaign medal' he was still wearing.

He unhooked it and let it drop into the darkness, thinking once again of the man who had pinned it there, smiling, looking him in the face, looking *everyone* in the face. What a piece of work. As he had mused earlier, they could only guess at how far back the beginnings of this thing lay. This guy, whatever his real name was, had to be an accomplished infiltrator: experienced and adept at the exhaustive duplicity of deep cover. The level of patience, planning, anticipation, calculation and contingency was soberly cold-blooded. He was a professional, all right, but a professional what?

Whoever, whatever he was, he wanted Parlabane dead – himself and several named others – even though Parlabane had never seen him before. In fact, he had never seen any of these people before. The only person he knew on the UML jaunt was Vale, and he was present at Parlabane's own invitation. Who were they? What connected them? Maybe there were no connections, except the one they each unknowingly had to whoever was behind it, and perhaps that was the perverse genius of it, of a mass hit. You invite the victims to their own murder, hand-picked: disparate, unconnected people you wanted dead for disparate, unconnected reasons. Perhaps, even, it was disparate, unconnected people who wanted them dead, too. A job lot of contract kills, erasing any apparent individual motive as the authorities searched for a collective one.

Wouldn't that be worth months of preparation and an investment outlay? For what kind of 'team' could they be

315

putting together but an assassination squad? Sure, between the sick thrillseekers and the testosterone-pumped thugs, the organisers knew they might not get many decent recruits, same as many of the participants knew they'd no chance of making the team. But that was about money: stake money for the future of Assassinations Inc. They were here, the prisoner had said, to wipe out threats. Clearly, someone somewhere still had a higher opinion of Parlabane's influence and abilities than he did these days, but at least there was a precedent for people wanting him dead. Who the hell was Joanna Wiggins a threat to? Or Uptight Emily, or an amiable eejit like Rory fucking Glen?

Night of the Eighties Undead 2

Rory looked at Emily again, each offering the other unconvincing but sincerely meant attempts at reassuring expressions. They stood side by side at the barricade, rapier and Sabatier.

'I like a girl who's handy with a kitchen knife,' he wanted to say, but couldn't bring himself. The self-aware chauvinistic double-entendre was the kind of patter that was sparking between them earlier, but while doing so now might offer a bit of laughter in the dark, for him it would only serve to underline what he was about to lose, even if they did get out of here alive.

They had relieved Toby and Sir Lachlan when Vale required them elsewhere, Toby being belatedly offered the chance to put his engineering degree to some practical application: something to do with gym equipment. Sir Lachlan was being ostensibly sought for his knowledge of the house, though Rory suspected he was being relieved from the barricade as much because he was in an increasingly bad way, losing blood despite Kathy's bandaging. Rory's own injury wasn't causing him too much discomfort, certainly not that he'd complain about for fear they'd threaten to pour more whisky on it. But he wasn't without his pain.

He and Toby had stood saying nothing for a moment as Toby prepared to leave the barricade, each knowing what the other wasn't talking about. Rory broke the silence, because he knew Toby wouldn't, not this silence nor the other one, without his consent. He was a good man, a far better man than Rory could ever hope to be. He was loyal, considerate, conscientious and utterly selfless. Toby had been young and stupid once too, but the difference was that one of them had grown up.

'Toby, it's time to tell them,' he said. 'For whatever it's worth.'

Toby had put a hand on Rory's shoulder for a second, then gone off to whatever Vale required of him.

'Tell them what?' Emily asked.

He wanted to put this off, and he did for a while. It was easy for them both to let the question slide, unanswered, amidst the kind of distraction that was around them: people hauling things about, nailing wire to doorframes; Ger and Vale coming by to collect the corpse that was lying in the hall outside.

Rory moved in a world where women were impossibly beautiful, rendered thus with the aid of digital manipulation, surgery or the regular application of two fingers towards the oesophagus. It set a benchmark that was so high as to be beyond even a natural ideal. Emily didn't resemble those women, and yet it felt a greater pleasure to look at her. Nobody would say she wasn't pretty, but it was something beyond the aesthetic and the physical that was touching him. Extreme circumstances like this could sell your emotions a dummy, he knew, but he honestly couldn't remember the last time he'd felt this way when looking at a girl.

There must have been such a time, though: a time before sex, a time when all you wanted was to be with that certain girl, to be hers, to be kissing her. Yes, you knew you'd want other things, but they seemed secondary, things that could wait. A time when mere smiles meant more than a glimpse of underwear – amazing as that was then too.

What happened? Where did it go? Was this what was meant by innocence? He hated that word for how it had been appropriated, and by whom. If their idea of 'innocence' was a lack of carnal desire, then there was no innocence about even fledgling sexual relationships. And yet there was truly an innocence to things that would appal the prudes: a journey of mutual discovery in those trembling shared acts, touches, partial undressings. Innocence wasn't lost in crossing lines and doing these things. Innocence wasn't lost in the passing of virginity when it was between two people who cared for each other. Innocence was lost when you stopped caring about the person and even stopped caring about yourself, only about the end product, and in his case product was definitely the word. Creature of Thatcher, he had become the quintessential consumer in his attitude to women, to sex, to life in general. It was all about what it brought him, what he could reach out and take, procure for himself. He wasn't on a journey like once before, encountering and experiencing. Instead it was gratification on demand, and not just in his sex life. That had been the motto of his *whole* life. Gratification on demand, and with deep pockets like his you could demand a lot. Material wealth and personal kudos brought most forms of gratification that he'd sought, and what they couldn't bring wasn't worth having.

Or so he'd thought.

In the currency required to give him what he wanted now, he feared he was bankrupt. If he wasn't already, then he certainly would be once Toby cashed his blank cheque. What would that leave? The knowledge of his worthlessness made Emily look all the more special, all the less attainable. Maybe the last time he'd felt this way was the last time he'd felt prepared to surrender so much of himself.

'Time to tell them this,' he said . . .

They were rearranging the deckchairs on the *Titanic*, but Alison was a rapt observer nonetheless. She knew she, Ger, Sir Lachlan and Charlotte were among the plus ones, simply

319

in the wrong place at the wrong time, but for that it felt somehow all the more imperative that there should be an explanation for why the others had been targeted.

She'd overheard Baxter ask people individually whether a tattoo of a boat meant anything to them, restlessly interrupting their tasks like it might precipitate some breakthrough that would change everything. He received no significant response, as she heard him stress to Vale. While they worked, waited and worried, posted around the grand staircase, the big question kept circling like a plane over Heathrow, with so far no sign of clearance to land.

'I wasn't aware I had any real enemies since Carol Clark stopped talking to me for three days in Primary Seven,' said Kathy. 'Why would anyone want all of us dead? Apart from the people we came with, none of us even knows each other.'

Toby spoke quietly as he re-fed a cable across one of his improvised siege-engines. 'That's not entirely true,' he said, instantly commanding the attention of everyone in earshot, which was pretty much everyone bar Parlabane and the four who were manning the barricades.

'Rory and I knew each other once,' he went on. 'But this is the first time we've seen each other since then.'

'Since when?' Kathy asked.

'Since we were students together in the Eighties. St Andrews. It's a small world; I suppose we were bound to run into each other again sometime, but that it turned out to be on this weekend might not be a coincidence.'

'Why?'

Toby sighed resignedly. 'It might mean nothing still, but no matter what, you're not going to like either of us much after I tell you this. Please remember it was a long time ago and we're different people now.'

'This doesn't sound promising,' Liz remarked.

'No. Well, I suppose we all found out where each other stands – or in some cases stood – politically last night. Rory and I met because we were both members of a campus Conservative group that was, shall we say, not at the wetter end of the spectrum.'

'The lefties were just spoilsports to me,' Rory explained. Emily nodded understandingly. After last night, none of this was exactly coming out of left – or should that be right – field, but it was early yet.

'I knew fuck-all about politics, I just knew they were the ones trying to take away my fun. And to me, student life was about having fun. My parents saw me all right, thank you, with my flat and my car and my endowment, and suddenly the benefits of freedom were at my disposal. Yet here were all these dedicated killjoys bringing down the party buzz by whining about everything and organising demonstrations. The country seemed to be doing very well from where I was standing, and yet they were determined to do it down and latch on to every negative issue they could lay hands on. If they couldn't find a native issue, they'd import them, like apartheid or whatever. I know, I know. You think I'm scum. These were important matters. They just weren't important to *me* at the time.'

'I don't think you're scum,' Emily said sincerely. 'I would have back then, but . . . well, maybe some of those issues weren't as important to me as I'd convinced myself. Perhaps I could have done with having a bit more fun. It wasn't exactly a barrel of laughs being a lefty. Do you know what it's like to feel guilty about every good time you have? Drank beer. Was that a Coors? They're funding the Contras. Bought a new top. Is it from Gap? Was it made with sweatshop child labour? Went to a club. What, while the rest of us were holding a candle-lit vigil outside the South African consulate? You're right, we could find an issue to get angry about every minute of the day.'

'I wasn't interested in issues, apart from us and them, us

being the cool, have fun, cars-and-girls set, them being the "carpers", as Thatcher called them. I came up with the name Conservative Student Forum because it abbreviated to CSF, which was close to "C as F": that's what we said to describe something we liked, and to describe ourselves. C as F. Cool as fuck.'

'Oh God,' said Kathy. 'Was that the lot whose little drinking song was: *Singing Thatcher, Reagan, Botha, Pinochet* to the tune of *She'll Be Coming Round the Mountain*? "Hang Mandela" T-shirts? Didn't Tebbit disband you for being too extreme? A bit like getting thrown out of Oliver Reed's house for being too pissed.'

'That was the Confederation of Conservative Students, to which some people I knew were affiliated, yes. But we were a localised affair, less bothered about Party policy and the like; being a national body, that was more the CCS's thing. We'd have had to actually know something about politics for that. We were just a glorified campus clique, a bunch of spoiled kids too used to getting our own way, brought together as much as anything by collective umbrage at the antics of the lefties. I don't know how much any of us believed what we thought we believed. There was a large element of posturing about it: adopting positions and professing statements in a kind of pee-the-highest contest to see who could outdo the others, or what we could do to outrage the lefties most. So yeah, if the lefties said "Free Mandela", we'd have said hang him, even if we didn't know who he was. It was schoolboyish tit-for-tat. You remember what it was like in those days.'

'I don't,' said Alison. 'My parents hadn't even met when Margaret Thatcher came to power. All I know about her is that my grandfather won't hear her name uttered in his house.'

'I'll place you on the spectrum,' Kathy said. 'How many

of the following do you hate: black people? Scottish people? The working classes? Gays? Intellectuals? Artists? The Irish? The French? Foreigners in general?'

'Eh, none of the above.'

'Then trust me, you and she wouldn't have gotten on.'

'Thank you, Kathy,' Toby said, 'for illustrating exactly what we were reacting to.'

'And how exactly did you react?'

'With much anger and self-righteousness. We felt inclined to fight militancy with militancy. I think the bottom line, the defining emotion, was a desire to shut the lefties up. They weren't in power, the overwhelming majority had voted against them, so we didn't see why we had to listen to them.

'Then came the Brighton Bomb. We saw it as an attack on ourselves, and part of the greater whole. It wasn't so much like Sinn Fein was the political wing of the IRA as the IRA was the paramilitary wing of this perceived lefty coalition, from Scargill to student agitators to the BBC. It didn't matter who they were, they were all out to do us down. And after Brighton we wanted to hit back. We wanted to defend ourselves. The SAS in Gibraltar felt like Mrs T was telling us that's what she wanted too.'

'What did you do?' Kathy asked accusingly.

'You remember the *Death on the Rock* programme? I think we felt more outrage over that than about the Brighton Bomb. It seemed like conclusive evidence of the enemy within, making our side look like the bad guys.'

'What did you do, Toby?' Kathy repeated.

'It was a fantasy that got out of hand,' Rory said. 'Haven't you ever wished you could just silence the people you disagree with?'

Emily nodded, an uncomfortable expression on her face, like she was feeling ashamed on his behalf, or maybe just having to work hard at politely hiding her disgust.

323

'We talked ourselves into believing . . . I don't know, everything seems so certain when you're that age. The SAS had just gone right in there, bang bang bang. Why couldn't it be like that, we asked ourselves. If people want to hurt us, let's show them we can hit them just as hard. Except, we weren't talking about the IRA. They were just one part of a bigger problem. What if we could silence these agitators, these enemies within, we wondered. Not up-front, obvious execution-style, because we saw from Gibraltar how that could backfire. But what if we could kill these people in ways that made sure no-one suspected a political assassination, or even a murder?

'It was just talk, just late-night fantasies. But the problem was, Toby met someone who wanted to make our wishes come true.'

'I was in the OTC, the Officers Training Corps,' Toby said. 'It's kind of the student TA. I got friendly with one of the army liaison guys, found we had a lot to talk about, having some of the same conversations with him as with Rory. The difference was, this guy was in the position to walk the walk. His name was Shiach. Maurice Shiach. He claimed to have connections in the intelligence services as well as the security services. More than connections, as it turned out. He was an informant. His role meant he had dealings with OTC and TA groups around the country, and he was officially supposed to be gathering intell on militant far-right elements in these reservist forces. There were a few such cells broken up around those days, but not on Shiach's watch. He was using his position to recruit like-minded volunteers for a little project he called the MoV: Ministry of Vigilance.

'It was going to do things for the defence of this country, Shiach said. Things that the government needed done but couldn't do for itself, or couldn't be seen to do for itself. He meant killing people who were, as he put it, a threat to

324

security. Killing them in ways that would deflect suspicion from those benefiting from their deaths. He hinted at unofficial sanction from higher up, but I'm not sure how true that was. There were certainly no resources forthcoming. At the time we were happy to convince ourselves, but let's face it, if the powers-that-be really wanted to set up a covert assassination bureau, they'd hardly pick students and TA weekend soldiers to do it.'

'They might if they wanted them to be disposable,' Kathy said. 'People they could easily disavow if it went wrong. Who the hell would believe you were anything other than fanatics acting off your own steam?'

'But that's exactly what we were. There *was* another intelligence agent involved, or so Shiach claimed. We never met him or learned his real name, because he was engaged in undercover work, infiltrating left-wing organisations. Shiach referred to him as the Architect, which suggested he was the brains behind the operation. He talked like this guy was the greatest, said he was a genius at blending in and earning the trust of the people he was there to spy on. You'd never suspect him in a million years: he could be your best friend, a guy you thought you knew inside out. You could look him in the eye and see no trace of deceit, yet all the while he was the enemy in your midst.'

'Campbell,' said Kathy.

'I guess . . . I don't know.'

'Of course it's Campbell,' said Baxter. 'You just described exactly what he did to me, what he did to all of us.'

'You don't understand. At the time, Rory and I weren't entirely convinced the Architect existed, and in retrospect I've always doubted he was anything more than a figment of Shiach's imagination, to help convince us we were part of something greater, something semi-official. He was also a convenient source of propaganda, allowing Shiach to gee us up with stories the Architect told him about just how evil and threatening these lefties he spied upon were. Rory and I came to the conclusion that in reality Shiach was the biggest fantasist of us all, just a nutter who was dragging us way out of our depth.'

'So you didn't go through with anything?' Emily asked.

'Of course not. We were just wankers, not murderers. We sat around thinking up schemes, ways of selling a murder as something else, such as the robbery-gone-wrong scenario. You find out where and when the target regularly buys his paper, say. You stage a botched robbery down the street, at the bank or Post Office, all masked up. Then in your plausibly erratically driven getaway car, you mount the pavement and run him down. It was my introduction to the ethics of advertising, you could say: selling an impression that disguised the truth. But believe me, the minute it threatened to get real, we bailed out. Shiach came up with a target, or rather, he said the Architect had. He wouldn't tell us the name, "for our own protection", but he was talking dates and locations. Toby and I, as they say in the common tongue, shat it. We told Shiach we weren't up to the job.'

'How did he react?'

'Spat the dummy, but it looked like the tantrum of a helpless man. He called us traitors and cowards and ranted about finding people who had the balls to go through with it. That didn't sound very likely, seeing as we were the best he'd come up with so far. And that was the end of it. We never heard from him again, and Toby and I didn't see much of each other after that either. Mutual disgust, it would be fair to call it. We'd learned some things about ourselves and each other that we didn't much like.

'I felt like I'd had a lucky escape. It taught me that I didn't care about politics, didn't even hate the lefties as much as I'd convinced myself. Toby was more chastened by it, though. He's got more character than me. We had a few mutual acquaintances, so I heard about him here and there. The summer after graduation, he went off and did some voluntary work with underprivileged kids in Tyneside. Ended up staying there and running his own charity. Meanwhile I just got on with what I always did best: pleasing number one.'

'I was pretty scared for a while in case Shiach showed up again. I half expected to see a news story reporting a death that bore a resemblance to one of the plans we'd discussed, or more likely to see that Shiach had got himself arrested in a failed attempt. But there was nothing.'

'Just because you noticed nothing doesn't mean nothing happened,' Kathy said. 'I mean, wasn't that the point? Unsuspicious deaths don't make the news.'

'True, but . . . a lot of these plans were things that *would* have been reported: they weren't all supposed to look accidental, just incidental. Innocent bystander scenarios, or—'

'Something that would conceal the true motive and intended target,' Vale interrupted. 'Such as a medieval massacre of unconnected strangers.'

'It's a lot more ambitious than anything we dreamed up, but the principle is the same,' Toby conceded. 'Though if it is Shiach, then at least we're not up against any kind of military genius. He was a failure, posted as liaison to the weekend soldiers because he was no use to the real ones. That's why he wanted to wage his own private war with his own secret army. If it hadn't been for the lefties, I don't know what he'd have done for an enemy.'

'The only thing the prisoner could tell us about the man in charge was that he had a tattoo,' said Vale.

'A boat,' Baxter added. 'I mentioned it earl—'

'He didn't say boat, he said ferry.'

'Sorry. I was being more general to widen the net.'

'Feriens Tego,' said Toby with a nod.

'What?'

'Feriens Tego. I don't know about a tattoo, but that was the MoV motto. Rory and I thought it sounded really cool, but then we were idiots who still thought the problems of the world could be solved by eliminating the people who disagreed with us.'

'What does it mean?' Kathy asked.

'Get your retaliation in first, attack is the best form of defence. Literally: "Striking, I defend". The kind of simplistic, half-witted macho bullshit that makes perfect sense to people who need an enemy in order to define themselves. It's Shiach, all right. And it sounds very much like Campbell was – is – the Architect. It's taken them more than fifteen years to get their project off the ground, but in order for it to succeed, they'd need to silence the people who can identify its hand. No use suiciding a dissident if there's people out there who recognise the MO.'

'Yeah, but what the hell did I do?' Kathy asked. 'Or Joanna, or Max?'

'Max said he was in the TA,' Liz told them. 'And he was pretty hawkish in his views last night.'

'But presumably not hawkish enough,' Toby observed. 'Otherwise he'd be on the *out*side of the building.'

'Brilliant,' said Kathy. 'So it's psychopathic right-wing extremists on the outside trying to get in to kill the right-wing not-quite-extreme-enough-ists on the inside.'

'And maybe it's not quite as simple as that,' Baxter said meekly. 'Rory and Toby aren't the only people here who knew each other in the past, nor the only ones with something to be ashamed of. Hate to break it to you, Kathy, but you're actually a plus one. Campbell hired Seventh Chime for the same reason he came to me, and he must have been pissing himself the whole time to know how much I was

328

squirming. So I guess your pal Emily didn't tell you the whole truth about her own student radicalism.'

It was slow going, more out of cautious necessity than Parlabane's physical abilities. He could have hauled himself along a lot quicker, but the greater his movements, the more sphincter-puckering the dip as the cable's brackets strained to support his weight. Keeping it slow, steady and smooth, his body tight to the spiral, lessened the bounce effect that threatened to bring his mission to an abrupt end.

Since being stabbed in prison, he had embarked upon an unprecedented commitment to his personal fitness in an overcompensating attempt to prove to himself that his recovery was complete. The approach of the big four-oh had also donned its own tracksuit and whistle, and between the two it would be accurate to say he was in the best shape of his life, other than missing a few feet of gut. It meant that he was ably disposed to haul his own weight and that of his burden across the blackened void without breaking too much of a sweat, but the irony of the bag's contents was as prominently vivid in his mind's eye as the prospect of what he was required to do with them.

He remained still for a moment in order to arrest the cable's swing, having reached the point where he'd have to descend. The outbuilding was a tantalising few feet to the left of the phone-line; once he'd climbed down far enough he could probably swing to its roof, but while he was already nervous about the strength of the cable, that was nothing compared to his dubiety with regard to Vale's improvised climbing cord. Parlabane hooked the crook of his right arm around the line in order to allow his left arm to wiggle free of one canvas strap. The bag then dangled beneath his back, requiring him to swing to and fro a little until his right hand could get hold of the zip. Immediately he pulled it, he could feel the weight inside press forward and squeeze into the opening gap, the touch of it against his knuckles a hideous foretaste of what was to come. He stopped the zip where it was. If he opened it any further, the whole lot would simply tumble out and disappear, which was admittedly a tempting prospect in isolation, but less so when the consequences were factored in. Turning himself on to his front, the bag now dangled in front of him, allowing him to get hold of the loose handle with his right hand. Another semi-rotation flipped him over again, this time leaving the holdall resting on his chest.

The smell was like low tide on the shores of Loch Shite.

Parlabane's motivations had had plenty of aspersions cast upon them in his time, rightly and wrongly. For the things he had done, the lengths he had gone to, the acts he had committed, he had been variously described as self-aggrandising, egotistical, self-loathing, isolationist, monomaniacal, eminently slappable and just plain nuts. Fair enough, he'd thought. Not even all-American comic-book superheroes were pure and uncomplicatedly altruistic in their deeds, and he'd never attempted to justify his activities by depicting himself as a champion of the people. Tonight though, he figured he must be on some kind of all-time shortlist of the selflessly heroic. Batman was out for revenge. Superman was trying to earn the approval of two dead father figures. Indiana Jones wanted fortune and glory. Luke Skywalker was a bored farmboy looking for kicks. Han Solo just wanted the cash and to grope Princess Leia's tits outside the force-field generator. Other than its necessity in helping stave off a massacre, there was no personal pay-off for Parlabane in taking twenty-five feet of human small intestine from a canvas bag and using it in lieu of climbing rope.

It was very slimy. This tactile aspect was naturally a major consideration in the potential boak factor, but an even greater one with regard to grip. Going down would be an express ride, but the return journey promised to be more

330

problematic, especially with a can of fuel on his back. Gagging reflexively at the combination of touch, smell and *Icare d'Afrique* recall, he tugged a length from the bag, letting it spill out until one end was free. It was going to be a long time before link sausages were back on the breakfast menu back home in East London Street.

Supporting himself with his ankles and the inside of his left elbow, he tied the end around the cable in a practised knot, yanking at it to check it wouldn't slide undone. His fist slipped along it at first, due to his reluctance to squeeze, but when he did, it appeared to be holding. He let the rest of the intestines drop from the bag and dangle into the darkness. There was so little light from the rear of the building that he couldn't see the ground, but from the free movement of the 'rope', he could tell it hadn't touched the bottom. He wasn't worried about the drop at the end, but if it was too high to reach when he went to climb back up, it would be gauntlet time.

Parlabane climbed forward a few inches and uncurled his right foot from the cable so that he could hook his ankle around the descendant. He was about to let go of the bag as a potentially entangling encumbrance when he heard the sound of hurried footsteps heading his way.

Keech.

He'd been made. All the way across, he'd been scanning, albeit upside down, for any sign of human activity on the horizon, but just because he hadn't seen them didn't mean they couldn't see him. If they were using those infrareds he and Vale discussed, he'd have been easier to spot than if he'd been doing this in daylight. His mind raced ahead, extrapolating scenarios. Armed only with a blade, the bad guy wouldn't be able to get him without climbing up himself, but he could call for help, which would mean someone shinning up the telephone pole and cutting the cable to bring him down. Could he make it back to the house before they made it to the top? Alternatively, of course, they could just shoot him in the head, or with one of those postulated tranquilliser darts. Again, survival would hinge on him reaching the roof before the shooter got a bead on him, assuming the guy whose footsteps he could hear wasn't packing a gun himself.

It was all rendered moot as the footsteps passed underneath and he saw the man, bearing a machete in both hands, charge forward, intent upon attack but oblivious to the target suspended above him. He watched in grateful disbelief as the man headed towards the house, his back now to Parlabane. That the guy had failed to see the intestines didn't augur well for the height of that final drop, but from Parlabane's angle it was hard to tell whether they'd have been in his line of sight anyway.

The man rounded the corner at the end of the house, where he slowed his run, pulling up like he'd twanged a muscle or was giving up on a forlorn pursuit. Parlabane watched him look around, cautiously at first, holding the machete now in preparation to defend rather than strike, then drop his guard altogether and wander rather purposelessly about the area. It seemed, as ever, incredible that he would not at some point glance up and spot Parlabane, even in this darkness, but the earthbound human tendency to survey only two dimensions had rendered him effectively invisible plenty of times before, and seemed to be protecting him again now.

'There's nobody here,' he heard the man say, though to whom was less apparent.

He walked around some more, poking half-heartedly at a shrub with his machete.

'Yes, I heard you, and I'm *standing* ten feet from the north-western wall,' he replied, to whatever had apparently been said in between. He wasn't holding a radio, but was clearly in remote communication somehow. 'Nah, it wouldn't be

332

the transmitter. More likely a clipping error with the wire-frame. The fucker's probably just inside. Yeah, okay. I'll have another quick check. Gotcha.'

WTF?

The guy had been running full tilt, determined upon something even though he couldn't see it. Determined upon some*one*, in fact, given that he was in machete-wielding mode. Then when that someone turned out not to be there, whoever he was talking to had insisted this target, this person, was a few feet from the north-western wall; insisted according to his faulty information, which involved a 'wire-frame' with a 'clipping error'.

Parlabane didn't consider himself a computer expert by any means, but he would lay claim to a solid grasp of modern PC fundamentals, such as how to bypass the office security to surf proscribed sites at work, and where in the system to hide certain jpegs so the wife won't stumble across them; as well as, naturally, the basic console commands for cheating at most of the best-known video games. Clipping was what you switched off when you decided it would be easier and/or more interesting to be able to walk, fly or drive your seventy-foot Japanese mechanoid through walls.

The bastard this bloke was talking to was looking at a 3D model. A transparent, wireframe one to be precise, and inside it he had a means of pinpointing the location of his targets. The machete bloke had been despatched to kill because according to their computer, someone was outside the building. However, the position had been wrong, perhaps because Parlabane was not only outside the wire-frame, but thirty-odd feet up at a point not triangulated in the model.

No. Even allowing for it wrongly positioning him on the vertical axis, it didn't explain why the guy was looking forty-odd yards away on the horizontal from where Parlabane was silently hanging on.

Unless it *wasn't* wrong.

The medal, the fucking UML campaign medal: that was the transmitter. Campbell had pinned one to each of them at the start of the evening, so that some swine with a laptop could keep track of everyone inside. He was then relaying that information to his cohorts via some form of concealed comms system, maybe an in-ear sub-vocal rig, and they were acting live on that information.

That was why they had launched an attack through the snooker room: they knew there were two isolated targets down there, with more on their way. Easy pickings and an encouraging start for the trialists, or it would have been but for that once-in-a-lifetime, unrepeatable circus feat. Then on the stairs, when they knew they'd meet resistance, they sent two guys to attack Rory, Liz, Joanna and Kathy *because they thought there was only one target*. The girls had gone to bed early due to events at dinner – Joanna in the huff, the others despairing of ever seeing dessert – leaving their medals in their rooms when they were roused. Everyone goes to assist Rory, leaving Alison and the medal-less Sir Lachlan vulnerable at the far end of the house: cue attack at the other stairwell. Right now they'd know everybody was sitting tight, waiting for the next wave, so the bastards could take their time and choose their moment, only reacting, as now, if someone appeared to be escaping from the house.

Parlabane feared that any degree of optimism in the current circumstances was the equivalent of saying 'so far, so good' as he plummeted from a skyscraper, but couldn't help thinking to himself that he might just have found the edge they needed. Which, of course, wouldn't count for dick if this guy looked up, something that seemed an excruciating eventuality as he ambled unhurriedly in Parlabane's direction, moving ever closer to where the human creeper was dangling from the phone-line. It was murkily dark and he didn't know how close to the ground the thing reached, but it had to enter the periphery of the bloke's vision at some point, surely.

He held his breath, aware he could make out even the bemused tuts and sighs of the man below, followed by a sharp bout of nasal inhalation.

'God, sniff that,' the man muttered distastefully, wandering within mere feet of the smell's source.

The next thing Parlabane heard was a splat as something dripped from the end of the intestine and hit the wet stone below. The man turned his head, zeroing in on the spot where the droplet had landed. There was only one place he was going to look next.

Parlabane had no choice but to let go of the cable completely and slide down the length of slimy bowel. He was already falling at speed as the man looked up, eyes and mouth agape, in time to be sprayed liberally in both by the matter that was being squeezed from the intestine by his rapid descent.

Up above, Parlabane's slimily lubricated knot slipped free under the strain of his weight, but his fall was broken by landing upon his erstwhile hunter, the pair of them tumbling to the ground a few feet apart. Parlabane reacted quicker in getting to his feet, less out of superior reflex than his opponent being temporarily blinded by faeces and convulsed by vomiting. The poor bastard was on all fours, wiping at his eyes with his sleeve while his stomach contents sprayed from his face. The machete lay on the monobloc closer to Parlabane, who quickly picked it up.

He stood over the man, wondering for a second what to do next. He had nothing to restrain him with, and even the dry heaves weren't going to keep him demobilised forever. Others, he knew, would have been sorely tempted to dish out what the bastard had had in mind for him, but Parlabane's vengeful instincts were far more spiteful than

335

that. Whatever these pricks were specifically here for, the general principle was to silence the people who posed them a threat, whether that be those who could bear witness to events tonight or those who perhaps had testimony of a more vintage hue. Killing people was a lot easier than winning the argument, a lot easier than explaining yourself or justifying your actions. These bastards were here because of arguments they couldn't win and deeds they didn't want to own up to. That being so, Parlabane wanted the fuckers taken alive. It wasn't easy when they were proving to be half-psycho, half-lemming, but it was the principle that mattered.

He stepped forward and kicked his conquest as hard as he could in the left temple. The man keeled over as though his body was dragged by his neck's recoil, then lay unconscious on his back. Parlabane knelt down and cradled the man's head, turning it on one side and then the other until the device he sought dropped into his waiting, cupped palm. He slipped it into his left ear and set about dragging his foe to the outbuilding.

'Maybe I should have worried a bit more about number one myself,' Emily said. 'Then I might have been a bit more balanced. You know what they say, you can't love anyone else until you learn to love yourself. When I was a student in Edinburgh, I was just guilt-ridden and angry all the time. We live in an age when communications media can immediately bring to our attention every last tragedy that can befall our fellow man, however remote, and every last cruelty we can visit upon each other. Wars and famines you'd never have even known about a hundred years ago, in countries you'd never have heard of.'

'But isn't that a good thing?' Rory ventured timidly.

'That is a good thing, yes, in that it keeps us aware of what we ought to sort out, but if you're sensitively inclined, half an hour in front of the box is enough to make you feel thoroughly inadequate, sheltered and privileged just to be alive, Western European, HIV negative, heterosexual, unraped, unbombed, unstabbed, unmutilated, unhandicapped, uncancerous, unaddicted, unburnt, unflooded, unmugged, unpersecuted, unshot, unmined, unmolested or unsacked.

'The girl with the weight of the world in her hands. That was me. My heart was always in the right place, but it was never done bleeding. I joined every demo and fought for every cause because I felt it was my responsibility. But as it was said last night – might even have been you – did I really care so deeply about *all* those issues? How can you? You can only feel like you ought to care. It's so pathetic: I was a vegetarian as a student because I moved into a flat where all the other girls were vegetarians and I didn't have the nerve to tell them I wasn't. It was like: shit, how could I have been so remiss, how could I have not got around to turning veggie? It was an orthodoxy that I accepted without asking myself what *I* wanted, what I really believed.'

'Bet you're wishing you'd stayed veggie tonight.'

'No, I'm wishing I'd indulged myself when I had the chance. I could die here tonight and I'm starting to realise how little I've really lived.'

'At least you tried to make a difference. Look where my ideas of student activism have got us.'

'Mine aren't blameless either. This must have something to do with me too.'

'How do you work that out?'

'Because of Baxter. It's not really for me to say, but it hardly matters now. That's not his real name. Campbell must have known that, known about both our pasts.'

'Not his real name?'

'His real name is Daniel Brown. We were fellow student lefties, him being about the only one more conscientiously

337

committed to absolutely bloody everything than me. He was a few years older, worked for a while then went back to nightschool to get his Highers. There was Danny, myself and a guy called Philip Young who were pretty close, considered everyone else trendy lefties or plastic socialists.'

'Philip Young. Why do I know that name?'

'He's a civil rights lawyer now, spokesperson for Taking Liberty. Max had a go at him last night.'

'Oh yeah. He's the guy they always wheel out for the TV news to denounce the Home Secretary's latest crime-prevention proposals.'

'Well, if you mean he believes we should retain the presumption of innocence until proven guilty, then yes. He's the only one who really went on to practise what he preached. Back then we were all on umpteen of the same committees, and Danny in particular seemed to be involved in so many things, I don't know how he ever managed to attend a lecture.'

'We were as sure of ourselves and every bit as self-righteous as Toby's CSF,' Baxter said. 'And ironically we perceived ourselves to be at odds with one of the same enemies: the media. It was all Tory-owned, all part of the grand right-wing conspiracy to silence dissent and spread their propaganda. We hated Rupert Murdoch and Roland Voss as much as we hated Margaret Thatcher and Ronald Reagan. And like Toby and Rory, we decided it was up to us to strike back.

'We hatched our own little gunpowder plot, to burn down Roland Voss's Scottish printing plant. You know, silence the mouthpiece of the oppressor and all that; or the same as Toby, silence the people who disagree with you. Well, we knew it wouldn't exactly silence them, but it would still be a blow. Best-case scenario would be they'd have to import the English editions, which would have buggered them up

338

editorially because the southern versions weren't quite so sensitive to Scottish feelings.

'It was pitiful. Three of us and a van full of Molotovs. Before the internet, it was actually a lot harder to learn your amateur anarchist basics. The plan was to drive there in the middle of the night and lob petrol bombs over the perimeter fence to the warehouse where they stocked their paper drums, then hope for a chain reaction. I guess we were also hoping for the staff to evacuate without getting burned to death, but we didn't give them a lot of thought. It was a mercy for all concerned that we never made it. If we hadn't killed some poor bastard in the warehouse, we'd have probably torched ourselves.'

'What happened?' Kathy asked.

'We got pulled over on the way there. No, actually, we didn't pull over, not at first. A police car came up behind us and put its blue lights on to signal us to stop. Danny was driving, and he panicked, just put the foot down. Like we were going to outrun a souped-up police Sierra Cosworth in our knackered old Honda Acty that could barely break forty with a steep downslope and a tail-wind. Turned out the police were only pulling us over because we had a broken tail-light, but obviously we'd just announced that we'd something to hide. They found the petrol bombs and took us in.

'The plot all came out. I might have considered myself a hardliner, committed to the cause, but when they told me it would go down better with the judge if I cooperated, I blabbed everything. They seemed to know a lot anyway, from the questions they were asking, so I suppose I wasn't the only one to crack.

'We were found guilty of conspiring to commit arson. The cops had scared the shit out of me by initially saying we'd be up on terrorist charges, but I think they just recognised I was a silly wee lassie who'd give them all they needed if they gave her a fright. Philip and I got suspended sentences. Ironically, our lawyers played the "good little middle-class kids who'd learned their lesson" card. We still had criminal convictions though, which didn't exactly make us hot prospects at the milk-round.'

'And what about Donald, Danny, whatever you call him?'

'He wasn't tried with us. He got taken away to London by Special Branch who were investigating his connections to other potentially subversive groups. He had previous convictions he never told us about; arrested on one too many demos. We never saw him again, just heard through the cops. He got jailed. Three-year sentence.'

'I've been rebuilding my life ever since,' Baxter said, 'and I suppose you could say I've come full circle, seeking the corporate shilling. But look where the revolution got me. I decided to change my name so that I could make a fresh start. Emily recognised me, but she was good enough to remain circumspect about it. Neither of us wanted to pick at that particular scab, but . . . I don't know. I thought I had escaped the past, but that the two of us were brought together under these circumstances would suggest other-wise.'

He picked up a claymore and began walking towards one of the corridors.

'I'm off to talk to her,' he said. 'She deserves the courtesy of knowing our sad little secrets are out in the open.'

Parlabane lay the unconscious body down less than gently next to the outbuilding's wooden double doors and reached into the still revoltingly damp bag for the keys and torch Sir Lachlan had laid on. Turning on the second revealed an absence of need for the first: the lock had been crowbarred, and another look at the doors showed that they were not closed properly, just pulled to. He nudged the overlapping one with his shoulder to give a gap of about three feet, then gripped his captive under the oxters and dragged him inside, wiping his hands on the guy's jacket when he was done. Parlabane reckoned it was some kind of miracle that he hadn't spewed his load tonight; indeed would have been relieved had his stomach decided to purge itself of his first involuntary helping of cannibal cuisine. Unfortunately, and perhaps disturbingly, his stomach seemed to like it just fine. There'd been no end of doner kebabs and late-night pudding suppers about which the same could not be said.

He played the torch around the inside of the building, his nose unusually grateful for the fusty smell of encrusted grass-cuttings. His beam picked out machinery around the floor, accessories and tools about the walls and shelves: a petrol-driven mower with a seat and steering wheel, like a scaled-down tractor; a v-shaped raking attachment; a leaf-blower, two edge-strimmers, a pressure-washer, hoes, spades, rakes and watering cans. There were a number of conspicuously empty spaces beneath hooks, Parlabane trying and failing to prevent himself guessing what they were there to accommodate. There were a lot of trees around here that would need regular TLC . . . Oh boy. Tobe-Hooper-tastic, as Rory the Tory might say.

The cans of petrol for the fuel-driven machines sat resting on a wooden shelf at the back, alongside lubricating oil, weedkiller and pesticides. It occurred to him that Vale would probably be able to make explosives, a space rocket and possibly a time machine out of the stuff in here, but the petrol cans were less than dainty so it was going to be no easy feat just getting back to base with what he'd come for.

Power was the priority, and it looked like he might still have time on his side to ensure it stayed on. The guy he'd flattened was not equipped with any night-vision gear, so it was likely none of his fellow trialists were either. They wouldn't kill the lights while they reckoned they could still

341

make use of their footsoldiers, whom Parlabane guessed probably had one more chance at proving themselves.

His captive moaned a little as Parlabane zipped the bag closed around the lightest of the petrol cans, prompting him to have another scan of the available equipment. The strimmers were electric, so there had to be extension cables here somewhere. He trained the torch below where the strimmers hung, and saw a pile of coiled orange flex sitting on the floor next to a heavy polythene refuse sack.

Perfect. There were two separate leads. One would do for the shit-gargler, and the other he could use for climbing: toss the end weighted with the plug over the phone cable and he'd have a double-strength, unlubricated rope to get back up with. He dragged the captive further inside and knelt down again, placing the torch on the floor next to him. With its light casting knee-high shadows upon the polythene sack, Parlabane looped the flex around his prisoner in a tight spiral from his ankles to his mouth, then down his back to where he bound his wrists together, and finally back to his feet where he knotted the plug end around the jack.

Time to go. He hopped over the prisoner to get back across to the second coil of flex, accidentally kicking the polythene sack as he landed. Something inside it shifted. Rolled.

It had felt solid yet soft, and Parlabane's stomach briefly considered (but declined) one more opportunity to eject his dinner as he realised it was the second time in half an hour that he'd kicked someone in the head.

Despite the movement inside it, the sack's neck remained mercifully folded over. He already knew what was in there; there was no need to confirm. Except that in the limited, low torchlight, it looked like there were four lumps, and as far as he was aware, they were only missing three: the chef, the waitress and the twat. He put his hand down and patted the plastic. It was no trick of the light: there was a fourth head in that bag, and he now had no choice but to open it.

342

Still suffering the cumulative effects of his intestine-squeezing descent, Parlabane felt he was seriously pushing his ick tolerance levels. He thus opted to spare himself the added tactile displeasure of lifting the heads out individually, instead taking the machete and ripping the sack apart. Three of them looked towards him with open eyes and lolling tongues, looks of permanent, horrified surprise cast on their features. He recognised two as the waitress Charlotte and poor, hapless Grieg. The third was unfamiliar, but it occurred to him then that he wasn't sure he'd seen Mathieson to know what he looked like. Perhaps the fourth would be similarly unidentifiable.

He wasn't granted any such mystery, any more than he was spared having to lay hands upon a decapitated napper. Parlabane turned the last head around and found himself staring into a face that told him what had for hours been staring into his own.

The face was that of Francis Campbell.

He wasn't the infiltrator and he wasn't the enemy.

But it was me who brought in him. Baxter had said. *I came to him*.

He wasn't lying, but as Blake put it, a truth told with evil intent beats any lie you can invent.

Baxter. The fly bastard was so subtle, he'd got them trying to persuade *him* Campbell was the spy. He'd got them to convince themselves of his own lie.

And yet the evidence had all been there. He'd come to the interrogation instead of joining Ger and Alison's search of Campbell's room, even though the latter would open the book on this guy whose deceit he was so avowedly furious about. He'd joined in the interrogation because he had to know how much the guy told them, and had to make sure he didn't finger the traitor in their midst. That was why the prisoner looked so baffled when he asked about 'the guy on the inside'. *He* was the guy on the inside, and it was his

343

way of warning the prisoner not to give him away. And then when he knew the prisoner had broken, knew he'd tell them anything to stop the torture, he'd pressed the accelerator to kill him.

He was everything they'd feared of Campbell and more: not only had he been observing them in the phoney war, but he was still among them right then, to monitor, maybe verifying what he feared they knew, picking up leads to further threats, future targets. He was an enemy agent walking free among them, able to choose his moment, to undermine, to sabotage, and secretly to strike.

Stronghold Opposition

There was a knock at the window. They both looked around to see Baxter send them an acknowledging wave through the small pane, a precaution against getting run through by Rory if he'd just opened the door and given them a fright.

'Rory, I'll take over here for a bit,' he said quietly, as though burdened. 'I need a word with Emily.'

'Rory knows,' Emily told him. 'Sorry.'

'Well, don't be. Everybody knows now. There's no secrets left tonight.' This last he said with a look to Rory. 'Don't worry,' Baxter assured him, 'they're not going to lynch you. I'll take over here, on you go.'

He looked as reluctant to leave as Emily was to let him, but awkward as it would be, she understood Baxter must need this moment. Rory shuffled past in the narrow stairwell, Baxter holding the door open for him.

'I'm the one who ought to apologise,' Baxter said as the door closed. 'But it would have been tricky to ask your permission before—'

'It's okay. It's nothing, in fact. It seems so small now, looking back. For years I've never been able to bring myself to admit it to anyone who didn't already know, and I've steered clear of most of them. But having finally told someone, it just looks like an overblown student prank. Everybody gets to screw up once when they're young, don't they? It's how we learn.'

'True. We were hardly going to bring down the state.'

'No,' she agreed. 'Couldn't see us edging Carlos the Jackal off the World's Most Wanted list.'

Neither, given that point, could she see why the pair of them constituted a threat. Why would Shiach and the Architect be worrying about a couple of failed radicals, so much so as to not merely invite but recruit both of them to this venture? Rory and Toby could identify Shiach and his methods, but what did Emily know that was so dangerous?

Then she saw that the answer was standing right beside her.

'Hey, can I see that knife a second?' he asked casually. 'I'll show you how you should be holding it.'

Oh shit.

'The Architect worked undercover, infiltrating all these left-wing groups,' Rory had said. 'Shiach told us you wouldn't believe how close he was to these people and they didn't have a clue.'

What about Donald, Danny, whatever you call him?

He got taken away to London by Special Branch . . . Danny was driving, and he panicked, just put the foot down . . . They seemed to know a lot anyway, from the questions they were asking . . .

She didn't just know he was the Architect, she now knew why she had been invited and who was next on the death list. She was the third side of a triangle connecting an MI5 agent, intent on building his own covert assassination unit, to a high-profile civil rights campaigner whose demise would suit the more hawkish elements of the security and intelligence services down to the ground; precisely the kind of 'enemy within' the Ministry of Vigilance had been dreamed up to get rid of.

Emily looked him in the face before she could stop herself, and he saw it immediately, saw everything she knew. He lunged for the knife, which she twisted in her grip to avoid his grasp and thrust into his chest just under his right arm. Baxter's own weight forced it deep through his armpit and into his shoulder, lodged so firmly that she lost her hold of it when he spun away, grabbing for the claymore he'd rested against the wall behind him. Emily slipped through the exit as the heavy steel blade clattered low against the edge of the open door, Baxter unable to get much power or control to his one-handed swing. She emerged into the corridor, where Rory was still in sight, turning as he heard the commotion.

'It's Baxter,' she shouted. 'He's with *them*.'

Rory began running towards the fire-door, rapier at the ready. She looked behind through the window and saw Baxter take something from his pocket then put it in his ear. He pulled clumsily at one of the mattresses in order to get down the stairs, the knife still lodged in his shoulder. Emily held the door open to facilitate Rory's charge, but before he got there, Baxter broke through the barrier and began scrambling down the stairs, talking to some invisible partner as he retreated.

'It's me,' he said loudly. 'I'm blown. Send in everything we've got, full assault, *now*.'

'You're fucking dead, Danny boy,' Rory shouted after him, but Baxter disappeared without retort.

Parlabane was thrusting his arm through the second coil of flex when he heard a voice and almost impaled himself on the nearest hoe in his startlement. It sounded so close that it could have been one of the heads addressing him, until he realised it was coming from the device in his ear.

'Charlie, get back here, I want everybody front and centre. Truck's ready, we're going in. This is it.'

'Roger,' Parlabane said, deliberately hoarse, after a gathering pause. A truck. Front and centre. They were going to pull the bloody doors off, or maybe just ram them down.

Well, fuck it, at least he could ditch the coil. If everybody was piling in the front, he could spare himself the climb and risk making a run for it at the rear. With his campaign medal lying in the flowerbeds, he was radar-invisible.

He stepped over the woozily struggling prisoner and lifted the bag. It felt a lot lighter now that he wasn't faced with lugging it up twenty-five feet of electrical flex and across fifty yards of telephone cable. There was just about room in the bag for a second can, and if he slung it satchel-style again, his hands would be free to carry something else. The generator was unlikely to need anywhere near that much fuel, but he had spotted something that could definitely use up the rest.

'They're coming,' Liz reported.

'This is it,' Vale called out. 'Take positions.'

Alison only *thought* she'd been scared before. What she'd felt during the waiting had been mere hyper-agitation, a flickering of pages depicting scenarios and possibilities, some of horror, some of hope, and none that she could bear to linger upon. It was the fear of not knowing, of projecting and imagining, even when you were trying not to. As she looked out of the empty windowframe, however, she felt something altogether different. This wasn't fear, but something heavier, duller, immovable and definite. This was dread.

There was a vehicle moving slowly towards the building, as though lumbering under its own weight. She didn't know much about the terminology of these things, but the phrase 'armoured personnel carrier' popped into her head. There were men walking behind it, fanned out on either side, dressed in camouflage greens, faces blacked, carrying swords, machetes and, in one case, a long-handled axe. She counted twelve, but couldn't be sure, as the ones closest to the truck were frequently obscured from her line of sight.

A man stepped from the cab of the truck just before it halted a dozen yards from the front door. He began talking and gesturing to the others, clearly the man in charge. Shiach, she guessed. He was squat and looked podgy, better able to command than to act. Tubby little ageing thug who was right now ordering her death, but wouldn't last a minute in a square go with Ger. The infuriating sight of him helped shake a little of the hollow, gut-tightening paralysis, but she didn't like to wonder how long her defiance would last, nor how it might end.

Baxter was gone, back among his murderous conspirators, and with him had gone vital information. He knew of the plan to use the emergency generator and he knew where they planned to fall back to. The infiltrator didn't know where the entrance to the underground chambers was, but it wouldn't take all night to find it, after which they'd be trusting their survival to whatever they could find to barricade the door.

There was no call of attack to begin the onslaught, though it was not without its herald. An outstretched arm from the glorious leader was accompanied by a chainsaw buzzing into action, the sound reverberating ominously through every head in the hall.

The chainsaw and axe-bearer broke away from the advancing party and headed to the west.

'That's our bloody chainsaw,' Sir Lachlan observed. 'And our bloody axe. They've been in the outbuilding,' he added gloomily, his tone conveying depressing implications.

'They're going to ram the door,' Liz said, though the truck remained in place, engine idling.

'Good,' said Sir Lachlan. 'Those stone pillars will do more damage to their truck than it will to them.'

He sparked up his lighter and handed Liz and Alison a bottle each, before picking up one for himself. 'When he's in range, aim for the windscreen.'

But at that point the truck began moving, turning around to face away from the building as the first of the footsoldiers drew near to the entrance. It reversed towards the hotel, then a length of heavy chain was tossed out of the back doors.

Below, four of the men picked up two of the corpses that were lying on the concourse, holding them with an arm and a leg apiece. They then peeled away to either side, gathering speed as they headed for the windows flanking the entrance. So much for the horror sapping their resolve.

Sir Lachlan held his lighter to the rag on his bottle, which depressingly failed to burst into flame. He tried it on Liz's, to the same effect.

The two pairs of corpse-bearers reached the front walls and swung their burdens against the glass. The panes shattered, but the mattresses held. They wouldn't for long though, and when they fell, the intruders falling with them would be those already dead. The first live ones through would be upright and ready, not sprawling and vulnerable as Vale had envisaged. Thank you, Baxter, you duplicitous piece of shit.

Sir Lachlan knelt down and held his lighter over the two rows of bottles, trying each for a second or so. None of them would light.

'The alcohol's not volatile enough,' he cursed. Alison remembered Ger heating those measures a few hours ago, and recalled her dad's attempts every Christmas to ignite a pouring of brandy over the plum duff, draining half the lighter before the briefest flicker of blue flame appeared and died again. It only ever caught once the heat from the dessert had warmed the booze. Sitting at the open windows, this stuff wasn't even at room temperature.

The ramming party picked up their burdens again.

'Oh, just fucking chuck them,' Liz shouted, and hurled her bottle down at the nearer pair. It missed one of their heads by a few inches and smashed on the monobloc. Alison threw hers too, her greater accuracy foiled by the warning of the first salvo. Her target dodged clear, though at the cost of dropping his hold of the corpse. She turned to pick up a second missile, and was handed one almost absently by Sir

Lachlan, who had stopped systematically trying the bottles and was instead checking the labels. He stood up again when he found what he was after: a 25-year-old special edition Speyside with a 47 per cent abv. He turned it briefly upside down to allow more spirit to soak the rag, then held the lighter to it. A blue flame licked around the neck of the bottle.

'Right. *Slainte*, you bastards,' he shouted, hurling it from the central window towards the open rear doors of the truck. It impacted on the tailgate, but not before its journey through the night sky had quickly extinguished its flame.

Beneath them, two more of the footsoldiers, one of them dragging the chain, had disappeared under the protection of the stone canopy, while the ramming parties checked above for incoming and prepared for relaunch.

The sound of breaking glass could be heard even through the fire-door, accompanied by raised and anxious voices. Vale's call had alerted them that the assault was finally under way, though it was an eerie half-minute or so after that before Emily heard the crashes that confirmed they were under attack. There was no sound from beneath them in the stairwell, so Rory was eyeing the door anxiously, having wondered aloud whether they would be better deployed elsewhere.

'They know we've got barricades here. Even mob-handed, it would be tough to launch an attack coming *up* these stairs. They've had plenty of time for a rethink.'

Emily looked at the kitchen knife she'd been given to replace the one lodged in Baxter's shoulder. It was half the size, a fraction of the weight, good only for stabbing if you were up close. If they did attack up these stairs, Rory might as well be on his own.

Then they heard another crash, this time much closer, and a buzzing sound like a small motorbike.

'That's a fucking chainsaw,' Rory announced, opening the door and heading into the corridor to investigate. 'Not exactly medieval.'

'It doesn't need to be medieval, just messy,' Emily remarked, following him out.

Once they were through the door, the buzzing became louder, joined suddenly by a repeated banging. Both sounds came from the side of the corridor to the front of the house.

The fourth of the arrhythmic bangs saw the blade of an axe jut an inch through the dining-room door behind which Grieg's incomplete remains had been locked. At the same time, the buzzing changed its pitch, slower and deeper as the chainsaw bit into the wood of the door to the adjacent drawing room. Another crash then sounded from the opposite side of the corridor, this time behind the door to the kitchen. They were trying to open up as many routes inside as they could, spreading the defences wide and thin.

'We need support down here,' Rory shouted. 'Now!'

The axe blade was withdrawn, then reappeared, coming through further, close to the handle and the lock. A hammering began from inside the kitchen, rapid and insistent.

'I said we need support here,' Rory shouted again. He looked to Emily. 'Get help. And if you can't get help, at least get clear.'

The chainsaw blade emerged through the drawing room's heavy oak. Across the corridor, the hammering from the kitchen repeated its indignant tattoo.

'I said we need support here.'

Alison heard Rory's second call for help, little as she was in any position to respond. The first had been drowned out by the revving of the truck's engine as it prepared to pull away, both ends of the chain now connected to a tow bar on its tailgate. As she'd watched them rig it up she'd been wondering what they might attach the chain to on the outside of the storm doors, optimistically picturing it yanking the brass handles free but leaving the doors locked in place. However, the two men who'd walked under the canopy emerged either side of it almost immediately, each trailing one end of the chain. It was only as the vehicle moved forward and took the strain that the scheme became apparent, each side of the triangle too obtuse for the base to be against the door. They had looped it around the columns and were planning to bring the whole canopy down. After that they could use the truck itself as a battering ram.

She had a glance back downstairs and saw Vale take off in response to Rory's call. He grabbed a canister from her kitchen collection as he did so, ignoring the weapon she'd worked so hard on loading. He'd been very serious when he said he couldn't afford to use it too soon, though surely too soon was better than too late, and too late wasn't looking very far off.

'A couple of hits and then they'll know how to protect themselves, you understand?'

She did, and it didn't boost her morale any that it made them sound like the bloody Borg: you only got a few shots before they adapted their defences to neutralise your ray gun.

The two manual ramming parties were persisting with their efforts, hampered by the bottles and cutlery that were raining down upon them. The group on Alison's side had at one point attempted to use their corpse as a shelter as well as a ram, holding him above their heads as they approached, but it had not proven conducive to getting much power behind the launch.

Liz had scored a direct hit with a litre of vodka, the sight of it in her hand giving Alison a taunting glimpse of happier times. She thought wryly how Liz wasn't the first person to get a result with a bottle of Stolichnaya.

The bottle had smashed into the side of the man's head as he moved to dodge another one fired by Sir Lachlan. He collapsed to the floor, causing his partner to drop their corpse before other comrades moved in to assist. The slug in command did a bit more pointing and shouting, then another figure emerged from the rear of the truck and knelt down to one side of it.

Alison stepped back from the window to grab a fistful of wooden-handled steak-knives. As she did, she heard Liz yelp and saw her recoil from her position, clutching a hand to her shoulder. When she lifted her fingers, she revealed a tight cluster of coloured fibres around a small patch of blood. Sir Lachlan turned around to see what had happened, then winced himself, reaching a hand around to his back. His fingers stretched in vain towards an identical cluster between his shoulderblades. He looked at Liz's injury with a pained expression that was more to do with what he saw than what he felt.

'Tranquilliser darts,' he said.

When she heard this, Liz made an abortive attempt at removing hers, her face immediately contorting with pain when she pulled on it. She took a couple of deep breaths, steeling herself for another go, but before she could do so, her legs buckled beneath her and she slumped to the floor.

Ger, who had been waiting on the grand staircase with the remainder of his own personal knife set, came bounding up to the gallery, ordering Kathy to follow.

'We've got to get them out the way,' Ger said, as Sir Lachlan wavered and put a hand out to Alison.

'Where?' Kathy asked.

'Other side of the gallery, for now.'

Alison could hear the engine whine and the tyres spin on the monobloc as the truck strained against the stone columns. She and Kathy held Liz upright between them, her arms across their shoulders, and began dragging her along one side of the gallery. Across the drop, Ger was propping up Sir Lachlan, as though helping a staggering drunk, but ended up hauling him, arms under oxters, as the older man's legs gave out. All the while, the securing bedsheets and curtains strained and tore as the mattresses were driven against them, now unhindered by aerial bombardment. Toby waited before the windows, his machines primed to deliver a desperate single shot each.

She'd experienced terror, shock, anger, loss, fear and dread, but this was the first time she really, really felt like crying. What her mind wouldn't allow her to feel – over Charlotte's death, over the horrors she'd endured tonight, over the people she'd never say goodbye to, the things she'd never do, all that *life* she'd never get to live – was threatening to swamp her now, like the hordes outside were about to swamp the building.

She glanced at Ger, but he was bent over Sir Lachlan, who appeared to be straining to say something, valiantly fighting the inevitable onset of unconsciousness. Like all the others tonight, it was just one more battle in vain.

Good Time for a Bad Attitude

'Fuck's sake, let me in, it's Jack,' called a voice from behind the kitchen door as Emily rushed past. She almost crashed into Vale at the dog-leg in the corridor, both of them running flat out in opposite directions.

'They're coming in, they've got—' she said breathlessly.

'I can see what they've got,' he replied, though she couldn't imagine how he'd be in much of a position to do anything about it, carrying as he was only a small blue cylinder. Perhaps it was bampot repellent.

She turned around again as he hurried past. Rory was standing between the two doors under attack, the one being chewed up by the chainsaw predictably closer to being breached. He held the rapier in both hands, pointing it upwards at forty-five degrees, his knees slightly bent in a defensive stance.

'Will somebody open this fucking door,' Parlabane's voice repeated.

'Be right with you, old chap,' Vale called. 'A bit tied up at the mo'.'

The chainsaw's pitch rose drastically as one more thrust broke through the edge of a panel on the drawing-room door. The buzzing, spluttering implement was then drawn inside and used, side-on, as a battering ram to smash the panel out completely. Rory made to step forward in defence, but Vale signalled him to hold his position. Vale moved to within a foot of the doorframe's near edge, his left hand flicking a lighter into flame with a snap of his fingers. A blackened face appeared in the gap, grinning and wild-eyed.

'Heeeeeere's Johnny,' the intruder shouted through the hole. The fucking macho prick was loving it.

Vale stepped in front of the door and blasted a spray of what Emily now recognised as oven-cleaner through the lighter's flickering tongue, sending a volley of instant napalm crackling into the chainsaw-bearer's face. It was accompanied by a hideous scream and the sound of a thump as his tool hit the floor and cut out, both of his hands pressingly required to hold his burning head.

It *was* bampot repellent.

'Johnny, meet Mr Muscle,' Vale muttered, before giving the door a surprisingly powerful kick. Already damaged, it flew open first time, the lock-housing clattering to the polished wood. The intruder was thrashing around on the floor, screaming to the point of rupturing his vocal chords. It was a sight and a sound Emily knew she'd be haunted by if she made it through this thing, but as he was part of the reason that was in doubt, she wasn't in the mood to shed any tears just then. Vale lifted the chainsaw and offered it to Rory. He accepted it with a narrow-eyed grin just as the axe delivered its telling blow on the dining-room door. It swung inwards, revealing another face-blackened assassin, six five if he was an inch, the long-shafted axe gripped in two huge and determined hands.

Rory pressed the button and the chainsaw screamed back into motion.

'My chopper's bigger than yours,' he told the axe-man, who concurred by turning around and getting off his mark.

'Yeah, you better fucking run,' Rory shouted after him. 'Tell them *all* to fucking run.'

The hammering resumed on the kitchen door.

'Any danger you could pleeease let me out of here,' Parlabane called.

'I think Alison's got the keys,' Emily told them.

'Stand back, mate,' Rory warned, before plunging the

chainsaw into the doorframe around the lock. There was a horrible grinding of metal as the chainsaw's teeth bumped against the housing, the only sound so far to rival the screams of the oven-cleaner victim in the blood-curdling stakes.

'Sorry,' Rory remarked, like it was a faux pas that needed any kind of apology. He was about to resume his cutting, but Vale opined that it was enough, and another powerful kick proved him right.

Parlabane was crouching on the floor, removing petrol cans, a machete and a pair of heavy-duty gardening gloves from a black canvas bag. Fragments of broken glass glinted on the tiles, testifying to his route back into the house. There was a yellow object beside him, trailing tubes and an electrical flex alongside a metal lance with a black plastic muzzle. It looked to Emily like something for spraying weedkiller or insecticide, though she couldn't imagine how such a thing would require electricity any more than she could imagine what Parlabane planned to do with it.

'Thank fuck,' he said, standing up and moving towards the open door.

'Watch out for the—' Vale warned, too late, as Parlabane walked into a length of piano wire stretched across the frame. It bit into his neck then sprang loose, one end whipping free from where it had been less than efficiently secured.

'Who the fuck put that there?' he demanded, putting a hand to his throat. The wire had broken the skin, but it could – indeed *should* – have been a lot worse.

'Actually, don't answer that,' Parlabane went on. 'I think I know. Because if it had been done properly, I'd be hosing the walls right now. Where's Baxter?'

'He's gone off to play with his real friends,' Vale told him. 'How did you find out?'

'Campbell gave me the heads-up, so to speak. Poor bastard didn't have a very proactive evening.'

'Ah.'

'So what else did I miss?'

'Oh, quite a fair few revelations. *In terrorum veritas.* I'll fill you in, but the condensed version is that I'm afraid, despite what you said last night, this time it *is* all down to a bunch of homicidal right-wing nutters out to kill all the lefties and silence the dissidents.'

'In a retro-Eighties stylee,' Emily added.

'And people say nostalgia's not what it used to be. So why didn't you let me out sooner?'

'Why didn't you tell us it was you?' Emily replied. 'You were just hammering the door. It could have been one of them.'

'This is why,' he said, taking something from his pocket. He held it up in the palm of his hand, ostensibly for the attention of Vale.

'Compact receiver and short-range sub-vocal mic,' Vale identified. 'Damn it, I'm slipping. I didn't spot one on our endurance runner.'

'You wouldn't. Sits pretty snug just inside the ear. I had to take it out before I could shout, so that they don't find out we're listening in. I started off just hammering the door because I made the crazy assumption you might suss it was me, seeing as the bad guys' attempts to gain entry so far haven't included knocking. Hey, maybe that's where they've been going wrong.'

'I can see why people end up trying to kill you,' Emily told him.

'They're not going that wrong, Jack,' Vale warned. 'We won't be able to hold out much longer at the front. And with Baxter knowing about our generator plans, I fear you made a wasted trip. We'll need to fall back for a last stand. Baxter knows about that too, but it's still our best hope.'

'Fall back where?'

'Underground chambers. Sir Lachlan said they go well

beyond the foundations. Lots of doors to get through. If we keep retreating as each one falls, they'd have to take it room by room.'

'And Baxter knows about this?'

'I'm afraid so.'

'Good.'

'Good? How?'

'Tell you in a sec. We just need a bit more time.'

A scream echoed from the central hall: Kathy's. 'They're almost through,' she shouted.

'Sounds like we're fresh out,' Rory said.

'Not so. Luckily, these days it comes in handy-sized tins.'

Parlabane handed Vale a heavy-looking can of petrol and picked up the yellow object, in closer proximity to which Emily could now read the words: HoseTek 440 Pressure Washer.

'My trip wasnae wasted, believe me.'

Kathy gave a scream, prompting Alison to turn around and face the front again. They had lain Liz down on her side after her eyes had closed, in order to protect her airway. Kathy had instructed Ger to do the same for Sir Lachlan, whose blood loss had caused him to succumb a few seconds earlier.

Alison looked over the balustrade in time to see the mattress on the left tear free of its crude rigging and topple forward, a decapitated body slumping down on top. Its counterpart billowed with the impact of another blow, ripping enough of the sheeting to suggest one more attack would finish it. Ger sprinted past her to the half-landing where he'd left his knives, while Toby took position behind his left-hand catapult.

The erstwhile human battering ram was dragged outside by the feet to clear the way in. There was a moment of incongruous stillness as the huge windowframe stood breached but empty, the sound of an angry engine and whining tyres that bit louder now that the mattress was gone. Then one of the ramming party, having retrieved his swords, climbed into the towering aperture and bent to help up his companion.

Toby pulled a restraining wire on one of the modified resistance machines, causing all of its suspended weights to drop from the highest point in its frame. These in turn rapidly pulled upon an already taut cable, and drove a sharpened broomhandle at speed along a channel formed between two chairlegs lashed to the machine's upward-angled bench. The sharpened tip snagged on something less than halfway along, causing the broomhandle to flip approximately one hundred and sixty degrees without the business end leaving the bench.

'Bugger.'

He leapt across to the other machine and began re-angling it to face the same window as the second intruder got to his feet on the table beneath. This time the broomhandle flew fast and true, hurtling through the narrowest of gaps between both men and disappearing out into the night.

'This kind of shit never happened to Hannibal Smith,' Toby remarked, looking around for support as the swordsmen jumped simultaneously from the table.

Ger picked his spot and launched a knife from the half-landing. It missed the head of the intruder on the right by millimetres, but it was enough to buy Toby a second to turn and run for the stairs. He spun and tripped on the bottom step, in panic Alison thought, until she saw the cluster of fibres jutting from his shoulder.

'GER!' she shouted, as he prepared to launch another knife. Alison pointed to the window, where the sniper was opening the breech of his gun, readying another dart. Both swordsmen began to charge, giving Ger three targets for one blade as the sniper lined him up as his next shot. He sent the knife over both advancing heads towards the window, causing the sniper to duck out of sight as the blade whistled through the gap. The resulting stray dart lodged itself in the balustrade less than a foot from where Alison stood, helplessly watching the situation unfold.

She heard the approach of hurried footsteps and looked to her right to see Parlabane and Vale crouch over something in the mouth of the corridor. Emily knelt behind them next to the wall, yanking a standard lamp's plug from its socket.

Toby tried to regain his footing, but tripped dizzily as the intruders drew near, one raising his claymore above his head, the other fixing his gaze on Ger. Behind him, two further assailants climbed on to the sill, carrying machetes. The other mattress had ceased billowing a few seconds before, which meant there'd soon be two more behind this pair.

Just then, Alison heard a thunderous bellow accompanied by a furious buzzing, and watched Rory charge from the corridor, thrusting a chainsaw before him. The first two intruders stopped almost mid-pace, trading an after-you-Claude look before stepping back to put space between themselves and this new opponent. Their reinforcements stepped down from the table and the four spread out, adopting cautious defensive stances as Rory tried to ward them away from the still scrambling Toby.

The sniper reappeared at the breached window, chambering another dart. Beside him, the next two intruders climbed through on to the table, bearing more steel. Ger stood, rooted on the half-landing, his last means of defence gripped tightly in one hand. At the window, the sniper was this time lining up Rory in his sights.

Then there came a clear shout from below.

'Rory, hit the deck.'

Rory obliged as all enemy heads turned to see where the cry had come from.

Vale stood in the archway, holding the lance from Sir Lachlan's pressure-washer in both hands, the feed-hose dunked into a twelve-litre can of petrol. Parlabane knelt to one side of him, a blue lighter-flame flickering above his glove-protected fingers.

'This game of soldiers is over,' Vale said grimly. He twitched the trigger and sent a searing plume of flame strafing across the frozen quartet.

'My God,' Emily said, her voice an awestruck, horrified whisper. The four intruders flailed and scrambled, crashing into the weight machines and each other as they fled screaming; clothes, hair and skin engulfed by fire. Behind them, the two on the table dived back outside as Vale swept the scorching jet towards the window. The burning men attempted the same means of exit. Two of them made it, though their fates would be no different to the two who didn't: the pair of them collapsing short of the table, breathing flame instead of oxygen.

Even yards back, Parlabane could feel the intense heat as well as hear their strangled cries and smell the burning flesh. He looked at his friend gripping the lance, his face filled not with hate or anger, but calm, solemn concentration. Now he really knew why they called him Death's Dark Vale.

I've done things I wish I hadn't had to; wished it had been someone else doing them; wished they hadn't been necessary.

Amen.

'Who the hell is this guy?' Emily asked him.

'We could tell you, but we'd have to kill you,' he said with a wink. 'Come on. We've got work to do.'

Vale torched the big reception desk blocking the front door, then the tables and mattresses either side. Behind in the corridor, Rory and Emily busied themselves by dragging several armchairs from the drawing room and piled them up to block the passage. Once they were clear, Vale set those ablaze too. Nobody would be coming through that way for a while either.

Parlabane unplugged the pressure-washer and pocketed the lighter while Vale grabbed the other petrol can. Ger stuck his knife through a belt-loop and helped Emily carry Toby up to the gallery. From outside, the sound of a straining engine still carried above that of the crackling flames.

'They'll be back,' Parlabane warned, climbing the stairs to where Alison and Kathy stood over the unconscious Liz and Sir Lachlan. 'They've no choice. We need to get our wounded holed up somewhere secure. Now, who knows where to find the entrance to the underground chambers?'

'Sir Lachlan,' Alison said glumly.

'Shit.'

'It's awright,' Ger informed them. 'He told me before he passed out. It's in the laundry, doon in the basement. Under one of the machines.'

'Perfect. Okay, Emily, go and warn Max and Joanna we're coming through. Alison, you've got the keys, right?'

'Yeah, but not to the—'

'You lead everybody to the tower and lock yourselves in.'

'The tower? But I thought you said we were going to the underground chambers?'

'No, that's just where they'll *think* we're going.'

Vale gave Parlabane the edited highlights as they and Ger made their way to the basement, the chef dragging two bedsheets behind him, one corner of each tied together. The campaign medals were pinned along the length of the knotted linen at irregular intervals, so that on the wireframe model it would appear that the group were making their way to the laundry, single-file and plausibly spaced.

They hadn't had time to stop and press Max and Joanna for where they reckoned they fitted into Shiach and Baxter's plans, but Parlabane was more curious about what had merited his own inclusion on the truly 'ultimate' guestlist.

'I'm also pretty hazy on where the hell they've been for the past decade or so. Unless it's like all those semi-retired rockers who hit a certain age and decide it's now or never to re-form the band for one last crack at glory.'

'Don't ask me,' Vale said. 'I'm clearly too old and rusty to offer any worthwhile insight. I used to be able to spot a spook at a thousand yards. Baxter was right under my nose the whole time and I never sniffed him out.'

'You didn't look too rusty upstairs, trust me. Besides, Baxter was good, I'll give him that. Sold us a pretty neat dummy with Campbell. He held his end up well enough. Seems like this Shiach nutter was the rusty one.'

'Let's not close the book on how rusty he is just yet, eh?' Vale warned.

'Good shout. Let's just check they're buying this.'

Parlabane put the receiver to his ear, Vale likewise with the device he'd removed from one of the flame-grilled fallen. He heard nothing for a few seconds, then Baxter's voice cut across the airwaves.

'Oi! Where the fuck do you think you're going? Get back here.'

'Bollocks to this,' replied a Cockney accent. 'I'm out of here. You told us it would be a picnic, not a fucking barbecue.'

'You can't escape this. Remember: once it starts, it has to be finished.'

'That's your problem, mate. It's your face they've seen, not mine.'

'I'm warning you, after we've finished with them, we'll be coming for you.'

'Then I guess it says it all that I fancy my chances more against you than against them. See ya.'

'Leave him,' said another voice, older, gruffer, East Coast: Shiach. 'We can handle this better without spineless scum.

They're pulling back, like you said. Bruce, get out of the truck. I'll take over. They've abandoned their barricades. Grab some darts and send everybody who's left in through the billiard room.'

Vale smiled. They were standing just outside the games-room door. He and Parlabane pocketed their receivers again, knowing they had to be used sparingly. A few words, perhaps uttered in the heat of the moment, and their advantage would be lost.

Parlabane told Ger to keep going while he knelt down and plugged in their improvised flame-thrower at a socket in the corridor. Vale grabbed books and board games from the shelves and cabinets lining the walls, tossing some on to the snooker table around the body of the Incredible Self-Decapitating Man, others on to the tennis table beneath the unbroken skylight. Together they shifted the sideboard until it blocked the route to the door, then they stood behind it and waited.

They heard heavy footfalls crunch on the gravel above, drawing near. Still they waited. They wanted these bastards to see them.

'Right,' said a voice above. 'You go first. No, leave the fucking sword. I'll drop it to you once you're down. You'll *see* why in a second.'

A pair of legs dangled into the empty skylight, cautiously dreeping down backwards. Parlabane lit the pilot and Vale let rip. The flame burst engulfed the protruding limbs and the man crashed down on to the snooker table, on to which Vale poured still more fire. He then ignited the tennis table and finally the sideboard, before they withdrew and closed the door.

'How many left, do you reckon?' Parlabane asked.

'Five, maybe six. Still enough anyway, while they're the ones holding dart guns. Plus we're almost out of petrol. Come on.'

Ger was waiting for them in the laundry.

'Baxter's fucked the generator, by the way,' he said. 'I checked it while you guys were busy. Cables are aw ripped oot.'

'Shit,' said Parlabane. 'That confirms they've got night-vision then.'

'Yes, but they're not going to opt for seeing in the dark with their goggles while they still think they can see through walls with their laptop. Let's get on with it.'

It took the three of them to move the enormous twin-cylinder tumble-dryer.

'I thought the lyre of Orpheus opened the door to the underworld,' Vale muttered, panting. 'Not bloody Electrolux.'

The warped wooden trapdoor revealed beneath was a couple of feet square, hinged in two places on the left-hand side. The handle had been removed in order that the dryer would have a level base, so Ger had to wedge it open with his knife. He reached down inside a foot or so and flicked a switch, a dim light glowing below in response.

'I don't know how far the electrics go,' he said. 'But I'm sure I read that Stormcrow did some vocal takes down in Willcraft's excavations. Stupit bastards thought it was haunted.'

From somewhere above, they heard a dull thud and felt a shudder of impact. The pillars had fallen, bringing down the stone canopy and leaving the front doors exposed for the truck to ram them.

'It's about to be,' said Vale.

'I feel like the pied piper,' Ger muttered, climbing down the steps out of sight.

'Well, you've sure got the troosers for it.'

Spectators of Suicide

Perhaps it was just an effect of the torchlight, but Rory reckoned Max looked sicker at the mention of the word 'Shiach' than he had when he discovered what he'd eaten for dinner. Max was sitting next to Joanna on the halfway landing, his legs resting a couple of stairs down, swords lying either side. There was a small window in the wall beside him, still open from Parlabane's earlier sortie to the roof. It would offer one last chance if the door was breached or the fire spread.

The tower accommodated a broad staircase leading up to a split-level honeymoon/VIP suite. It didn't offer a lot of floorspace, but was presumably intended to make up for it in privacy and the views afforded in daylight from windows looking out on four sides. There was a bathroom and living area on the lower level, bedroom with four-poster on the upper, from where a trapdoor and a pull-down ladder accessed the turret. All the movable furniture bar the over-size bed (but including the mattress) was piled in front of the door. Rory stood in front of the jumble holding his chainsaw, Emily sitting close by at the foot of the stairs. Kathy and Alison kept watch over the unconscious trio above.

Rory was giving his fellow guards a breakdown of what they'd missed, but it was clear Max could fill in a lot of the blanks himself once that single name had been uttered.

'You were in the TA, weren't you?' Rory put to him pointedly, to let him know he'd filled in a few on Max's behalf.

Max nodded reluctantly. He didn't look in much of a mood to talk.

368

'Secrets are a luxury we can't afford tonight, Max,' he urged. 'Just give me the bullet points.'

'Okay,' he said, as though coaching himself. 'Okay. I was in the TA. Met Shiach, got talking. You know how he worked it.'

'Only too well.'

Max sighed, pausing again.

'I drove a car, that's all. I only drove a car. He didn't tell me anything else, for my own protection. Just said I had to drive this car somewhere, and that would be enough to start with, to prove my commitment. I had to wear gloves so I left no prints, so I knew it was something dodgy, but there was no getaway, no hit, I just drove this bloody car to where he told me. It was at night, to ensure no-one saw me getting out and into that old white Beetle of his for him to drive me back home. After that, I never saw him again. Never. It was like he disappeared.'

'Where did you leave the car?' Rory asked, a horrible feeling taking hold of his insides. He didn't already know the precise location, but he could have provided a shortlist.

'A carpark next to the Severn Bridge.'

'Oh, Christ,' said Joanna, sounding like Rory felt. The Severn was on his shortlist.

'What?' Max asked.

'It's a suicide spot, Max,' Rory told him. 'People jump off it, and the tides often take their bodies out to sea, so they're never found. I'm sure the car owner's never was, but not because he went off the bridge.'

Rory looked expectantly at Joanna, whose eyes were brimming with tears. 'You know who it was?' he asked.

'Nigel Franklin,' she said, the name causing her to break into sobs. She rested her head on Max's shoulder for a few moments and gradually composed herself, sniffing more tears away before she spoke again. 'He was a lawyer, in Liverpool. That's as much as I knew anyway, until after his death. His obituary said he was involved quite high up in CND, links to Militant too.'

'How did you know him?'

'I slept with him.' She swallowed back another sob. 'I mean I was *paid* to sleep with him.'

Joanna shook her head and sniffed away more tears.

'It's all right,' said Max.

'It's not fucking all right,' she retorted, her voice distorted by her crying. 'I was a student. I was skint. I didn't have a rich mummy and daddy to finance my studies.' She eyed Rory accusingly, which he took on the chin. 'I turned a few tricks. I was very different then: slim, trendy, more outgoing. A friend got me into it. No street-corner stuff, strictly through contacts. I told myself it was easy money, the end would justify the means, all the usual lies. I wanted out of it as soon as I was in, but once you get used to having a few bob, it's hard to let that go, especially when you've got some regulars.'

'Franklin was a regular?'

'No. One of my regulars introduced me to a guy who said he had a business proposition. I had to seduce Franklin, basically, and make him think he had pulled me. He said he was a friend, that it was a favour to give the guy a boost because he was going through a sticky patch in his marriage. Wife was a bitch, making him feel worthless. I'm not sure I bought the story, but it was a lot of money to me, so I went along with it and didn't ask questions.

'Franklin's car was found at the Severn Bridge a couple of weeks later. It was reported that he was thought to have committed suicide because he was being blackmailed over an affair. There were photos sent to his office a few days before, of us going into the hotel where we'd had our one-night stand. They'd blanked my face, apparently, so I couldn't be traced. Mind you, that was the least of my worries. *I* was feeling near-suicidal, to have played a part in something that led a man to kill himself. Eventually though, despite my capacity for guilt and paranoia, I had to accept that nobody was going to come looking for me. I got on with my life, but I can't say my self-esteem ever fully recovered. My self-image certainly never did. And now that I know he didn't kill himself over me, I can't say it makes me feel any better.'

'Yeah, well, you think you feel bad?' Rory said to her. 'That plan was *my* fucking idea. It was one of the ones I dreamed up. I ended up killing somebody after all.'

'Come off it, Rory,' Emily appealed. 'You designed the gun, but you didn't pull the trigger.'

'Yeah, but if nobody designed guns, nobody would get *shot*.'

Parlabane, Vale and Ger listened as the raiding party checked every basement room except the blazing one for the hallowed portal they sought, then watched from behind two strategically placed laundry hoppers as the raiders finally made their entrance. The three of them were peeping unseen between gaps in towering piles of fluffy white towels, but Parlabane felt they could have been sitting on the bloody hoppers whistling a tune and still not have been noticed, their visitors intent to the verge of hypnotised by their point of focus now that they'd found it. They approached the trapdoor cautiously, one of them kneeling and wedging it slightly with the tip of a machete while another trained his dart gun on the spot. The door was hauled open on a silent finger-count of three, then a second gunman led the way down, slowly and quietly.

Parlabane listened in with his receiver.

'Nothing so far,' he heard one of them croak.

'They're well inside,' informed Baxter's voice. 'Twenty yards, maybe. The wireframe's got no schematic for down there. Take your time, play it steady. They aren't going anywhere.'

Parlabane looked to Vale, who gave a holding signal.

'Vinnie, bring the axe,' said a whisper. Parlabane removed his receiver because he feared he couldn't suppress a giggle. This was partly due to nerves but mainly due to the fact that these eejits were about to chop down a door that Ger didn't even have the keys to lock.

On the sound of the first axe blow, Vale gave the nod and the three of them ran from behind the hoppers on light feet. Ger closed the trapdoor with the utmost gentility, then they put their collective strength into sliding the huge tumble-dryer back against the wall. The dryer in place, they then slid two enormous, concrete-ballasted washing machines tight up against it, making sure no amount of combined effort from below could even rock the thing. Muted banging ensued a few seconds later, suspicions raised by the grinding of metal their efforts had raised. It was entertainingly futile. Parlabane was kind of disappointed nobody shouted: 'Let me out.'

'I counted four,' he said. 'Baxter's still out there. Did you figure any of them for Shiach?'

'Shiach's a wee bald dumpy guy,' Ger said. 'At least, that's who was giving orders out front, and he never went down the hole.'

'Fuck.'

If there'd been one left, it was as good as over, as it would take at least two to shift the machines and free the others. Two kept the game alive, especially two with dart guns.

'Let's see what they're saying,' said Vale, putting a hand to his ear and a finger to his mouth.

'—dio silence from you fucking idiots,' was what they were saying, or Shiach was anyway. 'We need peace to think.'

'Shit, that's . . .' said Baxter before tailing off, at which it became apparent that it wasn't only the eejits down the trap-door who'd ceased transmission.

The silence lasted a frustratingly long time, easily a minute. Not exactly a marathon endurance, but it felt that way when there were three men standing wordless in a basement, waiting for some kind of clue as to their next move.

'Okay, fuck it,' Baxter resumed. 'It's clean-up time. I'm going to the substation to cut the electricity. A couple of the bastards will be guarding that trapdoor, and the rest must be holed up in the tower: that was their other fallback. You grab your night-sights and head for the basement.'

Parlabane and Vale removed their earpieces again. A certain look from Vale meant he didn't need to verify what each had drawn from the information.

'We know what we have to do,' Parlabane said.

'Indeed.'

'What?' Ger asked.

They told him.

'Sounds pretty risky,' he opined. 'But I cannae suggest an alternative.'

'And time is of the essence,' Vale reminded.

'I need a blade,' said Parlabane.

Vale reached behind the hoppers for the rapier he'd received when Rory traded up. Vale's own weapon of choice jutted from his hip pocket.

'Just because they haven't used real guns yet doesn't mean they don't have them, Jack,' he warned. 'And they're definitely down to last resorts.'

'So are we – it's a chance we have to take. I think we should trust each other's proven abilities.'

'I know mine, what are yours?'

'Winding people up until they want to kill me.'

'These people already want to kill you.'

'Then I'm off to a flier.'

'It's not shifting. Whatever's up there weighs a fucking ton. It was a trap, it was a fucking trap.'

373

'I've found something. Shit. It's the medals. They're all pinned to a sheet.'

'This place is creepy as hell. It's like fucking catacombs or something.'

'Bollocks, one of the bulbs just went.'

'Boss, you need to get us out of here.'

'And I need radio silence from you fucking idiots,' Shiach hissed. 'We need peace to think.'

'Shit, that's . . .' Fotheringham put a finger to his lips. He removed the receiver from his ear and gestured to Shiach to do the same.

'They're listening,' Fotheringham said quietly, clutching the device inside a balled fist.

'You sure?'

'Definitely. They found out about the medals and they must have picked up at least one of these things too.'

'And you weren't aware of this?'

'It must have been after I left.'

'After you *ran*,' Shiach reminded him. 'You didn't bag any of them and you couldn't warn us that they'd tumbled our transmitters. Remind me again what the hell you were doing in there?'

'What I do best: gather intelligence, listen to people talk. You know that, so don't give me any of your shit. I needed to discover how much they really knew, in case there were any further loose ends we'd overlooked.'

'We haven't tied up these ones yet.'

'Well, it's not my fault you brought in a bunch of fucking no-hopers. I held up my end.'

Shiach bit back a retort: squabbling was the last thing they needed.

'Okay, enough. Let's stay focused, analyse the situation. If they're not in the underground chambers, where are they?'

'The tower. That was the other fallback mentioned. Not easy to get into, certainly not with just two of us, but for the time being we can consider the ones up there as out of the equation; some of them are unconscious already. But there must be others on the loose who laid the trap.'

'They'll be guarding it too, to stop us releasing our men. That settles it, then. We hit the basement, take them out, regroup our numbers and then take the tower. We'd better grab spare dart guns to save reloading. It could get hectic down there.'

Fotheringham shook his head.

'I'm not walking into a dead end to face down some bastard with a flame-thrower. Who knows what other traps they've set.'

'Well, if that's where they are, what they hell else are we supposed to do?'

'Let's bring the mountain to Mohammed,' he said, popping the sub-vocal back into his ear. 'Okay, fuck it,' he resumed loudly. 'It's clean-up time . . .'

Learning How to Smile

Poor Rory. He looked crumpled and almost tearful, like the bad guys could come in right then and he'd just offer himself before their blades because he had it coming to him.

They were alone again, Max having taken Joanna upstairs for a drink of water and some much-needed hankies. Emily looked at the pile of furniture blocking the door: the others would have sufficient notice to get back down here if the enemy arrived outside, and there was definitely no need for Rory to be standing to attention. She beckoned him to come and sit next to her on the stairs.

'It was just a horrible idea, Rory. Who hasn't dreamed up some wicked scheme in their time? In fact, I'm sure you've had even more horrible ideas, like altering the shape of an actress's tits to flog personal loans.'

He smiled a little. She thought for a second he was going to laugh, but it would have been asking too much.

'I should be devising ads for famine-relief campaigns,' he said. 'That's what I'm going to do if I get out of here.'

'If you're making desperate promises like that, maybe it's Liz you should be talking to. She'd be in a position to see you kept them.'

'I'm not saying it out of contrition. I'm saying it because I'm a better man for the job than the charities have been using so far. Never mind TV spots and posters that appeal to bleeding hearts – they'd be coughing up anyway. It's the minted selfish bastards you want to be milking, and I know how they think. I devised one once, still got the storyboard in a drawer somewhere. Handsome black guy in a business suit, briefcase in one hand, his little son holding the other. Their clothes disappear layer by layer as the background changes from outside a semi in the burbs to a mudhut, until they're both standing there in loincloths, swollen bellies, bare feet and the briefcase has been replaced by an empty, cracked bowl. Tagline: Famine is killing your neighbour. Why won't you help?'

'Hmm. I think if you reverse the sequence you could probably sell it to the government for their next anti-racism initiative.'

'I wouldn't be looking to sell it. It's about time I gave something back. I've only ever taken responsibility when it actually served my interests. Can you believe that I remained sober on Christmas Eve from the age of twenty-one to thirty-four?'

'And what's irresponsible about sobriety?'

'Depends why you're sober. It was a Christmas tradition among some friends and myself. Started when I got my first Porsche, a twenty-first present from mater and pater. We would meet up at four in the morning at a carpark next to the Kelburn roundabout, just outside Port Glasgow, everyone sporting their best wheels and fake plates. Have you ever noticed how little traffic there is on Christmas Day?'

'Practically deserted.'

'Believe me, the most you've seen during the day is rush-hour compared to four a.m., and where there is no traffic, there are no cops. The pubs and clubs have all emptied, the night buses have finished, the streets are dead.'

'I see where this is going.'

'Abington Services is where it's going, where the M74 meets the A702. That was the finish line because from there we could head back up through Biggar and on to Fair Edina. We'd race along the M8 through the city, then down the M73 and M74, or A74 as it was when we started. You've never known a rush like it, between the speed, the overtaking what few other cars were around and the lingering fear of flashing blue lights. You drove as fast as you dared, given the aforementioned considerations. Risking the lives of innocent fellow drivers, you may note, wasn't one of them.'

Emily looked at Rory's self-flagellatory expression. She knew she was supposed to be appalled, that Rory needed her chastising disapproval for purposes of confession. Instead she found herself wishing she was on a deserted M8 before dawn, pedal to the metal over the Kingston Bridge, past the Mitchell Library and down beneath Charing Cross.

'I jacked it in because Reflected Gleam won a Scottish Executive account for devising an anti-speeding campaign. I knew that if I got caught – and to be honest, those roads were getting less quiet every year – it would be a major disaster. The campaign would be tarnished, Reflected Gleam would be tarnished and HMG would make damn sure nobody they had any influence on hired us again. I only gave up my festive thrill-ride because it threatened my meal-ticket.'

Emily couldn't help but smile. He looked like a wee boy owning up to his mammy, expecting punishment but honest enough to take his licks. She wanted to give him a hug. Actually, she wanted to give him a bit more, but didn't imagine she was exactly Rory Glen's fantasy, even if she had caught him ogling her tits. She was a woman who hosted parties and made sure everybody *else* was lightening up, while she was endlessly worrying. Worrying about the guests, worrying about the party, whether it was having the impact the client wished; worrying about the worthiness of the client's enterprise (and her own) in the grand scheme; and of course worrying that she's making a living hosting soirées in restaurants while in Africa etcetera etcetera etcetera.

'Rory, here's a promise you *can* make to me if we get out

of here. Give something back, absolutely. Just make sure you don't give it all. I could do with somebody to show me how to have a good time.'

'You don't call this a good time?'

The Trap

Parlabane's eyes began to sting as he approached the end of the corridor. The smoke wasn't exactly billowing, yet, but there was still more hanging in the air than he'd seen since fags were banned from tabloid newsdesks. He pulled his shirt-tails from his trousers and ripped away a length of material, holding it over his nose and mouth before venturing into the reception hall. The barricades and corpses were still blazing and the fire was threatening to spread. He looked at the balustrades and the wood panelling lining the walls on three sides around him. The highest flames were waving a couple of feet below the underside of the gallery at the front. It would be touch and go whether they climbed high enough before consuming the materials that were sustaining them, but if the gallery did catch fire, the whole place would go up.

There was a narrow path through the flames where the truck had smashed its way in. The big reception desk had been driven to one side and now formed a blazing avenue pointing to the exit. Fragments of wood still clung to a sole iron hinge, mangled and dangling where the front doors had hung. Beyond them, the storm doors had been thrust asunder, deadbolts and locks ripped from the wood to force them apart. He could see the front of the truck out on the concourse next to three bodies: two blackened, one head-less. Headlights smashed in and bumper crumpled, it looked like a beaten-up face, but its expression said, 'You should see the other guy.'

Across in the far corridor, the armchairs burned with a laziness that was a credit to their kitemarks. Their advertised flame-retardant properties were presumably not supposed to withstand that kind of test, but it did look like it was mainly the petrol that was burning. He'd still have to get past them though: walking straight out the front door would be making himself kind of obvious, even if, according to Ger, the substation lay in that direction.

Narrowing his eyes and taking a deep breath through the shirt material, he ran to where the reception desk had originally stood and grabbed the fire extinguisher strapped to the wall. Fortunately, it was a proper, full-on foam number and not one of those glorified soda-streams. It extinguished the armchairs with a few sustained blasts, though they were still far too hot to touch, so moving them out of the way was not an option. He lobbed the rapier over them first, then drew a few steps back before taking a running dive over the top.

From there he made it outside to the rear through the kitchen, then ran flat-out towards the end of the building, retracing his earlier route at a lower altitude and a far greater velocity. He skidded slightly on some matter, the nature of which he was glad to have no time to contemplate, before regaining his balance and treading more lightly over the last few yards. Upon reaching the corner, he knelt down and waited, tight to the cold stone, peering around to look towards the front concourse and the single-track road leading away from it. Again, the direct route was void; he'd have to take the path less travelled by.

There was a clicking sound in his earpiece, the only interruption to a sustained radio silence. He had a look across at the position of the truck, calculating the angles by which it might provide cover. There weren't many, but enough to dictate his route.

Another breath, then he ran from the corner on to the concourse, keeping his body as low to the ground as carrying the sword allowed.

'That's far enough,' said Baxter's voice, this time audible in both ears.

Parlabane pulled up, stumbling, then slowly turned around. Baxter stepped out from against the wall, pointing a dart gun with his left hand. His right arm was clutched to his side, bloodstains soaking through a bandage around his shoulder. The bad guys had brought a first-aid kit. And there was him thinking they'd been complacent.

A second figure emerged from the rear of the truck: squat and balding as Ger described. What was it with short-arses and rampaging militaristic ambition? He also carried a dart gun, though Parlabane noted neither had night-vision goggles. Bollocks. He and Vale had given them too much credit. Cutting the power had never been the plan; Baxter had merely trashed the generator to keep them believing it was.

'Is this it?' Parlabane asked Baxter. 'The Minister of Vigilance who's gaunny save Blighty from her enemies? This wee fanny?'

'Says the man with two guns pointed at him,' observed Shiach. 'Perhaps you should think before you sound off.'

'Perhaps you should engage the grey matter yourself. Have you considered how boring the conversations are gaunny be once you've killed everybody who disagrees with you?'

'We don't have to justify ourselves to you, Mr Parlabane,' Shiach replied. 'That's always been your type's tactic. Get the authorities to justify every slightest action they take in defending this country, while our foes are running rampage in our midst.'

'Ach, your maw's got baws and your da loves it. Save it for the judge, baldy.'

'Told you he was a charmer,' Baxter remarked.

'It's okay, David. Insults are all he has left, and he knows it.' Shiach smiled, cruel and smug. 'There's two ways this

382

can end, Mr Parlabane. And in both of them, you die.'

Parlabane reluctantly swallowed back a retort to this quite unsurpassed display of cheesy machismo, and eyed Baxter instead.

'Do I get to know why I made the list, or should I take it as a general compliment to my investigative journalism?'

'Oh, you get to know,' Baxter replied, enjoying the moment. 'Your reputation was part of it, yes. The police have to follow rational and logical lines of inquiry, but a paranoid prick like you with the bit between his teeth . . . This would have been victuals and drink. You made quite a nuisance of yourself the last time somebody left a pile of bodies in a Scottish country-house hotel, didn't you? And that's what I want you to know, before Mr Shiach here takes your head: my old acquaintance George Knight says hello . . . and goodbye.'

'You knew Knight?'

'A kindred spirit, you could say. We still correspond. He warned you he would have you killed one day, didn't he, and I believe you gave him the impression you were just too clever for that to happen. But if you were that clever, you'd have remembered your own trick from the game on Friday.' He pointed to his ear. 'No use eavesdropping if the other side know you're listening in.'

'True,' Parlabane conceded. 'But do you remember how the game ended?'

'Same as this one. With you getting shot just when you think—'

The realisation hit him a fraction of a second before Vale's volley, Baxter's eyes suddenly widening all the better to let in more liquidised chilli. Shiach was hit by a second round from the paintgun less than a heartbeat later. Parlabane dropped to the deck to avoid any desperate, blindly aimed darts, but the pair of them had discarded their guns, each staggering and screaming as he clutched his hands – or one hand, in the injured Baxter's case – to his acid-burning eyeballs.

Vale and Ger came sprinting from their positions on the opposite side of the concourse, from where Vale had notified Parlabane of his readiness with a pre-agreed signal: a single click of the tongue relayed by the sub-vocal. Yes, no use eavesdropping if the other side know you're listening, but neither is it wise to try selling your opponents a dummy if they *know* you know. A minute of total radio silence, not so much as a 'What do we do now?', then straight out with all the details of your next plan? Come *on*.

Parlabane helped Vale wrestle Shiach to the ground, the Minister of Vigilance thrashing and bucking more in agony than resistance. Vale grabbed his head and cracked it off the stone beneath, giving him a merciful unconsciousness the bastard didn't deserve, then set about the more daunting task of pulling Ger off of Baxter.

'Come on, you've got more important things to do,' Vale persuaded him. 'We need to get the others out before the fire spreads.'

Ger sent in one last kick then stepped back, while Parlabane patted Shiach down and located what he was after in a buttoned thigh pocket.

'Got a mobile,' he announced. 'And a signal.'

'Who you gaunny call?' Ger asked.

'Nine nine nine for the deluxe package: fire, police and ambulance.'

'But how are they gaunny get here if the bridge is doon?'

'Who said the bridge was down?'

'Baxter,' Ger replied. 'Ah,' he added, getting it.

'On the strength of what we've seen, do you think these fucking idiots would know how to handle explosives?'

'What about the bang?'

'That's all it was, I'd bet. A sound effect. Fireworks at most.'

Vale picked up one of the discarded dart guns and examined it. 'Still loaded,' he observed, walking towards where Baxter was writhing on the stone.

'Aw, naw, no way,' Ger objected. 'You're no' knockin' him oot. That cunt doesnae get to miss any of this.'

'We need him restrained while we evacuate the others,' Vale pointed out. 'And we've no rope.'

'Give me two seconds,' Parlabane said. 'I've got just the thing.'

Later

In the end, they departed the estate much as they had arrived: driven in a minibus along the meandering track, through the ancient darkness of the woods and over the conspicuously unexploded bridge. The experience was not quite so neatly bracketed once they reached the other side, partly because their cars had indeed been uniformly sabotaged, but more pressingly because they were being driven by the police to a hotel in Auchterbuie. There they would be allowed some shut-eye and a shower before having a crack at explaining individually to the polis precisely how McKinley Hall had come to be ablaze, and why there were headless and chargrilled corpses lying all about the place.

Not everyone was on board. Toby, Liz and Sir Lachlan had regained consciousness but left in an ambulance on the advice of the paramedics, who said they'd need to be kept under observation, the latter pair also requiring proper treatment for their wounds. Sir Lachlan went along under protest, claiming nothing he had sustained overnight would match the assault he'd be facing when the missus got back.

'I can hear her now,' he lamented. '"I leave you in charge for *two* days . . ."'

The fire brigade had been on the scene with impressive haste, in time to assist with the evacuation of the tower and well ahead of the first cops. All three emergency services having been called at the same time, it transpired that the local firemen had needed the least information or directions for finding the place.

'We long had this place doon for the maist likely insurance

fire in the Highland region,' one of them explained to Parlabane. He almost seemed disappointed that there was a less mundane cause for the blaze.

The arsehole formerly known as Baxter was bundled along with the unconscious Shiach into a police-escorted ambulance. The polis were awaiting armed reinforcements before they attempted to arrest the subterranean contingent, and rather unsportingly rebuffed Parlabane's suggestion that they cut the electricity supply down there in the meantime.

He climbed into the police minibus and joined Vale on the back row, feeling the cumulative fatigue of the past twenty-four hours catch up as the seat took his weight. A black polythene bag was sitting next to Vale's thigh, his hand resting on it to prevent it slipping as the bus lurched and bumped.

Nobody spoke as the vehicle left McKinley Hall behind, the tense and awkward jousting of the journey there seeming a lot longer than a mere two days ago.

Parlabane asked Vale if he could borrow the mobile he'd confiscated from Shiach. The final edition would already be printing by now back in Edinburgh, but they'd surely consider an old-style, literal Stop Press for a tale like this. If not, there was still the online version to consider.

'Don't have it, old chap, sorry. Had to hand it over to the boys in blue.'

'Shit.'

'Never mind, *every*body's gone to press,' he consoled, reading Parlabane's mind as usual. 'It'll still be your exclusive. And the only one with photos,' he added.

'You got your camera out of there?'

'I took a brief detour before the firemen began dousing the place, yes,' he said with a smile, patting the poly bag. His grin said there was more to his detour than a digital camera, and the bulge in the bag concurred.

'What else have you got in there?'

Vale reached into the bag with both hands, twisting something in his grip.

'Fifty-year-old Springbank,' he said, holding up the bottle. 'He'll be claiming it on the insurance anyway.'

'You're a fly bastard, Tim,' Parlabane told him, before eagerly accepting a proffered swig.

Vale then passed the bottle forward to Max, who initially refused with a disapproving frown, then changed his mind and had a large, warming, medicinal chug. The bottle then made its way around the seats until reaching Rory last. He took a hearty mouthful, wiped his lips and stood up.

'So,' he said. 'Same place next October for the reunion bash?'

Later Still

McKinley Hall reopened in the spring of 2003, following extensive repair and refurbishment work, its new decor tailored to enhance the *Gothic Nightmares* and *Haunted House* theme breaks advertised in its publicity literature, which now makes shamelessly lurid play of the building's 'cursed' past. It has been operating close to capacity most weekends and public holidays since, and has hosted a number of horror- and supernatural-related conventions. The impetus for this change in direction came from Sir Lachlan, who finally concluded that, as Death had settled in the area first and clearly showed no intention of leaving, he might as well offer his troublesome neighbour a job and get the bastard working for him.

Ger stayed on as chef. He now commands a full complement of staff and exercises absolute authority over supplies, in particular butcher-meat. He is reputed to be open-minded and experimental in his cooking and has enthusiastically improvised a number of recipes around suggestions from Lady Jane, but is known to have an irrational aversion to ostrich.

Alison left on her travels after Christmas 2002, having deferred entry to Strathclyde University. Her last postcard to Ger was marked 'Cairns'.

The Reflected Gleam Agency's controversial anti-racism TV spot was launched in May at a reception in Leith, organised by Seventh Chime. Emily and Rory moved in together shortly afterwards. They both voted Liberal Democrat at the last election.

The Dawn Yuill nipple-shot turned out to be a fake. It was her head, but Anne Robinson's body.

Extract:

Case number 35812. Statement transcript 04.4. Recorded 27/10/02, 11:25-14:50 approx, Auchterbuie Police Station, Interview Room 2. Witness: John Lapsley Parlabane. Special Branch Detective Superintendent Andrew Lomax interviewing. Also present: Special Branch Sergeant Colin McIntosh, Special Branch Detective Constable Stewart Rowan.

DET. SUP. LOMAX: You used *what*?